The
Rabbit Hutch

TESS GUNTY

ALFRED A. KNOPF New York

THIS IS A BORZOI BOOK
PUBLISHED BY ALFRED A. KNOPF

All rights reserved. Published in the United States by Alfred A. Knopf,
a division of Penguin Random House LLC, New York,
and distributed in Canada by Random House of Canada,
a division of Penguin Random House Canada Limited, Toronto.

www.aaknopf.com

Knopf, Borzoi Books, and the colophon are registered
trademarks of Penguin Random House LLC.

Illustrations are © 2021 by Nicholas Gunty.

Library of Congress Cataloging-in-Publication Data
Names: Gunty, Tess, author.
Title: The rabbit hutch : a novel / Tess Gunty.
Description: First edition. | New York : Alfred A. Knopf, 2022. |
Identifiers: LCCN 2021054987 (print) | LCCN 2021054988 (ebook) |
ISBN 9780593534663 (hardcover) | ISBN 9780593534670 (ebook) |
ISBN 9781524712235 (open market)
Subjects: LCSH: Apartment dwellers—Fiction. |
Middle West—Fiction. | LCGFT: Novels.
Classification: LCC PS3607.U54827 R33 2022 (print) |
LCC PS3607.U54827 (ebook) | DDC 813/.6—dc23/eng/20211222
LC record available at https://lccn.loc.gov/2021054987
LC ebook record available at https://lccn.loc.gov/2021054988

Jacket image: (heart) Adobest/iStock/Getty Images
Jacket design by Linda Huang

Manufactured in the United States of America
Published August 2, 2022
6th Printing

"If you don't sell them as pets, you got to get rid of them as meat. Them guys are all meat. But see, they start doing this to each other."

Woman points to rabbits.

"What's that?"

"Peeing on each other and stuff like that, when they get older. If you don't have ten separate cages for them, then they start fighting. Then the males castrate the other males. They do. They chew their balls right off. Then you have a bloody mess. That's why you got to butcher them when they get a certain age, or you have a heck of a mess."

—RHONDA BRITTON, Flint, Michigan, resident, 1989

Invisible and eternal things are made known through visible and temporal things.

—HILDEGARD VON BINGEN, Benedictine abbess, 1151

PART I

The Opposite of Nothing

~~

On a hot night in Apartment C4, Blandine Watkins exits her body. She is only eighteen years old, but she has spent most of her life wishing for this to happen. The agony is sweet, as the mystics promised. It's like your soul is being stabbed with light, the mystics said, and they were right about that, too. The mystics call this experience the Trans-verberation of the Heart, or the Seraph's Assault, but no angel appears to Blandine. There is, however, a bioluminescent man in his fifties, glowing like a firefly. He runs to her and yells.

Knife, cotton, hoof, bleach, pain, fur, bliss—as Blandine exits herself, she is all of it. She is every tenant of her apartment building. She is trash and cherub, a rubber shoe on the seafloor, her father's orange jumpsuit, a brush raking through her mother's hair. The first and last Zorn Automobile factory in Vacca Vale, Indiana. A nucleus inside the man who robbed her body when she was fourteen, a pair of red glasses on the face of her favorite librarian, a radish tugged from a bed of dirt. She is no one. She is Katy the Portuguese water dog, who licked her face whenever the foster family banished them both in the snow because they were in the way. An algorithm for amplified content and a blue slushee from the gas station. The first pair of tap shoes on the feet of a child actress and the man telling her to try harder. She is the smartphone that films her as she bleeds on the floorboards of her apartment, and she is the chipped nail polish on the teenager who assembled the ninetieth step of that phone on a green factory floor in Shenzhen, China. An American satellite, a bad word, the ring on the finger of her high school theater director. She is every cottontail rabbit grazing on the vegetation of her supposedly dying city. Ten minutes of pleasure igniting between the people who made her, the final tablet of oxycodone on her mother's tongue, the gavel that will sentence the boys to prison for what they're doing to Blandine right now. There is no such thing as right now. She is not another young woman wounded on the floor, body slashed by men for its resources—no. She is paying attention. She is the last laugh.

On that hot night in Apartment C4, when Blandine Watkins exits her body, she is not everything. Not exactly. She's just the opposite of nothing.

All Together, Now

~~

C12: On Wednesday night, in the nine o'clock hour, the man who lives four floors above the crime is staring into an app called: Rate Your Date (Mature Users!). The app glows a deep red, and he is certain that there is no one inside it. Like many men who have weathered female rejection, the man in Apartment C12 believes that women have more power than anyone else on the planet. When evidence suggests that this can't be true, he gets angry. It is an anger unique to those who have committed themselves to a losing argument. The man—now in his sixties—lies on his sheets in the dark. He is done with the day, but the day is not done with itself; it is still too early to sleep. He is a logger, past his professional expiration date but lacking both the financial and psychological savings to retire. Often, he feels the weight of phantom lumber on his back like a child. Often, he feels the weight of a phantom child on his back like lumber. Since his wife died six years ago, the apartment has seemed empty of furniture, but it is, in fact, congested with furniture. Sweating, the man cradles his large, bright screen in his hands.

nice enuf, like a dad, but fatter then his prof pic. his eye contact = wrong. doesnt ask about u and seems obsessed w/ the prices. **velcro wallet,** user Mel-Bell23 had commented on his profile two weeks ago. *smells like gary indiana.* ★ ★ ☆ ☆ ☆

The only other comment on his profile was posted six months ago, by DeniseDaBeast: *this man is a tator tot.* ★ ☆ ☆ ☆ ☆

Noise rumbles from an apartment below. A party, he assumes.

C10: The teenager adjusts his bedroom light to flattering bulbs of halo. He runs a hand through his hair, applies a lip balm. Smears a magazine sample of cologne on his chest, although he knows the gesture is absurd. Angles the camera so that it catches his best shapes and shadows. His mother is working the night shift, but he locks his door anyway. Does thirty jumping jacks, thirty push-ups. Texts: *Ready.*

C8: The mother carries her baby to the couch and pulls up her tank top. He's not supposed to be awake this late at night, but rules mean nothing to babies. While he nurses, he demands to bond, and the mother tries. Tries again. Tries harder. But she can't do it. He fires shrewd, telepathic, adult accusation upon her skin. She can feel it. He sucks hard and scratches her with nails too tender to clip, long and sharp enough to cut her. With her free hand, she checks her phone. A text from the mother's mother: a photo of Daisy the bearded dragon, wearing a miniature biker costume. Cushioned helmet strapped to her spiky coral head, black pleather jacket strapped to her belly. In a Hells Angels font, the back of the jacket reads: DRAGON DISASTER. The reptile peers at the camera from her perch on the dining table, her expression unreadable. The mother zooms in on Daisy's dinosaur eye, which seems to observe her from another epoch, 90 million years in the past.

U got ur baby, I got mine!! wrote the mother's mother, who now lives in Pensacola with her second husband. *HA HA HA! Roy found the costume. . . . . . . 🛞 🔥 ☠️ isnt she a RIOT???* 🐲 🦖 🐉 *God bless u and my sweet Grandbaby* ☺ 🖤 🙏

Agitated, the young mother swipes out of the text thread and drifts between three social media platforms, feeling the weight and warmth of her baby beneath her right arm, cherishing his tiny sounds of contentment as he nurses. As usual, predators are wreaking havoc on the internet. Predators are the only people in town. If she had to summarize the plot of contemporary life, the mother would say: it's about everyone punishing each other for things they didn't do. And here she is, refusing to look at her baby, punishing him for something he didn't do.

The mother has developed a phobia of her baby's eyes.

He is four weeks old. For four weeks, she's been living in the cellar of her mind. All day, she has been feeding her anxiety with Mommy Blogs. They are dreadful, the Mommy Blogs, worse than the medical websites, but likewise designed to exploit your Thanatos. *Mothering is the most valuable work you will ever do,* the Mommy Blogs declare with rainproof conviction. Before clicking on them, the mother prepared herself for what she previously believed to be the worst possible diagnosis: *You are a bad mother.* But that was not, in fact, the worst possible diagnosis. *You are a psychopath,* the Mommy Blogs concluded. *You are a threat to us all.*

On her sofa, cradling her baby, the mother begins to panic, so she self-soothes. *Deep breath in, exhale the tension. Let the forehead, eyebrows, and mouth go slack. Hear nothing but the whirr of the ceiling fan.* She's supposed to imagine her body as a jellyfish, or something. Visualize the boundaries between her body and the rest of the world dissolving. Her cousin Kara taught her these tricks, back when they were roommates.

Before she was a mother, the mother was Hope. "It's funny that your name is Hope," Kara once said. "Because you're, like, so bad at it." After high school, Hope got a job as a waitress, Kara as a hairdresser. Together, they rented a cheap house near the river. Kara had a taste for neon clothing, cinnamon gum, and anguished men. Her hair color changed every few months, but she favored purple. She was a bafflingly happy person, often belting Celine Dion and dancing as she cooked. Frequently, Hope wondered what it would be like to vacation in her cousin's psychology. When they were twenty, Kara found Hope in the fetal position on the bathroom tile at three in the morning, sobbing about how frightened she was, frightened of everything, an everything so big it was essentially nothing, and the nothing swallowed her, swallowed everything. The next day, Kara drove Hope to the Vegetable Bed, the only health food store in Vacca Vale—a small cube of flickering light that beguiled them both with its perfume of spices and variety of sugar substitutes. They returned with a paper bag of homeopathic remedies that Hope could neither understand nor afford: aconite, argentum nitricum, stramonium, arsenicum album, ignatia. Whenever Hope would nosedive into one of her electrocuting shadows, Kara dispensed a palmful of remedies, brewed lavender tea, subscribed walks. Meditation. Yoga. Magnesium. Often, she'd put on an episode of Hope's favorite television show, *Meet the Neighbors.* "Wear this necklace around your neck," Kara would say. "It's amethyst—the tranquilizing crystal, great for fear. Dispels negativity. Here, do this breathing exercise with me." As Kara often informed men at bars, she was a Myers-Briggs INFP ("the mediator"), an

Enneagram Type 2 ("the giver"), an astrological Virgo ("the healer"). It was her vocation, she believed, to nurture.

Now, in her apartment, Hope can still hear Kara guiding her through a breathing exercise, her lilac voice hovering in the room. *Deep breath in. Exhale. One, two, three, four, five, six, seven, eight, nine, ten. Again.* As she breathes, Hope can feel her baby against her skin, warm and soft.

Her fear is not so mysterious, she reasons. Her husband has been gone at the construction site all day, and there is no sleep in her recent history, just a lump of an oncoming cold in her throat. Her breasts are swollen to celebrity size, there are bolts of electricity zapping the powerlines of her brain, and without any assistance from coffee, her body has awakened itself to the pitch of animal vigilance. The hormones have turned the volume of the world all the way up, angling her ears babyward, forcing her to listen—always listen—for his new and spitty voice. She feels like a fox. Like a fox on Adderall.

Not to mention the greater body-terrors. After the birth, it stopped being a pussy and went back to being a vagina. She is discovering that pregnancy, birth, and postpartum recovery comprise three acts of a horror film no one lets you watch before you live it. In Catholic school, they made Hope and her peers watch videos of abortions, made them listen to women weep afterward, made them watch the fetus in the womb flinch away from the doctor's tool. But did anyone ever tell them what would happen when you pushed the fetus out of your body and into the world? No. It was "beautiful." It was "natural." Above all, it was a "miracle." Motherhood shrouded in a sacred blue veil, macabre details concealed from you, an elaborate conspiracy to trick Catholics into making more Catholics.

Afterpains strike the mother's body like bolts of goddish lightning when she nurses. Nursing is not intuitive, and pumping makes her feel like a cyborg cow. Whenever she sneezes, she pees. To address this, she's supposed to do Kegels, an exercise from Hell. The internet instructs her to imagine she is sitting on a marble. *Then tighten your pelvic muscles as though you're lifting the marble.* "Quite frankly," the mother said to her husband the other night, after reading the instructions out loud, "what in the fuck?" She describes her physical states to her husband compulsively, in detail, as though she is a dummy and a ventriloquist is making her do it. If he doesn't share the cost, she will force him to imagine it.

But she doesn't need to force him. When she starts to speak of the toll the birth has taken, he holds her hands, her gaze, her pain. "I wish I could take it," he says. "I wish I could take it all from you and put it into myself." Then he kisses her neck, gently defibrillating her back to life. He wants this, he tells her. He wants the gore; he wants four in the morning; he wants the beginning and the middle and the end; he wants to fix whatever he can fix and be there through the rest; he wants the bad and the good; he wants the sickness and the health. "I want you," he says. "Every you." He calls her a goddess. A hero. A miracle.

No, the mother thinks. No, she is not losing it. And, yes, it is normal to feel abnormal, after a body has left your body. Despite the absence of her particular condition online, the mother reasons, it is not so freakish to mortally fear your own baby's eyes, when so much weather is raging inside you, and Twitter is cawing the news. Gunfire, murder, oil spill, terrorism, wildfire, abduction, bombing, floods. Funny video in which a woman opens her car to find a brown bear sitting in the driver's seat snacking on her groceries. Murder, murder, war. The internet is upset. To experience reality as a handful of tap water, at a time like this, is to find oneself in good company. The baby blues—could they be like this? Neon and shrieking?

What is it *about* her baby's eyes? They are too round. Permanently shocked. The baby catalogues each image with an expression of outrage, inspecting the world as though he might sue it. He doesn't blink enough. She tries to engage him—jangling her keys, refracting light in an old jam jar, dancing her fingers—but visual stimulation overwhelms him, and whenever she tries something like this, he gets upset. The baby prefers to behold plain and unthreatening surfaces, like the walls. And they are arresting, his eyes, almost black, always liquid, often frantic. A feature inherited from his father's family—a handsome tribe, each cousin moody and gorgeous and good at puzzles. The mother *loves* this pair of eyes, this pair her body formed like valuable carbon minerals under pressure. She loves his eyes as much as she loves his microtoenails, his fuzz of black hair, the scent of his head, the rash that resembles a barcode on his chubby, lolling neck. She loves her baby in colors she's never seen before, just as the Mommy Blogs warned that she would. But love does not preclude terror—at twenty-five, the mother knows that the latter almost always accompanies the former. His eyes terrify her.

The mother tries to determine what the eyes evoke. A security camera. A panther's gaze in the dark. A stalker in the bathroom. The eyes of the man who repeatedly thwacked the driver's side window of that old van, years back, while she idled at the drive-through, dreaming of fries and sweet tea.

The man had used a child's shovel to hit her window. Yellow plastic. He did not blink. There was no language in his throat, just ripping growls, his motivation unclear. A man who had lost it—and that was the right phrase, it contained the right holes. At the drive-through, the man's eyes were dark, scared, and open. Lost it.

She had cranked down her window and offered to order him something, but he didn't seem to hear her.

"Look at me," he said over and over. "Look at me."

She rolled up her window, wishing it were automatic so that this gesture of disregard wasn't quite as violent, afraid of him but also, suddenly, bound to him. The coincidental nature of all social collision has always troubled the mother, even before she was a mother. To have a nationality, a lover, a family, a coworker, a neighbor—the mother understands these to be fundamentally absurd connections, as they are accidents, and yet they are the tyrants of every life. After she rolled up her window, she approached the drive-through speaker and ordered. The man hit the glass of the next car with his beach shovel, his eyes wide open.

Now, when the baby pushes away, the mother offers him milk from her left breast, but he refuses it. She burps him against her toweled shoulder, flooded with chemical love for this fragile being. He fusses. She rocks him. Within fifteen minutes, he's asleep again. This is life, she has learned, with a newborn: it's easing someone into and out of consciousness, over and over, providing sustenance in between. As though infants inhabit a different planet, one that orbits its sun four times faster than Earth does. If you want to understand the human condition, pay close attention to infants: the stakes are simultaneously at their highest, because you could die at any moment, and at their lowest, because someone bigger is satisfying every need. Language and agency have not yet arrived. What's that like? Observe a baby.

She places hers in his crib and cracks her neck.

When her husband returns around half past nine at night, his head shelled in the construction hard hat, his boots dusty, his odor of perspiration and sunblock a kind of home, their baby is still asleep. For the first time, the mother realizes she hasn't spoken to anyone all day. She meant to take the baby for a walk but forgot. Television and radio did not occur to her. Fourteen hours tense and alone, panning the day for peril.

She hands her husband a plate of fish sticks and ketchup.

"What a feast." He smiles, kissing her bare shoulder. "Thanks, baby."

Don't call me that, she doesn't say. You're welcome, she means to say, but she can't remember how to transport words out of her head and into the world. It's been years, she feels, since she tried.

"Hey, I'm really sorry about Elsie Blitz," her husband says as he washes his hands. "That must've been sad for you."

The mother blinks rapidly, as though trying to clear something from her vision. "What?"

Elsie Blitz is the star of *Meet the Neighbors*. It was Hope's mother who first introduced her to the mid-twentieth-century family sitcom. Perhaps because *Meet the Neighbors* showcases a fraught but affectionate alliance between a conventional housewife and her rascal of a daughter, watching the show was a kind of matrilineal tradition in Hope's family: when Hope was a kid, her mother viewed it alongside her, just as Hope's grandmother had viewed it alongside Hope's mother. Hope still summons the show to her screen when she can't sleep, gradually identifying more with the mother than the daughter; maybe she'll watch it with her own child, one day. Elsie Blitz plays Susie Evans, a trouble-loving spitfire at the center of the series. Elsie Blitz was a child so optimally childish, she came to represent all children to Hope. She had a face like an apple, a sunny grin, plentiful confidence. She could tap-dance, sing, and whistle. Her disobedience, however reckless, was always redeemed by the fun that it generated and ultimately forgiven by authorities. As a kid, Hope measured her deficiencies against the idealized Susie Evans, but neither the character nor the actress inspired envy. Just sisterly aspiration. In Hope's mind, Elsie Blitz was forever frozen at the age of eleven—the age of Susie Evans in the series finale. It had been so nice to know that at least one person in the world would never have to grow up.

Her husband sits down at the kitchen table, his posture freighted with guilt, like he's accidentally disclosed someone else's secret. "I thought you would've heard by now." He frowns. "I'm sorry. I wouldn't have brought it up otherwise."

"Why? What happened?"

"She passed away today," her husband replies. "She was in her eighties."

The mother braces for a feeling that never arrives. It's as though she's underwater, and the news exists above her, on a dock. "Oh," she finally says. "Sad."

Her husband studies her with concern but drops the subject. While they eat—while he eats—she considers telling her husband about the eye phobia. She has considered telling him every night for four weeks. *Hey,* she could say, once she remembered how to talk normally. *There's this weird thing. This weird thing that's been happening, sort of funny, nothing crazy, just weird.*

"How's our big guy?" the husband asks between bites.

The mechanics of speech return to her, jerky at first. "He's . . ." Not big. *He's tiny,* she wants to scream. He needs to be rescued from his own smallness, like everyone else! She swallows a glassful of water in one breath. "Babies. What I like about babies." Her eyes lose focus.

"Hm?"

"Babies know that just because you have it easy doesn't mean that life is *easy.*"

Her husband chews a fish stick. "So he's alive?"

She nods.

"Terrific." He smooths her eyebrow, his finger rough. "I love you," he says. "You're tired, huh?"

"There's this . . ." She fixes her eyes on the smoke detector. "This funny thing, that's been happening."

"Oh yeah? What's that?"

She hesitates. Her husband believes that she is a good mother, a normal person, a worthy investment. "I'm scared. . . ."

Her husband puts down his fork, takes her seriously. "What?"

"Nothing." She begins to cry as quietly as she can. "I'm—so—tired."

Her husband wipes his mouth and studies her with his dark and searching eyes. "Babe," he says. He stands and takes her back in his hands, kneading muscles and skin, and she wonders who designs costumes for bearded dragons, what species will study evidence of hers in 90 million years, and what misunderstandings will result. What would a nuclear explosion feel like? Would the death be instantaneous? Are there physical buttons involved? Will her busted vagina ever resume its life as a pussy? Where did the dead mouse land after she flung it out of their window? Where is that man she saw at the drive-through, and what is he doing right now? Is this the most valuable work of her life? Is she a psychopath? Is she a threat to them all?

"Oh, babe," he says. "Of course you are."

"What?"

"Of course you're tired."

C6: Ida and Reggie, both in their seventies, sit in their living room, smoking cigarettes and watching the news on high volume. Bad factory fire in Detroit, Michigan. Pageant queen starts nonprofit phone-case business, proceeds funding dental care for refugees. Superpest destroying monocrops of pepper in Vietnam.

Ida remembers what she wanted to tell Reggie earlier that afternoon.

"Reggie." She coughs. "Reggie."

"What?"

"Can you hear me, Reggie?"

"Huh?"

"Turn it down."

"Huh?"

"Turn it *down*. I got to tell you something."

He presses a gnarled thumb to the remote. "What?"

"Frank's in jail again," announces Ida.

"Tina's Frank?"

"What other Frank do we have?"

"What'd he do this time?"

"What do you think?"

"Another robbery?"

Ida nods. "This time he had a gun."

"I thought that knee surgery would keep him out of trouble."

"Bad knee can't stop a dog like Frank."

"Well, feels good to be right all along, I guess." Reggie takes a long drag. "We did what we could."

"He had that flashy car," mumbles Ida. "Those stupid boots."

"I just hope Tina knows she can't come whining to us, hauling her kids over to do 'chores' around the place and expecting us to pay them."

"We should've tried something different," says Ida. "One of those barefoot schools. Piano lessons. Vitamins. No gluten. None of the kids turned out right."

"Ida, it's done and gone now. Tina's a grown woman. The best thing we can do for her is let her take care of herself."

Ida bobs a cigarette between her teeth.

"And you're wrong," Reggie says. "The kids turned out fine." He restores the volume of the news. Australian parents beg national governments to rescue their daughters and grandchildren from camps in Syria. Their Australian daughters married ISIS members, and now they face unspeakable violence. Can scientists successfully grow a human kidney in a pig? Not yet but stay tuned. Groundwater contaminated in North Dakota. Celebrity baby born with hypertrichosis, colloquially referred to as *werewolf syndrome*. A thirteen-year-old girl goes viral for shaving bars of soap. "It's just a simple supply-and-demand kind of situation," she says with a shrug when questioned. Her channel has made her a millionaire. "I listen to what the people want."

When the news anchor asks her to explain ASMR to boomers, she takes a deep breath, like she's bracing for liftoff. "Okay, well, it stands for *autonomous sensory meridian response*. It's these tingles some people get around their skull? And kind of down their spine? You feel like—like you're shimmering or something. It's the best feeling I know. There are all sorts of triggers. The rustle of leaves or whatever, someone taking your photograph. A really special present, made just for you. Haircuts. Bob Ross. Anyway, I get it whenever someone's paying very close attention to something else. Back when I was little, I thought either everyone felt it and nobody talked about it, or nobody felt it except for me. Either way, I knew to keep my trap shut. But then, when I was maybe eleven, there was this thing in the news about it, and suddenly we all found each other. It was like a revolution. I mean—revelation. I started watching these videos, and I realized there was an opening in the market. But this soap-shaving stuff? That's not my thing. It does nothing for me. I just do it for the masses."

The news anchor laughs uncomfortably. "So is it like a—is it like a . . . ?"

"What?"

"Is it like a . . . ?"

The girl watches him impatiently. "What? Like a dirty thing?"

"Well—"

"No. It doesn't have to be, at least. And geez, I'm thirteen. Why are you asking me that?"

The news anchor laughs again, turns to the camera. "Well, you heard it here first, folks!"

Cut to leafy monocrop in California. Doleful scientist in a white coat. Kale could be poisonous.

"Reggie," Ida says. "Reggie."

"*What?*"

"Turn it down. Something else I forgot."

He sighs but obeys. "Well?"

"I found another dead mouse on the balcony."

He blinks. "So?"

"It was killed in a trap."

"You set a trap out there?"

"*No,*" Ida says significantly. "That's what I'm trying to tell you. I *didn't* put a trap out there."

He waits. "Okay?"

"Did you?" she asks.

"No."

"Then it's what I thought!"

"Thought *what?*"

"It's those kids upstairs!" cries Ida like a detective in an old, bad movie. "Those newlyweds with the baby!"

"What're you talking about?"

"*Reginald.* Listen. You're not *listening.*"

"I *am* listening!"

"Those newlyweds are dropping their dead mice out the window."

Reggie dabs his cigarette on the steel ashtray and considers. "Well, what would they do that for?" he asks reasonably.

"Who am I to say? Laziness. Selfishness. Socialism. I'm telling you: they trap the mice at their place, and they don't want to deal with the bodies themselves, so they just—poof. Drop them out the window. Trap and all." Ida smooths her thin white hair.

"You sure it's them?" asks Reggie.

"All but positive."

"How?"

"Saw it, once."

"When?" demands Reggie.

"Last week. I was standing in the kitchen, making beets. What do I see? Dead body, falling from the sky."

"You don't think it's somebody else?"

"Who'd it be? *Alan*? Sweet *Alan*? No—these kids, they don't care about *community*. They have no concept of respect. First the sex, sex all the time, phony Hollywood sex—"

"We were all there," mutters Reggie.

"And then the wailing baby. And now *this*! I'm telling you, Reggie."

"Okay." He angles the remote at the screen.

"I'm not finished."

"*What?*"

"You need to drop it on their doormat."

"Drop *what?*"

"That dead mouse. Trap and all."

"Ida."

"You have to do it. They need to learn their lesson."

Reggie thinks, then smashes his fist on the armrest. "This is how wars start!"

"Oh, *please*." Ida rolls her eyes.

"I mean it!"

"You're so quick to call *me* dramatic, but the minute I ask you to do something you don't want to do, you go and say a thing like—"

"Why can't you let it go?" asks Reggie. There are some questions spouses ask each other over and over for decades, starring a fatal flaw that one has perceived in the other. Between Reggie and Ida, this is one such question. "Why can't you let anything *go*?"

"I live here!" Ida yells. "And I think a person who's lived here for over thirty years has a right to a peaceful home! A right to a balcony without any *corpses* on it!"

Reggie studies his wife. "And why can't you do it?" he asks slowly.

Indignation twists Ida's wrinkled face. "What?"

"Put the trap on their doorstep. Why can't *you* do it? If you're so bent on teaching a lesson?"

She gestures to her ankles and wrists, invoking her arthritis with a look of disbelief. "Often, I think you *want* me to die first!"

There is a dirge of an ambulance on the street below. They listen until it fades.

"So will you?" Ida prompts.

Reggie lights another cigarette. "It's late."

"Reggie."

He says nothing.

"Do this for me. Just this one thing. For your *wife*."

"After the news," Reggie concedes.

C4: Three teenage boys. One teenage girl. A stranger. A goat. A neighbor. Curdled plans. Punishment. Punishing who. Each confused. Each frightened. Laughter perched. A room of kicking hearts, kicking faster. Scent of roses. Pocketful of clovers. Good intentions. Tears on her face. A knife in his hands. No. Please. No. Stop. No. Don't. One of the boys films on his phone, grinning. This will get so many views.

C2: A jar of maraschino cherries waits on a lonely woman's nightstand, a small fork beside it.

PART II

Afterlife

~~

Around five in the evening on Monday, July fifteenth—two days before she exits her body—Blandine Watkins stops at the laundromat before heading northeast and wonders if the night's impending activity will reveal her to be a moral or immoral person. Power is one translation of virtue, she knows, and she believes that there is no such thing as amoral activity. Blandine recalls a passage that Hildegard von Bingen wrote about nine hundred years ago: *The will warms an action, the mind receives it, and thought bodies it forth. This understanding, however, discerns an action by the process of knowing good and evil.* Blandine has plenty of will—*the will is like a fire baking every action in an oven,* according to Hildegard—and some thoughts, but does she lack moral understanding? After considering the question for a few minutes, she realizes she's not very invested in it.

Sitting on the laundromat bench, Blandine tries to uncramp her muscles, clip herself from her body, and focus on the slobber of the machines. A dull financial angst pounds around her kidneys. She thinks of the urban revitalization plan that is about to destroy the last good thing in Vacca Vale: a lush expanse of park called Chastity Valley. Blandine is sick of cartoon villains. She prefers her villains complex and nuanced. Disguised as heroes.

Two heavy corduroy bags wait at her feet like a pair of guard dogs. The presence of free coffee at this underfunded laundromat always moves Blandine. She tries to focus on the smell of it, but a violent energy is brewing inside her. Her knees bounce uncontrollably.

The laundromat is usually vacant on Mondays, but this evening, another woman sits opposite Blandine, her eyes pinned to a forsaken sock on the linoleum. Unblinking, unseeing. The woman's hair is the color of mouse fur, her bangs are cut short, and she is wearing woolly knitted clothes despite the heat. Forty-something. She has the posture of a question mark, a stock face, and a pair of nineteenth-century eyeglasses. Her solitude is as prominent as the cross around her neck. You could be persuaded you'd never seen her before, even if you passed her daily. You could be persuaded you saw her every day, even if you'd never passed her before. You'd ask her for directions; you'd tag her with a name like Susan and with a job in accounting; you'd assume that she keeps a bird feeder. She could be your neighbor. She could be your relative. She could be anyone. Frightened by the energy building inside her, Blandine resolves to talk to this woman.

"Do you live in the Rabbit Hutch?" asks Blandine. "You look familiar."

The woman twitches. "Yes." Her voice is like a communion wafer—tasteless, light. Blandine was never baptized, but she sometimes attends Catholic Mass and receives communion anyway. It's not like they check your ID.

"What floor?" asks Blandine.

"Second."

"I'm third. What's your door?"

The woman inspects Blandine as though X-raying her for sinister motives. "C2."

"That's directly below ours," replies Blandine, smiling. "We're C4."

"Oh?"

"It's weird, right? Living so close to people you know nothing about?"

"Indeed," responds the woman politely. She attaches her gaze to the machines, obviously longing for a return to the standard script, which demands nothing of strangers in public spaces but the exchange of a few half-smiles, to indicate that you won't knife each other. She caps and uncaps a bottle of detergent in her lap.

"What's your name?" asks Blandine.

The woman clenches her jaw, her shoulders, her hands. "Joan."

"Joan. Nice to meet you, Joan. I'm Blandine."

Joan waves feebly.

"Do you believe in an afterlife?" asks Blandine.

"Pardon?"

"Afterlife."

"Afterlife?"

"Life after death?"

"I understand the term," says Joan.

"Do you?"

"Understand the term?"

"Believe in an afterlife?"

Joan's attention escapes to a clock. "I guess so. Yes. I'm Catholic."

"It sounds like you're on the fence."

"I'm not on the fence. I just didn't expect the question."

"It sounds like maybe you're on the fence."

Joan crosses her arms. "I'm Catholic."

"Maybe you're holding out for evidence."

"You don't *need* evidence when you have faith," answers Joan. Then she blushes.

"Right, right. Faith is predicated upon an absence of evidence." Blandine pauses. "But I always found that a bit awful of God. To *withhold* evidence, if the Cosmic Egg is so important. That's how Hildegard von Bingen puts it—*the Cosmic Egg.* But yeah, it's suspiciously stingy to give us nothing but a couple of self-professed messiahs every three thousand years. Prophets whose stories don't align. Mary on toast. Somebody's cured muscular dystrophy. It's a lot to ask of us without collateral, don't you think? Especially when there are so many competing stories, and the stakes are so high. Inferno or paradise. Forever."

"I suppose," says Joan.

"But Hildegard says that God told her—wait, I'll find it—hang on. . . ." Blandine flutters through *She-Mystics: An Anthology* and, to Joan's horror, begins reading out loud. "So God told Hildegard: 'You, human creature! In the way of humans, you desire to know more about this exalted plan, but a seal of secrecy will be imposed on you; for you are not permitted to investigate the secrets of God more than the divine majesty wishes to reveal, because of his love for believers.'" Blandine closes the book, squints her eyes. "I don't know. Seems like an easy exit, to me. God just *loves* believers so much? The hubris of it!"

Joan bristles. "Well, I don't know."

"Have you read Dante's *Divine Comedy*?" asks Blandine.

Joan reacts like she's being ridiculed. "No."

"Read *Purgatorio*, if nothing else. It's just like Vacca Vale. Like a travel guide. Honestly."

Joan's body contorts with the desire to be elsewhere, and Blandine sees it. She wants to stop haranguing this poor woman, but she feels like she'll drown in a current of her own terrifying energy if she stops talking. "I've been reading about Catholic female mystics lately," Blandine says.

"Oh?"

"Do you know much about them?"

"No."

"They loved suffering," says Blandine. "Mad for it."

Joan picks a cuticle. Her nail beds are catastrophic. "Hm."

"They were spectacularly unusual, the mystics. Blessed Anna Maria Taigi, for example? She said she could see the future by looking into this—this sort of sun globe? And Gabrielle Bossis—a French actress— she wrote a book transcribing her conversations with Jesus. *Word for word*, can you imagine? Therese Neumann never ate or drank anything besides the Eucharist. Marie Rose Ferron had her first vision of Jesus at the age of six. In *Massachusetts*, no less. And then there was Gemma Galgani. *Daughter of passion*, they called her. People were always walking in on Gemma in the middle of divine ecstasy, sometimes levitation. She had regular visions of her guardian angel and Jesus and the Virgin Mary—the whole crew—just kind of hanging out. She had a 'great desire to suffer for Jesus.'"

A watery smile. "Too funny."

"Blessed Maria Bolognesi's another good one. She had a rough childhood—malnourishment, illness after illness, abusive stepfather, so forth, we've all been there—but then to top it off, she was possessed for about a year. There were the usual symptoms: afraid of holy water and priests, couldn't enter churches, couldn't receive sacraments, compulsively spat on sacred images. But my favorite part is that sometimes, invisible forces would pull at Maria's clothes, and it would spook the living daylights out of her friends."

Joan raises her eyebrows. "Invisible forces?"

"You know, that's not even the part that strikes me most. It's the *friends*. Maria maintained an active social life, while *possessed*." Blandine places her hand over her heart. "Incredible."

"Very unusual," says Joan.

"Eventually," Blandine continues, sprinting via language from the storm inside her, "a bishop snuck a blessing on Maria when she was on her way to a psychiatric hospital, allegedly exorcising her. A lot of the mystics were diagnosed with mental illnesses, as you'd expect. And just when things were looking up for Maria—demons gone, a spot of safety, a taste of health—she had a vision in which Jesus slipped a ruby ring on her fiancé finger." Blandine pauses. She normally tries to avoid saying *in which* out loud, to minimize the number of people who find her insufferable. "And when she emerged from the vision, she saw the *real, physical* ring, right there, on her left hand. Bang."

It's clear to Blandine that this intrigues Joan against her will. "What did she do?"

"Oh, she freaked out. Then Jesus was like, *You're gonna sweat blood.* And you know what? She did. All the time. Would stain the sheets and everything."

"*Why?*"

"Why what?"

"Why sweat *blood?*"

"To suffer for Jesus, I guess."

"But why *that?*"

Blandine considers. "The book never explains it."

"Curious!"

"You know what's even weirder? According to her friend, after Maria would do her thing—sweat blood—the whole room would fill with this . . . this kind of perfume?"

"What did it smell like?"

"I don't know. They say it was sweet."

"Horrible," says Joan darkly.

"I know. But it wasn't all bad. Jesus helped Maria prophesize the end of World War II, got her little sister a job . . . personally, I find the engaged-to-Jesus rhetoric creepy as hell, incestuous at best, but it's quite a phenomenon. Most of the female mystics report similar experiences. Jesus appears to them and—you know—*proposes.*"

Sweat is blooming from the woman's face. "I don't like that."

"A lot of them had stigmata—where you bleed from the wrists and feet and side? For no medical reason? Holy Wounds, they say. Wounds corresponding to the ones Jesus received during crucifixion."

"Is that so?"

"According to accounts. But who's to say, really? Most of the female mystics starved themselves in favor of 'purer nourishment.' They were always very sick. A lot of them died young. Skeptics say that their visions were really just migraines. I think that we see whatever we fear, whatever we want. We look at the world, absorb thirty percent of its data, and our subconscious fills in the rest." Blandine cracks her knuckles. "I'm not sure I believe in God."

Joan removes her glasses and massages a lens with her long skirt. "Reading can be a nice pastime."

"Sometimes I think they were just hungry."

"Who?"

"The mystics."

Joan considers. "Possible."

It is Joan's reluctant engagement with the conversation, not her protest against it, that motivates Blandine to muster all the willpower she possesses and force these leaping, punching words to stay inside her head. It's like closing a cellar latch against the winds of a tornado, and her knee springs wildly as she does it, but she succeeds. Joan appears relieved.

Among the many objections Blandine harbors against the Catholic female mystics, the one she can't overcome is the fundamental selfishness. The *individualism* operating in their lives. Even within religious communities, among the mystics, there was a premium on seclusion, and it's clear to Blandine that when a person is in the middle of divine ecstasy, she's really just interacting with herself. An elevated form of masturbation. Many convents devoted themselves to people who were poor, elderly, sick, displaced, ostracized, imprisoned, disabled, orphaned. But the mystics—the ones Blandine admires—they didn't get out much. They viewed solitude as a precondition of divine receptivity. Most spent their lives essentially alone.

So how, wonders Blandine, would a contemporary mystic challenge the plundering growth imperative, if that were her goal? She'd have to break out of her solitude. There's no way to overthrow the system without going outside and making some eye contact. No matter how small your carbon footprint, you can't simply forgo food and comfort and sex all your life and call yourself ethically self-sacrificial. In order for her life to be considered ethical, thinks Blandine, she must try to dismantle systemic injustice. But she doesn't know how to do that.

Blandine sighs. She always knew that she was too small and stupid to lead a revolution, but she had hoped she could at least imagine one. She takes a deep breath, attacked by an awareness of how impossible it is to learn and accomplish all that she needs to learn and accomplish before she dies. She's spiraling down thoughts of the albedo effect and the positive correlation between climate change and most mass extinctions on the geologic record when Joan drops her detergent cap. It rolls beneath a machine. Blandine stands and retrieves it for her.

"Here."

"Thank you," replies Joan. "How old are you?"

"Eighteen."

"Eighteen!" Joan exclaims. "But you can't—are you really?"

"Yes. Why?"

"You don't seem eighteen."

This accusation depresses Blandine more and more each time it is leveled against her.

"I don't know how else to seem," she mutters.

"You just . . . you don't *sound* like you're eighteen."

You can't exist, the world informs Blandine daily. You're not possible.

"Well," says Blandine. "I am."

"You're very . . ." Joan squints at her as though she's an abstract painting, then trails off. "Are you going to college?"

Blandine touches her neck, upset to find it there. "No."

"Oh, well," says Joan sweetly. "It's never too late. You should think about it. They have a lot of people like you there. I went to VVCC, myself."

Vacca Vale Community College. "That's nice," says Blandine. "Maybe I'll apply."

"Yes." Joan smiles. "I think you'd enjoy it."

They sit in silence. Blandine forces herself not to say anything, hoping that Joan will engage with the mystics' fetishization of suffering.

Perhaps Joan's just reflecting. But soon it becomes clear that Joan is waiting for the topic to pass, like a flash of hail. Loneliness grips Blandine
with the force of a puppeteer.

"Do you have a bird feeder?" Blandine asks, changing course.

"Pardon?"

"You just—you look like the kind of person who would have a bird
feeder."

"No," replies Joan.

"Really?"

"Yes."

"Have you ever had a bird feeder?"

"No."

"Not even as a child?"

"Never."

"Huh." Blandine tucks the library book back in her bag. "Well, Joan,
between you and me, I'm giving mysticism a go, myself. I think I have a
real shot. From what I can tell, theism isn't a necessary prerequisite. All
I want is to exit my body."

Joan coughs. "Ah."

"I think we should all take each other a little more seriously."

A pause. "Perhaps," whispers Joan.

"Sometimes I walk around, bumping into people, listening to them
joke and fight and sneeze, and I don't believe anyone is real. Not even
myself. Do you know what I mean?"

Joan looks her in the eye for the first time. "Yes."

"It's like what Simone Weil says. 'To know that this man who is hungry and thirsty really exists as much as I do—that is enough, the rest
follows of itself.' Simone was a bona fide mystic." Blandine bites her nail.
"What's the rest, I wonder."

Another silence.

"I'm glad we met," says Blandine. "Strange to remain strangers with
your neighbor, don't you think?"

"Oh. Sure."

"We're all just sleepwalking. Can I tell you something, Joan? I want
to wake up. That's my dream: to wake up."

"Oh. Well. You'll be okay."

"I feel better, having met you. Like, ten milligrams more awake."

Joan blinks. "That's nice."

"But I know I'm not doing it right."

"Oh?"

"Pop religion and demons and little biographies. Sweating blood. You must think I'm bananas."

"No." Joan checks her phone in a clunky, theatrical gesture. "No, no. Oh, late. I should get going." She stands abruptly. "Nice to meet you." Abandoning her load of blues, she exits the laundromat and slips into the evening as though trying not to wake it.

Alone, Blandine grips her forehead. She's certain that she has some kind of social impairment; she just doesn't know what it's called. Internet quizzes never know what to do with her. In general, she feels too much or too little, interacts too much or too little—never the proper amount. It seems to her that she's spent her whole life sitting in a laundromat, freaking people out. The energy mounts and mounts; she should have brought her vaporizer. She forces herself to sit in quiet. Then she checks her watch. Finally, it's time to go.

She lifts her corduroy bags, which are stocked with bottles of fake blood, several voodoo dolls fashioned from sticks, bags of dirt from the Valley, latex-free gloves, her library book, and small animal skeletons. She power walks into an enchanting Midwestern dusk and makes her way northeast to the Vacca Vale Country Club. It's hot, but her hands are numb.

A Threat to Us All

Vacca Vale Gazette

~~~

By Araceli Gonzales　*Vacca Vale Gazette*
Tuesday, July 16, 8:50 a.m. ET　Updated 2 hrs ago

CELEBRATION INTERRUPTED BY DISTURBING ACT

Last night, officials met at the Vacca Vale Country Club for a wild game dinner, celebrating the official launch of a <u>development</u> plan. Unfortunately, the developers did not have the opportunity to taste the fruits of their labor. Derailed by a mysterious attack, the dinner ended before it began.

At 7:18 p.m., two large ceiling vents opened in the banquet hall. Immediately, several small animal bones and large quantities of dirt fell from the vents, littering the table and attendees. These items were followed by roughly two liters of what was first assumed to be real blood but later determined to be a persuasive imitation. Last, <u>26 voodoo dolls</u> dropped from the vent. The dolls were fashioned from twigs and string. They had X's for eyes.

To understand who might be responsible for the attack, private detective Ruby Grubb says that it is important to understand its context. "When you're dealing with a group or individual who commits organized sabotage," she told the *Gazette*, "it's almost always politically motivated. To track them down, you look for a motive. You look at the whole story. Not just personal history, but the history of their town, their country, their world. I think the first clue lies in the redevelopment proposal itself."

The Vacca Vale Revitalization Plan will generate an estimated $4 million in local tax revenue annually and create thousands of jobs, provided that the general campaign is successful. The plan takes advantage of Chastity Valley's natural beauty, and will construct luxury condominiums in the hills, transforming Vacca Vale from a dying postindustrial city into a startup hub, attracting talent from around the world.

Last year was particularly difficult for Vacca Vale, with unemployment at an all-time high of 11.7% and the rat population surpassing the human population by an estimated 30,000. (Who could forget the time a rat fell from the ceiling of a Ta Ta's restaurant onto a patron's fries?) Meanwhile, the cottontail rabbit population surpassed the rat population. Crime was on the rise, and last year alone, the town logged 319 murders and non-negligent manslaughters; 21,068 instances of theft; 14,472 burglaries; 907 cases of rape; and 644 acts of arson. In September, the city suffered a 1,000-year flood, which caused over $3 million in damage, exacerbated by the 500-year flood that occurred just a few months before. Vacca Vale ranked first on *Newsweek*'s annual list of "Top Ten Dying American Cities." By February, Vacca Vale was forced to declare bankruptcy, and the city faced unincorporation.

By March, Vacca Vale's plight caught the attention of developer Benjamin Ritter. An urban designer based in New York City, Ritter is known for his extraordinarily successful campaigns reviving small towns across the Rust Belt. Swiftly, Ritter partnered with Mayor Douglas Barrington and local real estate developer Maxwell Pinky, founder and CEO of Pinky LLC, to pull Vacca Vale out of the red and into the black. Within four months, the plan was underway. Ritter says Chastity Valley is the perfect site for renovation. "Vacca Vale's got a whole history of reinvention," he told the *Gazette*. "It's really buzzing with American spirit."

Construction will begin this upcoming August. The revitalization plan will renovate vacant Zorn Automobile factories, transforming them into the headquarters for three different tech startups whose identities have yet to be made public due to ongoing negotiations.

Benjamin Ritter, Maxwell Pinky, and Mayor Douglas Barrington were present at last night's dinner, along with 23 other men. Before the food was served, Ritter and his team projected a short film, which featured lifelike simulations of the plan, along with positive interviews with members of the community who say they are looking forward to a new economic era. The presentation concluded with a sneak peek at a commercial—the first of many that will air all over the country this year.

Following Ritter's presentation, the country club staff unveiled the food, set on chinaware that bore the new town flag—a result of last year's design contest.

After Pastor Wheeler led the group in prayer, Mayor Barrington addressed the table of men. "It's been forty years since Zorn left us, and it's true that we never quite recovered," Barrington said. "But now is the time to pull ourselves up. Not by our bootstraps, but by our innovation. Our grit. Our hands. Each other. Now is the time to start over. There is nothing more American than resurrection." After applause, Barrington added, "Except, maybe, a hearty meal you hunted yourself!"

The supper featured venison, elk, hare, pheasant, turkey, quail, goose, and American coot, all of which were hunted from the surrounding region by the developing team and prepared by lauded Windy City chef Danny Fiorentino, who was invited to Vacca Vale for the occasion.

The dinner, however, was thwarted.

"I've never seen anything like it," said Maxwell Pinky, age 34, whose white suit was splattered with dirt and fake blood. "It was very troubling. An act of aggression like this is a threat to us all. We're here to help and protect this town—to foster community—and this was, like, the antithesis of that."

"Rest assured we are doing everything we can to identify the aggressors," said Officer Brian Stevens, who is leading the investigation. Officer Stevens and his team arrived on the scene at once, but they found no evidence of the aggressor(s) in the ventilation system or surrounding area. Surveillance captured nothing unusual.

Officials have, however, determined that the fake blood was made from water, corn syrup, flour, cocoa powder, and red food coloring.

"Obviously we don't have much to go on," Detective Grubb told the *Gazette*. "But if I had to guess, I'd say it's an ecoterrorist. You've got to chop down a heck of a lot of trees to build that housing in the Valley, don't you?"

According to Officer Stevens, however, it's too soon to speculate about the perpetrators. "But we do have reason to believe the people behind this act are experienced criminals," he said. "There were no fingerprints, no DNA on any of the items. All we know is that whoever got into the ventilation system had to be pretty small."

Some officials theorize that the invaders were animal-rights activists, protesting the wild game aspect of the dinner.

A veteran of small-town development, Benjamin Ritter has a different theory.

"It seems obvious to me that this was a protest against the Valley development. I mean, twenty-six voodoo dolls? When exactly twenty-six developers were present? Come on," Ritter told the *Gazette*. "I see this kind of resistance all the time. It can be painful for inhabitants to watch their town change. Usually, we see this in folks who are attached to the local history—often the older generation. They're worried that we're the Big Bad Wolf, coming to blow down their favorite diner and replace it with a chain, bulldoze the mom-and-pop supermarkets and build up megastores, take away their church parking, put up a stadium that nobody ever uses. And they have a right to be skeptical—urban revitalization plans have failed countless residents in the past. But we won't fail you. I think when people realize how beneficial our work will be for them, their children, their grandchildren, they won't be so scared."

He went on to say that if he could send one message to the aggressors, it would be: "We're on your side."

Officer Stevens and his team do not believe that the developers face any significant threats, but they are cautioning residents to remain alert and to report any unusual occurrences to the local police department. The event may be connected to a series of power outages that occurred during a charette this past spring.

If you can contribute any information about this event, please call or text 1-800-CRIMEFIGHTER, which will give you the option to place an anonymous tip.

The *Vacca Vale Gazette* will provide updates as they are made available. The revitalization plan will proceed on scheduled pace.

Where Life Lives On

～

Joan Kowalski is forty years old. Whenever she's forced to provide a Defining Characteristic during a corporate ice breaker, she reveals that she has freckles on her eyelids but nowhere else. Group leaders always demand that she prove it. After she closes her eyes, at least two good-natured strangers make comments like, *Oh my,* or, *I'll be damned,* or, *Very nice.* Joan never feels closer to anyone afterward, never feels like a defined character, and doesn't understand why people are so eager to break the ice.

Joan works at Restinpeace.com, *Where Life Lives On,* screening obituary comments for foul language, copyrighted material, and mean-spirited remarks about the deceased. "You would be surprised," she often tells people, "by how cruel people can be to the dead."

After a lethally stylish coiffeur described Joan's hair as "the color of February," she began to trim her bangs herself, at home, shorter than any stylist ever permitted. This performance of autonomy never ceases to exhilarate her. Like most denizens of Vacca Vale, Joan has never lived elsewhere, and she now occupies a small apartment in La Lapinière Affordable Housing Complex, on the corner of Bella Coola and Saint Francis. At the laundromat, once, she overheard two women discussing the origin story of their building: saddened by the economic decline of his hometown, a wonky Christian philanthropist—now a resident of Quebec—decided to donate money to fund an affordable housing complex in Vacca Vale. He had one stipulation: it must look and sound chic. So he chose a French word he liked and fastened it to a deteriorating building with vintage charm, prioritizing aesthetic over functionality. La Lapinière Affordable Housing Complex was born. The building is located in the southern edge of downtown, with abandoned Zorn factories to its west and Chastity Valley to its east. In the early twentieth century, the building housed factory laborers. The donor selected a darling rabbit wallpaper for the lobby, along with brass rabbit lamps he wished to place in every apartment. Developers eventually vetoed the lamps in favor of updating the building's water heater. After suffering a few more rejections, the donor stopped trying to influence the design. Now, most tenants of the building call their home by its English translation: the Rabbit Hutch.

Joan can eat an unnatural amount of watermelon in one sitting—a skill she sometimes employs to amuse friends and coworkers to the detriment of her digestion. She likes to ride the South Shore train to visit her aunt Tammy in Gary, Indiana. As the train pulls her across her state, she likes to watch the factories breathe orange fire into the sky, likes to imagine that she is a stowaway orphan headed toward a Big City Adventure. On the South Shore, she likes to read Charles Dickens because he pays attention to pollution but also makes her laugh, which makes her feel that it is possible to laugh in her own polluted city. Joan has never confidently traversed a crosswalk in her life, and she profoundly distrusts people who claim they don't like bread.

On the afternoon of Tuesday, July sixteenth, Joan Kowalski sits at her desk, scanning an article that appeared on her newsfeed. A coworker that Joan wanted to impress and befriend brought a watermelon to lunch an hour earlier; performative gorging ensued. In the end, it was all for nothing. Joan said something irreverent about a member of a royal family, acutely upsetting the coworker. If Joan had known that the coworker was the sort to get defensive about monarchies, she wouldn't have been so eager to impress her. But the damage is done.

According to the internet, threats associated with overeating watermelon include nausea, diarrhea, bloating, indigestion, and a "weak or absent pulse." Joan decides to distract herself from this information with the local news. She adjusts her drugstore glasses and leans closer to the screen. She can hear Sylvie crunching company Moon Chips in the adjacent cubicle. CELEBRATION INTERRUPTED BY DISTURBING ACT, reads the front page.

Joan doesn't care much about the Valley development—she could take it or leave it—but this event does unnerve her. Especially the voodoo dolls. Although she would never admit it, Joan is positively drugged with superstition. The supernatural—witchcraft, God, bad luck, astrology, time travel—has a death grip on her. She remembers the spectral girl at the laundromat last night, inquiring about the afterlife. Some odd name. The girl was pale, white-haired, elven, thin. Pretty in a strange way. Phantomized. Come to think of it, the girl was exactly as Joan imagines the Ghost of Christmas Past whenever she rereads *A Christmas Carol*. She thinks of the women who starved themselves—the fiancées of Jesus. Sweating blood.

Suddenly, Joan wants witnesses. Could anyone else see that girl?

"Joan?"

Joan quits the browser in a spasm of disgrace and spins. Her superior, Anne Shropshire, stands at the entrance of her cubicle. When Rest in Peace downsized two years prior, offices became stalls. To increase each employee's sense of audial privacy as spatial privacy diminished, a white-noise soundtrack was installed in the ventilation. The office now sounds like a transatlantic flight. As a result, Restinpeace.com employees do enjoy intensified audial privacy, but they also frequently scare each other on accident. The office is rather tense.

Joan's heart thuds. Relief that her pulse is neither weak nor absent briefly eclipses her shame.

"Sorry to bother you," says Shropshire, "but I wanted to bring a little oversight to your attention."

Joan folds her hands on her lap and waits. In the spotlight of direct attention, she becomes conscious of behavior programmed to operate unconsciously, like breathing and eye contact. She stares too long or not long enough, blinks too often or too little, inhales at irregular intervals, yawns in moments of suspense. Three avian pins are fastened to Anne Shropshire's blouse.

"As I'm sure you know," says Shropshire, "the Elsie Blitz obituary has drawn quite a lot of traffic. Your job as a screener is always very important and very valued here at Rest in Peace, but on high-profile obituaries like Elsie Blitz's, your job is even more important. *Supremely* important."

Joan needs to blink but worries that this would be a creepy time to do so. Her eyes water.

"Maybe you didn't see the comment posted at four thirty-nine this morning by user Abominable Glow Man?"

Joan swallows incorrectly. "I—"

"I hope you didn't, because I know that you know that it is our mission to foster a safe space. I hope that if you *had* read the comment, it would have been obvious to you that such a comment grossly violates our Respect the Deceased Policy, and you would have deemed it unfit for publication."

Joan nods at an ambiguous diagonal. Sylvie's crunching has paused.

"This is why we assume that you did not, in fact, see the comment. It would be alarming to us if you actually *read* the comment and approved it anyway."

"I got an," Joan begins, but the words are stuck in her throat. "I missed." She gives up.

"Sorry?"

"He emailed me."

Joan is proud of herself for delivering a whole sentence at a time like this, but Shropshire frowns.

"What? Who did?"

"The user. I—I tried to . . . delete his comment. But he." Joan is shaking. "Emailed."

"And?"

Through the bureaucratic obstacle course of the *Contact Us!* feature, user Abominable Glow Man managed to find Joan's work email and inform her, politely, that he was the son of Elsie Jane McLoughlin Blitz, and as such, he found Joan's censorship inappropriate. As her son, the user claimed, he had a right to contribute a frank appraisal of her life. A quick google search confirmed that the name on the email matched the name of Elsie Blitz's real son, although Joan understood that this proved nothing. Joan didn't reply to the message but restored his comment, deciding that he had a point: standard filters ought not apply to family members of the deceased. In any case, hundreds of new comments flooded the Elsie guest book every minute, burying his. Better to leave it buried, concluded Joan. It was her favorite conclusion to reach, and she applied it to numerous quandaries.

"And he was—he said—was her son," Joan stammers.

Anne Shropshire closes her eyes and flares her nostrils. It is interesting for Joan to see patience expiring in real time. "And because some completely unknown user, likely a troll, claimed to be *related* to the deceased, you thought their comment was appropriate?"

"I had—got—"

"And let's assume this stranger *was* telling the truth. A totally improbable claim, but let's just assume for a moment. Do we have a provision for sons, Joan? Does the guidebook say that foul language, copyrighted material, and mean-spirited remarks are acceptable *so long as they come from the family?*"

Joan desperately needs to blink. It's like her eyes have been pressed against a scanner. She shakes her head no.

"No. It does not. We pride ourselves on protecting *all* of our online grievers, Joan," Shropshire says. "We strive to provide refuge for those otherwise drowning in agony. That's our mission. That's the whole point of us. But we can only accomplish this if each and every screener is dedicated and alert."

When Rest in Peace downsized, they eliminated the coffee in the office kitchen. If you want us to be *alert,* Joan would say if she were an entirely different person, give us back our K-Cups!

"You could be someone's guardian angel," Shropshire continues, "or you could ruin someone's week. Next time you're scanning your comments and emails from terrorizers, I urge you to picture the *grievers* on the other side of the screen. Just picture them. The grandkids, the coworkers, the siblings, the parents, the spouses and *real* sons and *real* daughters of the deceased. Sitting in their little chairs in their dark little rooms, pillaging the internet for solace. I want you to picture their distress when they stumble upon your mistake. That *one* comment from that *one* troll on their beloved's life summary, published because he claimed to share blood with the departed. I want you to imagine these poor souls as *your* error twists the knife of grief right in the heart of their guts. Can you picture that? Can you see them? Our grievers?"

To stave off an anxiety attack, Joan is breathing to the beat of "Ave

Maria." She tries to picture the grievers—tries to picture the knife of grief right in the heart of their guts—but sees only an inexplicable beagle in a sweater, glowing before a desktop.

"Every day, you need to ask yourself: Am I going to be a guardian angel today, or a knife-twister?"

Joan blinks. It is the wrong time to do so, but it feels spectacular.

"We value you," Shropshire repeats. "But that's not enough. You have to value yourself."

Anne Shropshire turns to go but stops. "One more thing," she says. "Defecation emojis are unacceptable. I thought that'd be obvious, but apparently not. Really, Joan. Wake up."

She leaves. White noise thunders. Sylvie's crunching resumes.

An Absolutely True Story

~~

Obituary >> Condolences >> Photo Reel >> Guest Book

Obituary:
ELSIE JANE MCLOUGHLIN BLITZ

Tuesday, 16 July

Dearest Loved Ones, Enemies, Voyeurs, and Fans,

One advantage of dying slowly is that you get to write your own obituary. I could have left the task to the kid of a friend with the poetry MFA, or the journalist with the serious hair, but instead I propose a new genre: the auto-obituary. Eighty-six years on Earth, condensed by the one who lived them. In an era of confessional status updates, factory-farmed memoir, and federal tweeting, it seems appropriate to deliver my own farewell address. I, Elsie Jane McLoughlin Blitz, pink-cheeked television sweetheart, activist, and—above all—devoted mother, hereby offer a sweeping assessment of my life *as it was lived*. I assure you it will have almost nothing to do with me. Part of it is considered a "listicle" by those who ought to know. I am nothing if not a modern woman.

At the risk of sounding terminally Los Angeles, I will begin by suggesting to you that we are interconnected and interdependent, no matter how fiercely narcissism reigns. I hope you will keep that in mind as you consider the pygmy three-toed sloth.

As you should know if you are a sentient creature alive in the Information Age, the pygmy three-toed sloth, Bradypus pygmaeus, is the most endangered of all Xenarthra, its minuscule population restricted to a single mangrove forest on an island off the Caribbean coast of Panama. The sloths have lived on these same 4.3 square kilometers for nearly nine thousand years, and they are thus invaluable specimens of evolution. Island dwarfism has made the pygmy three-toed sloth the smallest of its genus. Because it is a perilously slow creature, the pygmy three-toed sloth depends upon camouflage for its survival and has thus developed a symbiotic relationship with green algae, which grows on the sloth's fur at no cost to its health. I now write to you from the only home the pygmy three-toed sloth has ever known, Isla Escudo de Veraguas, where I currently sit on an orthopedic mattress, on which I have requested to die. Half of my ashes will be tossed into the sea, where the resplendent sloth often swims, and one-fourth will be scattered at the roots of the red mangrove trees, in which it lives and on which it feeds. Scientists estimate that fewer than eighty of these individuals persist on the island, due to illegal mangrove destruction, climate change, and poaching.

What about the last fourth of my ashes, you ask? The last fourth of my ashes will be sold to the highest bidder on eBay, proceeds benefiting the EDGE campaign to save the pygmy sloths. So bid while the ashes are hot, my darlings.

First, I will share a selection of life lessons, in no particular order. I will then provide a list of valuable items I have lost, followed by a few notes, and then an absolutely true story. Because most of us have so little tolerance for negative space, unreality, and nonutilitarian language, you will find a reward for reading said story. Finally, I will offer my concluding reflections on fame and death.

If you miss me after I perish, you will find my spirit virtually lingering here. I also recommend the somewhat outdated but nevertheless extraordinary documentary *Hanging with the Sloth*—a collaborative effort between Jeri Ledbetter and Bill Hatcher, two visionaries I admire very much.

A Selection of Life Lessons, in No Particular Order:

1. Supplement therapy with boxing lessons. Energy can neither be created nor destroyed.
2. When you're thirteen years old and actor Charlie Newman offers to teach you chess, accept, even if you already know how to play.
3. When you're sixteen years old and game show host Henry Hawk offers to teach you something in his hotel room, decline.
4. If you fail to decline, don't whine about the emotional aftermath, because you knew what you were getting yourself into when you removed your rings.
5. Always get on the sailboat.
6. If someone refuses alcohol, never ask why.
7. Tell no one, excepting your agent, that you can cry on command.
8. Open bathroom doors cautiously. Especially in Manhattan, Paris, Budapest, Berlin, Singapore, Abu Dhabi, Havana, and San Francisco.
9. Beaver fur is underrated.
10. Natural births are overrated.
11. Always order dark drinks at charity events, in case you encounter the likes of Darlene Pickens, so you may spill the drink on her dress, which will be white, because she lacks a personality.
12. Bring pot brownies to your private bankers and flirt with them, if possible.
13. If you see someone weeping on a bridge, always stop and place your hand on that person's shoulder.
14. Winter in Gruyères, Switzerland. Summer in Colmar, France. Autumn in Castiglion Fiorentino, Italy. Spring in Monemvasia, Greece.
15. The more attractive the stranger, the greater the imperative to use a condom.
16. Marry at least twice.
17. Forgo social media.
18. Believe in ghosts but not God, unless your conception of God is much like a ghost.

19. Take a pottery class in the fall; you will never be short of Christmas presents.
20. The streets you walk, the food you eat, the job you work, the method of transportation you choose, the beauty products you purchase, the shows you watch, the links you click, the way you sit on a train, the way you speak to waiters, the way you take your coffee—everything affects everyone. Find a way to *believe* this, even when sober.
21. Do not let your children become casualties of your damage.
22. Do not have children if you cannot ensure the above.

Three Lost Items, Which, if Found, Must Be Sold to Benefit the EDGE Campaign to Protect the Pygmy Three-Toed Sloths:

1. A leather notebook of handwritten recipes, to-do lists, prayers, and uplifting quotes. It has my mother's name on the back cover. Margaret Deirdre McLoughlin. Robin's-egg blue. (Last seen: winter, 1983, Geneva.)
2. A ruby-red coffee thermos with the initials *E.J.M.B.* inscribed on the base, given to me by my father, who seldom spent money, and hated coffee, and was an exceedingly good man. (Last seen: fall, 1964, Los Angeles.)
3. A taxidermic golden pheasant, lost in a cross-country move. (Last seen: April, 1990, somewhere between Los Angeles and New York City.)

An Open Letter to My First Husband:

Although I forgive you for the incredible pain you inflicted upon my young and tender heart, I am glad we never reproduced. You mugged my twenties. It is shocking to me that you are still alive.

An Open Letter to My Son, Moses Robert Blitz:

Hard to believe that my little blond baby is fifty-three years old. And no hope of grandkids! Ha! Though we have our differences, I love you beyond language. Your body is healthy, Moses—there is nothing sprouting out of it. And for Christ's sake, I insist that you quit your bizarre charade. Don't be surprised, Moses. Of course I know of it. If there's one thing money can buy, it's surveillance. Listen to me very closely: being looked at is not the same as being seen. If I can teach you anything before I die, let it be that.

An Absolutely True Story:

Back when my cells behaved, I believed that I would live forever. If you share this belief, do whatever it takes—go to church, get an app, break formation, get a tattoo, anything—to hatch out of this delusion and into the truth. Because one day you will die, I promise, and mortality does not care if you believe in it.

All my life, I just tried to have some fun. I was an artist of fun and a failure at everything else. What we need, at the end, is a parent or two. A leash and a fence, a bedtime, a tooth fairy. Milk on the stove. But if we're lucky, we are furthest from childhood at the end of our lives. If we're lucky, we are closest to our parents, but they evade us until it's officially over. What we get instead of these comforts is a meet-cute with Death. He is always early.

I met Him one March afternoon outside a shoe store in Florida. I was gazing into a fish tank from my wheelchair, seeing myself in the glass, seeing America in the fish, who were busy and doomed and theistic. As usual, I was making plans to rectify the crimes of my motherhood when He interrupted. I was eighty-five years old. Sex had long evacuated my body, and yet when He marched toward me, my ovaries did a little jig. I have never found it easy to distinguish between arousal and a fight-or-flight response. His scent *alarmed* me—I could have accepted decay, but this scent was antilife, the scent of absolutely nothing, less alive than rock. He knelt and batted His eyelashes on the top of my right hand— that's how He says hello, how He royals you up. I didn't recognize Him at first, although He emitted an aura of celebrity.

"Can I take a selfie with you?" He asked me.

I never say yes to a selfie, but then I saw His scythe.

"You bet," I said.

He snapped three. Then, in view of the security guard, He slipped his hand into my pocket and took something. After that, he left.

The security guard didn't notice. My son was the one I wanted to call.

My assistant emerged from the store with three pairs of shoes for me. She opened one box like a casket and offered me the ruby walking shoes inside. An absurd gesture, all things considered. She nestled my feet into them with care. "You look like death," she said. "Anything I can do for you?"

I told her to dial my son. She did, although we both knew it was futile; he had blocked me months before. She feigned surprise.

Later, my phone buzzed during tea. I jumped and beamed, sure it was him. But it was Him.

Text from an unknown number. A photo of the thing He took in a vase on a toilet.

How did you get this number? I typed. I am a slow typer.

He sent a rabbit emoji.

At once, I knew that this was, as they say, the beginning of the end. Soon, I would have to do a lot of agonizing. *This is it, isn't it,* I texted Death. He sent me a GIF of a walrus vigorously nodding, with the caption: *Indeed, indeed, indeed, indeed, indeed.*

I wanted Him on my side, so I summoned some friendly banter. In the following weeks, we stayed in touch. I had heard from the clergy that He gives you some time to organize your affairs, so I asked Him for an extension. We negotiated. *Three months,* He settled. One more birthday.

He is not a barbaric captain—somebody has to do the dirty work. Nor is He a philosopher, thank God. The last thing you want to do at the end of your life is math. I am not His detainee, and He is not my boss, and I am not His client, and He is not my muse, but neither of us is free. I misjudged Him when we first met: He's very DMV about his work. All business, despite the inefficiency. No sex. Not even dinner.

The doctor called a week after I met Him. I was nonplussed, but everybody else wept.

"What can I do for you?" asked my assistant.

"Rewire me," I said. "My selfishness."

She ordered me a massage.

People caught wind of it. My end. After decades of paparazzi, gossip columns, interviews, and talk shows, they wanted more. They wanted to know the Real Me. Crowds materialized outside my neighborhood like invasive pests, destroying the landscape. After the internet was invented, I often riffled through my son's browser history—that's how I got to know him. But how could anyone get to know me, when my history, browser and otherwise, has already been exposed? *If you want to know me, memorize the wine stains on my sheets,* I tweeted reluctantly. *I am sorry I cannot be of more service. I have only seen myself three times.*

Once while observing a female wolf at my hometown zoo.

Once at the Temple of the Feathered Serpent in Teotihuacán, Mexico.

Once at the fish tank outside of the shoe store in Key West.

Suddenly, it was a Friday in the four o'clock range, two weeks before my death—my most loathed hour. A purgatorial hour, neither afternoon nor evening, too early to eat and too early to drink, an hour that encourages its hostages to tally up their failures, an hour that portrays one's entire life as a parking garage. I stared at my phone.

"What can I do for you?" my assistant asked me.

"Tell him I'm dying."

She did.

As my son knows better than anyone, I am Olympic at walking away, even after the wheelchair. Your gift is your cross, my mother always said. She was very Catholic and did not know how to have fun. That night, there was a fire chuckling in its marble throne. Blistered carrots, lamb shank, and hot pearled couscous with lemon and tahini on my plate. Fresh pomegranate juice in my glass, black and white on the television, an email from the estate lawyer in my computer, never-ending company in my house. Nothing from my son.

"What can I do for you?" asked my assistant.

I gave her the destination. She arranged a journey to my beloved sloths and held my hand on my plane as she wept. I told her to pull herself together. I told her I wanted an American flag in the room where I would die. Billowing white veil. I told her things I never told anyone: I confessed that the supporting roles I took after the lupus were existential pool noodles. I never quit smoking. Rehab, by some measures, was the best time of my life. I am still haunted by what my son said to me on the balcony, during my sixtieth birthday party: *Here you are with your five-hundred-dollar cake, and still you want to jump.* I left the party to box an angel oak tree and cry. I love best in snow, and I sing best in stairwells, and I pee best on trains. Sometimes I make a pile of Himalayan pink salt on my palm and lick it, just lick it. When I wear socks to bed, I have the most erotic and transporting dreams. Half my life, I have been waiting for someone to yell: *Action.* The other half, I have been waiting for someone to yell: *Cut.* All my life, I have been cute. These conditions make you selfish, and America knows them well.

Then one day you find yourself in a boutique of terminal illness, forced to purchase something in order to use the bathroom, and from then on, you have nothing to think about except a catalogue of the instances you took when you could have given.

My assistant said, "You are not alone."

"There is no time to update my software," I snapped at her the next day, from my deathbed. "Who in God's name cares if my cursor's disappeared?"

"What can I do for you?" she asked. That dreadful refrain. She offered me a cottage, a precious director, a bottomless brunch. The window was open, and the breeze was hot, and the pain was totalizing.

"Blamelessness," I told her. "Doctor my biography."

"A pillow," my assistant said. "I'll get you the world's best pillow."

My son is the first call I make in the morning and my last call at night. He knows that I will not live forever, but I want to tell him that *he* will not live forever. I want to tell him that everyone—*everyone*—is wrong about mortality. Across every season of every year, I nursed on summer, but now its milk is dry. I want to tell my son that I am so sorry. Death is in the room with me now, doing squats beside the air conditioner. We wear identical socks. Socks embroidered with white rabbits. While I wait, I Command F my life for mentions of my son, details that might justify his absence. Or maybe I'm looking for a contradiction, a counterargument, proof that I wasn't such a bad mother, after all. No matches. I shut the screen, inconsolable because my cursor is gone.

Do Not Read This Unless You Have Read the Absolutely True Story:

In Rock Paper Scissors, pick rock first. Most people choose scissors. This is my most painful tip to relinquish, as its advantage is dependent upon its secrecy, which is why I offer it as reward.

<u>Concluding Remarks on Fame and Death:</u>

They're both so lonely and boring.

Bisous,
Elsie Jane McLoughlin Blitz

Hear Me Out

~~~

The animal sacrificing began when we all fell in love with Blandine. This past winter, in the Rabbit Hutch. Six months ago. Maybe it's her golden leg hair. Maybe it's because she's the only girl. Maybe we were just bored.

One thing for sure is that we all hate her phony name, still do, and not even love cured that.

We'd been living together for five months when the love hit. We moved into the Rabbit Hutch last summer, and we didn't think much of Blandine at first. She avoided us, and we avoided her. She was weird from the start, either ignoring us completely or unloading a speech about the end of the world. She carried around enormous, freaky books and used annoying words. I don't think I ever saw her consume anything other than spicy ramen, spicy chips, spicy seaweed, and big green leaves. Plus a lot of pot and sweet tea. When all four of us were home at the same time, it was like she didn't even see us. Sometimes I'd hear her walking around the kitchen in the middle of the night—we were both pretty nocturnal—and I'd think about leaving my room to talk with her, but something always held me back. She was beautiful, but in a spooky way. Eyes too far apart. Skin and hair as white as the walls. Graveyard clothes.

I didn't spend much time with Todd or Malik at first, either. We had our own lives and jobs, or at least we pretended to. In retrospect, I think the seeds of everything—the love, the sacrificing, this—were planted last September, during the flood. We'd been living together for a month. Everyone in the Rabbit Hutch was supposed to evacuate the building, but we lived on an upper floor, and none of us had anywhere else to go, so we just locked the door and drew the curtains and stayed. When the power went out, Blandine brought some candles out of her room and lit them for us. Her lighter had the Virgin Mary on it. Todd made everybody tomato sandwiches. Malik brought out a pack of cards and a bottle of whiskey. It was awkward at first, and we all resisted playing, but before long, we were three rounds deep, howling with laughter. We didn't even notice that the doorframes were flooding—sort of weeping—until the water touched us. It was coming from the roof, I think. I caught Blandine looking at me, then, her face flushed from the drink and her eyes all twinkly, and I felt something. Like waking up.

But I didn't feel it again until four months later. That's when the love attacked me, Todd, and Malik for real. All at once. Synchronized. We were three teenage guys hot out of the Vacca Vale foster system, living on our own for the first time, and we believed we were free until that winter morning. I think Malik fell for Blandine the hardest, and Todd the softest, and me in the middle. Seemed to me that Todd fell more for Malik than he did for Blandine, but he wanted to fit in, so he started to drool at the sound of her hiccups like the rest of us.

It happened in January. Fresh snow outside. New year. She got up late that morning, walked into the kitchen, squinting. Malik was making chocolate chip pancakes, like a douchebag. Blandine doesn't really walk—she slinks. Cattish. It was a Saturday and none of us had to work, which was rare. The hair on Blandine's head was bleached white, the hair on her arms golden, her zits out and about, nipples poking through her shirt. Most people are beautiful because they look like the average of everybody else, but Blandine is beautiful because she looks bizarre. Asymmetrical. Scrawny limbs. Something alien about her. A beauty that should be ugly but isn't. She yawned and said, "Fucking mattress."

And we fell in love.

I know it seems implausible that it happened like that, all at once. But Todd, Malik, and I have been over it again and again. It's the truth for me, and I believe that it's the truth for them, too.

If Blandine knew that we had fallen in love with her, she was too smart to show it. In hindsight, it's clear that the dynamic was fucked in one way or another from the start, and nothing could be done to save it. Three nineteen-year-old guys lusting after the same eighteen-year-old girl in one hot apartment, running low on pot, jobs minimum-wagey and back-achey, independence a sham. On top of that, getting snubbed by the girl, who hates attention, hates being close to anybody who wants anything from her. We hardly knew Blandine, but that much about her was clear.

The four of us met in an "Independence Workshop" that prepared foster kids to transition out of the system. We would've aged out of it at eighteen anyway, but if you completed the workshop, they helped you find a place, a job, healthcare. They give you a little money for a security deposit and a stipend in your first year. You just have to pass a monthly drug test and prove you haven't spent the money on immoral things. In class, I liked Blandine's white-blond hair. It scared me.

Blandine doesn't talk about the bad stuff that happened to her before she met us, but you can tell her bad stuff was fucking *bad*. Can tell by the way she scrubs her hands raw with the steel wool in the kitchen. By the giant religious books she lugs around. The bird nests and twigs and valley shit she collects. Animal bones. Sometimes, when she's not home, I snoop around her room, which smells like weed and roses. Glass bottles of spiky plants crowd the windowsills. Above her bed, she's taped depressing internet biographies of people no one's ever heard of. She keeps a lot of Venus flytraps.

No one has it easy in the Vacca Vale system, but Blandine had it the worst, being so smart and female. People want things from the Blandines of the system, and I'm sure her brain didn't help. Thinking too much can zap you dead, and Blandine—she just shuts herself in rooms and thinks. Thinks and thinks and thinks herself into all kinds of doom, and by sundown she's afraid of the doorknob. She's the only one of us who didn't graduate high school, but also the only one of us who would've gone to college. Once, I found a letter in her bedroom from some guidance counselor—an email she must've printed out—pushing her to apply to the Ivy Leagues. The counselor said she had a real shot at admission. We have no idea why Blandine dropped out. She was a scholarship student at the only fancy high school in town. Only one more year to go. She never talked about it. If you ever mentioned any kind of school to her, she'd either lecture you about how fucked-up the American education system is or she'd bolt.

Since she wouldn't let us love her, Malik, Todd, and I started spending all of our time with each other.

I'm not embarrassed to admit that the animal sacrificing was my idea. Malik was getting on my nerves one night in February—a month into the love—because he wouldn't stop cooking for Blandine, wouldn't get out of the kitchen, and I wanted to make myself a goddam quesadilla. Thing about Malik is, he has absolutely no acne. You look at him, with his dopey, perfect smile and his dopey, perfect skin, and you feel a special kind of hatred. Plus, Malik is the only one of us four who has a good relationship with his foster family. He still goes to their place for holidays and takes their calls, laughing a lot when he does. Todd never talks about any of his families. When you bring it up, he gets that look on his face—the same look Blandine gets, actually. Like they're trapped in a flooding car.

I'll admit that Malik is the most attractive of us three guys, as far as physique, brains, talent, teeth, and disposition go. Then me and then Todd. Poor Todd. He looks kind of undercooked—like he didn't spend enough time in the womb. As for me, I'm a six or a four, depending on who you ask. I'm under no illusions—I know that my body has faulty proportions, like I was designed by a five-year-old, and I know that I don't really have lips. But I have a good personality. I can bench 225. And I can do fantastic impersonations.

Still—Malik is Malik.

So I super-hated him, in that moment, that night in February, as he stood shirtless in the kitchen, showing off his muscles and his skin, stirring all these sauces, flipping some goddam pancakes, bags of crazy groceries all over the floor, jazz fizzing from the shitty speakers that I found on the sidewalk, months back, on my own.

"Can you *move* for chrissake?" I asked.

"Almost done."

"You keep saying that."

"Just five minutes."

"Come *on*."

He didn't reply, just kept wrapping raw steaks in strips of raw bacon.

The kitchen faces the living room, where Todd was sitting, staring at the screen we thrifted, watching this show called *Tough Love,* where spoiled parents send their spoiled tweens to live in places like home-less shelters or maximum-security prisons or sometimes soft-core war zones, depending on how much of a shit the kid is, to Build Character. Todd was breathing wetly, chewing radishes, sitting cross-legged on the couch. When the kid on the television fell into a puddle of mud, Todd laughed.

~~~

You probably think that Todd is the reason I'm talking to you now. What if I told you that he was the gentlest of us three? The one who hated the animal sacrificing the most?

On many occasions I've walked in on Todd watching a shaving tutorial—mostly lathering. Which is weird enough, but even weirder because, as you can tell, Todd has absolutely no facial hair. Not a speck. Picture it: some prepubescent kid, watching dad after dad teach the inter-net how to shave. When I asked him about it once, he just shrugged, said the videos relaxed him. Never elaborated because he didn't care what I thought. But when Malik made fun of him for it, he shut the computer and locked himself in his room. Humiliated.

Malik went to school on the west side, but Todd and I graduated from Vacca Vale High. We weren't close in school, just acquaintances, eager to carve out separate lives once each of us found out the other was in the system. In school, I watched Todd from a distance. He was usually with friends, but they seemed more like props, or self-defense weapons. They rarely spoke to each other. At lunch, Todd drew in a sketchbook. Our junior year, he won some kind of national award for a piece he did in art class, and the school put it on display in the lobby. I didn't know what the hell the drawing was about, but I could tell it was good.

Malik and I often say that he puts the Odd in Todd, but the truth is, I envy Todd's capacity for mystery. Maybe I read people too quickly, but I also read them accurately. Normally, I can hear the message under-neath the message, you know? The true conversation inside a false one. But not with Todd. With Todd, information always seems like it's miss-ing. There's something un-American about him that's tough to describe. Like he belongs to no place. He hates teams. He's obsessed with raw vegetables. He's got glass skin. In high school, I'd never seen Todd join any kind of group. Never seen him fired up or ashamed, follow any trend or try to look cool, partake or submit. Todd wasn't a leader, wasn't a follower—just a drifter, happy that way. Until he met Malik.

Ironically, Todd's probably the one Blandine would've liked best.

I was always fascinated by other kids in the system. Studied them like they were my blood siblings. Todd's the one who told me about the Independence Workshop that could launch you out of the system and into your own life. He just came up to my locker one day and mentioned it—time, place, website. Left before I could reply.

During our sophomore year, Todd was suspended for a week because he disappeared from a field trip in Chicago. It was a history class, I think—I wasn't in it. They were supposed to go to a museum. Traveled three hours to get there. But as soon as they got to the lobby, Todd broke off, hopped on a bus, and went to Ikea. He had never been to one before, only heard about them. He says he was dying to go. He spent the whole fucking day there. Says he read three comic books in three different family rooms, ate meatballs on a fake terrace, and took a nap on a totally black bed. No one bothered him. They just let you loiter, he says. Like a dream. All these cubes of clashing, imaginary houses, side by side, making no sense together. Then, around dinnertime, he found his way back to the bus that his class was boarding and went back to Vacca Vale with everybody. The school contacted his foster family—everyone was foaming at the mouth with hatred for this kid, this weird and selfish kid. No one believed him at first when he told them where he'd been, but when they *did* believe him, they hated him more. Convincing us you'd been kidnapped or worse, for fucking *Ikea*?

Todd says he'd do it again. It was the best day of my life, he says.

~~~

Back in our apartment, the first night of the animal sacrificing, as Malik made bacon steak in the kitchen, I turned to Todd.

"Can you believe this guy?" I asked him, pointing to Malik. Todd didn't respond, just bit off another radish head. "Isn't she a vegan?"

"Is that where you don't eat meat?" asked Todd.

"That's vegetarians. Vegans don't eat anything—no eggs, cheese, milk, chicken, tilapia, nothing," said Malik. "And she's *not* a vegan."

"You sure about that?"

"Believe me, we'd know if she was. Vegans make themselves known."

"I think she said she ate rabbit once," said Todd. "At her foster family's. Or maybe she said she refused to eat it?"

"Well, it doesn't matter," I said. "Because she's not even hungry." Blandine had just told us so before she locked herself in her bedroom with her vaporizer and a jug of sweet tea.

"She is," said Malik. "She will be. She just doesn't realize it. I'll make her *realize* she's hungry."

"You're a fake," I said.

"What?" asked Malik.

"You just do things for her to prove that you'd do things for her."

"So?"

"Don't you see how fake that is?"

"There's nothing fake about proving you'd do anything for someone you'd *legitly* do anything for."

I rolled my eyes. "You would not do *anything.*"

"I would too."

"Oh yeah? Prove it."

He gestured to the meat. "I am proving it."

"No. For real."

On the television, the camera zoomed in on a kid's bare calves, which were covered in red, oozing sores.

"What do you mean, 'for real'?" asked Malik.

"Put yourself in danger. Be a man."

He scoffed. "Coming from *you.*"

"Would you kill for her?"

"Come on."

"I would," I said, suddenly feeling so angry I knew that I meant it.

"You would not," added Todd, without looking up from the screen.

"I'll kill for her right now."

"You won't." Malik flexed his whole upper body, his eyes on the meat in his hands. "You'd never."

I put a switchblade in my pocket and left.

R.I.P. Tho

~~~

Obituary >> Condolences >> Photo Reel >> Guest Book

Featured Memorial:
ELSIE JANE MCLOUGHLIN BLITZ

July 16
Excellent lady and excellent obituary!! Gotta love her spunk for writing
it herself! Of course, she always had spunk, that Elsie! Ha! Ha! She was
an Original! ;) Rest in Peace, Dear Ms. Blitz, you will always be remembered as one of the world's greatest juvenile stars, & a devoted activist,
& mother. So many ppl are ruined by fame, especially when they get it
at a young age, like you did, but all fame did, was give you a sense of
hu3mor! You are safe now.
—**Terri Collins**, Deer Park, MD

July 16
RIP sweet Angel. . . . . JESUS will welcome You into His lovng
Arms. . . . . Pain is finish now. . . . . many PRAYERS for u
and ur Family. . . . never Forgotten dear One
—**Agnes Silvers**, naples, FL

July 16
"Ohhhhhh JEEPERS, Pastor Bill!"

ruhet in frieden
—**Dietrich M.**, Heidelberg, Germany

July 16
well that "absolutely true story" was 5 minutes of life i'm never getting back but peace out god bless
—**justin**, Henderson, NV

July 16
"It matters not how long you live, but how well you live." Elsie Blitz lived both long and well. She is a sweetheart of golden age American television and she will be sorely missed. My prayers and condolences go out to her family. God be with them and with all who grieve.
—**Dr. Juan Alvarez**, Sante Fe, NM

July 16
wew I do not kno what to say that "still life of death" too much for me wew wew ~ but good luck to her i guess + clutch tip re: rock paper scissors!!!!!!!!! /// have a nice afterlife elsie you;re international trea-surrrrrrrrrrrrre
—**wesley sugar**, poulsbo, washingtonnnnn

July 16
if she can die, everyone could. o i am so sad.
—**Dhrubo A.**, Kolkata, India

July 16
Cheers to Elsie Blitz: Voice of the Pygmy Sloths!
—**Mohammed Patel**, London, England

July 16
sorta creepy that she wrote her own obituary hahahaa but r.i.p. great life lessons
—**Adam Pejewski**, Denver, CO

July 16
PLEASE ALLOW ME TO EXPRESS MY DEEPEST AND MOST
PROFOUND SYMPATHIES TO ELSIES FAMILY. I DIDNOT
KNOW HER BUT I HAVE LONG ADMIRED HER WORK AS AN
ACTRESS AND FOR THE WORK SHE DOES FOR THOSE POOR
CRITTERS IN GUATEMALA. IF YOU LOVED ELSIE BLITZ
AND YOU MISS HER JUST REMEMBER SHE WILL ALWAYS
BE THERE BECAUS LOVENEVER DIES. YOULL SEE HER IN
A TULIPS AND A SUNSET AND YOULL HEAR HER VOICE
IN THE WIND SHE LIVES IN BEAUTY. HANG IN THERE IN
THIS PAINFUL TIME ALL WHO KNEW HER. YOU WILL GET
THROUGH THIS!!!
—HATTIE PRESTON, BOISE, IDAHO

July 16
um wth is up with that 'true story' ummmm *crickets*
—nicole sassafrass, Nantucket, MA

July 16
Lol! Had no idea she Lived such an Excited life!!! ;) i've never heard such
an old person talk about sex before lol wusnt she like 200 yrs old??? guess
she had to keep herself busy after Meet the neighbors wrapped up rofl;)
well either way We'll miss you, SUSIE EVANS i mean ELSIE BLITZ
hahahhha <3 and Great work with the sloths!!!!!!! :) the world lost a
CLASSIC today ~I<*.::.oO^Oo.::.*>I~
—Gwennie, Nova Scotia, Canada

July 16
Love her. Love the obituary. Love the absolutely true story. Love life.
Love words. Hate death.
—Ishani K., Mumbai, India

July 16
So "He" is Death. But who is the "Son?" I do not understand. Is there
anyone who knows the answer? And what did He take from her pocket.
Why? Sorry my English.
—ElsieBlitzFan, Kyoto, Japan

July 16
ugh i used to do rock first & i always won
 r.i.p. tho
—joey shmoey, montreal, canada

July 16
😭😭😭😭😭😭😭😭😭😭😭😭😭😭😭😭😭😭😭😭😭😭😭😭😭
—Bee.D.P., Stockholm, Sweden

July 16
omg wut the heck what a lady what a thing who knew elsie was trippy as frick im gonna start volunteering at a nursing home firreal what a time!!!!!!!!!!!
—Liv F, Pasadena, CA

July 16
i hope she died with out pain. i pick white chrysanthemums for her and put them on fire. always Elsie.
—cheung hyunsoo, Hong Kong, China

July 16
Shouldve won a juvenile academy award for that scene where the house burns down. Also poor John Griffin haha.
—Z., South Bend, IN

July 16
grew up watching reruns of "meet the neighbors" with my parents and brother at dinner. best show ever. have such good memories watching it after finishing homework and eating instant mashed potatoes and spill-ing milk and stuff. simple times then. she may be elsie Blitz to some ppl but she'll always be little susie evans to me. my brother and me still do the handshake susie and peter make up when the truck breaks down after the harvest festival and they steal the sheep without farmer sebas-tian noticing. good wholesome family entertainment they dont make it like they used to do they. now my brother lives in atlanta and i don't see him much but wenever i do we do the handshake. he's got kids and a wife and there all photogenic. im still here in arkansas taking care of

mom because now she's got dementia. pretty hard i must admit but she sure does perk up everytime she hears that "meet the neighbors" theme song. i downloaded all the seasons and i watch them with mom just to see her light up like that. i forgot how funny and awkward it is when they switched to color in season 4 and everyone in the show says stuff like "golly its so bright over here!" haha. love the part in that 1st color episode when susie paints the dog blue bc she says everythings "topsy turvy" that still makes me laugh so hard. even tho it probably wasnt a good day for the dog tho. mom doesnt recognize me so well anymore but she sure does recognize those sweet characters. RIP little susie evans my heart goes out to you and your family. america will always love you. thank you.

—**Mary Jensen**, Jasper, Arkansas

July 16

THIS WHOLE #OBITUARY IS A BOLD-FACED LIE. WHOEVER WORKS AT THIS WEBSITE NEEDS SOME FUCKING #FACT-CHECKERS. I AM AN #INSIDER. I KNOW FOR A FACT THAT #ELSIEBLITZ DIED AT #CEDARSSINAIMEDICALCENTER ON BEVERLY BLVD, NOWHERE THE FUCK NEAR PANAMA. ON TOP OF THIS ELSIE WAS A #SHITTYMOTHER. IT IS TIME PEOPLE KNOW THE TRUTH ABOUT ELSIE BLITZ. SHE WAS A #LIAR & A #COLDSLUT A #NARCISSIST AND AN #OPIOID ADDICT. SHE'S NOT #AMERICASSWEETHEART AND SHE NEVER WAS. SHE RUINED MY LIFE & MANY OTHER PPLS LIVES & DOES NOT DESERVE ANY SADNESS OR NICE WORDS. DM ME FOR DETAILS. #THETRUTHABOUTELSIE BLITZ #ELSIEBLITZ #OBITUARIES #TRUTH #LIES #FACTS

—**Abominable Glow Man**, Like I'd Ever Tell You Where The Fuck I Live

Intonation

~~~

When Moses Robert Blitz tells people that he writes a mental health blog, their follow-up question is always the same.

"Are you a psychologist," asks a pregnant woman. She uses absolutely no intonation. They're standing at a cocktail party in a loft on a warm and polluted evening. It is Tuesday, July sixteenth, and his mother is newly dead. He chose to attend this party because it's a music crowd, not a Hollywood crowd, and he suspects that no one here will ask about Elsie. The Arts District always troubles Moses—he prefers to avoid evidence of mental illness, drug addiction, and poverty, although he admits that these forces plague every street in Los Angeles. He just doesn't like to see them! On the way from his car service to the door of the Walnut Building, a man asked Moses for something to eat, and when Moses gave him a twenty-dollar bill, he beamed. "Thank you—bless you," said the man, accepting the money. "And hold her close, do you hear me? Hold your girl close." Moses, who was walking alone, frowned. Then he passed a barefoot woman sitting against a building with a tabby by her side. "I'm a god, I'm a god, I'm a god," she said.

Now he stands in a loft that serves as the host's studio. Tastefully arranged shadows make the furniture appear more expensive and the people more fertile than they actually are. It has a high, angled ceiling and a skylight through which they can see no stars. Exposed brick. Original windows. It's a party meant to celebrate the tenant's album release, but he has refused to play the music, suddenly ashamed of it, and has retreated to the bedroom with two very young women and one cocker spaniel.

The guests are uptight and fragrant, dressed in experimental athleisure and feeling very sexual. Except Moses, who wants to unzip himself from his skin. He feels the fibers, again, pricking and biting like ticks. He has a condition. He doesn't like to talk about it.

"What?" he asks the pregnant woman, already claustrophobic inside this exchange.

"Are you a psychologist," she repeats.

"No."

"Have you ever studied psychology."

"No."

"Psychiatry."

"No."

"Psychoanalysis."

"No."

"Medicine."

"No."

"Counseling."

"No."

"Sociology."

"No."

"Anthropology."

"No."

"Critical race theory."

"No."

"Queer theory."

"No."

"Indigenous studies."

"No."

"Women's studies."

He takes a deep breath. "No."

"Then what qualifies you to write a mental health blog."

She's alluring but dull-eyed, and her lack of affect tugs at Moses's nerves. He feels violently white and male in her presence, and he can't explain why. She's white, too. He scratches his neck with both hands, multicolored fibers mushrooming up from his pores, but his scratching is insufficient. He fantasizes about taking a fork to his skin.

"Well, I exclusively chronicle my own *personal* mental health," he says. "So."

This is in fact the opposite of the blog's intention, since it's formatted as an advice column for anonymous help-seekers, but Moses prioritizes figurative truth over literal truth.

"Then how does that qualify as a mental health blog," deadpans the woman.

Were you raised by robots? he decides not to ask. "Just trying to engage."

"Your blog sounds just as navel-gazing and bereft of meaningful content as everybody else's blog."

"Well." He is stung. He is itchy. "Each man is an expert on himself, so—"

"Person."

"What?"

"Person."

"When I say 'man,' I mean 'mankind,'" explains Moses.

"Your speech is codified in patriarchal microaggressions."

Moses hates himself.

"Go on," she instructs.

He is sweating. He's afraid he will do something drastic—he feels bad behavior coiling inside him like a wild cat. He'll throw a lamp out the window, he'll begin mooing or stripping, he'll push this woman onto the floor. No, no. No. "Well, each *person* is an expert on *him* or *her* self. Or themselves." He downs the rest of his whiskey pickle juice. "Understanding one's *self* helps one understand *others.*" And then, in a burst of conviction: "That's why we have consciousness!"

He's feeling weird, now, and it's impossible to tell if she can tell. Can she tell? This pregnant mannequin? What is she thinking? Can she mourn or yearn? Hers is the kind of presence that registers as an absence. Motherly.

She grips a tumbler of toothpick-impaled olives. Slowly, she selects one, brings it to her mouth, and chews without breaking eye contact. Why would she *do* such a thing? Moses focuses on the sleeplessness that her puffy eyes betray, visible beneath her makeup, even in the candle-light.

"Oh," she says sarcastically. *"That's* why we have consciousness."

He doesn't know this woman. Some philanthropist wife of some has-been director. Why should the threat of her disapproval activate such extreme perspiration? He scratches his neck raw.

"If we can understand our own motives and desires," he begins carefully, "we can better predict the motives and desires of others." He is panting. "Predators, superiors, mates. So forth."

"Didn't consciousness evolve as a by-product of language."

"The theories aren't mutually exclusive."

"You didn't present yours as a theory."

"What?"

"You presented it as a fact."

"You say 'oyster,' and I say 'erster.' " He grins beseechingly. He needs to leave.

"Excuse me." She places her glass on a bookshelf stocked with encyclopedias that are still bound in their plastic membranes. "I think I'm going to throw up."

Moses watches her waddle to the restroom, then exhales.

Misbehavior averted. He contained himself, his skin contained him, the fibers contained themselves inside his skin—what a miracle. Moses checks his phone the way a regular person would. 10:34 p.m. He thumbs a screenful of texts, voicemails, missed calls, emails, direct messages. People wishing him well, people sorry for his loss, people asking how he's doing. And who among them cares? He has a red-eye to Chicago in a few hours, and he hasn't packed yet. From Chicago, he'll rent a car and drive to Vacca Vale, Indiana. He should be at home in Los Feliz right now, preparing himself. Attending this party was an untenable choice.

As he locates his blazer—sapphire velvet, a fifty-second birthday gift from Jamie, before she fucked that chubby startup fucker and—behave, breathe, behave—Moses notices a splotch of glowing neon on his hand in the shape of a tiny lung. He'll have to be more careful.

Big

~~~

Blandine Watkins works four shifts a week at a diner called Ampersand, fielding the apologies and smiles and the Sorry to Bother You
Buts and the If I Could *Just* Get Anothers of excessively thankful free-
lancers. Ampersand is the only non-chain establishment in Vacca Vale
that approximates a coffeehouse. Opened by a pair of optimistic hip-
sters, it attracts a disproportionate number of people in berets. A vintage
botanic wallpaper encloses them—a wallpaper that Blandine loves, most
of the time. Today, it makes her feel murderous about deforestation.
Ampersand serves avant-garde pie; that's their thing. They donate fifty
cents of each pie purchase to the women's shelter. Blandine spends most
of her shifts scowling at customers from her register, resenting their
phony manners. Stacks of the *Vacca Vale Gazette* wilt on a chair beside
the door. All morning, Blandine has watched people read the article. She
tries to feel amused, or victorious, but she just feels tired.

On the morning of Tuesday, July sixteenth—the day before she exits
her body—Blandine watches two oppressively polite customers negotiate seating.

The first is a woman in a baby-yellow dress with bad highlights, a
good manicure, and a young daughter. The woman fidgets across from
her child at the communal table, twisting a napkin. The second is a
bespeckled twenty-something with a satchel slung across his chest and
the radiant complexion of a vegan. What are all these people doing in
Vacca Vale, Blandine wonders, and where do they live, and when will

they leave? She never sees people like these outside of Ampersand, in the wild.

"Mind if I sit here?" the young man asks, touching the chair beside the woman.

"Oh," says the woman, flustered. "Um."

"Taken?" he asks.

"Well—the thing is—see, we're actually waiting for someone, actually."

"Oh okay, no problem!" With his smile, and those jeans, it's evident to Blandine that no one has ever truly criticized this young man to his face, and that he's a product of extreme parental love. He believes that the whole world ought to love him like that, Blandine assumes. "Is that one taken?" He gestures to the chair beside the child.

"Um." The woman's features crumple into panic. "He might want that chair, actually."

"Okay." The young man places his hand on the chair he initially requested. "So this one's free after all, then?"

Eyes of café patrons lift from mugs and screens, intrigued.

The woman swallows. "Sorry, it's just—it's just that the person we're waiting for is her dad? And he's on the way? And he's big. Big guy. Like, really *big*. So he'll just need like a lot of space?" Her pitch has climbed, the paper napkin now shredded in her lap. She appears as collapsible as an umbrella. "He likes having lots of space."

The young man blinks. "But . . . he's not going to take up two chairs on opposite sides of the table, surely?"

"I just—I just don't want *you* to be uncomfortable."

"I wouldn't be uncomfortable."

"I want you to be *comfortable*."

"Whatever's most comfortable for you."

They beam at each other.

"But what if—" the woman begins, "it's just that he might—"

"I'd be happy to switch with him, if he wants this chair instead. I'd be so happy to do that."

Wordlessly, the woman implores her child for help. The child smashes two plastic toys together, indifferent. One is a brown rabbit, and the other is a Tyrannosaurus rex; the former is three times the size of the latter.

"He's a really big guy," the mother insists quietly, and Blandine notices, for the first time, that the woman's arms are stitched in cat scratches.

Finally, the young man understands that an anxiety unrelated to seating has materialized, for this woman, in the form of a seat. He took an Introduction to Psychology class at the junior college, Blandine imagines uncharitably, and now he thinks he's an expert. "Okay." He smiles, addressing the woman and her child as though they are the same age. "No worries. I'll just sit right over here."

He takes a stool by the window, tossing glances of sympathy at the woman and her child as he unpacks his satchel. Blandine hates this undemanding caricature of sympathy, which so often manifests as pity. She believes it is native to the overly loved and the never-truly-criticized.

Shortly after the exchange, another man arrives, bell chinking behind him. Bound in a dark leather jacket, the odor of cigarettes, and a fresh tan, his presence exerts its own gravity. He'd be well suited for a men's deodorant commercial, Blandine thinks: handsome enough to serve as a vessel for positive self-projection, but not so handsome as to threaten the consumer's personal sense of masculinity. Blandine senses that he has many tattoos, although she can't see them. He wears his testosterone like a strong cologne.

The café patrons collectively notice that the man is short.

"Oh," says the woman, her voice falling. "I remember you being bigger."

"Huh?"

"Hi," she corrects.

He sits beside the child, ruffling her wispy pigtails. "Heya, kiddo."

The child glares at him. "I do not want to sit next to you." Her tone is dark and deliberate. She appears to be five years old.

"Sweetie, stay by Daddy," orders the woman, watching the father, who watches the child, who watches Blandine, who watches back. "He came all this way to have breakfast with you. Isn't that nice? Wasn't that so *nice* of him, sweetie?"

Betrayed, the child transfers her glare to the mother, then returns to the toys. As far as Blandine can tell, the rabbit is winning.

"This is what happens when I try," complains the father.

"Oh no, no, no—she's just hungry, is all!" Bright laughter spouts from the mother's throat. "You know, it's funny; I feel so silly—I just, I thought you were much bigger. I was telling everyone you were big. I was like, 'He's so big, he's so big.' But you're actually not. That big."

He crosses his arms. "What's that supposed to mean?"

Her smile twitches. "It's just funny."

They read their menus.

Eventually, Blandine approaches the table and waits for them to speak. She knows that she is not a good waitress—she lacks a pleasing disposition, often aims to displease—but she is too exhausted to counter her deficiencies today. The mother orders pancakes with a side of avocado, a grapefruit juice, an apple juice, and an extra plate. The father orders coffee, blackberry pie, bacon, and eggs. "Really runny." He grins, his teeth snowy, his eyes flicking to Blandine's chest. "Basically raw." He winks.

Customers often wink at Blandine. After the wink, they tend to offer unsolicited, intimate facts about themselves. Unaware of her odd beauty—indeed, repulsed by her body—she suspects the phenomenon has to do with her compulsive eye contact. Last week, while his wife was in the bathroom, an elderly man revealed that he's "center right, on the spectrum of sexuality, far right being fully homosexual." The next day, a teenager confessed that she provides topless photos for her middle-aged youth minister. "He's in love with me," the girl said hopefully. Just yesterday, a park ranger from Michigan admitted that he sometimes leaves cutlets of raw salmon near campsites, hoping to see a bear.

Blandine does not enjoy lugging around the secrets of strangers. She wants to transcend herself, wants to crawl out of the grotesque receptacle of her body. How can she accomplish such a thing when strangers treat her as a storage unit for their heaviest information? She frowns at the winking father.

"We don't have blackberry pie," she says.

"You sure?"

"Yes."

"Because I've had it here before."

"We've never served it."

"Yes, you have," the man insists. "I ordered it the last time I was here."

"No," Blandine replies, aware that she is sublimating her general opposition toward this man into one pointless opposition, but unwilling to surrender. "That's impossible."

"Maybe it was before your time."

"I've worked here since it opened."

"Well, it's a real shame you're not serving it today." The man scowls. "A real shame. What's on offer?"

Blandine turns to the blackboard at the front and reads, "Lavender lamb, avocado rhubarb, black mold, strawberry tomato vinegar, banana charcoal, and broccoli peach."

It's as though she told him that their pies are stuffed with shredded human thighs. Horror fills the man's face, rapidly setting into rage. Sensing danger, the woman busies herself with a tissue, unsuccessfully exhorting the child to blow her nose.

"Is that some kind of joke?" asks the man.

Blandine clenches her jaw. "I am dead serious, sir."

"You've got to be kidding me."

"Look at the chalkboard."

He does. "Black *mold*?"

"It's a sour cream pie with black licorice powdered on the—"

"No pie for me. No pie. Jesus." The man crosses his arms and shakes his head. The universal performance of moral disgust. "This place has gone downhill since I left."

After placing their orders, Blandine resumes her perch at the register, studying the family bitterly. Neither parent wears a ring. The mother collapses further and further into herself as she chatters about her hair and skin, then the child's hair and skin. "Doesn't she look so cute, today?" she asks repeatedly. "In her pigtails? And her pretty white dress? I wish I wore a white dress, kind of. To match." The father remains taciturn, but occasionally tries to pet the child, who flinches away from him. This continues for some time.

Blandine retrieves and delivers their meals.

"Thanks, sweetheart," says the father, eyes on her chest again, and Blandine is glad she sneezed on his eggs. The child guzzles her juice as soon as she receives it, as though she's been stranded in the desert for days.

"I used to get really tan, you know," the mother says as she transfers two of her three pancakes to the child's plate. "But now my skin is so sensitive to the sun that I can't even be outside for more than like fifteen minutes without SPF. It's crazy. We were at the Dunes over the weekend—because you know, I'm teaching her how to swim and stuff?—and I had to keep applying and applying and applying and she had to help put it on my back and I still got burnt like all over, maybe you can tell, you probably can, but I don't know, it's been a while since you've seen me so maybe not." Her speech tumbles to a halt, and she blushes. The daughter gives her a stern look, appearing disproportionately huge for a moment, like Jesus in paintings of Madonna and Child.

"Syrup," commands the daughter.

The woman applies syrup to each point the child indicates.

"It's just crazy," concludes the woman in a small voice. "Because I used to get so tan."

"And yet you still talk too much." The man slices himself a quarter of the woman's remaining pancake.

"I'm sorry," she whispers, folding her arms and legs to her core, compressing herself limbless. She examines the father as he chews her pancake. A frothy laugh. "It's funny."

"*What* is funny?"

"I just—I thought you were so big."

Please Just

~

Noise pollution triggers a feeling best described as murderous rage within Joan Kowalski. This reaction is especially violent at libraries, at work, and during the week before her period. Lately, the noise above her apartment—where that pack of teenagers lives, including the spooky white-haired girl from the laundromat—has become unbearable. Furniture crashing. Boys yelling. *Bongos.*

Three months ago, on a train to visit her aunt Tammy in Gary, Indiana, Joan sat a few seats away from a man who snored louder than she thought possible. Joan felt, for the first time, that she was capable of killing someone. It was spitty and gross, the snoring—indescribably gross. Joan had already transferred from the café car because a young man who looked fresh out of a fraternity spent an hour joyriding from one phone call to the next. She stood from her seat to confront the snoring man, shaking from the fear of confrontation and the anger at having to confront.

"Excuse me," she said, but the man snored on. She tapped his shoulder. "Excuse me." Nothing. *"Excuse me!"* When he snorted awake, he looked so embarrassed and fatherly that most of Joan's anger retreated into apology. "I'm sorry, but, um, I'm trying to read?" she began gingerly. "And I'm very sensitive to noise? And I was wondering if there was a way you could maybe, um, stop snoring? I'm really sorry. If not, that's okay. I know it's an unreasonable request. It's just that I have trouble focusing when there's . . . noise."

The man flushed and nodded. "I didn't realize I was," he said. "Snoring. I didn't mean to fall asleep. I've got sleep apnea, so I normally don't sleep too well, but last night my son was sick, so I didn't sleep at all. He's got the flu, we think. I guess I must've dozed off. I'm really sorry about that—I'm so embarrassed. I'll try to keep it under control."

Joan apologized three more times, then returned to her seat, feeling evil. As usual, when she confronted the world about one of its problems, the world suggested that the problem was Joan. She vowed to pry herself out of her misophonia and be a better person, from then on.

But on the evening of Tuesday, July sixteenth, as Joan Kowalski attempts to read on the tram home from work, she is tested again. The tram is red and flashy, brand-new but nostalgic, evocative of early locomotives and vintage American optimism. Normally, Joan drives an inherited station wagon to and from work, but her tank is empty, and she doesn't get paid until Friday. Recently, the preparatory stage of Vacca Vale's revitalization effort spawned the tram and its artery of tracks. To encourage transit use, the city has provided every denizen with one free monthly pass. The promotion worked, and now, during rush hour, there are at least ten people in every car.

Despite the severe air-conditioning, the interior is cheerful. Joan grips a Venetian detective novel that her aunt Tammy mailed to her, still stinging from her earlier interaction with Anne Shropshire, hoping to distract herself from lingering shame, but the cackles and squaws of three tween girls overthrow the words on the page, infuriating her. They sound like chimpanzees. Just when Joan thinks the tween cackling will stop, it gets louder, engulfing her flammable peace along with the compartment. The tweens screech like they can't see anyone else. Joan is confident that nothing in the world is that funny.

After shooting a glare at the girls, Joan transfers tram cars, running between them to make sure she doesn't get left behind, feeling ridiculous. The next car is quiet until three people in their thirties start to yell.

"Just you wait!" shouts a very tall man. "Males will bear children, soon enough!"

"It's only a matter of time!" adds a second, sunburnt man.

"I hope you do!" declares a woman in a camouflage jumpsuit. "I really hope you and all your balls get pregnant!"

Joan can't tell if they are outraged or thrilled.

She transfers cars.

The quiet in the next compartment lasts nearly two stops. Then, a child pulls his sweatshirt on backward, conceals his face in the hood, and stalks like a zombie, screaming. His father stares at his phone, noise-canceling headphones clamped over his ears.

The last of the tram's cars is empty but for a woman and her service dog. Both the woman and the dog are beige. DON'T PET ME, reads the dog's vest.

Joan steps inside and clears her throat. "Mind if I—"

"Please shut up," says the woman, her eyes closed. "Please just shut up and leave me alone."

My First Was a Fish

~~~

Just a lousy, half-dead fish I found by the river. Bronze and thin, no longer than my hand, base of palm to fingertip. Almost cute. When I found it in the frozen mud, it was only an inch or so from the water, but there was no tide to pull it back in. I swear it saw me. *Witnessed* me. For a minute it was just the fish, a couple opossums, a load of rabbits, and me. Silent besides a look-how-big-my-dick-is motorcycle revving on the road. Frigid, too, since this was back in February, and my coat was shit, so I was shivering a bit. The fish's gills were pumping like they still had water to breathe. I took it by the tail and carried it a mile back to the Rabbit Hutch. Pinched its scales between my fingers. Slimy. The fish sort of flailed once or twice, but then it died for real.

I know that it was only a fish, and I know that most people wouldn't feel bad about its death, but that night—bear with me—it was like the fish was teaching me something about my soul. Teaching me that my soul was faulty. I know this is stupid, but it's what I thought, and I wasn't even high. I thought the fish was saying: Yes, Jack, you are wicked. Something went wrong inside your machinery, maybe in vitro, maybe in childhood, and now you're wound to the wrong moral time zone, maybe even to the wrong solar system. You, Jack, are coldhearted. And you have no excuse. You may have been trapped in the system, the fish said to me, but you got lucky—nobody hurt you. They put you with Cathy and Robert, those older Catholic folks, when you were eleven, and you honestly can't remember much before that, when you lived with your grandma, but you're pretty sure you were fine. Not great, but fine. Your grandma worked a lot, but she took care of you, didn't she?

When I was still in the system, therapists were always trying to extract pre-eleven memories from my mind, but I never had any to offer. Nothing specific, at least. Just vague things—Grandma would smoke in the car; Grandma had a gumball machine that she kept stocked; Grandma wore hot pink lipstick; Grandma used a perfume that smelled like nothing from the natural world. When we were driving somewhere far away, the smoke-and-perfume combo would make me carsick, but instead of changing her habits, she just rolled down the windows, even in the dead of winter. I remember I had to cross some old train tracks to get to the bus for school, and they were always flooded with rabbits. Grandma made me Cream of Wheat in the mornings when it was cold, and even though the utilities would sometimes go off, we always had enough to eat. In the winter, she'd pile three blankets on me as I slept. She was a cashier at the grocery store.

One psychologist suggested I was repressing traumatic memories, maybe dissociating, and I wanted to believe him. It would explain how fake everything felt, how lonely and digital. How often I wanted to hurt somebody, just to see if either of us was real, just to move someone's face around, just for the fucking thrill of it. But two other psychologists told me my childhood passed the smell test. There was no record of abuse in my file. It didn't sound easy, they assured me, but it didn't sound so bad. One therapist suggested that I couldn't remember anything because I smoked too much pot.

I talk big and flex like the next foster kid when I have to, but Cathy and Robert were good to me. They were gone a lot, hoarded angel figurines, kept creepy parrots in the sunroom, and almost never looked me in the eye. But they cared, in their way. Paid for my jujitsu out of pocket. Rarely went into the basement, definitely not into my bedroom, so it was easy to sneak girls over, when I could convince them—mostly Anna, this curvy chick a couple years older, from the community college, who actually enjoyed having sex with me, bless her soul. Sex with Anna was the brightest thing in my whole overcast life. She had these freckles on her shoulders that I loved. During sex, she liked to take control, always telling me exactly how to touch her and what to say. She said her parents hated her, said I was lucky I didn't have any. The miracle of Anna got me through junior year of high school, until she met a full-time boyfriend in a class called Money, Banking, and Capital Markets. Then she cut things off. If Cathy and Robert knew about Anna, they never said a word. Cathy taught me stick shift, Robert grilled three different meats on my birthday, they never criticized my grades, never forced me to read or pray, never hurt me, never turned a blind eye to somebody who might. Gave me freedom. A reasonable curfew. A phone. What I'm trying to say is, Cathy and Robert never subjected me to the kind of shit that mutates your life forever, the kind that basically every foster kid I know has to take. A girl like Blandine would have faced it from Day One. It's hard to believe that our hands were dealt from the same deck of cards.

Cathy and Robert hosted two other kids, but they weren't from the system—they were exchange students from China, sent to Vacca Vale by some godforsaken program that mistook Vacca Vale for a worthy American place. The students were named Wang Wei and Li Jun, but in Indiana they went by Tyler and Chip.

Tyler and Chip stayed in the basement, but I barely interacted with them. They saw Anna all the time, but never acknowledged or reported her. We had an understanding: live and let live. On Christmas one year, Tyler left a box in red paper outside my door. It was a handmade notebook with some royal-ass pattern on the front in blue, and even though I knew I would never be caught dead with that fruity notebook, as I held it, I felt like Tyler was my brother. It sounds dopey. It felt dopey. But it also felt real. I opened the cover, my hands hot. Inside was a notecard that said: *for your writing.*

Which is when I remembered the dinner where Cathy and Robert asked each of us what we wanted to be when we grew up. Chip said aerospace engineer. Tyler said, "A judge for children." After some questioning, we figured out that Tyler wanted to be a child advocate attorney. When it came to me, I shrugged, took a big bite of potatoes, but Robert pressed. The English teacher liked me, said I had a gift for essays, kept leaving books on my desk. "Writer," I said on an impulse. "Screenplays. I don't know." It sufficed. And then everyone went back to their barbecued chicken.

On Christmas, after receiving the notebook, I ran out and bought Tyler a pack of cigarettes because he was always smoking "secretly" in the alley behind the garage. Bought Chip a bottle of General Tso's sauce because he said it was his favorite American food, and it seemed wrong—creepy—to buy a gift for Tyler alone. Wrote *Merry Xmas* in Sharpie on the front of both. Left them outside their doors in the basement. Fled the scene.

But despite all that, life with Cathy and Robert never felt realer than a video game to me. Despite their natural clove mouthwash, Robert's mustache trim in the sink, the classical station they played while they cleaned, their tendency to purchase too many condiments, the growth on Cathy's eyelid—despite all this proof of them, I never *believed in them,* or the parrots, or myself. Definitely not Tyler or Chip, who only stayed for two years. I believed in Anna while we were fucking, but otherwise she was unreal, too. I spent six years between the same walls as Cathy and Robert, and still we were strangers. I had a recurring dream that I stood in front of a burning house, and I knew they were inside, and I felt nothing. If I was evil, I had no one to blame.

As I carried the dead fish back to the Rabbit Hutch, I was coming to terms with all this. Well, I thought, it's settled. It turns out I'm the kind of guy who'll pluck a dying fish from the mud to make his friends feel crappy about themselves. I'm officially fucked up, and no one can tell me why.

The fish was super-dead by the time I reached our door. I was starting to doubt my choices, but the uncertainty made me double down. When I walked inside, the apartment was cloudy, and I noticed the smoke detector gutted on the counter. Malik was sitting at the ping-pong table, which doubled as a dining table. He'd set it with a sad stubby candle, napkins, two glasses of blue Gatorade, and two plates of food. I'd been gone about half an hour.

"Where the hell did you get *cloth* napkins?" I asked.

Staring at Blandine's door, his posture was stiff, his expression bewildered and hurt. The expression that all widely adored men wear when they get rejected for the first time. Malik was no virgin. Everywhere he went, he charmed girl after girl. It's important for a charismatic, handsome, lucky person to catch a glimpse of normal life every now and then. It's like when celebrities have to use public transit. I'd never seen such a desperate look on his face—Malik is the one who keeps people waiting. Todd was still watching television. Todd hadn't moved. In all our time living together, I can't recall him blinking, not even once. I know that's not possible. I'm just telling you what I remember.

I held up the fish. "Killed it."

"A fish," said Malik, no life in his voice. "That's the best you got?"

"Told you I'd kill for her," I said, losing my nerve.

Malik stress-rubbed his eyes. "Fuck if I care."

"Sleepwalker could kill a fish," added Todd. "Baby could kill a fish. Cucumber could kill a fish. That's not *impressive,* Jack. Are you impressed, Malik?"

"I am not, Todd," said Malik, his attention still bound to Blandine's door.

"Just proving I'd do it, is all," I said defensively. "Told you I would."

Todd changed the channel, glancing at Malik for approval. "Whoop-de-fuckin'-do, Jack."

For a moment, Malik studied the fish in my hand, his eyes unblinking and unfocused, then he got up from the table and marched over to Blandine's room. He banged on the door. Real macho knocks. "Blandine? Yo, Blandine? You there? I made you something. I know you said you weren't hungry, but I just—I made too much food, and I thought we could maybe—"

"Not hungry," came her low voice behind the door.

"Maybe if you just saw it, you'd get hungry, or—"

"Not *hungry,*" she said, a few notches louder.

"Or just smelled it," he pressed. "You know how that happens? You think you're not hungry, or that you don't have to piss, but then you smell some popcorn shrimp, or you hear a fountain, and you realize—"

"I'm going to bed good night," she said in one breath.

Malik's back flexed. Todd had muted the television. Malik turned to us, head down. "Whatever," he mumbled.

He sat back down and slowly cut through strips of bacon, through the steak, which was burnt on the outside and bloody on the inside, the whole thing sprinkled with little green flakes. To tell you the truth, the little green flakes sort of broke my heart. But then I remembered that Malik was the enemy. A stack of depressing pancakes—"They're not *pancakes,*" Malik snapped when I commented on them—drooped in yellow sauce next to the meat. Malik chewed like somebody rationed his bites.

I didn't really know what to do with the fish, hadn't thought that far ahead, so I just stood there, watching Malik and Todd and the muted television for who knows how long, trying to remember the point of all this. Everyone on-screen was a shirt to me. For a second, I recalled grabbing the fish out of the river with my bare hands and smacking it to death against the bark of a tree. Beating my chest and howling at the moon. Shit I'd never done.

I didn't expect Blandine to come out of her room, but at some point, her door opened. White hair tied in a mess on her head, scrawny body looking even scrawnier in baggy shorts and a basketball jersey. As she left her private world and entered ours, Malik half stood, then froze. Blandine didn't look at us as she made her way toward the bathroom, but I stepped in front of her, fish clutched behind my back.

"What?" she asked, irritated. "What now?"

"I've got something for you."

"I'm not in the mood for this, all right? Any of it, with any of you, so quit playing. I'm tired and I want to brush my stupid teeth."

Malik stopped chewing. He was crouched over the ping-pong table, a stance that was awkward to witness, and I felt embarrassed on his behalf.

Slowly, I brought the fish between me and Blandine, dangling its slimy tail. Fish don't have eyelids, which I didn't plan for. You don't want a dead body to look you in the eye.

Blandine observed the fish for a moment, her striking face blank.

"Got a—got a bouquet for you." I could feel my heart in my brain and my blood in my eyes.

And then something miraculous happened: she laughed. *Laughed.* Laughed and laughed, doubled over, crossed her arms over her stomach and squeezed her eyes shut until tears slipped out the creases, and when she finally caught her breath, she put her real hand on my real chest—the first time she'd touched me since the love hit—and I finally understood the phrase *time stopped.* "Oh God," she gasped. "That's a good one." She touched my chest one more time, and I felt her everywhere. I tugged my shirt over my pants, grinning like an idiot. She walked to the bathroom, sighing a few leftover laughs. "You clown." As she shut the door behind her, I saw that she was smiling.

A hot and happy silence.

"Are you," Malik began, face murderous, still crouching, "fucking kidding me."

Todd had finally looked up from the screen, his vision now attached to the brown scales in my hand.

I smiled big, then walked over to Malik, dropping the dead fish on the plate he'd fixed for Blandine. It sagged on her food, eyes open.

"I would," I said. "I did."

Chemical Hazard

~~

Sometimes, Moses Robert Blitz—only child of Elsie Jane McLoughlin Blitz—paints his entire body with the liquid of broken glow sticks, forcibly enters the house of an enemy, and wakes the enemy. Then he flails around in the dark, naked and aglow.

He doesn't mean any real harm. He just likes to fiddle with people.

In the cover of glow, Moses finds relief and control. He feels seen on his own terms. The formication—the fibers, the bugs, the creeping, maddening activity beneath his skin—quiets until Moses removes the chemicals. He thinks the glow is somehow bad for the fibers, which makes him love it like a medicine, or a parent. He is fifty-three years old.

It's not so dangerous, his act, especially now that he uses a glass-free brand of glow stick. As a novice, Moses used glow sticks that contained a glass vial of hydrogen peroxide in phthalate ester, floating in a tub of phenyl oxalate ester. He'd crack the tubes until the glass in each one broke and the chemicals mixed, reacting together to radiate. Then he'd clip off the heads and tails of the sticks and methodically work the fresh luminous chemicals into his skin, before concealing himself in a long coat, a ski mask, and gloves, at which point he would surreptitiously make his way to the victim's location. But after cutting his legs on the glass in preparation for the Bussini attempt this past winter, he decided to switch to a different brand, which contains no glass but *does* employ the chemical dibutyl phthalate—DBP—the use of which is banned in the European Union for cosmetics and children's toys.

But so what if DBP can enhance the capacity of other chemicals to produce genetic mutations? So what if it can cause developmental defects, provoke unwelcome changes in the testes and prostate, reduce one's sperm count, interfere with hormone functions, and impair fertility? So what if it's toxic to aquatic organisms and young children, capable of causing liver failure in the latter? None of this bothers Moses Robert Blitz. In no material sense is he a child or an aquatic organism. He has no interest in reproducing and is surely mutated beyond repair already. Besides which, he believes the European Union has a tendency to overreact. He has his policies: avoid the eyes and mouth, don't ingest, keep away from pets, thoroughly wash in hot soapy water and follow with a generous application of baby oil. Eager to brew his own batch of glow, he recently discovered an online recipe: sodium acetate, ethyl acetate, dye, hydrogen peroxide, and a powder called CPPO. He's waiting to hear back from a CPPO source in Russia. He has never understood the appeal of immortality.

It took no more than a brief google search and three emails to identify the woman who deleted Moses Robert Blitz's comment on his mother's obituary. He found her home address without even trying. After his email, she restored his comment, which was surprising. But then she deleted it again! How could he let an offense like that go unpunished, when he's already punished lesser ones?

He had never heard of Vacca Vale before the obituary affront, but he likes to visit Middle America, likes to investigate and report back to the coasts. Their churches and their supermarket smiles. Their canned corn, which travels thousands of miles before returning to the land that produced it. Their American flags in the yards, their minivans and Christian schools. The roads, the unwalkability, their hard and friendly R's. Sweet gas station clerks. The faith and anger and geometry. All highways and God. Moses only understands contemporary politics when he's in the Midwest.

It's around three in the morning on Wednesday, July seventeenth, and Moses is about to board his red-eye from Los Angeles to Chicago. While he waits, he types an itinerary for himself into a beige app on his phone:

- 7:30 a.m.: Arrive in Chicago. Rent car. Drive.
- 9:30 a.m.: Arrive in Vacca Vale. See sights. Kill time.
- 10:30 a.m.: Check into motel. Nap.
- Afternoon: Walk around. Find nice park. Stroll. Museum? Food. Booze. Olives. Most important = feel good!!!!!
- Evening: Update blog. Read. Martinis. Glow prep.
- 2 a.m.: KAPOW!
- 2:30 p.m.: Return flight, ORD–LAX. Call estate lawyer about the Zorns.

Moses swipes out and smiles, pleased with himself. Crafting schedules makes him feel like a real adult.

At the gate, people sit body-to-body, gazing into their screens, everyone terminally addicted to that blue light. Moses inspects the starless, navy sky through a glass wall. A sleepy toddler tips over his father's coffee, which the carpet absorbs in disturbing totality. It should be illegal, Moses thinks, to take toddlers on red-eyes. He prefers night flights because they make him feel important, as though his life is stocked with obligations. He's got insomnia, anyway. Tiny planes meander on the tarmac, and even tinier people in orange vests make decisions. Moses admires people with jobs. He knows he should feel exhausted, but instead, in his seat, he buzzes. Not with a desire to hatch from his flesh, but with a desire to gently punish Joan Kowalski.

A pair of young women sit beside him, cased guitars at their feet. They could be twins or lovers, he's not sure, but they have clearly spent years in the same home, stepping over each other to get to their lives. "We have all this stuff, and yet we're still so sad," says one to the other.

"Why don't you write a fucking screenplay about it."

"Don't be a bitch."

"Don't be a cartoon."

"Of what?"

"Of a millennial."

"Your dog is at a spa!"

"Your voice is like gasoline."

"*Your* voice is like *coal!*"

Each is silent for some time as they retreat into their screens. One twists her hair moodily, her thick brows furrowed, legs crossed, white sneaker bobbing. The other applies coat after coat of lip balm, then sanitizes her hands with an orange-blossom spray that momentarily reunites Moses with an enchanting cocktail he drank a decade ago in Beirut. Eventually, the first girl giggles. "Watch this," she says, tilting her phone and resting her head on the other girl's shoulder. "You ever seen a bat on a treadmill?"

Moses dislikes all generations, dislikes the very concept of them, but this is the generation he dislikes the most. He retrieves his noise-canceling headphones and listens to "Fourteen Ocean Waves to Soothe Your Baby" on high volume. It sounds great. He googles Joan Kowalski again, to prevent his hands from scratching the fibers that burst from his pores.

Joan Kowalski has the kind of sloppy online presence of a person who believes that no one will ever google her. It's obvious that securing her own privacy—deleting that unflattering image of herself squatting beside a trash can shaped like a whale, for instance—would not only register as an act of vanity, but also of delusion.

A leather bag of glow sticks occupies the seat to Moses's right, and he feels its presence like that of a crush. The glow sticks puzzled security, but Moses shrugged, said he was organizing a music festival. The airport upholstery is a shade of orange endemic to the seventies, and it makes him nostalgic. He observes a wasteland of factories, construction, and dead grass on Google Maps. Moses scrolls through the search engine results, validating his suspicion that Vacca Vale is yet another American blemish—one of those disposable, expired towns responsible for electing the demagogues who reduce their country to a trash fire. A town that needs a good babysitter. And a lot of education! He comes upon a photo of a lush park whose splendor appears accidental in context, like the only beautiful child in a family of ten. In another image, cows huddle in a snowy field. Moses would like to tip one over.

After skimming Vacca Vale, Indiana's online encyclopedia page, he stumbles upon a section that makes him gasp. The young women glance at him, concerned. *Zorn Automobiles,* says the link. Moses had no idea that his mother's favorite car manufacturer was based in Vacca Vale, and the coincidence makes him itchy, makes him suspect that forces are conspiring to send him a sign that he doesn't want to receive. Elsie owned several Zorns and loved them more sincerely than she loved the people in her life. When Moses was sixteen, he stole her 1932 Presidential Coupe, drove it down the Pacific Coast Highway at full speed at four in the morning. When she found out, she enrolled him in an intensive Old Norse language program and shipped him off to Reykjavík. She didn't speak to him for the rest of the summer.

He is missing his mother's funeral to punish Joan Kowalski, but he is not missing his mother. As he sips an oversweet cappuccino, an emotion that approximates happiness circulates through his body. Once he arrives at the airport in Chicago, he'll have to take a bus to the rental car agency. He hasn't ridden a bus in years, and the prospect makes him feel like a man of the people. Like he should run for office. He'll have a whole day in Vacca Vale to plan his attack. Joan will be so easy to frighten.

He stows the phone in his pocket and scratches his arms, harder and harder until people begin to queue. He removes his headphones. A businessman on the seat across from him with absolutely no neck talks into a phone. "I invite her over for a shower, see where things go." He chortles. "So what."

"Now boarding Zone One, now boarding Zone One," an androgynous voice announces, and Moses stands without checking his ticket. Maybe that's his problem, he thinks. He's never had to check his ticket to know that he's in Zone One.

Variables

~

In this equation, the variable of Y could be a producer, a gas station manager, the Sun King. On more than one occasion, he has been the president of the United States. X could be his employee, his stepdaughter, a wild plot of land, but he must believe that X is his. Most often, X is human. X is not always female. X always wants to be seen, and Y always wants to see her, or him, or them, or it. In the process, they often discover that Y wants to be seen, too. It has happened before—in rental video stores, churches, and meat lockers. It will happen again.

This time, Y is a man named James Yager, a music teacher at St. Philomena, the only private high school in Vacca Vale. Like many high school music teachers, James never wanted to be a high school music teacher. He accepted the job as a consolation lifestyle when both his band and the health of his mother failed, at which point his future in Vacca Vale ossified. He regularly uploads home-recorded music under the name Vu. Cares for students but not for pedagogy. Most call him by his first name. He's forty-two, handsome in a sleepy sort of way, sometimes brilliant and often depressed. The Cool Teacher.

This time, X is a seventeen-year-old named Tiffany Watkins. Only a junior and she's already seen too much. Bleached hair, wraithlike complexion, bad posture. Wide-set eyes. Panoramic vision suited for prey. Tiffany is insecure, cerebral, and enraged. Pretty in an extraterrestrial sort of way. Addicted to learning because it distracts her from the hostility of her consciousness; she has one of those brains that attacks itself unless it's completing a difficult task. Her fellow students live in the suburbs and spend their lunches complaining about the cruises that their mothers foist upon them. They exchange How My Parents Surprised Me with My First Brand-New Car stories and wear coats from luxury outdoor brands, as though driving to high school is an extreme sport. They are members of a decaying aristocracy, descendants of Zorn money, increasingly pointless but lousy with trust funds. They remind Tiffany of the royal family. The students smelled like dryer sheets— every last one of them. Tiffany won a coveted scholarship to attend St. Philomena's and spends her lunches in the library, hunched over homework. The teachers like her because she is brainy and tragic. When discussing her among themselves, they call her "less fortunate," "at risk," "atypical," and "gifted." Her essays, although polluted with typos, frequently elicit suspicion of plagiarism: how could such a quiet, luckless girl produce such compelling, sophisticated arguments? *With all that going on at home?* Reverently, the teachers cite her GPA and standardized test scores. She is special, they say. Still, they keep her at a distance, and she returns the courtesy.

As a civilian, Tiffany buys her clothes at the thrift store, always a size too big. At Philomena's, she wears a uniform. The school had to pay for hers, and when she told the dean of student formation what size she wanted, he raised his eyebrows but did not object. The school, like its entire Catholic county, considers modesty a young woman's most admirable virtue.

One winter morning, between passing periods, the English teacher delivers Tiffany to James's music room. "She needs to act," announces the English teacher. "You should have heard her reading Perdita just now."

James looks up from his desk to see a scrawny girl in oversized clothes. Her pale skin reminds him of the glow-in-the dark polymer clay that he buys for his children. You bake it—the clay. James coughs. As soon as he sees Tiffany, he wants to get away from her.

Tiffany picks a cuticle. As soon as she sees James, she wants to touch the stubble on his chin, taste his coffee, try on his glasses. She blushes.

"Okay," says James impassively. "Come to auditions on Thursday."

He's directing the spring play: a dark dystopian comedy about four teen-agers who worship a mannequin. It was written by an obscure, multi-disciplinary artist who drowned herself in 1923.

Tiffany gets the lead.

It's true that she is a volcanic actress. She has a gift for performance, reaction, and imitation—instincts cultivated by a childhood of unpre-dictable caregivers. But it's the inhuman quality of Tiffany that entrances James most: she is cold and faraway. Otherworldly. Astral.

It's true that James is a charismatic teacher, too big for his tank. But it's the extra-human quality of James that entrances Tiffany most. He is burning and loud and there, right there. He is beloved, he is sexy in his insomnia, he looks famous if you squint. She can see his pulse in his neck. She can tell that his front incisor is fake. She can reach out and touch him if she wants. She wants. She doesn't.

It goes like this: a week into rehearsals, Tiffany starts smiling too long at James, daring him to smile back because he is the only person alive that she wants to touch. One evening, she tells a joke that makes him laugh himself breathless, and this is their first mutual shot of sero-tonin. It's clear to her that he would be happier in a coastal city. It's clear to him that she would be happier in a different species. By December, it is clear to both variables that each could capsize the other.

For weeks, other students in the play covet the attention that James reserves for Tiffany, but they temper their suspicion. They know her story. Pity her. Assume that he does, too.

～

The beginning of James and Tiffany is math, while the ending between James and his wife is erasure. Meg spends more and more weekends at her parents' house with the kids, justifying her absence by reminding him that Lillian and George could die at any moment.

"This is our last chance," she says, and James's heartbeat races.

"For what?" he asks.

"For the kids to build a relationship with their grandparents," she says. "You can't come, obviously."

Her parents hate him. James assumes the character mutation that has only become legible to him recently must have been apparent to them all along. His own parents are dead.

Tiffany and James begin for months, but James and Meg have been ending for years. Lately their fights have increased in frequency and duration, paralleling the hurricanes, droughts, and wildfires around the world. James's children sustain a series of minor emotional earthquakes that they do not have the vocabulary to describe. They refuse their luxury vegan desserts. They grow fussy at bedtime. They scratch at their tags. Emma, age eight, develops the unnerving habit of studying her father for a long time before asking, "Do I *know* you?" Then she laughs.

~~~

At St. Philomena, James becomes Tiffany's mentor. It's nice to have a word for it. He coaches her with special attention and tongue twisters in rehearsals. She is brilliant, he tells her. She is exceptional and singular. Over time, he builds validation in her body like a ship in a bottle. He asks her to stay late, demands that she practice tiring mental exercises to excavate her character. They idle long after the school floods with the odor of fish guts, a gift from the dog food factory across the street. The factory pauses production during school hours and restarts after three in the afternoon—an agreement between St. Philomena High School and Daydream Pet Chow that took five years to reach. After the last students leave, carpooling to their gated communities, Tiffany asks James: "Is it unusual for a dying city to have suburbs?"

"No," he replies. "That's how they die."

"I guess the dentists have to live somewhere."

Which makes him laugh, which makes her laugh, their pleasure locked in a positive feedback loop until she feels like her head will pop off and champagne will spill forth, out of her body, into the school.

Another day, alone in the music room, James asks Tiffany what she fears most. Tiffany finds it neurologically impossible to lie to him. It's all predetermined until a principle wrestles down a feeling. "Infinite loneliness," she tells him. "That's what I fear most." It sounds false when she says it out loud, but it's the truest thing about her.

James and his troupe of gloomy, dramatic teenagers have a five-hundred-dollar budget, no functional sound system, no costume designer, no understudies. But they rehearse as though competing for a Tony.

The other students watch Tiffany and James warily. Text each other about it.

James begins to contact Tiffany outside of rehearsal. Emails her articles, clips, music, advice, misspellings. Gives her personalized assignments: Wong Kar-wai, Samira Makhmalbaf, Rungano Nyoni, Károly Makk, Bernardo Bertolucci, Denis Villeneuve, Jean-Luc Godard, Chetan Anand, Viêt Linh. He gives her his log-in information for streaming services and reimburses her for video rentals. An eager student, she watches every film he recommends with a speeding pulse and a surging body temperature. The films leave her catatonic. One makes her cry every night for a week.

When no one else is listening, Tiffany tells James that she never knew films could tell the truth. She tells him that she loves *Paradise Lost*. She tells him he's good at his job. She tells him loneliness is an occupational hazard of consciousness. She tells him she hasn't had it so easy. He tells her to speak up.

"Louder," he says. "I want to be able to hear you from the parking lot."

One rehearsal, James pulls Tiffany aside and articulates her potential with the kind of mathematical precision she has spent her life yearning to hear, and she has to leave the room. All the girls' restrooms at St. Philomena resemble bomb shelters: windowless constructions of cinderblocks painted the color of sharks. In the far stall, Tiffany breathes each breath on purpose, because sometimes you have to. He's just being fatherly, they separately assure themselves, a father to a fatherless girl. But James has misinterpreted Tiffany's problem: she's had an overabundance of fathers, not a scarcity.

From her stall, Tiffany hears two girls enter the bathroom.

"See, it's this medication I'm on," says one to the other. "It does this to my skin."

"What?"

"Look at me. It's like my face is falling off my face."

~~~

It goes like this: as the weather gets colder, Tiffany and James play emotional apocalypse by email, script, art, and eye contact—all talk, no touch. She gets to be the world, which makes him the ending. There is no revelation. He orbits her. She spins. Gradually, they become orphaned from their morals, and they feel that something has died, but also that something's been born. Among everyone Tiffany's ever met, James takes the most from her, gives her the most. It's his fault, it's hers, he isn't, it doesn't matter, it matters most. Fellow students begin to look like children to Tiffany. She believes that she is in the middle of her life. James becomes her friend, despite the odds. She becomes his recreational drug, a bad habit he tries to conceal from others and from himself. They both feel violently understood. For months, Tiffany and James fuck without touching. It's been done before.

~~~

One night after rehearsal, when he thinks the students have left, James sits at the upright piano in the music room and plays the first movement of a Maurice Ravel suite. Tiffany is still there; James's subconscious knows she is there; James's subconscious no longer considers Tiffany a student.

She stands several yards away, leaning against the doorframe, her arms crossed over her baggy blue uniform. With her fair skin, white hair, and purple-shadowed eyes, she looks like she's been dead for days. When the suite ends, James catches Tiffany staring at him, her expression revealing something akin to fear.

"*Gaspard de la Nuit*," says James, clearing his throat. "Took me seven years to learn."

"Gaspard?"

"It means something like 'treasurer.' Treasurer of the night."

"That was long."

"What?"

"The suite."

"Oh, yeah. Seven minutes."

"So you learned a minute a year."

"Well, that was just the first movement. There are two more, all based on the *fantaisies* of this French poet named Aloysius Bertrand. Published in the early eighteen hundreds, I think." He cracks his knuckles. "You'd love the poetry. Surreal as hell. Never succeeded in its time. Never succeeded at all, actually. You take French, right? Or Latin?"

"*Les deux. Tum ex illis.*"

"My translation has French on one side of the page, English on the other. I'll lend you my copy."

"And what was that?"

"What was what?"

"The movement you just played."

"Oh. It's called 'Ondine.' It's about a mermaid seducing a mortal."

Embarrassed by the thematic relevance, which had not occurred to him until he said it out loud, James scrambles to other facts, flexing his music theory degree. He maunders on, louder and louder, but Tiffany says nothing. To get himself to shut up, he retrieves a pair of headphones from his bag and crosses the room to her. It's something to do.

"Do you have some of these already?" he asks. He knows that she doesn't.

"Headphones?"

"Yes."

Tiffany keeps her eyes on the piano, as though she's afraid it might spring to life. "Why?"

"Rosie spilled juice on my laptop, so I had to get a replacement yesterday," says James. "They had a deal for teachers. Buy a laptop, get headphones. Take them, I'm serious. I got them for free."

"What about you?"

"I have others."

"Better ones?"

"Yes."

When their hands touch, Tiffany hardly feels it, because it seems to her that they have been touching for weeks. James feels it and withdraws at once. The dog food smells especially like sewage today. For a moment, they hold their breath and study each other in the faulty electricity of St. Philomena. Then James marches to the piano and collects his bag.

"Excuse me," he says professionally, almost angrily, as he pushes past her. She exits the room as he flicks off the light and locks the door.

For a moment, they hesitate in the dark hallway. After hours, the entire high school feels like a set to Tiffany, insisting on the fraudulence of everything that occurs there. The sports, the calculations, the dissections, the assemblies on drunk driving, the fire drills, the chicken tenders, the virginity gossip, the imitation friendships. Nothing counts. It's all sudoku, a controlled experiment, a relentless series of practice tests. Tiffany conceives of her peers as baby predators, biting and scratching in the den while their mother hunts. She wants something—anything—to count but is also emboldened by the conviction that nothing possibly can.

James pockets his keys, looking fractious and skinnier than usual. Smudged glasses, beard gleaming with nickel. Tiffany doesn't fit in his life because his life is too big; she'd slosh around like a hamster in a swimming pool if he let her inside it. He would never let her inside it.

He takes a deep breath and walks purposefully toward the exit. "Drive safe in this weather," he calls, although he knows she rides her bike. If he were a decent man, the decent thing to do would be to offer Tiffany a lift. As it stands, the decent thing to do is to extract himself from her presence as soon as possible. He marches to the faculty parking lot without looking back.

Tiffany drifts to the student exit like a ghost with nothing to haunt. When she steps outside, the frigid December rain is a relief on her hot skin. Aggressively, Tiffany pedals to the grocery store and does not shiver in the fluorescence, although her clothes are wet and she runs cold. Now she's pink and sweating and feverish, altogether carnal, like a contestant on a tropical reality show. She can't remember when she last enjoyed corporeality. Had she ever? She feels exuberant, drugged, libidinous. A man gazes at her as he feels up the avocados, his mouth open, and for the first time in her life, she enjoys the sexual attention of a stranger. Go ahead, she thinks. Look at me. Inside her backpack, the headphones radiate. She can feel them. Tiffany tears leafy greens from their misty perches and thrusts them into her basket, beaming uncontrollably. Bok choy, endives, spinach, kale, baby kale, swiss chard, mustard greens, collard greens, micro greens, beet greens, watercress. Salivating, she concludes that she probably has an iron deficiency, but knows she will never schedule an appointment to find out.

"Oh, my." The cashier smiles. "Do you keep rabbits?"

The total appears on the screen: two weeks of tips from her job at the diner. Tiffany pays in cash.

"Something like that," she replies.

～

Tiffany's current foster parents are gentle but weary. Treading in debt. It's her fourth family, and her best family. They have three biological sons, all grown and out of the house. By the time Tiffany reaches Wayne and Stella's fifties ranch house on Arcadia, they're asleep, and she is heavy with rain.

Hope you had a good day at school, reads a note in Stella's writing. *Leftovers in the fridge.*

With the sharpest knife they own, Tiffany butchers the vegetables, blisters them in olive oil and salt, and prepares enough to fill two salad bowls. In her bedroom, Tiffany opens her laptop, on loan from the school, and finds the suite that James played. The headphones are cordless, futuristic, like a gadget from science fiction. She sheds her damp clothes, replacing them with soccer shorts and a large T-shirt that says BLOOD DONOR across the chest. She once tried to donate blood but she didn't meet the weight requirement. As she eats, she listens to *Gaspard de la Nuit* in its entirety—over twenty minutes. She burns her mouth on the greens but eats ravenously, savoring the bitter taste, the oily slip of the leaves. She finishes one bowl and listens again. In "Ondine," Tiffany can hear the water flirting, she can hear the peril of desire, she can hear the splash. Someone dies in "Le Gibet"; she senses the end of a life that nobody wanted to conduct or sustain in the first place. "Scarbo" sounds like the panic attack of a genius. She doesn't know, she'll look it up later, he'll lend her his copy. Listens to the suite until her laptop dies. Brushes her teeth until she can't feel her gums. Showers until she can't feel her skin. At three in the morning, she screams into her pillow, obscenely alive.

～

Three miles away, in a renovated mansion built in the American Queen Anne style 143 years ago by Woodrow Huxley Zorn III, cofounder of Zorn Automobiles, James makes love to his wife for the first time in months, inducing seismic orgasms from them both. But he feels her fall sad afterward, turning from him too soon, abandoning him for her private interiority, which he imagines as the library of a castle they once visited in Ireland, spectacular and haunted and damaged by cannon fire. He has yet to catch his breath, and she's already in the bathroom. As he listens to her pee—she has never had a urinary tract infection in her life, her hygiene a kind of religion—he tries to compute why he finds one person's distance alluring while he finds his wife's distance funereal.

The faucet pummels water in the tub; he listens to his wife pull the metal valve and wonders how much water is lost as it is rerouted between the faucet and the showerhead. James never lost interest in his wife, even after the color drained from her hair and her laugh, but she lost interest in him. By the time her shower ends, he feels even more energized than he did during sex—but it is a rabid energy, this drug, hijacking him, driving him recklessly away from himself. When his wife reenters the room, smelling of vetiver, he fights an alarming urge to lunge at her, pin her down, and make her laugh.

"Remember the girls have the dentist tomorrow," she mumbles from the opposite shore of their mattress.

Around three in the morning, James pulls on some clothes and goes for a jog around their neighborhood, feeling sick and extraordinary. Tree roots rebel under the historic brick roads, thrashing like snakes and making him stumble. He passes rows of dignified houses from the nineteenth century, none of which are as opulent as his. The air is cold and damp, the neighborhood dressed for Christmas. Fake deer in the yards, wreaths on the doorways, champagne lights twinkling on trim. Nearby, men are yelling, but James can't see them. Can't hear what they're saying. Many armed robberies have occurred in his neighborhood in recent years, prompting an exodus to the suburbs, and James knows he should be cautious, but his strongest impulse is to track down the voices and join them. His pockets are empty.

After running for twenty minutes or so, James stops at the bridge that connects his neighborhood to downtown, watching his breath in the tangerine streetlights, listening to the river as it churns below. Inspired by their favorite picture book, his daughters often tell him that they want to be lamplighters when they grow up. He imagines Emma and Rosie hovering through the city at dusk, planting flames in glass cages like pixies. He doesn't have the heart to inform them that Vacca Vale isn't illuminated by gaslights anymore; instead, high-pressure sodium-vapor streetlamps sprout like saplings from the pavement. When electricity passes through the sodium, the sodium gets excited and glows. Efficient and cost-effective, the lamps cast his city in the dim orange luminosity of a dream. James enjoys facts, but unlike his student Tiffany, he does not mistake them for wisdom. Still, like Tiffany, he longs to amass information until his education becomes the inverse of itself, until he is absolutely stupid with knowledge. James once found the Vacca Vale River—mostly sewage, by the time he was born—depressingly impotent. Three months ago, it flooded the town with a force that James interpreted as repressed fury, like it was avenging itself for centuries of mistreatment. The flood spared his neighborhood, which was built on a hill.

On the bridge, his ears stung by wind, James stretches. His ankle throbs from a sprain he got when he was seventeen. Soccer match. Winning goal. An injury that never healed right.

~~~

The next day, as they block the final scene, James refuses to meet Tiffany's eyes. There are consequences, he reminds himself. This isn't a fucking rehearsal.

~~~

In February, James gives Tiffany his phone number, accompanied by a reason. Will she babysit his children on Friday night? Although, at first glance, inviting Tiffany into his home and introducing her to his family seems antithetical to his newfound conviction, James is obeying an instinct: he needs to recast his time with her as nothing but acceptable. Needs to extract her fangs and declaw her. He struggles to articulate this to himself, but inviting her to babysit is the answer to some sloppy math: the best way to ensure that nothing ever happens between them is to show her to people. To the people who matter. Besides, once she becomes both a student and a babysitter, he couldn't—he wouldn't . . . *two* clichés? Yuck, he thinks. No way. Plus, James has a curious urge to verify Tiffany. She could be a hallucination, a psychological crisis, the ghost of an ancestor! His domestic life—his *real* life—will puncture and deflate this thing between them. He will hypostatize her to his life, and hypostatize his life to her, and then they will retreat to their barricaded realms, and all will be well. All will have always been well.

"Our regular babysitter is going on a silent retreat," he explains unnecessarily. "And my in-laws are busy."

He does not ask if Tiffany has experience with childcare. Presumes that being female is sufficient qualification for the job.

"I don't have a car," Tiffany responds.

"One of us can pick you up and drop you off."

She rolls her neck. "What time?"

~~~

On the drive, James fiddles with the radio as Tiffany plunders her life experiences for something interesting to say. They both settle on silence.

Most of the houses for rich people in Vacca Vale depress Tiffany. One of her foster families—a family she tries not to think about—lived in the suburbs. The idea of the suburbs excited Tiffany until she arrived there at the age of twelve: a panopticon of beige, no imagination in the architecture, no life in the brick and vinyl paneling, so much wealth in a desert of taste. Megachurches. Whole neighborhoods copied and pasted into existence, besieged by industrial farmland. Sometimes Tiffany would wander miles from her foster family's house to watch a field of horses. THESE HORSES ARE HAPPILY RETIRED, said a sign near the pasture. She never saw any humans there, just a black barn in the distance. The horses would approach her curiously, and she would feed them apples through a honeycomb of chain-link fence.

Because James is rich, Tiffany assumed he lived in the suburbs, too, so she is surprised when he pulls into a neighborhood only seven minutes from Stella and Wayne's. A row of historic houses near the river, just north of downtown. Brick fucking roads. He parks in front of a mansion—a *mansion*—and Tiffany's jaw drops like that of a cartoon. She clicks it shut. Spire work, wraparound porch, bay windows. Stone and brick and shingles. Two chimneys. More square footage than all of Tiffany's foster houses combined.

"I thought you'd live in the suburbs," she says idiotically.

"Why?"

"I don't know." She gulps and sweats like she's facing a dragon. "This house is very . . . it's so—"

"It was passed down on my wife's side of the family," he says gruffly. "I have nothing to do with it."

Plucked from another era, the house is inconveniently magnificent. The house is hard to take. Before, Tiffany knew that James's wife came from Zorn Automobile money—money that continued to multiply even after the company orphaned Vacca Vale in the sixties—but she didn't imagine a fortress. He leads Tiffany inside, depositing her in the entryway like a bag of groceries, and suddenly he's gone, replaced by his wife. Marble table, ceramic vase, woodsy bouquet of branches. Emerald details. His wife smiles. "James is just getting ready," she says. "He'll be down in a second." Her voice is limpid and cool, pond-like, her vocabulary casually vigorous, her posture assured. Prior to this evening, Tiffany understood the *concept* of James's wife, but not the reality of her. Now she is here, in three dimensions, as real as Tiffany is—probably realer. She has eyebrows, chapped hands, a personality, a master's degree in public health, a cautious laugh—the laugh of an adult who was constantly hushed as a child. She even has a name. Her name is Meg. Her presence makes Tiffany feel like a prototype of a woman, not the real thing. Tiffany dashes to remove her shoes, realizing that she failed to do so upon entry, feeling unduly ashamed of this faux pas.

"It's so lovely to meet in person," Meg says, perceiving Tiffany's discomfort and seeking to remedy it. "James speaks the world of you. Thanks for taking care of our girls on such short notice."

Meg leads Tiffany to the kitchen, where she orchestrates small talk with gymnastic dexterity. Despite herself, Tiffany wonders about the money: Would it amount to much in a big city, or does it merely coronate Meg and James within the shipwrecked economy of Vacca Vale? Up until now, Tiffany had assumed that Meg would wear thick makeup and strong perfume, balayage her hair, partake in trends like rompers and basket purses, receive fancy manicures in hip colors twice a month, and harbor few informed opinions. Tiffany's not sure why she assumed this. In fact, Meg is earthy and bookish. Articulate. Intelligent. Barefaced. Kind. The brutal fact of her unnerves Tiffany. "Are you okay?" asks Meg as Tiffany coughs. Tiffany is having some kind of allergic reaction to the house. When Tiffany notices the water and power bills on their kitchen island, shame roils inside her. Don't they know that she is a child, too young to care for fellow children?

A health, culinary, and lifestyle blogger, Meg writes vegan cookbooks. She has a YouTube show in the works, along with half a million followers on social media—facts she manages to relay to Tiffany without bragging. She says Tiffany should help herself to the roasted paprika root vegetables in the fridge, then describes some of her favorite recipes. They all sound folkloric. "Would you like some elderflower soda?" she asks Tiffany. "Lavender lemonade? Rosemary rhubarb fizz? Dandelion and rosehip tea?"

Perhaps noticing that Tiffany is too distracted by the house to select a beverage, Meg gives her a tour of the first floor. Her sister Gwen is an architect in Copenhagen, she explains. "She helped with the renovation. Some of my family updated the place over the decades, and a lot of their choices were appalling. James and I wanted to honor the home's history, so our changes were mostly about unearthing the past rather than imposing the present. We wanted to restore the house to its original beauty." Frightening oil paintings. Relics of travel. Creepy, gratuitous technology. Engraved wooden doorways. Stained glass windows. Imported rugs with stories woven into them—stories that belong to other people, other eras. Tall ceilings and sublime windows. A bewitching scent that seems to emanate from the floorboards. Tobacco and cedar and vanilla. Frankincense. Tiffany breathes and breathes, unable to get enough.

"The city keeps trying to buy the house from us," Meg explains, "but we're determined to keep it in the family. They say they want to turn it into a museum honoring Woodrow, local history is sacred, blah blah blah, but remember what they did to Cecil's estate? Oh, you didn't hear? It's just a few blocks down from us—you should swing by at some point. The city couldn't pull the funds together to update it, so they just left it vacant until the pipes burst, and the roof collapsed. Now they say that the museum conversion is on 'indefinite hold.' Next thing you know, it'll be a parking lot. No thanks."

All of the children's toys seem to come from the eighteenth century: no plastic, no batteries, no jingles or flashing lights. Hardcover books stock wall-to-wall shelves; the cats match the furniture; the furniture is surprising. Logs in the fireplace. Mahogany floors. Tiffany treads in this flood of beauty, overwhelmed nearly to tears. She feels like one of those cows in the wake of a hurricane, swimming without a destination, doomed by a task that she was not designed to perform.

Presently, Meg leads Tiffany down a hallway that displays a gallery of black-and-white portraits. "Ancestors," explains Meg. "Impeccably dressed and miserable—every last one of them. A family trait." In both size and magnitude, the portrait in the center is the greatest: a steely, suited man in his fifties. Walt Whitman beard. Hollowed Renaissance eyes, pitched in shadow, staring. Tiffany recognizes him from history books. "Yeah, that's Woodrow," says Meg, her expression unreadable as she studies him. "Woodrow Huxley Zorn the Third. The founder himself. He's not my great-grandfather or anything. We're related pretty distantly. But I was the only member of the family who stuck around in Vacca Vale, so when my parents got too old to maintain the house, it made sense for me to become the . . . the steward, I suppose. I grew up here, so I feel some obligation to it."

Abruptly, Meg turns from Woodrow and walks on. "Enough of him," she says. The hallway deposits them into a small room wallpapered in repeating minimalist bird drawings. Blind contours. They look like hawks to Tiffany. At the center of the room stands a grand piano, its gold feet perched in Moroccan wool. *Bösendorfer,* says gold script on its side. Tiffany tries not to ogle it, but she can't look away; it is the most enchanting object she has ever seen. "This is James's room," says Meg. "I don't have a musical bone in my body, and the girls despised their lessons, so we gave up. But James is a genius at the piano. Have you ever heard him play?"

A bit too violently, Tiffany shakes her head. "Never."

"Oh," replies Meg. "He could've been a professional—he's totally transfixing. Maybe we can force him to perform for you, one day. In any case, the kids go to bed around seven, fall asleep by eight." Tiffany's coughing again, but Meg has the grace to ignore it. As she speaks, she leads Tiffany through the first floor, back to the foyer. "All the doctor information and emergency contact stuff is taped to the fridge—you'll see it. Dinner's all prepared; you just have to serve it. We never force them to finish anything, but they know they don't get dessert unless they eat the vegetables. Emma will be happy to explain their bedtime routine to you—she's the boss around here. They'll want you to read about eleven hundred stories. We try to limit it to three. What else? Oh—we keep the cats out of the kids' room at night. Just call or text if you have any questions."

That's when Tiffany notices James ambling down the stairs, tucking an Oxford shirt into navy slacks. Flushed and clean, scruff grown out, hair unkempt, laugh lines pronounced, altogether taller than Tiffany remembered. He devastates her. Hardly noticing the children trailing him, Tiffany offers James a normal smile like she is a normal student, like she is a jolly nameless babysitter, like her nerves have not just burst into opera for the dad on the stairs. Her body reacts to James exactly as it reacts to his house: all this splendor, precisely calibrated to her innermost desires, and none of it will ever be hers.

"Godspeed," James tells Tiffany.

The neutrality with which he delivers this greeting cancels all other evidence. Tiffany understands, with a force that nearly shoves her to the ground, that she has misinterpreted everything. She is delusional, foolish, disposable, grotesque. Humiliated.

"I love you," says James. "I love you so much."

His daughters cling to him, begging him to stay. Only Meg can wrench them from his legs. "Be good, my loves," she says, kissing their heads. "You are both so good."

After a few more reassurances that Tiffany can call them at any point, the parents leave.

As the children—ages five and eight—peer up at Tiffany, she is reminded of a pair of macaws she once saw at the zoo. At first, they stare at her with suspicion, then fascination, then delight. In their matching NASA pajamas, they resemble neither their father nor their mother, but they are copies of each other.

"I'm *starving*," says the older daughter, Emma. "Do you like tagine?"

Feeding them is bafflingly difficult. They keep bolting from the table and sprinting in circles around the first floor, cackling like mad scientists. They make animal noises at random and refuse to use forks. Rosie, the younger one, has a lisp. They shout, "TIMBERRR!" as they drop throw pillows from the couch to the floor. Tiffany admires the untempered weirdness of children in general, and these in particular, but she is already exhausted, and she's only been there an hour. After dinner, the children lead Tiffany upstairs and scream about strawberry toothpaste.

"We could've had different rooms," says Emma. "But we share, because *she* doesn't like to go to sleep alone." She points at Rosie, who is crossing her eyes in the mirror.

"And do you like sharing a room?" Tiffany asks.

"Yes," replies Emma. "*I* don't like waking *up* alone."

Rosie curates a stack of books while her sister explains why they have so many toothbrushes. "Our dad is always buying toothbrushes,"

Emma says. "He always thinks we're out of toothbrushes. He's always saying: 'The good news is, I remembered to buy toothbrushes!' "

Under the sink, there are about two dozen packs.

Changing her tone, Emma gravely points to a bottle of pain reliever. "You know when something shows the 'actual size' on the label?" she whispers to Tiffany. "That really freaks me out."

Tiffany knows exactly what she means.

She reads to Rosie and Emma from a tattered corduroy rocking chair. Of all the dazzling furniture, this is Tiffany's favorite piece. Worn, blue, out of place, and almost ugly, it feels familiar to her. It is the only thing in this house that she is not afraid to break.

James's habitat exposes a type of affluence that Tiffany never encountered in Vacca Vale before, one she associates with foreign capitals. The wealth that Tiffany has seen before ensures that everything is storyless and new, but James's wealth ensures that everything is storied and old. It contains art and history. It possesses Tiffany. Her former disgust with fortune once made her proud, but now she sees that all this time, a kind of wonky elitism has been growing inside her. She finds the effects of bewitching real estate on her body deeply troubling, and she cannot reconcile it with her budding ideologies about private property. Who allowed this foster kid to give a damn about artisanal furniture? To value hand-knotted rugs like a fucking aristocrat? Who does she think she is?

These are the contours of her thoughts as she reads a rhyming cartoon to the girls about the evils of capitalism. Rosie snuggles beside Tiffany on the corduroy chair while Emma makes snow angels on the sheepskin rug—"Wool angels!"—quietly reciting the words as Tiffany reads them. Their room is wallpapered to resemble a forest. Fairies crafted from cloth, glitter, and pipe cleaner nest in a web of lights above. Tiffany never dreamed of such a scenic childhood when she was growing up in the system, passed from house to house like a cursed heirloom. Padlocks on the refrigerators.

"When we go to thleep, *they* wake *up*," whispers Rosie, pointing to the fairies.

"Yes, and they change the thermostat," reports Emma. "They make it colder."

Before going to bed, the children ask Tiffany to cut the tags from their pajamas, claiming the itch keeps them awake. Tiffany recognizes this as an innovative form of stalling, but their sensitivity, she thinks, indicates that they are geniuses. She snips the tags but saves them for the laundering instructions because she assumes that's what rich people do. In her own life, Tiffany has never read laundering instructions, much less obeyed them. After she reads the last book of the night—a rhyming cartoon about deforestation—she switches off the light in the girls' bedroom, descends the stairs, and stands in the kitchen.

It's the kind of ringing silence that follows a concert. She places the pajama tags in a ceramic fruit bowl, then gazes into a pantry of exotic balsamics. Takes a picture on her cheap flip phone. Deletes it immediately.

She wants to be his kid and she wants to be his wife and she wants to be him.

He's showing his life to me, Tiffany realizes, so that I don't murder it. *Actual size.*

~~~

By the time James drives Tiffany home, it is clear that the night has exorcised them from each other, just as James had hoped. All they had to do was step out of their private, fake world and into the public, real one. The thing that possessed them—call it Ondine—could only breathe imaginary air, in the theater of St. Philomena. Oxygen kills it, witnesses kill it, and now, rejoice, it is dead.

Outside the house on Arcadia, James puts the car in park and pays Tiffany too much money.

~~~

"What do you want me to do to you?" James asks Tiffany, his mouth on her neck. "What do you want from me?"

~~~

Questions 19–21 refer to the late-nineteenth-century photograph below by journalist Jacob Riis. Advocates for individuals such as those shown in the image would have most likely agreed with which of the following perspectives? *Everyone is overreacting. People just want to gossip, there hasn't been a scandal since Mrs. Lansberry got that DUI. I think he just feels sorry for* her. (A) The Supreme Court's decision in *Plessy v. Ferguson* was justified. (B) Capitalism, free of government regulation, would improve social conditions. *Speaking of scandals, did you hear that Kayla gave three lacrosse guys pterodactyl? Oh my God, you haven't heard of this? It's three guys, one girl. The guys stand side by side, in a row. She blows the guy in the middle, then gives the other two hand jobs. So it looks like she's trying to fly.* (C) Both wealth and poverty are the products of natural selection. (D) Governments should act to eliminate the worst abuses of industrial society. *But why does Tiffany stay after everyone? My mom says we should tell Mr. Rayo.* "The history of mankind is a history of repeated injuries and usurpations on the part of man toward woman, having in direct object the establishment of an absolute tyranny over her. To prove this, let facts be submitted to a candid world. He has never permitted her to exercise her inalienable right to the elective franchise. He has compelled her to submit to laws, in the formation of which she had no voice." *Maybe she thinks she's too good for boys her age.* Seneca Falls Convention, Declaration of Sentiments and Resolutions, 1848. *She doesn't even have social media. Everybody's always feeling sorry for her, but I think she's a total snob.* Many supporters of the declaration in 1848 broke ranks with which of the following groups by the 1870s? (A) Social Darwinists. (B) Supporters of Southern secession and states' rights. (C) Supporters of the Fifteenth Amendment. (D) Isolationists. *I've never seen her talk to another student, except when she was like, dissecting a fetal pig. People try to be nice to her, but she thinks she's better than the rest of us.* What is the direction of the current, if any, induced in the loop as seen in Figure 3? *Obviously, she has no boundaries.* (A) Clockwise. (B) Counterclockwise. (C) Undefined, because there is no current induced in the loop. Justify your answer. *He wouldn't do anything weird. He's a good person. If you seem lost, he's the kind of teacher who will take you under his wing.* Select and clearly identify two works of art depicting the male figure that support or challenge attitudes toward men within their cultural contexts. *I don't know. I've never seen anyone so deep under anyone else's wing.* An arctic food web includes the following organisms: orca, polar bear, ringed seal, arctic cod, krill, diatom. Note: Figures not drawn to scale. *I know everybody thinks he's a dreamboat, but he's only hot for a teacher. If you passed him on the street, you wouldn't look twice.* Other than showing which organisms are consumed by other organisms, describe what is indicated by the direction of the arrows on the diagram. *Speak* *for yourself. I have a sex dream about him every time I'm ovulating. You think I'm joking? I'm dead serious. He's a* man, you know? *And have you ever seen him play piano? Good God.* Pullo attacks and is attacked. *Do you think she's pretty? I can't really tell. She creeps me out, but I feel like you could use her to sell something. She's memorable.* Translate the following passage: *I heard she's in foster care because her mom was an opioid addict and her dad's in jail. Yeah, oxycodone. I hear she had to get an attorney at birth because the mom was high and the dad was nowhere to be found. Can you imagine? Needing a lawyer the moment you're born?* Midiocri spatio relicto . . . *No, her mom is dead now.* Maria has been chosen for the lead role in the play. She is both nervous and excited about this opportunity. *Did you hear how she fumbled her lines when he touched her arm? Is he even allowed to touch us?* Part A: Explain how each of the following concepts may help her performance in the play. *Context-dependent memory *Acetylcholine *Kinesthetic sense *Selective attention. *Isn't she supposed to be a genius or something? She's top of the class, right? And I hear she got a perfect score on the PSAT. Why do smart people always do such stupid things? She's putting him in real danger. He has a wife and kids—I met them at the auction, and they're the cutest family ever.* Part B: Explain how each of the following concepts may hinder her performance in the play. *Proactive interference *Yerkes-Dodson law of arousal *External locus of control. *Look at the way she's staring at him. It's disgusting. If she really cared about him, she would leave him alone. He has everything to lose.* Vous aurez six minutes pour lire le sujet de l'essai, la source numéro un et la source numéro deux. Sujet de l'essai: *Do you think they'll fuck for real?* Evaluate $(d^2y)/(dx^2)$ at the point on the curve where $X = 1$ and $Y = 1$. *He'd never, but I bet she's trying her hardest.* Solve for X in terms of Y. *She has no one. She has nothing to lose.*

~~~

"Can I have," Tiffany whispers to James in his three-hundred-dollar sheets, "a glass of water?"

~~~

It goes like this: they detach throughout February. Then, in March, James texts: *Come over.* Minutes later, Tiffany replies: *Pick me up.*

She tells Stella and Wayne that she is going over to a friend's house, which is true enough. She might spend the night, she says. They are so pleased by the mention of a friend that they ask no further questions. Tiffany takes a careful shower, pushing a razor against her skin until she feels her shinbone. Honeysuckle shampoo and Stella's fancy lotion. Wet hair, side braid, no makeup, soft clothes. Quick heart. Hot blood. It's the first Sunday of spring break, and the slush outside is cruel.

In the car, Tiffany and James act maniacally normal.

As they enter his house through the side door, the awareness that Tiffany is embarking upon a Major Life Event caffeinates her; her body trembles, her senses sharpen, and all the colors saturate. She feels more alive than she thought possible, and she understands that she has finally graduated from an imitation of life. Now, she stands inside her real one for the very first time. In the kitchen, James appears nervous, running his hands through his thick hair and spilling the wine as he pours it. He gives her a glass of pinot noir, like an equal. Drinks his very quickly, then pours himself another. Somehow, without explicitly saying so, he communicates that his kids, his wife, and his in-laws are vacationing in Key West. The desperation with which Tiffany wants to like the wine makes her actually like it, but when she asks for another glass, James says, "Maybe not." They wander around his house like it's an Ikea, sitting on various pieces of furniture, chatting about childhood, and imagining alternative lives until they land in the music room.

"Play it," Tiffany commands when she sees the Bösendorfer.

"Play what?"

"*Gaspard de la Nuit.*"

He obeys without demurring, grateful for something to do with his hands.

As she listens, Tiffany doesn't cry. Doesn't compliment him. Doesn't pet the cats. These are tough accomplishments, but she accomplishes them nonetheless. When he finishes, his face flushed, she steadies herself by pouring herself another glass—he doesn't object—and asking a lot of questions about the piano. He explains that the piano has a satin ebony finish. It was crafted from an Austrian high-altitude solid spruce, with a maple and red beech pin block and a walnut veneer top. A traditional cast-iron plate. Hand-wound single-looped strings.

The piano was a wedding gift from his wife's family, a product of their evergreen wealth, and no one has ever associated it with James as intimately as Tiffany does that night. His wife's fortune, once so alluring, now repels him like a funhouse reflection. It makes him feel misshapen, carsick, malnourished. Increasingly, he has felt like a tourist in this house. But in Tiffany's eyes, all of this is his.

"Hand-notched bridges," James says. Tiffany is standing inches from him, her delicate hand hovering over a B minor chord. She's examining the Bösendorfer's open anatomy. Carefully, as though petting a carnivorous bird, he touches her wrist. "Spruce keys," he mutters. He can feel her holding her breath, can see her whole body react. "You are beautiful," he says, shocking them both.

Her face turns pink. A sudden dusk. "Fuck you," she says, punching his arm and backing away. A moment of silence. James wonders if he has shattered everything.

"You make me unlonely," she finally whispers, her eyes on the piano. "You make me feel real."

Tiffany and James finish emotionally undressing as the Bösendorfer watches. Then they ascend to the bedroom and take off their clothes.

~~~

When dawn arrives, Tiffany stops pretending to sleep. She sits up in bed and unleashes her braid, watching James's back rise and fall with his breath. Her hair is still wet from the shower she took at Stella and Wayne's, still fragrant with honeysuckle shampoo, and this bewilders her—a different woman took that shower. Tiffany tiptoes to the bathroom and pees as quietly as possible, humiliated by the fact of her body. When she returns, James is awake, looking a decade older in the glow of his phone. "Hey," he says, his tone cold. "Better get dressed."

He throws her clothes to her, and she dresses quickly, sensing that something critical has gone wrong. They descend the stairs and enter his sublime kitchen, foraging for conversation strong enough to chase the shame. He brews espresso for them both using a loud and complex machine but then seems to regret it. As they sip crema from ceramic, they speak of weather, favorite types of oatmeal, the personal histories of his cats. One is black, the other white, both longhaired and agitated. Through narrowed eyes and accusatory body language, they watch Tiffany as though they know exactly what she's done. When James feeds them rabbit pâté, Tiffany wonders aloud why their interactions are so consistently plagued by the odor of pet food. He doesn't laugh, doesn't seem to hear her at all.

She smiles. "What do you think it means?"

"Probably nothing," he snaps, his attention on his phone. "Not everything means something."

An hour before Tiffany's ACT prep class begins, James deposits her at a coffee chain close to school.

"We'll be in touch," he says to the windshield. He hasn't looked her in the eye since last night.

"Sure," she replies, a sob building in her throat.

When Tiffany vomits her scone into a toilet at St. Philomena's, what upsets her most is the waste of money.

<center>~~~</center>

The evening after the Night, James sends her a text message.

I just want to reiterate my respect for you. You should know that my behavior has always been guided by an investment in your well-being.

Tiffany feels her pulse in her eyes as she stares at the screen. That distressing formality again. She tries to feel indignant, as she's supposed to feel, but instead she begins to weep. It would be a blinding relief to believe him. She replies: *Can we talk?*

And then nothing. Absolutely nothing. Each day after the Night, Tiffany stares at her phone, freshes and refreshes her inbox, receives nothing, tells no one, googles his face and zooms in until she can't tell who it is. She listens to his stupid music with the stupid headphones he gave her. Each listen grants Tiffany a clearer awareness of his narcissism. What's more, he's ridiculous. *Vu.* Ridiculous! In her bed, Tiffany eats an entire jar of cornichons, stares into her laptop, taps pause, loses her grip. She doesn't sleep for thirty-four hours, then sleeps for fourteen consecutive hours. He never lent her his copy of *Gaspard de la Nuit,* and now she knows that he never will.

She only leaves the house to work her shifts at the diner. As she bikes through the industrial wasteland of Vacca Vale, she keeps mistaking her setting for the afterlife. This year, Vacca Vale ranked first on *Newsweek*'s bafflingly heartless list of "Top Ten Dying Cities." Nobody was surprised. At Ampersand, Tiffany is mean to customers and often forgets to speak altogether. Desiring James has always felt like a mental illness, but this is the first time it's felt like a crisis. At work, she takes too many bathroom breaks. Ransacks her phone each time.

After the fourth day of no contact, she begins mouthing, *FUCK YOU FUCK YOU FUCK YOU, YOU FUCKER* when she checks her empty electronics. Sometimes she addresses this to herself. Eating, sleeping, and breathing become unnatural tasks. Teeth chattering, color draining from her vision, temperature dropping, red cold wind ripping through her body. Nausea oppresses her, sometimes making her throw up. Stella and Wayne conclude, endearingly, that she has the flu. They materialize with cups of ice water, tomato soup, and berry-flavored medicine. She takes the medicine, willing it to treat whatever she has.

"He loves being seen and it shows," Tiffany tells her Venus flytrap on the fourth night. It hasn't eaten in a long time because the house is too clean. You're supposed to feed one of its heads once a month, but Tiffany keeps forgetting. "Only live bugs," said the lady at the store. "It only likes the live ones."

<center>~~~</center>

Six days after the Night, James chews the plants his wife left in the fridge but tastes very little. He pictures himself as a Brachiosaurus, munching the forest canopy, irrelevant and doomed, wrinkles everywhere, his contemporaries extinct already. He has spent the week washing every sheet, pillowcase, duvet, quilt, throw blanket, and bath mat in the house; it felt too murderous to exclusively launder the bedding in which he fucked his student. Now, as he eats, he listens to the hum of the washing machine and makes a list of tasks to complete, knowing that he will not complete them. After clearing his plate, James cancels his therapy session by text message. The death of his mother had prompted the revelation that therapy was indispensable to his health, which made him wonder how he had survived for so long without it. It was like discovering fruit at the age of thirty. He doesn't know anyone else in Vacca Vale with a therapist.

In the afternoon, Meg FaceTimes from Florida. "There's a hurricane that will obliterate all of this next week," she monotones in the dazzling sunlight, showing him the house her parents are renting. "So we got here just in time."

That evening, as the tub fills with water, James rummages in the cabinets until he finds a jar of bath milk. He had given it to Meg as a birthday gift a couple years ago. For far too long, he deliberated at the farmers market stand, asking the vendor outrageously specific questions until he decided that Meg would prefer the eucalyptus spruce over the chamomile rose. Now, the jar is dusty and unopened. *Restore, energize, uplift,* reads its label. He pours a third of it into the tub and lies in the fragrant water until it surrenders its heat to the clock. He does not feel restored, energized, or uplifted.

In one of the guest rooms, James sleeps on his back, hands folded over his navel like a corpse at a viewing. Across from the bed, Meg fastened a print of *The Unicorn in Captivity,* which makes him want to eat his own hands. He wakes before dawn in a museum of his wife's magnificent stuff and spends the day shuffling from room to room, curiously unable to go outside. The cats make themselves scarce. He avoids the Zorn Family Hallway, which has always given him the creeps, and now also gives him esophageal spasms. He doesn't believe in ghosts, but he accepted their presence in this house long ago. They dress him in cold wet blankets. They fuck with the electricity and the cellular service and the Wi-Fi. They call him Farm Trash. They know what he's done. He tries to kindle a fire, prods and reconstructs, uses all the newspaper in the house, but the wood refuses to light.

On Saturday, he eats nothing but a bag of venison jerky that he hid from Meg months ago and stares at the television for many minutes before remembering to turn it on. He spends the evening crunching ice between his molars and gazing into a digital clock as its numbers shimmy. He pours himself a large mug of gin and apple juice—the drink that he and his brother favored when they were teenagers, secretly getting drunk in the abandoned corncrib on their parents' property, discussing quantum physics as if they understood it. Now, he sips his drink in the girls' room, mentally archiving their books and toys as though he might have to flee the country in the middle of the night, falling asleep on the sheepskin rug to the distant wail of a car alarm.

If Tiffany believes that she is the only one they injured, she is even younger than he thought.

Sunday arrives—the seventh day after the Night. Spring break is over. Tomorrow, Tiffany and James must return to school.

In preparation for the sluggish psychological brutality that Monday is sure to inflict, Tiffany has forced herself out of Wayne and Stella's dark, low-ceilinged house and into the world. She's three pounds lighter than she was a week ago; she can feel herself minimizing. She stops at the gas station and purchases a blue slushee to cheer herself up. Now she stands in the Valley, the only place she's ever loved, inhaling the pollen and dirt of a forest too wild for the town it inhabits, dyeing her tongue blue and trying to circumvent a brain freeze. It's the first warmish day after a relentless winter, and this is the Valley's most public meadow. It seems the whole town is there. Attached to a fence, a banner advertises the condominiums that will sprout in the hills and demolish this park in the summer—Phase One of an urban revitalization plan that makes Tiffany want to unvitalize. The day breathes sanguine and gray, melting the last ice, and the scent of petrichor is so lovely it makes her eyes water. Lines from the play fire through Tiffany's brain on an irrepressible loop, and she's trying to stop them when her phone rings.

She jumps. Gasps. He's never called her before.

"Hello?"

"Hi."

"Hey."

Their hearts pound on separate acres. This wasn't his idea, and he wasn't hers, but here he is, in a cliché he especially hates, and there she is, in a cliché she especially hates, and what can you do.

James stands in his kitchen, shaking from a third espresso, aware that he has no reason to be so tyrannically awake at 4:14 in the afternoon. His wife is returning in a few hours. They got into a fight on the phone earlier—a fight that had nothing to do with anything. A fight about time.

In the meadow, Tiffany trembles in white cotton, aware that she's suitably dressed for her role as disposable ingénue.

Neither of them feels capable of change, this month.

He waits for her to speak, like she was the one who called. Finally, he asks, "What's up?"

"Good."

"How are you?"

"Nothing." She flushes. "I mean—"

"Yeah." He smiles. She hears it. It hurts her. "I know."

Have you mentioned me to your therapist? Tiffany wants to ask. Either way, she'd be offended. Instead, she chews the straw of her Chug Big and stares at a pink tree to prove that good is, indeed, what's up. James is a child but different, both of them children but different, so in the static they say nothing. Tiffany wants to exit her body. James wants to stay rooted in his. It's why a lot of people fuck—there's nothing to see here—Tiffany wants to scream.

Beneath the tree, a young woman cuffs her jeans and laughs into her phone. Tiffany studies her like an anthropologist. Unlike Tiffany, the laughing woman is real. Whomever she's speaking to speaks back like they want to, and Tiffany envies her. She wonders if there's a word for the opposite of solipsism, wonders if such a term could accurately describe her psychological disorder. It's Sunday but it feels like Wednesday. It's spring but it feels like fall. It's warm but Tiffany shivers. She feels drunk.

Tiffany thought she just wanted James's voice until he said Hi like he had to, and now she revises—now she just wants his voice if it'll hold her name like it did that Night.

"I should've called sooner," James says.

"You don't owe me anything."

But neither of them means it.

Up until James, Tiffany had led a small life in dark rooms, and she was hoping to expand, but this bright empty space embarrasses her. In the grass, she sees a piece of trash and relates to it. Tiffany is not designed for a big life—she does not meet the height requirement. She is seventeen; she feels seventy. She is seventeen; she feels seven.

"Still, I'm sorry," he says.

"What for?"

"Well." He sighs. "Pretty much all of it."

He is trying to do the right thing, but instead he is pulverizing her.

Here's what they wanted—it is what they always want: Tiffany wanted to preserve James's sadness like an endangered species because she thought it made them both more interesting. James wanted to preserve his youth in hers. He is forty-two, but he never made it past fifteen. He didn't want her to interview him, but he needed her to ask him questions. They weren't sure if they wanted to have *sex,* per se, but they wanted to know what would happen next. He is forty-two and he is terrified. She didn't need a future-inclusive tense, but she needed him to wring the pleasure from her voice just once. Once he did, she did not know what she wanted. What she ever wanted.

"Listen," he says on the phone, but discards the rest.

Observing how open and spacious the Valley is, Tiffany's eyes water. Not far off, someone uncorks a bottle of wine. A very human man approaches the very human woman beneath the pink tree. Their flesh looks soft and packed with organs. He carries a metal pipe.

"Excuse me," he says, pointing to the branches. "I gotta get that down."

The woman looks up, irritated, then crosses the grass. "Sorry," she says to the other end of the line. "There was a drone. Go on."

The very human man hurls the pipe again and again at the tree, shedding branches and blossoms. A dog barks, children scream, someone plays a harmonica, and Tiffany sips until she has sucked all the blue out of the ice. "WE ARE LIVING WITH THE ENEMY!" bellows a child, pitching a branch at her brother.

"Jesus," says James, sounding annoyed. "Where are you?"

"At the park. I was reading." She did bring a book, but she wasn't reading it, just bullying the ink into sense. "It's pretty good," she says. "It would be brilliant if it weren't the literary equivalent of a shirtless mirror selfie, you know, like, if the author only flexed when he had to lift something. But I guess no one is spared the primal dispossession of psychosexual pressures. Not even the geniuses."

She blushes. All she meant to communicate was that James is not her only story, but now she's gone and revealed precisely what she vowed to conceal. This always happens with him.

"You should probably watch more television," James says.

It's been done before, and it will happen again, but when it happened to them—when it was done to her—there were some diversions from the formula. For example: Tiffany seemed to enjoy the actual sex more than James did. On his bed seven nights prior, Tiffany and James tried to guide their hips into something, but she moved like a kid, and he hardly moved at all, so they made something up. By the time it happened, they both understood that fucking was beside the point, but they were determined to see it through. It was polite, then fearsome, then euphoric, then over. Before this experience, everyone who touched Tiffany relished it precisely because she didn't. Masturbating had never occurred to her. She wouldn't know how; her intelligence was restricted to the immaterial. But that night, in the flicker of a tobacco candle, James—apparently more interested in her pleasure than he was in his own—introduced her to feelings she had previously considered unattainable. She used to believe that sexual bliss was a luxury reserved for other people, like skiing. Now she mourned that belief.

He pulled the dress over her head, unclasped her bra, and ran his hands over her skin as though it was offering him instructions in an emergency. She watched as he removed his shirt, his belt, his pants. Imperfect body perfect because it was his. Pressing against the navy cotton of his briefs, she saw an erection that was his but for her, for her and because of her, and the astonishment of it made her whole body bloom open, hot and stormy and alchemized. He looked undressed, but he did not look nude until he removed his glasses and placed them, gingerly, on a nightstand. Confronting his naked, endangered face for the first time was like seeing a tiger at the zoo, subdued and therefore doomed, and it sent a shock of pity through her, made her want to look away but also save his life. She closed her eyes, felt his heat, felt his cock press against her leg, felt his stubble on her neck, breasts, thighs. And with his mouth between her legs, she felt something entirely new, the activation of a sensory system she didn't know she possessed. The whole room flickered, flooded, sang.

"What do you want?" he asked once he brought her to the verge of herself.

"You."

"Say it."

"I want you."

"Want me to what?"

"To everything."

When had he lit the candle? Later, when Tiffany reviewed the details of the night like a detective on a murder case, this seemed important; it indicated premeditation, thus the severity of the offense, thus the severity of the sentence. She wasn't on birth control and he didn't have a condom, but neither of them gave this much thought. On her back, in his bed, all she experienced was molten rapture. By the time James entered Tiffany, reason had evacuated her. Improbably, she orgasmed almost right away. She didn't know if this was supposed to be embarrassing—she had never orgasmed, before, never had sex on *purpose,* before—but this microclimate of luminosity exiled shame. She would never forget the pride on his face, like her pleasure was the greatest accomplishment of his life. Orgasm, she discovered, simultaneously possessed and exorcised you of yourself. As the chemicals lifted her from one realm into another—due to increased stimulation of the right angular gyrus, she later learned, a region of the brain associated with spatiovisual awareness, memory retrieval, reading, and out-of-body experiences—Tiffany felt like a mystic. James took his time.

Afterward, with his boxers, he wiped evidence of himself off her chest. Entwined and almost sweet, he stroked her hair, her neck, her collarbone. He traced the outline of her breasts and told her that she was brilliant, otherwordly, important. Propping his head on his fist to face her, he began to speak.

"Was it your first time?" he asked.

She hesitated, then shook her head. "No."

"Good. That's good." He paused for a moment, studying her collarbone. "Listen, Tiffany. I want you to know that I respect you tremendously." He touched her neck like she was fragile and valuable. A cracked iPhone. She couldn't tell what was more alarming: his sincerity or his formality. "All of this . . ." he said, vaguely gesturing between his chest and her thighs, "was motivated by that."

A freaky guffaw was flapping in her throat. She swallowed it down.

"Thanks," she replied.

"You should pee," he said.

"What?"

"It prevents UTIs after sex. Didn't anyone ever teach you that?"

That's when she let herself laugh.

"No." He smiled. "Really—I don't want to cause you pain. Of any kind. Trust me."

"Fine." She blushed. "But wait, where are my . . . ?"

"Hm?"

"I lost my . . ."

"Your what?"

She knew, as a general rule, it was good to avoid fucking people in whose presence you couldn't bear to say the word *underwear.*

"My . . ."

"Your underwear?"

Relieved that he didn't use the word *panties,* she sighed and tried not to burst into flames. "Yes."

He rummaged in the bedding and handed them to her. It was not possible to put them on sexily, but she tried. Then she crept to his bathroom, turned on the faucet, and peed. She didn't flip on the light, didn't want to see the evidence, couldn't stomach the sight of another woman's soaps and razors and hair tools. The rightful woman.

When she was done, he took her place in the bathroom, using it without any discernible shame. He returned in a fresh pair of boxers, looking serious in the moonlight.

"I know this is . . . well, forgive me for even asking, but . . . we won't tell anyone about this, right? We'll keep it between us?" A beat. "It would be bad for us both."

He wasn't asking.

"Oops," Tiffany deadpanned. "I live-tweeted it."

He didn't laugh.

In a quieter voice, she added, "Who would I tell?"

In one study, stimulating the right angular gyrus made a woman perceive a phantom behind her. In another study, it made the subject believe he was on the ceiling. Tiffany felt it all.

What Tiffany remembers best from that night is her name in his mouth when he was in her.

Now, in the Valley, certain sentiments boil and spit in her chest. What I love most about you, she wants to say, is your piano. Weren't we safe until you got your shiny, pricey Bösendorfer involved? Yes, I wanted to touch your stubble, drink your coffee, and wear your glasses. Yes, I wanted your mind and your words and your face and your sadness and your sensitivity and your power and your talent and your age and your imagination and your hair and your music, but ultimately— ultimately—I wanted to fuck your piano.

On the phone, in the Valley, she says, "Warm day."

"Sure is."

"Are you upset?"

He pauses. "Why would I be upset?"

She can't figure out how to reply, and that's when he says it: her name.

But it's not what she wants, after all. Now, in James's voice, her name isn't held; it's diagnosed. Tears fill her eyes, but she feels detached from them, the way she feels detached from the behavior of her knees when the pediatrician taps them to test her reflexes. She still has a pediatrician, and recalling this makes her cry harder. Suddenly, Tiffany remembers that James has children—it's a fact that always upends her. How could a dad like him invade a kid like her? Like that? A dad in no glasses and absolutely no condom? She pictures him standing in front of his kitchen window, drinking elderflower soda. She pictures him naked without meaning to. She looks around the park, astonished that no one can hear the noise inside her body.

"What do you want from me?" he asks wearily. He wants credit for calling.

"Stop asking me that."

"What do you mean?"

"You're always asking me that. Please just—"

"You wanted this, too." An accusation. Then, softly: "Didn't you?"

"Wanted what?" she snaps.

He sighs. "How should *we* know."

"How old are you?" Tiffany demands. Anger has hijacked her speech, and she wants him to hear it.

"Seriously?" he asks.

"Forty?"

He pauses. "Forty-two."

He does not ask how old she is.

"Well, I'm seventeen." She wants to arrest him, and chiropract his guilt, and marry him, and beat him up. She wants to launch herself into outer space. *Our night was as illegal as it felt.* But it wasn't. Not in Indiana, where the age of consent is sixteen. She looked it up. "Seventeen."

When he speaks again, his voice is gentle. "You should expect more from people."

"You should expect more from yourself."

Tiffany can no longer see the point of this, or anything else. She ends the call.

Finally, the very human man dislodges his drone from the tree and walks away, leaving a carnage of petals behind him.

~~~

As time passes, Tiffany comes to think of the Night as the Situation because she knows they fucked in one sense or another even before they did it with their bodies. Now, when the Situation reappears in her mind, the facts are tangled and rearranged, some missing, some deformed, like a puppy got to them first, and many seem to have been swallowed whole, looping and knotting questions inside her gut. What did they choose? What was chosen for them? Who undressed whom? *Had* it been pinot noir? He entered her, he exited her, but what happened in between? Did he give her tea or coffee the next morning? Was it Stella or Wayne who picked her up from her ACT prep class? Was there anything salvageable about this? Was there anything interesting about this? Did James and his wife get divorced? She wanted, and he wanted, but what exactly did they want?

Tiffany reads *The Waste Land* over and over, which makes more and more sense to her on every read, although she has no idea what it's about. *Here is Belladonna,* writes Eliot, *the Lady of the Rocks, the lady of situations.* Tiffany is not a lady of situations—everyone assumes she is, but she's not. This is her only Situation.

In the aftermath, Tiffany picks up more shifts at Ampersand. She legally changes her name to Blandine, after a teenaged martyr who stoically endured public torture at the hands of the Romans. Blandine persuades her foster parents that she needs some time off. She finds a book on female mystics in the library and reads it in one night while drinking Wayne's Yukon Jack. She rents two more books and requests a third from their partner branch. The mystics were sick and wonky geniuses, often hilarious, always alone.

Hildegard is Blandine's favorite mystic because she is about a hundred people in one body. Hildegard of Bingen: prophet, composer, botanist, abbess, theologian, doctor, preacher, philosopher, writer, saint. Doctor of the Church. A veritable polymath. She didn't ask anyone's permission to be these things, to be everything; she just did it. She was always writing letters to male members of the clergy, telling them to get their act together. They weren't *blowing the trumpet of God's justice,* was the problem. She wrote recipes. The tenth of ten children, she was born to a noble German family who donated her to the Church as a tithe, an alarmingly common practice of the time. Hildegard was born sickly, as the mystics always were, and experienced visions since she was a child but didn't tell anyone about them until she was in her forties. In her writings, she adopts an annoyingly gendered humility, painting herself as some idiot savant, some silly little woman. This initially annoyed Blandine, but upon reflection, she realized that it was a brilliant choice: it was the only way her exclusively male superiors would let her assume as much spiritual authority as she did, lecturing priests and publishing her books. *Kings* consulted her.

Blandine was born sickly, too. She made her social worker explain it to her once: she was born with neonatal abstinence syndrome. On the Finnegan scale, she scored a ten. Her biological mother was high at the time of the birth, and as soon as Blandine arrived in the world, she began to experience withdrawal. "You were treated for three months," explained the social worker. "Your symptoms became subacute over time. Your foster family took great care of you, though. Do you remember them? The Millers? They really loved you."

Later, Blandine looked it up: babies with neonatal abstinence syndrome required pharmacological treatment. A controlled dosage of morphine. They have tremors and a fever. You have to minimize light and sound, hold the baby a lot—almost all the time.

Now, studying a book of Hildegard's chaotic and luminous writing, Blandine tries to remember if she ever had visions as a child. Slowly, images return to her: worlds of cotton candy and light, mothers and geometry, lilac triangles and little jumping goats. Voices telling her that she would be free, one day. That she would be held.

She did have visions. Didn't everyone?

<center>~~~</center>

Three weeks pass this way. Wayne and Stella accommodate Blandine because social services warned them that Tiffany had experienced repeated trauma and that she coped far worse than she appeared to. Social services also warned Stella and Wayne that Tiffany was unpredictable and possibly dangerous. Blandine enrolls in an "Independence Workshop" that will expedite her transition out of the foster system and into independence, which Wayne and Stella encourage. Neither of them attended college, and they find her resistance to it sensible. They tell St. Philomena that Tiffany—*Who now goes by Blandine, by the way*—is taking a leave of absence.

"For her health," Stella says on the phone. "Your school has worked this girl to death."

The Independence Workshop is hosted at Vacca Vale High and taught by an irrationally chipper man named Micah, someone with a background in youth ministry. You could see the God all over him. He loves his wife, his kids, his dogs, his grill, his aboveground pool. He's the lead singer of a Christian rock band. As far as Blandine can tell, the worst thing that had ever happened to him was the alcoholism of his grandfather, who got sober well before Micah was born. Whenever students answer questions correctly, Micah distributes Smarties. "Smarties for a smarty!" He grins, and the whole class scowls. Despite herself, Blandine feels affection for this man. Maybe it's pity. His optimism is embarrassing, yes, but she finds herself helplessly rooting for him. The course involves watching a lot of videos from the nineties about how to balance checkbooks and triumph by bending the truth in job interviews. During breaks, girls deal weed in the bathroom. For the hell of it, one shows off the knives she keeps in her jacket. In class, under the guise of note-taking, Blandine writes unhinged spiritual advice in the voice of Hildegard von Bingen. Through the psychological fog of that summer, she sees that she is only partially real, partially alive. Unfit for human contact. She sees that this has always been true.

At the workshop, she sits behind a boy named Todd who draws exquisite comics with a left hand and a fine-tipped marker. She loves to watch him conjure whole worlds from nothing but ink, paper, and thought. When a handsome guy named Malik stops Blandine after class and asks if she wants to live with him and two other boys in a four-bedroom apartment near the river, Blandine says sure. Later, she'll wonder what made her accept his offer so swiftly: an investment in her life, or an indifference to it? She's got to live somewhere, she reasons, and boys don't scare her. Men don't scare her. Nobody scares her. Nobody can break into you if you break out of your body first. In 177 AD, not a single hungry beast touched Blandine of Lyon in that arena. "Cool." Malik smiles. He looks like an actor. Not a specific one—all of them. "If we get it, we'd move in on August first. I think they'll like our application more now that there's a girl."

The rent he found is cheap.

Blandine forbids self-pity, but she permits rage. When she takes inventory, she grants that many aspects of her Situation were enraging: in the end, she was insignificant to the person who was most significant to her; she freely entered a power dynamic that was prematurely fucked; she allowed herself to participate in the fracturing of a family, even if they remained together; her behavior was surely anti-feminist, although she hasn't worked out the particulars of this, yet; she invited one person in the world to see her, and as soon as he did, he fled; she never returned to school, although the college counselor pushed competitive courses and applications on her, and learning was her drug of choice. Almost every teacher from St. Philomena contacts her, plying her with descriptions of her worth, urging her to return. James does not contact her at all. *If you don't come back, you will not only break my heart— you will break your future,* writes her English teacher, whom she loves. Blandine deletes it. She hates melodrama.

She prefers the anger of the principal, apparent in his email:

You may conceive of the decision before you as a strictly personal one, Ms. Watkins, but it is not. Your arrival at St. Philomena's resulted from the generosity of our community, and your experience here thus far has resulted from the generosity of our teachers. Your departure would betray this collective generosity. Your merit qualified you for the Aquinas Scholarship before you enrolled, your talent and work ethic allowed you to thrive once you arrived, and you owe it to your own astonishing potential to stay now that you only have one year left, but you are not the only person involved in this choice. The year you were awarded the Aquinas Scholarship, St. Philomena received 748 applications. That's 747 students—about the population of our student body—who could have benefited from the valuable resources that our committee chose to invest in you.

As you make your decision, please consider your responsibilities to the community of St. Philomena. Consider the donors who have funded your education thus far. Consider each student who would have made the most of the Aquinas Scholarship had he or she received it. Consider your teachers, who have tirelessly advocated for you, devoted hours before and after school to your advancement, and prepared you to qualify for a place at the best universities in the world. Consider the precedent that you will set for the rest your life if you terminate your studies now. The decision before you will either fortify a pattern of resilience or initiate a pattern of defeat. We—donors, advocates, administrators, students, priests, nuns, and teachers—have devoted our goods and services to you because you were and remain one of the most promising students ever to enter this fine institution. You only have one more year of work to go, and you have the entire staff on your side. It will be a gift to all if you stay, and a disloyalty to all if you quit. Do not betray us, Ms. Watkins.

Which was also enraging.

But the most enraging aspect of all the aspects is the Situation's banality. Blandine is thereafter cursed with the knowledge that one of the defining events of her life was nothing more than a solution to a tired equation. The internet pummels her with proof: an actor sleeps with his nanny; the head of the International Equestrian Games has fucked at least sixteen participants; yet another intern blows yet another president; a philosophy professor proposes to an advisee who was born when he was fifty. One nation flashes its nuclear weapons at another. Most of the world's debt belongs to one guy. Rich countries are fucking up the weather in poor countries. In a nature documentary, a low-ranking chimpanzee rises to power by wreaking havoc in his community for a week, until the other males begin to submissively groom him. In the Valley, Blandine overhears three preteen girls tell a fourth preteen girl that she smells like socks. The redevelopment will begin its renovation of Zorn Automobile factories this summer, and demolition of the Valley will begin after that. At the Vacca Vale Zoo, the male polar bear eats one of his cubs while the mother looks on, too depressed to intervene. The moment Blandine felt most alive, she was nothing but a variable.

The rage shovels her out of herself, like it's mining her for something to burn.

~~~

One evening in July, Blandine sits on a stump in the Valley and holds a translation of a letter that Hildegard von Bingen wrote to Richardis—her friend and fellow nun—nearly nine hundred years ago. An earlier rain makes the woods breathe, and the fragrance of mud perfumes the air. All over the world, millions of people are managing not to think about James Yager. How do they do it? He has appeared in her consciousness every day, every hour, since the Night, and Blandine is glad that she has heard nothing from him, or at least that's what she tells herself because she can't trust her reaction to his attention—her reactions so far have been involuntary. Messages build themselves in her mind, in her hands, but she never sends them. She knows that not contacting James is the right thing to do, but God—how much like a sneeze unsneezed it feels.

Hildegard wrote the letter in the early twelfth century, shortly after Richardis was removed from Hildegard's convent and appointed Abbess of Bassum. Hildegard, so opposed to earthly attachment, ardently loved Richardis and fought her relocation. She wrote a letter to the archbishop in the voice of God—first person!—condemning the decision. When that didn't work, she wrote one to Richardis herself. Blandine reads the letter, then contemplates the open notebook in her lap, which is a relic of St. Philomena, a tool originally purchased to ferry Blandine from one school to the next, paper once covered in physics. She has ripped out her school pages and filled the remaining lines with drafts of letters to James that she will never send.

My grief rises up, wrote Hildegard. *That grief is obliterating the great confidence and consolation which I had from another human being.*

If there was anything unethical about our arrangement, wrote Blandine, it wasn't that you were a teacher and I was a student, or that you were the director and I was the actress, or that you were married and I was a kid, or that you were rich and I was poor, or that you were a father and I was an orphan, or that you were forty-two and I was seventeen. It was the fact that this was always going to mean infinitely more to me than it meant to you, and you fucking knew it from the start.

Which means that a human being must look to the living height without being obscured by love or by the weakness of faith, which the aerial humour of the earth can have only for a short period of time.

You always already mattered. I did not.

A man should not wait upon a person of high rank who fails him like a flower that withers; but I broke this rule in my love for a certain noble human being.

My whole life has educated me against investments whose rewards depend upon the benevolence of others. For seventeen years, it was impossible to unlearn this lesson and then, in a span of months, impossible to learn it.

Alas for me, a mother and alas for me, a daughter. Why have you forsaken me like an orphan?

You are a metaphor. I don't know what you represent, but you're not just yourself. You're also not a *father*, if that's your conclusion. I am not so cause-and-effect.

I loved you for your noble bearing, your wisdom, your purity, your soul, and all your life! So much so that many people said, "What are you doing?"

What were we doing, James? What were you doing?

⁓

Blandine receives the email one evening at the end of July, long after dropping out of school. Next week, she'll move out of Stella and Wayne's and into La Lapinière Affordable Housing Complex. *U can hav the biggest bed room,* texted Malik that morning. *Coz ur a girl.* Then he sent a winky face. Now she's sitting at a sticky computer in the Vacca Vale Public Library. Confused, she leans closer to the screen: the sender is Zoe Collins, a student from St. Philomena's—a senior when Blandine was a freshman. The year they overlapped, Zoe was the lead in all the theatrical productions. After she graduated, St. Philomena often bragged about her—she won a scholarship for piano performance at some prestigious institute of music. Twice a week, on her way to World History, Blandine would pass a photo of Zoe in the hallway, smiling merrily, her teeth bright under the banner: ALUMNI EXCELLENCE. Blandine has never spoken to Zoe before. As dread pulses in her stomach like a war drum, some animal part of her knows the content of the message before she reads it.

No subject.

So he got you, too?

PART III

It Wasn't Todd's Idea

~~~

After the fish incident in February, Blandine avoided the apartment, as though she sensed a shift. I told myself that the fish was a peculiar, one-time case, but I knew, deep in my body, that our ritual had been gaining momentum since we moved into the Rabbit Hutch. I knew we would kill something again.

The next time it happened, Malik was strumming on a shitty guitar, and Blandine was out. Nighttime, March, all of us a little bit drunk. Malik was sitting on the futon, and Todd sat on the floor, glaring at the TV. It was a Wednesday night, as it always seemed to be in those days. The heating in the Rabbit Hutch was too intense, and we couldn't control it, so we had the window open, even though it was blustery outside. While Malik worked out a song, I was throwing a ball of rubber bands into a bushel basket that we'd sliced the bottom from and nailed above the door. He assured us that once he was finished, he would upload it to his numerous channels. Fame, riches, and sex would follow.

"How does this sound to you, Todd?" Malik cleared his throat and started to sing, striking the same three chords over and over in different patterns. And you know what? Motherfucker has an excellent voice. Makes you think of apple cider and somebody else's childhood.

"Your eyes are like the ocean, yeah, your soul is like a bird. Do you wanna go home? If you do just say the word. Our home, home, home, our home's the same home, home, home, so if you feel alone, alone, alone, I'll loan you my phone."

"What ocean?" I asked. "What fucking ocean, Malik?"

"No one asked you, Jack," snapped Todd.

"No really. I'm curious. Have you ever touched an ocean? A lake, even?"

Malik ignored me and continued to the next verse. *"You don't have a phone, and I think that is so damn bold, and your hair is like a moonrise, yeah, your hair is like white gold. Blandine, baby, blondie, you're a weirdo, yeah it's true, but my God, you smell like roses, and girl, there's no one else like you."* Malik stopped strumming and beamed at Todd. "S'all I have for now. Still working it out, you know. The kinks. But what do you think?"

There was something deeply wrong with the rhythm.

"First of all," I said, "why would she have to borrow your phone if you're both going back to the same home, home, home?"

Todd pulled his ear and thought hard. For the first time in about a decade, Todd took his eyes off the TV. He reveres Malik so much, it hurts to witness. "Okay, well, I'd have to say, my main feedback is 'phone' and 'bold' for sure don't rhyme. The white gold thing was nice. But I don't think she smells like roses. Does she *actually* smell like roses?"

Malik shrugged. "How should I know."

"She does," I admitted. "Like a funeral."

Then a commercial came on for some crazy Vacca Vale tourism campaign.

We all watched the commercial in silence until it came to an end.

"Such garbage," commented Malik.

"Vacca Vale: Welcome Home," scoffed Todd, but he looked sort of emotional to me. "What the hell kinda slogan is that."

"More like—*Vacca Vale: Don't Touch the Rust,*" said Malik.

"Vacca Vale: Excuse Me, Sir, Are You Lost?" I added.

"Vacca Vale: We'll Clean It Up in the Morning," said Todd.

We laughed. We warmed. We didn't know who we were trying to impress.

"Vacca Vale," joked Malik, *"We Used to Make Cars Here!"*

"Vacca Vale: Where the Churches Outnumber the Humans."

"Vacca Vale: Where the Rabbits Outnumber the Churches."

"Vacca Vale: Where the Soil Is Poisoned."

"Vacca Vale: At Least You Can Still Fuck Here."

"I recognize zero of the places they showed," said Todd. "Do we even *have* a farmers market? And that garden definitely doesn't exist."

A scuttle behind the stove. We turned. More rodents in the walls of the Rabbit Hutch than all the sewers of Vacca Vale. You get used to them, almost feel for them. But a mouse had been banging around in our kitchen for months, and even though I never saw it, I was sick of knowing it was there.

"The trap'll get it," said Todd. "Just wait."

"I put peanut butter in it and everything," I said. "They love peanut butter."

"I'm telling you—this generation of mice is *advanced*," Malik said. I missed a shot, and the ball rolled toward him in the living room. He picked it up and, from the opposite side of the apartment, sunk the ball through the basket in one try. Annoyed, I retrieved the ball but didn't shoot again. Just gulped my beer. "They outsmart you at every turn," continued Malik. "I know a guy from work who had a trap out for months, and you know what happened? One morning, he woke up, tiptoed to the kitchen real quiet, and what did he see? Two mice eating the cheese out of the trap, from the outside, with their little hands. Like without getting smashed. For real. He clapped his hands, and they didn't even scatter, didn't give a fuck. He said they ate a whole loaf of bread. Can you believe it?"

"What I can't believe is that you think this is an interesting story."

"Fuck you, Jack."

Malik stood, put down the guitar, and stalked toward the kitchen. "What's it doing? You think it's in the stove?"

"Leave it alone," said Todd. "I don't want to see it."

"I do," said Malik. "I want to shake its fucking hand. Maybe it's not even a mouse."

"What else could it be?" I asked.

"I don't know. A bunny. The tooth fairy. A ghost."

"The ghost of Woodrow Huxley Zorn the Third," said Todd. "I'd have a few words for him."

I stood from the floor and joined Malik in the kitchen. The kitchen is always very clean because Todd scrubs the place to death every night. He's very particular about the arrangement of everything. Sometimes Malik shifts something just to fuck with him, and then we watch Todd pace the kitchen until he figures out what's wrong. As he fixes it, he usually blames Blandine. That night, the counter was perfectly blank except for a jar of twigs and white clovers. Blandine was always leaving shit like that around the place. I was surprised Todd hadn't trashed them yet.

Malik got on his knees and peered into the space between the wall and the stove.

"Do you see it?" asked Todd nervously.

"Nah . . . it's all . . . I mean, I can see its shit all over the place, but . . ."

A flash of gray on the counter. I spun toward it.

"There it is! Todd, look!" I launched the ball at its body, but the mouse sprinted out of sight, and the ball ricocheted off the wall.

Todd hopped onto the couch, his eyes wide. "Where?"

"There! Near the TV!"

"Where?"

"It's hiding behind the cabinet right now—watch it!"

Malik took off his basketball shoe. "Todd! Catch!" He pitched the shoe across the room, where it struck Todd hard in the belly and left a streak of brown on his white T-shirt.

"Jesus, Malik!"

"Pick up the shoe, boy!" ordered Malik.

"I don't want to touch your filthy-ass shoe!"

"Pick it up!"

"*Why!*"

"So you can kill the mouse!"

"I don't wanna—"

"*Pick it up!*"

Todd fumbled, bending to retrieve the neon shoe from the floor. It looked massive in his pale and tiny hands.

"Throw it at the fucker when you see him!" shouted Malik.

"But—"

"Do it!"

"I—"

"*Do it!*"

"But it's not—"

"Don't be a fucking pussy, Todd!"

When the mouse darted from the TV stand toward the couch, Todd pounced like a cat, slamming the shoe over the little guy's body in one fluid motion. Then again, and again. Then over and over, harder and harder, grunting, until all we could see was a little bloody pulp on the floor. I squinted. Smallest foot I ever saw in a heap of red, twitching.

Silence.

"Damn, bro," said Malik, finally. "Knew you had it in you somewhere."

Todd sniffed and looked at us like he was the one who got beaten, his hands shaking. He dropped the shoe to the floor, stood, and backed away a few steps, averting his eyes from the blood. Behind him, a reality show about paranormal activity in rural Ireland flashed on the television. Todd's face was white and wet.

"It's just . . ." he began in a weak voice. "It's a baby."

Malik pulled a beer from the fridge, cracked it, and walked over to Todd. Clapped him on the back. "Proud of you, son," said Malik. He placed the beer in Todd's trembling hands. "You did it for Blandine."

It's fair to say that things got a little out of hand from there.

Namesake

~~~

According to the internet, it was the year 177 AD in Lyon, France, during the reign of Marcus Aurelius. Blandine—non-Roman and enslaved—was taken into custody with the Christian who bought her. They tortured Blandine until her resilience exhausted her executioners, who then bound her to a stake in an amphitheater and released an armada of hungry beasts upon her. But the beasts wouldn't touch Blandine, wouldn't go near her, not for days. Frustrated by her indestructibility and embarrassed in front of their fans, the executioners removed Blandine from the amphitheater, scourged her, and half roasted her on a grate. They enclosed her charred body in a net, which they then tossed to a wild steer, whose horns impaled her. But she would not die. "I am a Christian, and we commit no wrongdoing," she is said to have repeated over and over when interrogated.

She was mystifying. She was invincible. She was fifteen years old.

After a week or so of failed attempts, her executioners resorted to a minimalist approach and stabbed her with a dagger. She finally died.

Infatuated by the idea of such a faith, starstruck by a person who existed nearly two thousand years before she did, a young woman formerly known as Tiffany Jean Watkins chose Blandine as her namesake in an effort to transcend the troublesome corporeality into which she was born and achieve untouchability. Blandine of Lyon: patron saint of servant girls, torture victims, and those falsely accused of cannibalism. Tiffany/Blandine found an account of the martyr online in Papyrus font, printed it out at the library, and taped it above her bed.

Six months after Tiffany/Blandine had submitted her court papers, proof of birth, and $210, she discovered that the name Blandine is Latin for "mild," while Tiffany is Greek for "manifestation of God."

Pearl

~~~

O n the morning of Wednesday, July seventeenth, fifteen hours
before she exits her body, Blandine walks from La Lapinière to
the Valley. She couldn't sleep last night. Now it's dawn, the city stirring
to life around her, and as she walks, Blandine remembers an article she
recently read about a woman named Pearl. Pearl's abdominal organs
were inverted from normal human anatomy, but her heart was in the
right place. Situs inversus with levocardia—a diagnosis that Pearl never
received. No one discovered this peculiar fact of her body until a group
of medical students opened Pearl's corpse to study her cardiovascular
cavity. After struggling to find a major vessel, they traced the mystery
through her biological design until it revealed its cause.

One in every 22,000 babies is born with the condition. Of those, one
in 50 million survives to adulthood. After living a relatively healthy life,
Pearl died at the age of ninety-nine. Natural causes, according to the
article. She owned a pet store. She had three adult children and five
grandchildren. In a portrait of Pearl from the fifties, her face was sym-
metrical, her cheeks rosy, her auburn hair curled into a cloud around her
face, her smile demure, a botanic emerald broach pinned to her collar.
Everything about her appearance belied the truth of her body, a body
who kept the spectacle, hindrance, and impossibility of itself a secret
from everyone. Even from its tenant.

To get to the entrance of the Valley, Blandine walks through the
southern part of downtown Vacca Vale, passing rows of foreclosed

shops and boarded-up houses. The establishments in operation include a sports bar, a fast-food chain, a tanning salon, a thrift store, a liquor store, a ramshackle church, and a vape store. She passes a tin-paneled shop with vacant lots on either side of it and plywood nailed to its windows. A rusty door. Vines reclaiming the brick foundation. LIL DADDY'S FASHIONS & ACCESSORIES, says its sign. Hand-painted with delicate lettering and roses. Down the street, another solitary shop of butter-yellow siding slouches toward the street. No windows, no visible entrance. Behind it, a small parking lot is empty except for a stroller. FOR A BED CALL——ANYTIME, says a board fastened to the shop front, but a block of yellow obscures the phone number. At the intersection menaces a large message board with replaceable black letters hanging from it as people might cling to a cliff. Many letters are missing from its original sentence. Now it reads: S. T A A E   O   P   R N   @   ALL   C   S T. Across the intersection, Blandine passes St. Jadwiga's Catholic Church. A gothic wonder built of brick and stone by fifty families from Poland and Germany in the 1800s. Modeled on a French basilica, two towers flank a rose window. Gold crosses rise from each peak of the church, and the baroque windows are frosted in white trim. Overall, the church looks like an impressive construction of gingerbread. Above the window stands a statue of St. Jadwiga, the first female monarch of Poland, with her hands outstretched. On its door hangs a sheet of computer paper with a message in Papyrus: *Welcome refugees, prisoners, prostitutes, and outcasts. Welcome to the sick, the disabled, the homeless. Fresh tomatoes. Cool beds. Bread bread bread this week.*

Birds chirp rebelliously in their metallic habitat. A few early-morning commuters drive sleepily on the roads. It's too early for the odor of cars, so Blandine thanks the air for its unpolluted splendor, inhaling the perfume of summer grass and recent rain. A lavender sky lights up, gestures wearily toward the future. As she walks through the warm morning breeze, Blandine fantasizes about someone emailing her the article about Pearl. The person would say: *Reminded me of you.* In the fantasy, the person knows Blandine better than she knows herself, and their message sinks through her skin like a poem, asserting its truth before revealing its meaning. It is not a normal fantasy, she understands. But who could call "normal" good, anymore? Who could call it anything?

Blandine suspects that if medical students sliced open her body, they would find a miniature Vacca Vale nestled inside it. No organs at all. A network of highways, disposable attempts at human ascendency, a plundered place existing despite its posture of nonexistence.

Splitting the center of her would be the Vacca Vale River, curving up and over and eventually pouring out of her head, into Lake Michigan. It's 210 miles long. Flooding more every year. In Vacca Vale, many bridges arch across the river, stitching the urban fabric of their city together, offering one equalizer: no matter who you are, how much money you have, or where you live, you're close to the river. Improbably— phenomenally—local fish activists installed a salmon ladder in this river, near the courthouse. The activists count and identify the fish that pass through it every year, chronicling the numbers as they dwindle. They publish their findings in the *Vacca Vale Gazette* every autumn.

Along the river, to the north of downtown, stands a neighborhood of historic houses. Mansions perched on sloping minty lawns in various states of majesty or decay, built by Zorn money in the early twentieth century. A few are now museums. One is a bed-and-breakfast. One belongs to—or at least, once belonged to—Blandine's high school theater director, a man whom she tries not to think about. He was everyone for a while. When she fails to avoid thinking about him, she pinches her thigh until her nails leave parentheses of red in her skin.

To the west of those houses scatter a few gloomy businesses: the Vacca Vale cinema, a strip mall, the Wooden Lady Motel, and the Zorn Museum. At the city's center, downtown is built in a ring, anchored by a collection of municipal buildings that now crumble like cakes. Across from the courthouse stands Ampersand, where Blandine has worked as a waitress for two years. Down the street from the women's shelter looms a compound of brick buildings erected in 1919 to house underpaid factory workers. Some were transitory and lived alone. Some shared apartments with other employees. Others lived there with their families. The apartments feature a dearth of windows and closets, small rooms, poor plumbing, retrofitted electrical and heating systems. A third of the compound was converted into La Lapinière Affordable Housing Complex, so Blandine knows the building well.

To the north of the historic houses sprawls industrial farmland, west to east, on both sides of the Vacca Vale River. Corn and soybean crops, freaky and inconceivable in scale. In the summer, they become an assault of chemical green, expanding like cultish odes to geometry for acres and acres. A patina of health desperately concealing and sealing a future of dust. Of drought. Of lifeless dirt that no machine, chemical, company, or person can defibrillate. This future is already materializing, and so now, when the land can sprout nothing else, it sprouts suburbia. Developers pounced on the opportunity, promising safety, man-made retention ponds, gated communities. A glut of beige. Two competing megachurches. Suburbanites can now buy their clothes at an enclosed shopping mall, buy their groceries at a supermarket that smells of imported turmeric and new paint. Deer keep stumbling into yards, confused and hungry. Drinking from the sprinklers.

Spared from such a brutal fate for a hundred years, Chastity Valley, the best part of Vacca Vale, lives southeast of downtown. Over five hundred acres, the Valley is shaped like an arrow pointing east. Constructed during the 1918 flu, it was Vacca Vale's effort to provide safe recreational space for a prosperous city during a pandemic. Framed in lush plants, the Valley meanders between manicured public fields and thickets of undisturbed nature. On the western edge, there is a small lake, now suffocated with algae blooms. A boathouse greets its edge, uniting the wanderer with a path that will take her through the parade grounds, past the barbecue area, past the memorial lilac grove, beyond overgrown soccer and baseball fields, through a small, serene paddock with an oval fountain at its center, past a sinister carousel, until, finally, the path deposits its wanderer into the park's largest meadow—the Valley itself. Of course, it's not a valley at all because no mountains flank it, but the designer of the park believed that the best nature words should belong to every person of every region. The Midwest, he believed, need not be as flat as its topography. In the large meadow, the wanderer will encounter picnics and babies, Frisbees and quarrels, wine and laughter. Increasingly: drones. Increasingly: her own homicidal fury at them.

If she wanders off the path through the forest to a southern pocket, she'll reach Lover's Hollow, a dipping overgrown sanctuary obscured by forest. From the sixties through the eighties, people escaped to Lover's Hollow at night for socially condemned sex, pleasure they couldn't safely enjoy anywhere else. That a place called Lover's Hollow existed within a place called Chastity Valley gave Blandine some hope about human resilience in the face of human brutality. Despite her research, she never figured out why people stopped meeting in Lover's Hollow in the eighties. Did others find out? Did police show up? Was the AIDS crisis responsible? Were the men attacked? Patterns of history force Blandine to admit: yes, yes, yes, and probably yes. Now Lover's Hollow is roped off due to damage from last year's flood. Half the park is. The city promises to repair the destruction, attaching their promises to the revitalization plan. Toward the eastern edge of the park, a grove of pine trees spells ZORN from above.

Finally, southwest of downtown, in a far corner of Blandine's body, medical students would find a campus of hollowed factories. In Vacca Vale, they haunt the sky and the birds with their remembrance of a supposedly better time, reliving their history over and over like a sad, drunk father who was once the high school quarterback.

Once the largest car manufacturing facility in America, Zorn Automobiles began as a humble wagon in 1852, born from the rough and wind-chapped hands of Woodrow Huxley Zorn III. At the age of twenty-four, he built the wagon to transport his family from Pennsylvania to Indiana. There, they would join his brother Cecil on a farm. The wagon traveled through the chill of November, surviving miles of mud and rain and the first snow of the season. When Woodrow, his wife, his three children, and their horse arrived in Vacca Vale, people stopped to admire their wagon. It was attractive, aerodynamic, sturdy. A design they'd never seen before. Impressed, townspeople began to commission Woodrow to make more. He needed the money, so he accepted.

Using his brother's barn as a workshop, Woodrow accumulated tools and labored alone. Plagued by self-criticism, shyness, bouts of depression, and a religious conviction that self-confidence was hubris, Woodrow fulfilled the orders mechanically, improving the design with each wagon he built, shrugging off the praise when he received it. When he finally accepted that he was not only competent but in fact brilliant at a hard and necessary job, Zorn Automobiles was born again. It was born a third and final time when Cecil—a garrulous, genial businessman at heart—said, "Together, we could make something great. Something that could last."

Over the decades, the wagons became buggies, then carriages. In 1904, Zorn made its first automobile. The original design was electric, but observing a trend in the market, Cecil pressured Woodrow to design a gasoline model instead. In 1920, Zorn made its last wagon, calling it: the Last Wagon. Zorn, a metallic family of winners, entered every endurance race, won most. In 1922, a Zorn automobile drove for seventy-nine hours and fifty-five minutes, from New York to San Francisco, winning first place. Zorns were known for their breathtaking and original designs, prettier and stronger than most houses that Blandine saw in Vacca Vale decades later. The 1926 Duplex Phaeton, red and glossy as wealth. The 1929 Vacca Vale Fire Truck, black leather seat in the front, no roof, gold embossment. Luxury saviors. The 1931 Roadster, the 1947 VD Pickup. The Zorns were not just cars—they were sculptures. Even presidents loved them. Ulysses S. Grant owned a Brewster Landau. Harrison owned seven Zorns, but his favorite was his Brougham. A Phaeton for McKinley. A black Zorn Barouche drove Lincoln to the theater where he was assassinated. The yellow Peg of 1909 shuttled congresspeople around the Capitol. Yellow, blocky, wacky. Futuristic. Those horse-drawn models were often roofless, and for good reason. Zorn was limitless.

Blandine recalls an elementary school trip to the Zorn Museum, where she was automatically transfixed by a peculiar 1922 model: marshmallow exterior, white tire rims, stained glass, a red velvet interior, and an actual lamp clinging to the panel between the windows, the design arresting her with its pointless beauty. It wasn't until she peered inside and saw a wreath of paper flowers over a small coffin that she realized it was a children's hearse.

For decades, Zorn Automobiles was a miracle, a heartbeat, an empire. Cecil Zorn believed that they had dominion because God wanted them to have it. Woodrow disagreed. The success of his company troubled him, and as his fame and fortune accrued, he became increasingly irascible. Minor flaws in manufacturing would send him into a rage, and he became so obsessed with the perfection of his models, he set up a bed in one of the factories, slept there all week in order to oversee every moment of production. His wife and children learned to predict his rages and sidestep them, which was easy to do in a many-roomed mansion overlooking the river, especially when Woodrow was gone.

In 1907, as Woodrow accepted his approaching death from stomach cancer, he left the company to his eldest son, Vincent. At the time, Vincent was living as a painter in Paris. He wanted nothing to do with

Zorn Automobiles, but after many desperate letters from his mother, he dutifully returned to Indiana, convincing Delphine, his Parisian wife, to accompany him. There, they threw opulent parties in the Zorn family mansion, neglecting the company but accepting its profits. It was Cecil's youngest son, Edward, who kept the company afloat throughout the early twentieth century. Edward Zorn devoted himself to an American dream of self-determination, self-reliance, self-actualization. His father was half right: Zorn Automobiles was great. In 1943, Vincent's son Claude took over the business and steadily drove it into the ground. Because they were American and because they were a dream, Zorn Automobiles could not last forever. Finally, Zorn Automobiles declared bankruptcy. They were wagons, buggies, carriages, automobiles, and then, after about a hundred years of supremacy, Zorn was nothing at all. Most of the remaining members of the Zorn family scattered across the globe.

Shortly after the factories closed, an anonymous report reached the Indiana Department of Health and Human Services: a storage tank at a Zorn plant had leaked thousands of gallons of benzene into the Vacca Vale sewage system, contaminating the groundwater. Benzene, the seventeenth most commonly produced chemical in America, is a volatile organic compound that quickly evaporates into air. A clear, flammable liquid with a sweet odor. In humans, benzene attacks the central nervous system and the immune system. Before the report even found the IDHH, the benzene had already ascended as a gas into the Vacca Vale air, polluting houses, workplaces, schools, churches. Unaware of the dangers, residents inhaled the vapor for months before state health officials finally tested. The symptoms were mild at first: headaches, eye irritation, fatigue, blurred vision, confusion, tremors, nausea. When the news finally broke, Zorn offered hotels and gift cards for residents forced to evacuate their homes. Lawsuit after lawsuit struck the company. But the real punishments wouldn't surface until it was too late to prevent them: anemia, miscarriage, birth defects, infertility, bone marrow dysplasia. Lymphoma. Leukemia. Zorn made fat checks to the families they shattered, but a check couldn't resurrect anybody. In total, Zorn paid a fraction of its yearly revenue.

After 1963, Zorn—a superhero in previous generations—became the Vacca Vale bogeyman. Zorn took away Christmas. Zorn was why parents drank themselves out of commission. Zorn was why you saw your dad cry. Zorn was why you didn't have a dad. Why he overdosed or dealt. Why he was doing time. Why he shot himself in the head. Even though there were plenty of questions—when, who, how much, how to clean, what to pay—nobody questioned Zorn's responsibility for the poisoning. By the time health officials conducted their investigation, the conclusion surprised exactly no one. Zorn Automobiles had abandoned the whole region, bankrupting the economy and slashing jobs, yanking pensions and insurance like tablecloths from elaborate sets of china. Then, as if the psychological and economic damage weren't enough, Zorn mutated the people they were leaving behind—that's how the residents saw it.

The story took root in the lore of the city. Teachers gave lessons on the benzene contamination in middle school. The residents were relieved to find a vessel for their anger. Even the children born well after Zorn closed needed someone to blame for their permanently overcast skies, the needles in the alleys, the robberies. Everyone wanted an enemy.

Graffiti now splashes across the exteriors of the factories. Once, Blandine bought a disposable camera to photograph the distressing pandemonium of expression she found there. GO FUCK YOUR UMBRELLA. FJP SOUTHSIDE. MAYOR BARRINGTON IS A FASCIST. MARRY ME, JESSIE. @BAXTER_BILLIONAIRE: BOSS DJ. LOCK UP THE SOCIALISTS!!! Someone painted over BLACK LIVES MATTER to write BLUE LIVES MATTER. Another sprayed over both to write ALL LIVES MATTER. Another drew an arrow to the chaos of messages and graffitied a weeping Earth. A machine gun. Angel wings. A falcon wearing an American flag as a cape. A marijuana leaf, grinning. LEGALIZE HAPPINESS, says the leaf. GET A JOB, someone wrote in response. A poster depicting a fetus between two burger buns. OBAMA BURGER, it says. The pope with an anti-Semitic speech bubble. Many cocks. Many hearts. Many initials. Messages and symbols of manifold xenophobia. A peace sign. A red rabbit in a crown and a despotic glare, nine feet tall, holding a smaller white rabbit by the scruff of its neck.

Taken in sum, the graffiti on the Zorn factories looks just like the internet.

Look at me, everyone says when no one's looking.

Downtown, as she nears the Valley's entrance, Blandine passes an alley of garbage cans, against which a large blue sign leans. WELCOME TO VACCA VALE, INDIANA: THE CROSSROADS OF AMERICA. The city speaks to her. Won't stop speaking to her. As she walks, she can hear the dead Zorn factories, even though she can't see them. She can always hear them. A hum, chilled and wet and dissonant. In 1967, a group of men tried to burn down the factory where they once worked, but its interior was too damp to catch fire. The factory's voices are loudest at night, in February, and after a week of insomnia. The factories pollute the air with their history, just as they once polluted it with dark chemical smoke. The price of overabundance.

Relics, ruins, ghosts—the Zorn factories insist on themselves. Listening to them now, Blandine realizes that they have no idea that they are about to be gutted and transformed into a bad imitation of Silicon Valley. One form of spookiness supplanted by another. Open concept, white walls, ping-pong tables, IPAs in the office fridge. Millennial pink. Fiddle-leaf figs. A corporate gymnasium and cafeteria, a home away from home so that workers would never leave work. Leather sofas, artisanal throw pillows, numerous ways to make coffee. Soon, these factories would resemble Instagram. Oblivious to the plan, the factories loom and groan. Rusty and trapped in their expired power, they march to the east until they vanish into the hallowed glimmer of the Valley.

Blandine doesn't need medical students to open her body to know that her city lives inside it. She doesn't need someone to send her the article about Pearl to know that she and Pearl are related. She doesn't need anyone else to hear the factories to know that the factories are addressing her, addressing everyone.

We will invade you with all of our nothing, the factories say, because it's all we have left.

Blandine pauses outside a frayed white shop front. She passes it every day but has yet to determine what it sells or whether it's open. Broken blinds and a shadowy interior. She peers through the cloudy glass to observe overturned chairs, stacks of paper, guts of sinks, apple cores. An upright piano, missing its teeth. A sign pressed against the window, facing the sidewalk.

NOW OFFERING LIGHT, it says.

The Rotten Truth

~~~

M oses Robert Blitz does not attend his mother's funeral on the morning of Wednesday, July seventeenth, but he finds himself in a church nonetheless. He can't check into his motel until ten in the morning, and it was nine when he arrived in Vacca Vale, so he's been driving around the city without a destination, looking for a site to see. Vacca Vale reminds Moses of the afterlife. He considered visiting the Zorn Museum, but it's closed—only open two days a week. So when he saw St. Jadwiga's Catholic Church, its Gothic Revival elegance out of place, Moses parked his rental car, leaving his bags in the trunk.

The sun blasts like a medical fluorescent light trying to expose the fungi. He is the fungi. Vacca Vale, Indiana, is intolerably hot and humid, and he did not pack the right clothes. St. Jadwiga stands across the street from his motel, at an intersection two thousand miles from his mother's ashes, and the force that drew him inside it was the same that drew him to a fast-food breakfast at the airport in Chicago this morning. He wants relief. He wants to get away from her. He wants America to dismantle the problem because America constructed it. Physical distance lost its impact on Moses around the time the internet was born, and although he recognizes this, he is still unsettled when he faces the altar, so far from Los Angeles, and sees only Elsie Jane McLoughlin Blitz. He sees her in the Grim Reaper costume she wore one Halloween, fifty years ago—the only Halloween she spent with him. There was—still is, he suspects—a photo of it, fraudulently framed in her mansion, as though parenthood defined her history.

On the doors of the church, a sign on printer paper blasts a message of radical Christian welcome that Moses feels too cynical and sweaty to read. Inside, a baptismal font gurgles and tall windows of stained glass fill the church with color. A banner in affable font celebrates St. Jadwiga's 170th anniversary. He sees no ventilation for air-conditioning, but the structure is chilly—either from strong insulation or supernatural forces, Moses concludes. He blesses himself with holy water, relieved when nothing happens, trying to clear his mother from the windshield of his psychology, thinking in social media posts. He is fifty-three years old.

When he was eleven, Moses was baptized, first-communioned, and confirmed, but it all happened in a rush, after Elsie nearly died of an overdose. In the spring following her accident, she clung to Catholicism—the religion of her parents and childhood—like the nearest flotation device in the deep end, initiating Moses as a kind of insurance. Moses did not object. He spent his childhood in a state of confusion, eager for organizing systems like math, science, and religion.

Against his will, he remembers Jamie, the last person he loved. Or sort of loved. Or at least *tried* to love. Jamie, with her crystals and tarot cards, essential oils and podcasts, astrology apps and sage. Dark angular hair chopped to her chin. Delicate face, theatrical cheekbones, soft skin. Flares of eczema behind her knees. Scent of cypress. Her youth was both a selling point and an embarrassment. "My ram," she would call him. "My egocentric Aries ram." Toward the end, she made many comments like: "I'm such an idiot! Aries and Libra are primal opposites in the zodiac—how could I expect you to respect my sexual boundaries?" Throughout their relationship, he found her devotion to the supernatural ridiculous, but now he can see that it was no different from his.

Walking deeper inside the church, he inhales as long as he can. He smells marriages, baptisms, funerals. Incense and bouquets. Beginnings and endings. He wants bacon. The architecture is gothic on a budget, with red carpet, a powder blue ceiling, dark wooden pews, stained glass, and a tabernacle that kindles Moses's nostalgia for monarchies. An organ looms in the upper wing like a bouncer, and he feels the crawl of surveillance, as he often does; he scratches his skin.

He walks along the edges of the church, studying the stations of the cross, which are truly horrific—worse than a horror film. All the characters look Polish. It occurs to him that *children* see these images on a regular basis. He steps close to the sixth station: *Veronica wipes the face of Jesus.* It's a mosaic of a woman holding a selfie of the messiah but marveling at the bleeding man. This one relaxes him. Veronica looks at Jesus like he is a shattering twist in the series finale of her favorite show. Moses finds her sexy—he finds all undivided attention sexy. Moses sits in a pew and retrieves his phone, investigating this church online to stave off an invasion of loneliness.

The search yields a website written entirely in future tense, a catalogue of St. Jadwiga parishioners over the decades. *Kasper Wiśniewski will be born in 1843. He will emigrate from Poland to Vacca Vale, Indiana, at the age of seventeen.* The website text is superimposed on a cartoon graveyard. Above it is a photo of Kasper, happy and young and training for war. *In 1865, he will marry Magda Mazur in St. Jadwiga Church. Magda is the daughter of Filip Mazur, a successful peasant.* There is no photo of Magda, and no definition of successful peasantry. *They will have thirteen children, five of whom will perish before adulthood. Kasper will die of yellow fever in 1901, and Magda will die of stomach cancer in 1926. He will be remembered fondly for his pranks and his laugh, and she will be remembered as an avid reader, too solemn for her beauty. Mr. and Mrs. Wiśniewski will be buried in Immaculate Conception Cemetery, in locations known only to God.*

The prophetic conjugation distresses Moses. Looking at the altar, he envisions Magda and Kasper linked in a chaste but enthusiastic wedding kiss. He wants to know more about Magda. He imagines her in a dirt yard, surrounded by a picket fence and a dozen yelping children, smoking a cigarette and glowering at a detective novel. He sees the youngest boy tugging at her skirt, saying, *Mama, Mama, look at this, look what I can do, Mama, look at me.* He sees her refusing to see him, reserving her beautiful, solemn attention for the fake paper world in her hands. He sees her in a Grim Reaper costume.

It is so natural for Moses to care about the people he finds online, and nearly impossible for him to care about the people he finds in so-called reality.

A bird cry jolts Moses from his screen. Three miniature cries follow. He looks around, bewildered.

"That'll be the falcons," says a man. "Breakfast."

Moses jerks out of the pew. A few yards away stands an elderly priest, dressed in black pants and a black shirt, his white collar glowing. Most priests give Moses the willies, but this one radiates something like— like *sanctity*, he admits to himself. Moses doesn't believe in sanctity, but here it is, obvious as a suntan. The priest appears to be in his seventies. He has a face designed for Christmas, a diminutive stature, and rimless spectacles.

"Sorry?" says Moses.

"A peregrine falcon built her nest here, in the spring," says the priest, "and we haven't had the heart to do anything about it, so we're just kind of coexisting. In fact, we've set up a live camera. You can watch them online whenever you want. There are three little chicks. I call them Ruby, Radish, and Rhino." He grins. "I don't know; it just makes me happy. She swooped down during communion, yesterday. The mother. Stole a wafer! Wasn't consecrated yet, luckily. It scared off some parishioners, but."

He waits for Moses to speak. Moses does not oblige.

"They're on the verge of extinction, peregrine falcons," adds the priest. "So we're keen to keep them safe."

The statement gently dissolves a wall inside Moses. "Oh."

"Anywho. I know it can be alarming. A falcon!"

After a pause, Moses asks, "What do you call her?"

"Who?"

"The mother. Did you name her?"

"Oh, yes. Dorothy the Second."

"Who's Dorothy the First?"

"My mother." The priest blushes. "My human mother."

Moses clenches his jaw and nods.

"I loved her very much," mutters the priest. He studies his shoes, then steps forward. "I'm sorry," he says. "I don't think we've met. I'm Father Tim."

"John," says Moses, shaking the priest's warm hand. "Nice to meet you."

"Welcome to St. Jadwiga, John. Are you new to the parish?"

Moses hesitates. "Yes."

"What brings you here?"

Moses begins to sweat.

"Are you here for confession?" asks Father Tim helpfully.

"Confession?" This had not occurred to Moses; he has only been to confession once before. "Yes."

"Great. It's right over here, whenever you're ready. Take your time."

Father Tim smiles again, then disappears into an archaic confessional booth on the other side of the church. A flash in the rafters catches Moses's eye: there she is, Dorothy the Second, yellow feet and matching beak, delivering something that Moses does not want to see into the mouths of her chicks. Her chest is speckled, her beak hooked, and she is pretty but haggard, like she works the night shift on the highway. He wishes that this bird had a spouse and a nanny, that she got paid time off, that someone would give her a massage. She sees Moses, stops what she's doing, and glares at him, her creepy animal wisdom confirming that he is the intruder in this place. Not she.

Moses checks the time, ignoring a screenful of vacuous sympathy messages. The fans will be crowding the pavement outside the funeral now—strangers who believe they know her, love her. They will flood blocks, these blank grievers, wielding their spectacularly fabricated relationships with Elsie Blitz, beloved American starlet, like tickets to the fair, trying to catch a glimpse of the corpse, even though she was cremated. Elsie would have adored the attention at first, then hated it. Adoration and hatred—the only energies she knew how to dispense and accept. "I used to think all relationships were imaginary," she told Moses from her nine-thousand-dollar mattress. Her hair, skin, and sheets were three shades of snow. She was eighty-six years old. "But now that I'm dying, I see the consequences. I see people existing outside my mind, making decisions, making dents. I see you—my Moses, my sweet angel boy. Do you see what I'm saying? I see how I've ruined you."

～～～

In the beginning, there was a mother and a baby. But the mother was not much mother and the baby was too baby. He needed everything; he was raging id. The baby would die without her, and the mother did not like to look at him. She needed everything, too.

The mother's problem was that she never turned around when she heard *Mom?* in a public space. She was an actress first and only. When she was four years old, her scarlet hair and greedy parents won her the professional lottery, and she had been working since the age of five, baptized in binary waters of worship and disgust.

You're perfect. You're doing everything wrong. Hush. Speak up. You're clever. You pretty little idiot. Show us your dance. Hold still. Give us a song. Be quiet. Imitate. Be an original. You're just like her, and her, and her. Dazzle us. Don't draw attention to yourself. All eyes on you. You're not the center of the universe. You're perfect. What's wrong with you?

She was the nation's supply of sugar in the acrid years following World War II. A time of traumatized fathers, economic prosperity, and an international deficit of psychological health. Her job never allowed her to be a child, so her psychology never allowed her to age. It was not advisable for a child to have a child, but she, so childish, liked to disobey.

In her teens and twenties, the actress built herself a fortress of glass and mirror and held whimsical parties there. Bad things happened to the young actress, as they often did: rejection, rape, anorexia, addiction. Cast aside by an older married man, her first love, as the director warned. Horrible wigs! But mostly, the violence was administered by the attention, which was the wrong kind of light—radiation that burned her, gave her melanoma of the spirit. She learned to grip and collect the things she liked, learned that pleasure was the intravenous nutrient that could keep her alive. To frame it that way was dramatic, she knew, but then again, she was dramatic. So what? she could say to the army of bad nights that appeared at her gate. I still have all these strapping good nights. She invented a religion of pleasure and dedicated herself to it.

She was petite; all her friends were enormous. She liked alcohol and drugs; she liked traveling between realms of consciousness without going through security or stamping her passport. She liked force—how, if you were strong enough, you could make anyone do anything. She liked avocado three days ripe. She did not like the ocean and accused people of bragging when they claimed to love it. Sometimes, she'd sit in front of the Pacific and try to feel something, but her heart was too landlocked. Too Midwestern. All she felt, when she looked at the ocean, was the presence of the absence of awe. She was too afraid of it to swim.

Her mother was Irish; the actress liked to listen to Irish jigs, Irish people reading books, Irish prayers. She liked making everyone wear blue to her parties. She liked growing orange trees in the yard, liked watching other people pick the fruits. Honeysuckle, lilacs, chlorine, thunderstorms, pine, bar soap, unwashed hair, matches, the incense of midnight mass, cigarettes, campfires, gasoline, fur: she liked these scents. When she told people about this, they lied and called her unique. She liked when people lied to make her feel good. She liked revenge plots and physical deformities. She loved Whiskey I, the miniature schnauzer who played her dog on *Meet the Neighbors*. She liked Whiskey II, his replacement, but not as much. She liked foam—all kinds. She liked having her photo taken, her figure drawn, her body examined at the doctor's office. She hated to be described.

Improbably, the actress reached adulthood. Because her childhood was a renunciation of childhood, she treated adulthood like a crackdown on adulthood, which is to say, she abdicated most responsibilities of living in a body and a world. Voting. Taxes. Dentists. Lunch. These things could terrorize her whenever she was forced to endure them on anyone's terms but her own.

She said her daily prayers. She liked private compartments on trains, men in their fifties, iconoclasm. She liked fucked-up pigeon feet; she liked pointing them out to her companions; she liked reading explanations of the phenomenon; she liked that, no matter where in the world you went, you could count on seeing fucked-up pigeon feet there. She liked endangered creatures. Smoked meat. To leave the lights on in her house, to drive with the roof down even when it was cold, to watch postwar films where nothing, absolutely nothing, went wrong. To scream when no one was there: in her blue ballroom, underwater in her pool, facing mountains on her porch. She liked strong flavors: espresso, bourbon, hot sauce, horseradish, Dijon, wasabi. She always let the tea steep too long. Her favorite meal was her mother's corned beef and cabbage, and one of her greatest regrets was that she failed to record the recipe before her mother died. She liked to trash all the expired and disappointing food in her fridge; she liked her radiant absence of guilt.

She loved Zorn automobiles, liked to park all four of hers side by side in the garage, liked to call it her stable. Loved the metal falcons perched on the hoods with their eyes narrowed and their wings outstretched. Loved to watch a man named Dominic clean and wax the perfect metal bodies of her Zorns, loved to feel the sponge slipping down her own skin as she observed him. She loved the look of her yellow 1932 Presidential Coupe the best. For novelty: the red 1924 Duplex Phaeton. For speed: the emerald 1959 Torpedo Hawk. But for driving, she favored her 1951 Commander Stardust Zorn. A bullet-nose convertible with a pontoon body, an exterior the color of cream, a V-8 engine, and a face that looked like a missile. Whiskey leather upholstery. Brass detailing. Orange steering wheel. If freedom had a smell, Elsie found it inside her Zorns. Three of her best orgasms took place in the Commander Stardust Convertible. High-voltage orgasms that brought her back to life when she was otherwise entombed in despair. When she drove the convertible, she felt that it understood her, felt that their bodies were two halves of one machine.

By the time she was thirty, she had constructed her life around her preferences; she presciently invested in likes well before the internet did. The likes she possessed and the likes she received. She didn't care who or what she broke as she reached for the pleasure on the top shelf.

In the actress's religion, pregnancy was heretical.

Like all of the people with whom the actress had sex, the father of the baby was vast and transient. He was a little bit royal; they agreed to keep it a secret. Elsie liked keeping the secrets of powerful men—it made the patriarchy more inclusive, palatable, and funny. The actress was a genius at attracting company, but she had no idea how to sustain it and didn't see the appeal. She'd received an abortion before. Had no qualms about doing it again. She took the test on her annual Blitz of July party, at her mid-century modern house in Malibu, where there was an abundance of glass and a crisis of privacy. She was already drunk. If the minute is even, she thought, I will keep the baby. She checked the clock around her neck.

Immediately, the fetus proved itself to be a resourceful parasite, with no equal in the natural world. The animal inside the actress had no interest in her preferences, and it had a vendetta against her pleasure. He liberated her from menstruation for nine months, but in its place, he inflicted a new program of anatomical hell. Room by room, he demolished her body and rebuilt it into his own. It seemed to be his mission to expose, over and over, the barbarism of female corporeality. The actress expected pregnancy to add weight, deplete her energy, and harden her breasts. She expected morning sickness and cravings. She expected to leak. She could cope with these taxes, but she was ill-prepared to cope with the rest. Nobody—not her friends or her mother, not doctors or books or television—had warned her about the rest.

One day, she stopped being a soprano. Her skin tightened. Her bones felt . . . *loose.* Her brain delayed and stuttered as though it had aged decades in weeks. It was like she had picked up a virus at summer camp: she was always sneezing, itching, overheating, forgetting, sweating. She could no longer dance. She developed bad breath that could not be controlled. All pipes of her internal plumbing malfunctioned. The veins on her breasts began to resemble the veins on bovine udders. Pregnancy ravaged her skin, separated her pelvic bone, sprouted hairs from her chest, doubled her blood volume, ballooned her joints, gave her acne and melasma and migraines and nausea and prophecies. It darkened her belly button. Her vagina *turned blue.*

For nine months, time slowed. And then time happened all at once. Suddenly, the doctors were saying that she needed a Cesarean. "Cesareans are for sissies!" she shrieked at them, then cackled. Or maybe this only transpired in her mind; she couldn't tell. She was, by then, pain incarnate. In the hospital room, the contractions were the Rotten Truth, and there was nothing beyond or before the Rotten Truth. "Oh, give it to me," said the actress. Her mother was beside her, wearing a yellow track suit, clutching a rosary. It was like an exorcism. "Give me the fanciest Cesarean you have!"

Afterward, her hair turned curly, and her vision prescription changed. He—the baby—wanted her—the mother—the actress—the *mother*—to see and be seen as his. He wanted to ruin her for everyone else. Something a charming suitor told her when she was twenty: *I want to ruin you for everyone else.*

When she got home from the hospital, Elsie stowed the baby in her mansion's only sunless room and told the nannies to keep language away from him, for now. She didn't want to deal with the repercussions of language. She needed to gather her wits, her whereabouts, her preferences. She needed to order new contact lenses. And there was the question of feeding. "You know what they say," said one of the nannies, who was too young, an aspiring actress with gossamer clothing and perfect skin and filthy, filthy shoes. She smiled. "Breast is best." Elsie fired that nanny, kept the ones in their sixties, but she decided to nurse the baby.

She only liked to look at the baby in his room, in the dark, where she could see nothing but an idea. In the abstract, it was an exquisite idea.

〜〜

"I'm afraid I'm not a very good person." Moses frowns to the confessional screen.

"Usually, you start by saying, 'Bless me Father, for I have sinned.'"

"Oh." Moses is shivering. "But I'm not sure if I've sinned, actually."

"We'll get to that in a moment."

"So what do I say?"

"Oh, let's skip it. Let's just make the sign of the cross. In the name of the Father, Son, Holy Spirit. Amen."

Moses forgets the order—forehead, shoulders, chest?

"Okay, John. How long has it been since your last confession?"

"Uh, forty-five years or so?"

"All right. Go ahead."

"I think I'm a bad person."

"But you don't think you've sinned?"

"Well, I think it's more of an identity thing than a behavioral thing."

"What makes you say that?"

"You can't tell anybody any of this, right? It's like therapy?"

"Right, this remains between you and God. I'm just an interpreter."

"How do I know you'll keep it quiet?"

"I'll be excommunicated otherwise."

"No."

"Yes."

"But what if a criminal tells you he's about to murder someone?" asks Moses.

"All you can do is counsel that person away from sin and toward God."

"I'm not, by the way. About to murder someone."

"Happy to hear it."

"But it seems like a faulty policy," says Moses. "The total secrecy, when someone's life is on the line."

"I don't make the rules."

"Well." Where to begin? "My name's not John."

Child-celebrity-turned-pygmy-sloth-preservation-activist Elsie Blitz christened the only child she carried to term Moses Robert Blitz because she met the urban designer Robert Moses at a dinner and found him bewitching. Robert Moses—bewitching! To Moses Robert Blitz, this fact alone evidenced his mother's derangement. Elsie knew that if she named her only child Robert Moses, the tabloids would have assumed that he was the father. So she flipped it.

"But I won't tell you my real name," says Moses.

"Do you want to tell me what compels you to hide it?"

Moses searches for a phrase. "I'm not at liberty to say."

"All right," says Father Tim. "Tell me what's on your mind."

"I'm missing my mother's funeral right now."

A pause.

"I mean, it's happening *right now*," continues Moses in a rush, "and I'm not there, obviously, and I'm glad I'm not there. I don't feel any regret at all. No guilt. None. Actually, I have no feelings about it whatsoever."

"Is that true?"

"She was a narcissistic opioid addict who never should have had a child," says Moses. "She neglected me and everyone else around her. I mean, all she saw when she looked at you was herself. Everybody loved her, but I'm the only one who knew her. If you knew her, you'd hate her." His heart is pounding. "She's an actress."

"Is the funeral in Vacca Vale?"

"No. It's in Malibu."

"So what brings you here?"

"Sometimes I cover my entire body with the liquid of broken glow sticks and break into the houses of my enemies," Moses blurts.

Father Tim pauses again, like a GPS system recalibrating after a wrong turn. "Okay. How many times have you done that?"

"Two so far."

"And what do you do once you enter the house?"

"I just kind of wiggle around in the dark. I don't wear any clothes. Just briefs."

"And you don't . . . you just leave, after that?" asks Father Tim.

"You think I steal or rape or something?"

"I didn't think that."

"You think I *murder* them, or something?"

"I wouldn't assume murder. Although it has come up twice already."

"I'm not a *psychopath*. I just like to fuck with people. After I spook them, I walk out. I just walk right out the front door and go home. I don't touch anything or anybody."

Father Tim thinks for a moment. "And do your . . . targets . . . how does this affect them? Do you know?"

"One thought it was a nightmare, I think. Like, sleep paralysis. Another was in a psychedelic phase at the time. So, you know. It hasn't had the intended effect, yet."

"What is the intended effect?"

When Moses does not reply, the priest tries again. "How did you choose these people?" Father Tim asks. "To target?"

"The first bullied me when I was growing up. I found out she still lived in West Hollywood, so I . . . I just . . ." Moses trails off. "I had a stutter when I was younger."

"Oh?"

"It was bad."

"When did it go away?"

"Not until college," replies Moses. "And it still comes back sometimes, when I'm stressed or tired or what have you."

"And this person ridiculed your stutter?"

"Yes. We went to the same boarding school. She also made fun of my weight. Other kids joined in, of course, but she was the leader. She made these little cartoons, she called me Moses the Moon. I was a sort of local planet, always haunting the school with my obesity and my stutter, in her drawings. She'd draw me in the sky, with students below, and the students would be running from me."

"That must have been very painful."

Usually, Moses hates when people say this, or versions of this, but from Father Tim, it sounds less like an exit from the aforementioned pain and more like an entrance into it.

"And what about the second person?" asks Father Tim. "What made you choose them?"

"Oh. He was my roommate from college. I took him with me on spring break one year—my mom had this place on Pumpkin Key—and he had some kind of . . . some kind of sex with her. My mother. Took some photos. Publicized it, sold the details and everything to a tabloid. Her people had to buy the story back to bury it."

The priest pauses. "Has there ever been a time when you wanted to punish someone but refrained?"

"Yes."

"What happened?"

"Well, I wanted to do this to my ex-girlfriend. Jamie. She was in special effects. She was twenty-five—I should have seen it coming, I guess. Cheated on me with some startup douche. Maybe that's redundant. *Startup douche.*"

"And why did you refrain?"

Moses considers. "She knew me too well. She might have figured it out. She was pretty smart, for an astrology wackadoo. And then what, you know?"

"Figured what out, exactly?" asks Father Tim.

"Who was to blame."

"You think she would have connected the event with you?"

"I know she would have. She was intelligent, like that."

"Tell me more about your mother," says Father Tim.

Moses notices a weird grin on his own face—one he can't control. He is relieved that Father Tim cannot see him. That's what he tells himself, at least.

~~~

When Moses remembers his mother, he sees a montage of Fourth of July parties. It was Elsie's favorite holiday—she must have been so grateful to die shortly after it passed. Every year, she threw a party that cost the average American annual income. The Best and Brightest always made an appearance, along with a bewildering abundance of small-town mayors. As a child, Moses was sent away for these parties. As a preteen, he locked himself in his bedroom. As a teen, he observed. In his twenties, he wrecked himself with drinks and drugs. In his thirties, his objective was sex. In his forties and fifties, he just stayed home.

It was hard for Moses to explain his mother's obsession with the military, which informed much of her personality, politics, and taste in architecture. Her obsession was further complicated by her identification as a socialist. She was blacklisted around the time her lupus took over and her opioid addiction began, by which point she had accumulated many reasons to retreat from Hollywood and did not need to be forced.

She used to display her collection of exotic weapons and taxidermy on the walls of her mansion for the party alone but over time decided to leave them as permanent decorations. She got the idea from a Scottish castle where she once filmed a period drama on family secrets. "It communicates that you are not to be invaded," she once explained to Moses.

The Blitz of July, as Elsie called it, was a scripted yet feral event, characterized by games, winning, abundance, overpopulation, glitter, and red meat. Even, twice, rooster fights. She had professionals install misters and fans across her estate to counter the heat so that all the skin glistened and all the hair fluttered; guests who were already prone to posing were practically hypnotized by these conditions, drooling at the enhancement of their own allure. There was always a trampoline, a chocolate Slip 'N Slide, somebody making clouds. An aquarium petting zoo. Every year, Elsie imported bands from around the world—her only stipulation was that the bands could not be American. There is nothing more patriotic, she believed, than importing another country's talent. Nobody listened to the music, but everybody loved it. The guests worked hard to make their power visible and their efforts invisible. Moses thinks of his mother and sees celebrities in one-of-a-kind swimwear, fluttering about like piles of trash on the streets of Manhattan. With the best skin, teeth, and hair that money could buy, they chatted about justice, speculated about the sexual lives of those who were even more powerful, and decried automation as if it were coming for *their* jobs. Service people were omnipresent, but Moses never saw them.

For as long as he could remember, Moses had a recurring dream that he was wandering a Blitz of July party, the scenes warped and fish-eyed, the music mutated, the hair unanimously blond. In the dream, he had information about an urgent threat—an assassin lurked among them, the house was surrounded by guerrilla enemy soldiers, terrorists were waiting on the roof, a drone was about to drop a bomb—but when he tried to warn the guests about it, he discovered that he was voiceless. He would scream and no sound would emerge.

"Well, that one's no psychological mystery," his therapist told him.

~~~

"My real name is Moses," he admits urgently.

"Interesting," says Father Tim.

"What?"

"In the Bible," begins Father Tim, but Moses sneezes six times in a row, as though allergic to the reference. He is a yell-sneezer.

"God bless you," says Father Tim. He waits for Moses to recover. "You okay?"

"Yes. Sorry. Go on."

"So in the Bible, Moses's mother stows baby Moses in a watertight basket to protect him from the pharaoh, who had ordered all baby boys to be fed to the Nile. He was afraid that a boy would overthrow him one day. She still fed him to the Nile, but she put him—"

"I know, I know," says Moses impatiently. "Everyone knows. What of it?"

"So Moses's mother abandoned him to protect him," says Father Tim. "What do you suppose your mother was trying to protect *you* from, by abandoning you?"

Moses does not want to pursue this allegory. "I wasn't named after *that* Moses," he says. "I have nothing to do with him. I was named after an urban planner. A monstrous one. A racist! Parking lot after parking lot. Highways everywhere. He wanted to build one through Washington Square Park!"

"Fame?" suggests Father Tim.

"What?"

"Was your mother trying to protect you from the fangs of fame?"

Fangs of fame—who is this joker? "No. In fact, she pushed me toward the industry. Relentlessly setting me up with auditions, screenwriting, production jobs. Said I wouldn't be able to make anything of myself on my own, so I was lucky to have her." Moses scratches his neck. "Is this how confession normally goes?"

"Every confession is different."

Moses can't quite recall his last confession, only the circumstances that inspired it—he had been thirteen, on a vacation in Rome with two boarding school friends and their nannies, when one of the nannies insisted. "We'll wait outside," said the other nanny. "No," said the first nanny gravely. "Everyone must confess." Moses and his friends concluded that she had just committed a crime. The next day's news reported that the tooth of a long-dead queen had been stolen from the manor they had toured. The nanny had a pixie cut of hair that changed color every month and a wardrobe of white jumpsuits. She was some kind of painter, without family or community, always hauling around French manifestos, clever and visibly exhausted by the human condition, although she was not yet thirty years old. The type to do such a thing.

She did not return to America with them; she boarded a train to Ancona instead. "Tooth fairy!" they yelled at her as they parted ways. "Thief! Witch! Slut! Cunt!" She did not look back.

Months later, Moses's friend explained what had really happened: he had broken into the hotel bathroom while his nanny was showering, opened the curtain, and offered her his erection. She physically kicked him out of the room. "Gave me a bruise, can you believe it? Child abuse! My mother didn't pay her for that month." But before quitting her job, the nanny ordered the boy to tell a priest what he had done. Forcing him into confession was her last act as his caregiver. He wasn't Catholic. Neither was she. Moses had a sensational time in Rome.

The Roman confessor told Moses's friend to do a year of community service, preferably at a women's shelter. This is why Moses likes religion: it has a way of dealing with incidents like these—summarizing them, interpreting them, offering a course of action.

"What was your mother protecting you from, by abandoning you?" repeats Father Tim.

Moses rolls his eyes. "*That* Moses's mother put him in a watertight basket. Mine basically put me on the back of a crocodile and told me to tip him."

"I'm not dismissing the harm she caused," says Father Tim. "I'm just trying to understand her. I find that's the best place to start, no matter how cruel someone seems."

"You *people*. You *Hoosiers*."

"Sorry?"

"Why do you assume that she was protecting me from something? Maybe she wasn't thinking of me at all, did that occur to you? People are selfish. Sometimes that's all there is to it. When they *seem* cruel, they *are* cruel." Suddenly, Moses feels like he is attached to a bike pump of rage. The Midwestern breed of narcissist, Moses reasons, must be much smaller and more docile than the breed they have in Hollywood—like those tiny foxes near the equator. But how can Father Tim know that? "But how could you know that?" Moses demands. "You live in this god-forsaken town, where your serial killers probably hold the door open for you. They probably ask you how you'd like it before they murder you. You have no idea what she was like."

For a moment, Moses feels relieved. Then he feels ashamed.

"Maybe," suggests Father Tim, "your mother abandoned you to protect you from herself?"

~~~

Moses Robert Blitz was twelve years old, recently acquainted with arousal and humiliation, and the date was the fifth of July. It was around five in the morning, and he had woken in a sweat, so dehydrated he felt like he was filled with sand. The problem was that there were no cups upstairs and he hated drinking from bathroom taps—it seemed dirty. He switched his light on and off several times before deciding to get out of bed and retrieve a glass from the kitchen. His dream had taken the form of a blooper reel—he had to act out the same scene over and over, making different mistakes every time, triggering eruptions of laughter from the people around him.

It was therefore disorienting when Moses heard real laughter as he descended the stairs. He froze. Detected at least five different voices. The various laughs of his mother funneled toward him: the tense one, the one that sounded like winter, the one that meant she was bored.

Carefully, he leaned over the railing to observe the scene below: Elsie and four of her friends—two women and two men, often the last to leave the Blitz of July—splayed their bodies in various poses around the fireplace. All wore blue. There were two couches, two loveseats, and four armchairs in this room, but they favored the shag rug. Glasses and bottles glittered around them like boats at sea. It was his mother's favorite room, with its skylight and white walls, twenty-foot ceiling and taxidermy—exclusively birds, suspended from the ceiling as though frozen midflight in a multispecies migration. An exodus. Moses could tell by their eyes that Elsie and her friends were drunk or high or both. Jazz howled and candles flickered. Someone was articulating a complicated opinion that ended in the word *earthmen*.

"But in the end, he gets stabbed."

"What do you *do* when someone gets stabbed? I've always wondered."

"Oh! Oh, I know this!"

"Check your enthusiasm."

"No, on *Roses Are Red,* my fiancé got stabbed and I had to—"

"Oh please, educate us with your soap opera knowledge. I'm sure it's medically valid."

"It is! They consulted an expert! You bind it. The wound. And then you apply pressure. I think you're supposed to elevate the wound above the heart, but they don't do that so much anymore. It's not as important as the pressure. You're supposed to lie them flat, though, and you can raise their legs. I think it's about, like, circulation?"

"Very useful information, Marianne. Thank you."

"Good morning, Moses."

Moses gasped. One of the men had noticed him, and now everyone except his mother stared. In the spotlight of their attention, he felt like some kind of swamp monster, emerging to prey on the hippos. *They* were the trespassers, he reminded himself, trying to summon the courage to speak. He lived in this house; they didn't. But he knew that confidence was as likely to descend upon him as God was. To summon something like that it must be inside you, or at least respond to your call.

"Look at those darling pajamas."

"You're a mess, Junior. You been swimming?"

"No, I have an idea, let's all give him advice—booze makes me wise, and Paul's an aficionado of—"

"For fuck's sake, Marianne. Have kids of your own."

"You hungry, big guy?" asked a man that Moses recognized as an Important Director.

"Bodies . . ." began Marianne prophetically, squinting at her glass, but did not continue.

"We've got snacks here," said the director. "Prosciutto."

"But not too much for *grasso,*" said a man in an electric blue suit. This man appeared at their house once annually, and Moses had no idea who he was. Moses did, however, hate the man with an intensity that did not correspond to their interactions. It must have been a response to a message only available to his subconscious. Wistfully, Moses thought of the

Christmas Island crab migration, which he learned about in school, and which was also an annual event, and which he would strongly prefer to witness than the Blitz of July. He imagined the female crabs, red and sturdy, marching en masse through the darkness to reach a high-tide beach. He learned that each crab carries a hundred thousand eggs that she must deposit into the sea—a treacherous endeavor because she can't swim. As soon as the eggs touch the water, they hatch, and the female leaves them to fend for themselves. Could you call such a creature a mother? Moses feared that if he ever attended the Christmas Island crab migration, he would step on one. "Yes, Elsie?" continued the hateful man in the blue suit. "It's not healthy to feed your child too much. It's abuse. You are a bad mother, my darling. But this is why you are interesting!"

Moses watched his mother, who did not look at him. Her auburn hair was pinned in a complex updo. Her skin gleamed with sweat, oil, sun, makeup. The rest of her gleamed with sapphires. She had changed into indigo silk pajamas but had not removed her jewelry.

"Do you know they took Fattest Domestic Cat off the list of Guinness World Records because it encouraged animal abuse?" contributed Marianne, who was the youngest and most beautiful of the five.

"Elsie, your son is hungry," said the director. "Do something about it. We're frightening him."

"We just tease you, my Moses," said Sabine, a Parisian costume designer in her forties, one of Elsie's closest friends. "You know that. You know we are just having a little fun because we are all very tired— very tired of ourselves."

"It's true," said Marianne, smiling. "You're like a godson to us, Moses."

"Elsie," said the director. "Feed him before we inflict lasting psychological damage."

"I'm n-n-n-n-not hun-hun—hungry."

Moses enjoyed a brief high after the expulsion of this sentence. He was then mobbed by embarrassment. The adults fell silent for a moment, and he noticed something watery about them, something dissolvable, as though they were the substance of a dream.

"Do not feel shame for your hunger!" cried Sabine, who was prone to dramatic interpretations of ordinary scenes. A feather boa was coiled around her neck, and it quivered when she spoke. Moses could track her exhalations. "If our boys feel shame for their hunger, what kind of men will they be!"

"Of course you're hungry, big guy," said the director, whose hand was resting on Elsie's ankle. It occurred to Moses in preteen abstractions that this man and his mother were fucking. "Come on. We won't bite."

"He is a growing boy," said Sabine. "Elsie, feed your growing boy."

"Too much growing," said the man who called him *grasso*, laughing and looking at Elsie for approval. Her back was turned, so Moses couldn't tell if she gave it.

"Moses, I want to apologize on behalf of us all," said Marianne, grinning at him. She was so pretty it was hard for him to determine the sincerity with which she said this, her beauty redacting all other data. "This is your house, and we're being rude."

"Where's Harriet?" asked the director, and Moses felt betrayed. Why did the director know his nanny's name?

"She took the weekend off," said Elsie at last. Although he couldn't see her face, he could tell that she was gazing into a tumbler of amber liquid. "Abandoned us during our busiest time of year for some kind of funeral. She's in Kansas. Maybe Wyoming. I don't remember. Somewhere flat."

"I'm—j-j-just—th-th-th-thirsty," said Moses, rooted to his stair.

"He's thirsty," said Marianne. "Did you hear that? Let's get him some water, for God's sake." She stood and turned toward the kitchen, but the director grabbed her hand.

"Marianne, you just act nice because you don't have a personality. That's your problem," he said. "And it's not your fault—it's the fault of society. No one ever *asked* you to develop a personality because you always looked so heavenly. Who can blame you for being nothing but nice? Who among us would have done the hard work of developing a personality if we weren't *forced* to?" His language was precise, but he slurred the delivery, his tongue heavy with booze. "But you should admit that there's nothing virtuous about niceness, Marianne, especially niceness unaccompanied by a personality."

"Cheers," said the other man.

Marianne yanked her hand free from his grasp, flipped him off, then marched to the kitchen. Moses felt sorry for her, although even at twelve he knew that he could not trust feelings inspired by the beautiful. He felt tears advancing and scrambled to construct a blockade.

"Elsie, you must do something," said Sabine. "Look, your child is hurt. We have hurt your child."

"My child?" said Elsie. She turned and looked at Moses for the first time, her face closed up like a shop after hours. "I've never seen this boy before."

~~~

"She got addicted from her lupus—had all these surgeries, and the doctors kept prescribing morphine. That was before they had the restrictions, you know. Not her fault, but she waited to get help until it was almost too late. She had a billion people around; she knew exactly where to go; she had the money; she had the time. I mean, eventually, she went to rehab, but she could have gotten help quicker than she did."

"Addiction alters the brain. It—"

"So does motherhood, they say."

Moses has no idea how long he's been in this confessional booth; he guesses somewhere between ten and forty minutes.

"There's room for your anger, even if you don't blame her for the addiction," Father Tim says softly.

"But instead of asking for help," continues Moses, "she asked for more and more and more morphine. The sick truth is that she loved being addicted, loved being a victim, loved feeling oppressed, loved losing control. She loved any excuse to spiral. She wanted to—to leave."

"What do you mean?"

"Get out of here. *This.* Herself."

"You think she wanted to die?"

"No, not exactly—death was too boring for her. She wanted the opposite of death. Which ended up looking a lot like death, to me, but she thought she'd reached some kind of nirvana."

"Many people would argue that death is a prerequisite of nirvana."

"I would argue that basic human decency is, too."

"What do you think your mother was trying to escape?" asks Father Tim. "The same thing she was trying to protect you from?"

"There are also multicolored fibers that burst from my pores," announces Moses. He understands that this conversation is a mess, but he doesn't know how to have clean ones anymore.

By now, Father Tim doesn't miss a beat. "What do they feel like?"

"You really have a way of rolling with the punches."

"Yes," he replies, coughing. "So I've been told."

"They feel like fake grass," says Moses. "Plastic grass growing out of you. Imagine that."

"I'm imagining it."

A pause.

"What do you think is the cause?" says Father Tim. "Of the fibers?"

"I don't tell people my theory unless they feel it, too," says Moses.

"Because you don't think people will believe you?"

"Because I *know* they won't believe me. They can't. They lack the capacity."

"Try me."

"Do multicolored fibers burst from *your* pores?"

"No."

"Then I'm not telling you my theory."

"Fine." Father Tim sighs. "Let's return to your mother. Why do you think she—"

"Look, I already have a psychotherapist, a psychiatrist, a counselor, and the internet. I don't need some priest from Nowheresville, Indiana, to analyze me, or my mother, or whatever. Truth be told, I had no intention of confessing today. I'm not convinced I've done anything wrong in the first place."

"Neither am I," replies Father Tim. "But you began this confession by saying that you thought you were a bad person. I'm just trying to help you see yourself."

"You want to confirm that I'm a bad person."

"On the contrary, I'd like to show you that you are good."

"You don't know me. You don't know if I'm good or bad."

"You're good."

Moses scoffs, then makes a deal with himself: if Father Tim says something about being created in God's image, he will leave the church at once.

"The Church teaches that we're born with original sin," says Father Tim. "The temptation to behave selfishly is something that we have to negotiate throughout our lives. But as we grow up, we also develop a capacity to override our temptations. That's what differentiates human beings from every other animal, as far as I can tell. If you had no choice but to obey every impulse, we wouldn't call it a 'sin'—we'd just call it an instinct. We don't call a dolphin *sinful* when he commits infanticide."

"*Dolphins* do that?"

"It's been observed."

"Well maybe we *should* call it—"

"A dolphin lacks choice. But you're free."

"Just because I don't commit infanticide doesn't mean I'm *good*. Or free."

"I didn't say you were good," says Father Tim.

"You just said I was good!"

"Did I?"

"Yes!"

"Well." Father Tim sighs. "Sorry. I didn't mean it. You're right. I don't know you at all. I haven't had coffee yet. I tend to make irresponsible claims before I've had my coffee."

Moses is surprised by his disappointment—what it reveals.

"Honestly," adds Father Tim, "I think this might be my last day."

"What?"

"Of the priesthood."

Moses feels the roles of listener and talker trade places, feels it like a change of a current. "Well—"

"There's a rot at the center of the Catholic Church," murmurs Father Tim, "and I thought I could effect change from the inside, but instead, all I feel is infection. I'm starting to smell the rot on myself. Especially when I'm alone. This collar is starting to choke me. Physically *choke* me. I feel cold, and damp, and gone, and God won't talk to me. God never talks to me. In all my years of prayer, God has never once called me back."

A weak bird cry from above. Moses listens so hard, he can't see what's in front of him.

"I want to travel," continues Father Tim. "I want to fall in love again. I want to meet someone who's suffering and talk with them as myself, not as some representative for a boss I've never met. If the boss is worth his salt, and he saw the data, he'd be pretty disappointed with the way we've been running his business. Women should be priests. Priests should get married if they want, have kids if they want. Folks of all genders and sexualities should be welcomed exactly as they are. Abuse should be condemned. Birth control should be encouraged. I mean, the last thing our burning planet needs right now is a population boom of industrial appetites. These are easy things, obvious things, unavoidably right and good, and yet I've come to believe that they're never going to happen within this decaying institution. I'm sick of following orders, meekly playing the game, waiting for the rules to change themselves. It's going to be hell to get free of this collar. But that's life, isn't it?"

It takes a moment for Moses to realize that he's nodding. "Yes," he whispers, his voice hoarse. "Yes."

"Anyway, I'm surprised I called you good not because I think you're bad. It would be absurd to describe a whole person as good or bad. You're just a series of messy, contradicting behaviors, like everyone else. Those behaviors can become patterns, or instincts, and some are better than others. But as long as you're alive, the jury's out."

Moses scratches his calves gently. "What was so great about Dorothy the First?"

~~~

In the end, there was a woman and a man. But the man was too much son and the woman was too little mother. She would die without him. She needed everything, and the son did not like to look at her. He needed everything, too.

She spent her final Fourth of July in bed at her mansion in Malibu. Moses hadn't spoken to his mother in a year, but Clare, the obsessive assistant, wore him down. When the calls, emails, letters, and morbid texted videos did not work, Clare hunted down his social networks and forced her message through them; when that didn't work, she showed up at his house near Griffith Park and threatened to smash his dishes until he agreed to pay his mother a visit on her deathbed.

When he arrived at Elsie's mansion, the nurses were on their lunch break, microwaving glass dishes of food in the kitchen, leaving delicious aromas in their wake, having a conversation together in Spanish. The overall atmosphere in the house was less funereal, more cheerful than

Moses expected. Rooms bright with Los Angeles sun, carpets recently vacuumed. Fresh flowers in the vases. Her staff present and pumped with life. Clare led Moses up the stairs, to his mother's bedroom, saying nothing as they moved. Her hair smelled of mint.

Throughout her life, Elsie had looked and sounded healthier than she was. It was an appearance generated by Botox and every other beauty-boosting chemical known to humankind, plastic surgery, a lifetime of pricey exercise, a private chef, thirty years of leisure, a self-replenishing bank account, and supernatural genes. The enemies of this appearance—substance abuse, insomnia, sun damage, mental illness—were no match for its defendants. She had, through a blend of will and science, bottled her youth.

But now, finally, death had announced itself in Elsie Jane McLoughlin Blitz. In her bedroom, Moses averted his eyes.

"Clare, leave," said Elsie as though speaking to a Labrador. "To the backyard. Go on. Don't come back until he's gone."

"Okay." Clare reached over to insert a straw into a smoothie on Elsie's nightstand.

"Clare."

She hurried away. "Yes, yes, I'm going. I'm gone."

Above Elsie's enormous bed hung an eighteenth-century oil painting of a massacre. The wall opposite the bed featured taxidermy: a whole pheasant, a chukar partridge, a rattlesnake, the heads of bison, buffalo, reindeer, bighorn sheep. A vampire bat. A beaver, looking transgressed.

Her room was too warm, almost foggy. Moses hadn't set foot in this house for years.

"Don't touch anything," croaked Elsie. "Common germs could kill me. Which is comical. You survive the unthinkable for eighty-six years, and then you die from something microscopic—from a cold. I'll have you know I'm in agony."

He scratched his skin.

"Stop that. For God's sake—*stop* that. You know it sickens me." She paused and closed her eyes, as though counseling herself. "But I do like your socks."

He studied them, grateful for the excuse to do so. They were neon yellow.

"I had a dream that *you* were the bogeyman, can you believe it?"

Elsie said. "It was all over the news, in my dream. Breaking news: they finally caught the monster who's been terrorizing children and the unstable since the dawn of time—and his name is Moses Robert Blitz! In the dream, they didn't even *mention* me. Can you believe it? That's what I found most upsetting. They failed to mention the most interesting thing about you!" She cackled until she coughed. "Just kidding, my darling. Oh, lighten up. You're so sensitive."

"This is going well, Mother. Thank you. You're making me so *grateful* I drove up here. She forced me to come—your servant. She said *you* were begging to see me. She said it was all you wanted."

Elsie cleared her throat. "Well."

"You have a fucking hysterical way of showing it."

He aimed one glance at her then looked away, unable to see what he saw. She was bald, bluish, ninety pounds, nonnegotiably mortal. But even when he looked at her, he saw her through a computer raster, a matrix of pixels and scanning lines rendering her unreal. He gripped the nearest object—a standing rack of top hats—to steady himself.

"Don't *touch* anything!" Elsie cried. It didn't seem possible that her feeble body could produce such a sharp, loud noise. "But of course you want to kill your own mother. You dream of it."

Moses recalled the advice his therapist gave him before this visit: *You do not have to tolerate her abuse,* she said. *Not anymore. If it gets to be too much, you can and should leave.*

"I'm going to leave," Moses announced flatly.

"No!" cried Elsie.

For the first time in his life, Moses glimpsed something like fear in his mother.

"I have exactly five requests," she whispered.

"I have no obligation to stay here, whether or not you're in agony. You never stayed when I was in agony."

Moses, whose attention was fixed on the beaver, mistook Elsie's ensuing silence for penance, until he heard the slurp. One more glance at her: she was leaning over the bed, wearing a sapphire gown, every bone visible, attempting to suck from the straw. But she lost her balance and knocked the glass on the carpet. A splatter of pulpy green on white.

"Damn," she muttered.

"I can get Clare," Moses said through gritted teeth. Unable to dim his biological reaction to this proof of his mother's suffering, fighting back angry tears, he relocated his attention to the bat. The bat's mouth was open, exposing four micro-fangs below a walnut nose. It looked ridiculous, its threat in life reduced to a joke in death.

"No," said Elsie.

"Fine. Tell me your requests. But I have a meeting soon, so—"

Elsie scoffed. He could hear his mother readjusting on the bed, her slow and labored movements, a rustle of sheets, effortful breathing.

"Do you want me to tell Clare to bring you another smoothie?"

"No," she replied. "I'll throw it up anyway."

He closed his eyes. "What is your first request?"

"I want applause at my funeral."

Of course she did. "Tell that to Clare. You know I'm not organizing it."

Elsie ignored him. "Second request: I want the reception modeled after one of those harvest festivals in European folklore. I want flame-throwers. Maypoles. Decorated tree trunks. I want bands playing little jigs, and beer, and sausage, and maidens in white, and strapping fellows with ruddy cheeks. Fairies. Witchcraft. Religious judgment. Candy apples. Dancing and proposals and garlands of daisies. Fainting. Sunbeams. Libido—lots of it. In essence, by the end of it all, I want everyone to feel very gratified and sticky."

"That's gross."

"It's what I want."

"Fine. I'll pass it along to Clare."

"My third request is that you check in on the pygmy three-toed sloths every now and then."

"*Check in* on them?"

"Just see how they're holding up."

"Mother."

"I've donated a considerable portion of my estate to their preservation, but it might not be enough. Money's not always enough, you know. I'd feel better if I knew that someone was looking out for them."

"You actually give a damn?" Moses asked skeptically.

"Of course I do!" Elsie exclaimed.

"Forgive me for assuming it was an act."

Elsie's voice lowered, and her words fell slowly. "There's almost nothing I care about more."

"Fine," Moses said, eager to get out of the house. "I'll check on the fucking sloths. Next request?"

Despite himself, he sensed a palpable shift of energy from his mother's bed, some unprovable but real change, and when she spoke again, her tone was imbued with decades of sorrow. A rush of vertigo made him stumble.

"Moses," Elsie whispered. "Avenge yourself against me and my motherhood. Don't forgive me—that's my fourth request. Please, never, ever, ever forgive me. My crimes are my only company, in this room. Clare and my crimes. I've been thinking long and hard about it, and it's obvious to me that I don't deserve clemency, even after I die. Even after you die. I was never able—I don't know why I was never able to—but I just wasn't—I *couldn't*. Even now, I try, and it doesn't come to me. Motherhood just doesn't come to me. I'm looking at you, Moses." Her voice wavered. "My love. My only. Moses, please."

Moses scratched his neck, then stopped, remembering that this compulsion upset his mother, then resumed, remembering that his mother upset him, then stopped, because she was dying. Manipulation—she had a PhD in it; she could lock you in the pool house for ten hours and make *you* feel guilty about it; she could do absolutely everything wrong for five decades and still make you cry at her deathbed.

"And the fifth request?"

"Look at me," Elsie demanded.

"I'm looking at you, Mom."

Finally, he was. For the rest of his life, he would consider this the most difficult thing he had ever done. When his eyes met hers, her cratered face split into a smile, splitting him along with it. West-facing windows cast her features into an eerie orange. This view was clear of pixels.

"I'm looking at you, Mom. What's your fifth request?"

"That was my fifth request."

~~~

"Dorothy the First?" asks Father Tim. "My own mother?"

"Yes. You said you loved her very much."

"I did, didn't I."

"Why?"

After they hatch in the moonlit sea, the crabs spend a month in the water, growing. Most years, almost none survive this period. Once or twice a decade, however, a great population of baby crabs emerges from the sea uneaten. For nine days, they journey across the island to the forest where their parents live, braving new threats, including, but not limited to, the yellow crazy ant. Moses will never discover what conditions encourage this abundance of life, or what kind of reception the offspring experience upon their arrival, or how they know where to go. But the crabs do survive, sometimes, despite the odds.

Father Tim is quiet for a long time. "Hey," he finally says. "Your mother didn't happen to play Susie Evans on that old show, did she?"

A List of Hildegard Quotes, Written in a Notebook on Blandine's Nightstand, Which Jack Reads on Wednesday Morning, Tracing the Word *Nothing* on His Skin with a Fingernail

～

But God watered some human beings so that humanity would not become a complete mockery.

Paradise is a pleasant place, flourishing in the fresh greenness of flowers and herbs and the delights of all spices, filled with exquisite perfumes, adorned with the joys of the blessed.

The earth which sustains humanity must not be injured. It must not be destroyed!

The horror buffeted the dark membrane with a massive impact of sounds and storms and sharp stones great and small.

The word stands for the body, but the symphony stands for the spirit.

Drink beer for health!

Even in a world that's being shipwrecked, remain brave and strong.

Humanity, take a good look at yourself. Inside, you have heaven and earth, and all of creation. You are a world—everything is hidden in you.

The Word is living, being, spirit, all verdant greening, all creativity. This Word manifests itself in every creature.

The living light says: the paths of the scriptures lead directly to the high mountain, where the flowers grow and the costly aromatic herbs, where a pleasant wind blows, bringing forth their powerful fragrance; where the roses and lilies reveal their shining faces.

Holy persons draw to themselves all that is earthly.

I will utterly destroy you, death, for I will take from you those by whom you think you can live, so that you will be called a useless corpse!

The soul is not in the body; the body is in the soul.

For she is terrible with the terror of the avenging lightning, and gentle with the goodness of the bright sun; and both her terror and her gentleness are incomprehensible to humans.

But she is with everyone and in everyone, and so beautiful is her secret that no person can know the sweetness with which she sustains people, and spares them in inscrutable mercy.

I am Hildegard. I know the cost of keeping silent and I know the cost of speaking out.

But because Lucifer, in his perverse will, wished to elevate himself to nothingness, all that he wished to create was indeed nothing, and he fell into it and could not stand, since he had no ground beneath him.

Purebreds

〰

About six and a half hours before Blandine Watkins exits her body, she stands with her roommate Jack in the loft of local real estate developer Maxwell Pinky. Two purebred Samoyeds pant at the door. The air-conditioning relieves all of them from the afternoon's humidity. Pinky leaves the air on for his dogs, Jack explains incredulously.

There's no air-conditioning at the Rabbit Hutch. Only half the tenants have window units, and the residents of Apartment C4—Blandine and her roommates—are not among them.

"I don't know, Blandine. He told me not to touch anything. I think he's got cameras and stuff. I can't lose this job. I keep getting fired from shit and I just—"

"Don't worry," she says, glancing back at him. "I just love architecture."

Blandine is familiarizing herself with the loft to prepare for Phase Two of her sabotage plan, which she refers to as the Undevelopment in the privacy of her mind. Jack knows nothing of her scheme, but he senses something felonious in her as she creeps from room to room.

They've been in the loft for ten minutes, and she hasn't touched the dogs.

"I guess it's a nice place, huh?" Jack is nervous, pocketing and unpocketing his hands, fiddling with the leashes.

"I wonder how much it costs."

"I think some are for rent and some are for purchase."

"I bet it's over two thousand a month," says Blandine.

"Two thousand!"

"I don't know."

Jack notices with a blend of disappointment and relief that, outside of Apartment C4, Blandine is only a bit prettier than the average girl. He assesses her sallow complexion and knobby limbs, her prepubescent body, her starched white hair, dark at the roots, her lack of ass. Still, there is something hypnotic about her. She emanates the same force he associates with ghosts, extraterrestrials, magic, miracles. He sees her flaws, feels a little repulsed, and yet he can't kick the enchantment out of his body. It occurs to him that he might actually like her personality.

"Who would pay that much to live in *Vacca Vale*?" he asks.

"Someone who wants to own Vacca Vale."

It's a renovated automobile factory, one of Pinky's luxury construc-tions, located downtown, on the banks of the polluted river, just a ten-minute walk from the Rabbit Hutch. The building is unoccupied now, with the air of a television set, but when the tech talent relocates in Vacca Vale, Pinky is confident that the condominiums will sell right away. He wants coastal urban people to feel at home in this complex. Sixteen-foot ceilings, cement floors washed in a hue of jade, large win-dows. Light pours in from all sides, despite Vacca Vale's permacloud. Perfect temperature, new appliances, showers with too many settings. Climate, safety, and music controlled on one's phone. A sauna and a gym in the basement, grills and sofas on the roof. The sun casts Blandine's hair into an aura around her skull. Jack fixes his attention on the bruises that cloud her legs.

Blandine studies the wooden beams on the ceiling, sucking in her cheeks, tipping her head back. There are too many lemons in this apartment—lemons on the kitchen counter, lemons in the ceramic bowl on the dining table, lemons in a glass jar on the bookshelf. She didn't think it was possible to hate Maxwell Pinky more than she already did, but the profusion of lemons does something to her. Blandine already knows where Jack keeps the key to this loft. Phase Two will be so much easier than Phase One, and the thought of it drugs her. Admittedly, it will be difficult to find a time when no one is home. She'll need at least seven minutes to hang the life-sized, white-suited voodoo doll from a rafter in Pinky's bedroom. She plans to stuff the doll with mud, leaves, and animal bones from the Valley, which will make it heavy.

"You say there are cameras?" Blandine asks.

"Yeah, he told me so on the first day. He thought I was gonna steal something, I guess. I didn't even tell him I was in the system before this because he already had all these, like, notions about me, you know? Just from looking at me. I can't describe what he did or said exactly, but I got this feeling that he *expected* me to be some kind of bad guy, and that really pissed me off, but I had to take the job, since I got fired from the hardware store, and . . . did I tell you about that? Oh, yeah, they fired me for being high too many times. So but what's nice about dog walking is you can be high whenever you want. The stakes are really low. And I guess it makes sense for Pinky to have cameras, though, since he's got a lot of people coming in and out of here—cleaning lady, me, his assistant, people dropping off groceries and shit. I guess he *has* to be suspicious of people, since he's so rich. Rich people are never alone, is what I've learned. There's an older lady who comes by all the time to clean the bathtubs and vacuum the curtains and stuff. Maybe he's fucking her, too. Maybe she's his mother. I don't know. He's always with this entourage of women who are about twenty years older than him? I don't really get it. But anyway, he's gotta have surveillance, with all the people coming in and out. Plus, that fucked-up thing that happened at the dinner. He's, like, tightened security since then, I think. That security guard in the lobby didn't use to be there." Chin-deep in his own babble, Jack gropes for some kind of ladder, hauls himself out of it. "Did you hear about that?"

"But *where*."

"Where what?"

"*Where* are the cameras?"

Jack eyes her. Sensing his distrust, she spins around, does a little twirl, tosses a flirtatious laugh his way. "I just love technology." She smiles. "We've never lived anywhere so futuristic. I mean, I haven't. Have *you*?"

"Of course not."

"And I didn't hear about the dinner. What dinner?"

"You don't know? It was all over the news."

"I can't keep up."

"It was all over social media, too."

"I don't have social media."

"Oh, right." He rolls his eyes. "Too good for all that."

She shakes her head. "Not at all. On the contrary, I'm too weak for it. I mean, everyone is, but I am especially susceptible to its false rewards, you know? It's designed to addict you, to prey on your insecurities and use them to make you stay. It exploits everybody's loneliness and promises us community, approval, friendship. Honestly, in that sense, social media is a lot like the Church of Scientology. Or QAnon. Or Charles Manson. And then on top of that—weaponizing a person's isolation—it convinces every user that she is a minor celebrity, forcing her to curate some sparkly and artificial sampling of her best experiences, demanding a nonstop social performance that has little in common with her inner life, intensifying her narcissism, multiplying her anxieties, narrowing her worldview. All while commodifying her, harvesting her data, and selling it to nefarious corporations so that they can peddle more shit that promises to make her prettier, smarter, more productive, more successful, more beloved. And throughout all this, you have to act stupefied by your own good luck. Everybody's like, *Words cannot express how fortunate I feel to have met this amazing group of people,* blah blah blah. It makes me sick. Everybody *influencing,* everybody under the *influence,* everybody staring at their own godforsaken profile, searching for proof that they're lovable. And then, once you're nice and distracted by the hard work of tallying up your failures and comparing them to other people's triumphs, that's when the algorithmic predators of late capitalism can pounce, enticing you to partake in consumeristic, financially irresponsible forms of so-called self-care, which is really just advanced selfishness. Facials! Pedicures! Smoothie packs delivered to your door! And like, this is just the surface stuff. The stuff that oxidizes you, personally. But a thousand little obliterations add up, you know? The macro damage that results is even scarier. The hacking, the politically nefarious robots, opinion echo chambers, fearmongering, erosion of truth, etcetera, etcetera. And don't get me started on the destruction of public discourse. I mean, that's just my view. Obviously to each her own. But personally, I don't need it. Any of it." Blandine cracks her neck. "I'm corrupt enough."

A beat.

"Well," says Jack. His eyebrows are raised. He was listening closely.

"I just . . . I want a life that's a little more lifelike," Blandine says. "Don't you?"

The Samoyeds whine in tandem, eager for their walk. Jack looks at them gratefully, like they've delivered a long-awaited cue, freeing him to walk offstage.

"We have to go," he says. "They really need to get outside. They have to piss and stuff."

"Just one more moment."

"Fine. But . . ." He studies her with a pained but stoic expression, as though receiving a flu shot. "Fine."

"So what was this dinner thing about?"

"Oh, it wasn't that big of a deal. I think it was just a prank."

"What happened?"

"There was this dinner that all the politicians and big renovation people had together. Somebody, like, attacked."

"Attacked?"

"Not exactly *attacked*. I don't know; they keep using that word on the news, but it was more like a creepy joke."

"What happened?"

"In the middle of the dinner, all this witchy shit fell from the ceiling, onto the food."

"Witchy shit?"

"Like voodoo dolls and blood and bones and shit."

"*Real* blood?"

"I don't know. Maybe. I think so."

Blandine pauses, and something about the vacancy of her expression gives Jack the chills. Then the moment passes, quick as a moth, and she laughs. Jack, who has only seen Blandine laugh three times—once when he offered her a dead fish—involuntarily laughs along.

"You're right," she says. "It's kind of funny."

"I mean." He chuckles, confused. "I guess."

Blandine's laughter fades as she paces the loft, examining the ceiling and bookshelves. Black-and-white photographs of Pinky with irrelevant politicians and B-list celebrities crowd the walls. "This is such a nice place," she says.

"Blandine, we really have to—"

"Lucky dogs. They have better lives than we do."

Jack sighs. "He really does love them."

Blandine finds Maxwell Pinky, Vacca Vale developer and city council candidate, the most abhorrent of the Valley Destroyers, because he's the only one who is *from* Vacca Vale. She considers him a traitor. His story is mysterious, and nobody knows who his parents are. Rumors suggest that his initial investment money resulted from a dark family lawsuit. To Blandine, Maxwell Pinky doesn't seem orphaned so much as fundamentally parentless. It's as though he emerged from the sludge of the Vacca Vale River, a jazzily dressed swamp monster willing to plunder his own home in order to eat. To overeat. On a table beside the entrance stands a fishbowl, empty of water but full of political pins. She remembers reading that Pinky founded Vacca Vale's first dog park—as if that could possibly compensate for bulldozing a place as rare as the Valley. Above the kitchen, a large banner reads: MAXWELL PINKY FOR VACCA VALE CITY COUNCIL. "HE KNOWS THE NEIGHBORHOOD!"

The quote is unattributed.

Blandine feels some herd of violence stampeding through her, toward the owner of this stunning habitat. She imagines fishing a pin from the tank, unfastening it, and dragging the sharp end down Pinky's back. Drawing a tree.

"Do you interact with him much?" Blandine asks Jack.

"Pinky?"

"Yeah."

"No, usually his assistant."

"Who's his assistant?"

"Guy named Paul."

"How old is he?"

"I don't know, college?"

"Do you know his last name?"

"Vana something? Vanacore? Something like that?"

Blandine makes a mental note to contact Paul Vanasomething. That's how she'll extract the travel schedule.

"Why?" asks Jack.

"I'm just curious about him. Aren't you?"

"Paul?" asks Jack. "He's not that interesting."

"No, I mean Pinky. He's thirty-five years old, and he's basically colonizing our town."

"Well, I don't know about that," says Jack. "I think that happened a long time ago."

"But you don't think it's problematic? What Pinky's doing to us?"

Blandine squints across the loft, into Pinky's bedroom, envisioning the doll she will place there, constructed entirely from Valley materials, fake blood in its mouth, hanging from a rope. Maybe she'll cover the floor with sticks and bones. The entire bedroom is white: the rug on the floor, the walls, the bedding, the shelves, even the *items* on the shelves—white ceramic, white lamps, and books arranged to show their pages, not their spines. Maybe she'll throw dirt all over his freaky white everything. Or maybe she'll try a different approach, something new, something that Jack could never trace back to her. She could install a camera of her own, simply harvest some blackmail.

"Look," says Jack. "I know what you want me to say. You want everyone to hate the Valley plan as much as you do. But I just don't. A lot of people are excited about it, and I think you're being sort of judgmental and shortsighted. I mean, a lot of people say it's going to help our economy and make jobs and stuff. And I've only met him a couple times, but Pinky doesn't seem that bad. From what I've heard, he grew up poor, he knows what it's like not to have what you need, and now he wants to help Vacca Vale get out of the gutter. Sure, he's making money off it. But so what, if it helps people at the end of the day? We need to get out of the gutter."

Blandine turns to Jack. She pauses for a moment, examining him with interest.

"Also," he adds, "you're wrong to say social media is pure evil. Good stuff happens there, too. I follow a lot of activists and stuff. I learn a lot from them—like, ways to talk about things, new ways to think, petitions to sign. All that. Think about all the protests, all the people leading movements around the world. Lots of it wouldn't have happened without social media."

She feels her face flush, and she looks away from him.

"What?" asks Jack. "What?"

"Nothing," she says. "It's just—that's a good look on you."

He clears his throat. "What?"

"Expressing an opinion that contradicts the one in front you. It's . . ." She drifts off, blushes harder. "It's cool."

"That's a condescending compliment," Jack says, but he looks helplessly pleased. He forces his grin into a weird scowl. "Why don't you just leave, then? If you hate what's going on here so much? Why don't you move someplace else?"

"Like where? Mars?"

He shrugs. "Chicago, New York City, Portland. Wherever. You clearly hate it here, is what I'm saying. You look down on everybody. You could go someplace with fancy people with fancy degrees and fancy opinions. You don't have to stay in Vacca Vale and sneer at everyone."

It's as though he's hurled the lemons at her. Blandine backs away, eyes wide with fear, injury, shock. "I don't sneer at everyone," she says. "I only look down at those at the top."

Jack shakes his head. "See, I don't think that's true."

"It *is,* though." She bites her lip. "It—it *is* true."

"Oh God. Don't cry. Please don't. I just—sorry. I didn't mean to offend you or anything. I was trying—"

"I'm not leaving Vacca Vale," Blandine cuts in. Now her voice is angry. "If I wanted to get out of here, I would have by now. But I don't *want* to, and I *don't* sneer at the people here. Do you understand? I am never, *ever* leaving Vacca Vale."

He looks at her like she's told him that the moon is actually a golf ball, hurled out of bounds and lodged in the sky. "Well, that's just insane," says Jack.

"What?"

"*I'd* leave the second I got the chance. Why the hell would you stay?"

"Are you serious? A second ago you were—"

"I was saying you can be a little snobby, that's all. I never said that Vacca Vale was some kind of paradise. If I ever got the chance to escape, I would fucking seize it."

"It's not like we're surrounded by a moat of sharks."

"Maybe I'll leave someday, but it's not as easy for me as it would be for you."

"What are you talking about?"

"Come on, Blandine. We know you went to Philomena's. We know you got that scholarship."

She looks outraged. "How—"

"It's all online, okay? I didn't look it up. Malik did. He's got a thing for you. He's actually sort of obsessed with you, but you didn't hear it from me. Anyway, it doesn't take a team of detectives to figure out that you had options that the rest of us didn't have. We hear the way you talk. The books you lug around? We know you go to those community meetings about the revitalization. You—you're . . . different."

She rolls her eyes.

"No, I'm serious. You had a shot to find something beyond this place, and you didn't take it. And I don't care what you say about your undying loyalty to Vacca Vale—I don't buy it. I think you desperately wanted to get out of here, and something went wrong. So what was it? Why'd you drop out of high school? Why do you serve screwy pie for a living?" He pauses, standing tall. "Why?"

Blandine's face goes hot. In the drawer of her nightstand, she keeps a printed email from her guidance counselor, Mrs. Wood. Nearly two years old, the paper is worn and delicate now, folded countless times in the same three places. The email was short and unadorned, but it filled Tiffany with a druglike euphoria when she first read it, tripling the oxygen available to her, stretching the ceiling several stories higher. She received the message at lunch, in the library of St. Philomena, on a stormy day in October. It was the beginning of her junior year, before her life collapsed under the weight of her stupidest desires. Immediately, Tiffany printed the email and stowed it in the front pocket of her corduroy backpack so that it would always be close to her.

Although the message now plunges her into very different psychological weather, Blandine still returns to it from time to time, reading and rereading the futures that Mrs. Wood had imagined on her behalf. A list of the most elite universities in the country. A serious inquiry into Tiffany's visions for herself, as though they were relevant to other people, as though they were achievable. The actions that she could take to realistically pursue acceptance into these mahogany worlds of choice, mobility, beauty. Tiffany understood herself to be woefully uninformed—she had turned seventeen just three weeks prior—but even then, trembling under fluorescent light, listening to rain on glass, inhaling the scent of library books, she knew that any one of the degrees described by Mrs. Wood ranked among the most powerful passports on Earth. Was it possible that education could not only distract Tiffany from the windowless waiting room of her life, but actually liberate her from it? *With continued hard work,* Mrs. Wood wrote, *it's clear that you could put forth an exceptionally strong application. While I can never guarantee an admissions outcome, I have no doubt that you merit the consideration of these institutions. At the very least, you have earned the right to their attention.*

In Pinky's sunlit loft, Blandine feels horribly visible, as though she is unclothed. "College isn't for everyone," she snaps.

"Right," says Jack. "It's for people like you."

"I'm not going to tolerate a lecture on education from *you.*"

Jack's not offended. "What?" he asks. "Because I didn't go to college, either? Come on, Blandine. Don't make this about me. I'm smart enough to understand that I'm not that smart. But you had—"

"You don't have to be a genius to go to college. From what I understand, it's easier if you're not."

"Doesn't matter. College wasn't for me, that's obvious. But—"

"You act like college is some kind of sanctuary. But it's a system, as corrupt as the rest of them. You can't just climb up some credits, out of your history, into a better life. You can't. You're trapped inside yourself no matter how many degrees you get. College is just another level in the game that oppresses us—oppresses everyone."

"I'm not lecturing you," says Jack. The tenderness in his expression catches Blandine off guard, makes the room glitter vertiginously. "And I'm not judging you. I'm trying to figure out *what happened to you.*"

In the ensuing silence, feeling skittish, Blandine spots a camera, situated atop a thick book called *Rust Belt: The Second Coming.* Easy to reach with a slingshot.

"We can't leave Vacca Vale," she finally murmurs, eyes on the fishbowl of political pins. "We're the only ones who can save it."

Jack doesn't say anything, but when she looks at him, he meets her gaze like a dare. He has understood something crucial. Some subtext has become audible to him, and he has listened to it. Evidence of this change is packed into his expression, and Blandine sees it. Feels it. In the loft, in his sky blue T-shirt and yellow baseball cap, buzz cut and summer tan, Jack looks sturdy, convincing, real. He glows with the radiant health Blandine associates with the Amish and the fatal obedience she associates with the military. She looks at him—truly looks at him—for the first time. Freckles splashed on his nose from the sun, facial asymmetry, speckles of acne, the bright and endearingly crowded teeth. His muscles have become more defined since the spring, his chest broader, his clothes tighter. Even though her roommates are a year older than Blandine, they usually strike her as a generation below. But right now, in the July light and immaculate loft and the buzzing aftermath of their first real conversation, Jack appears her age.

It occurs to her that she could walk up to him, touch his shirt, and kiss him. Undress herself in a shrine of someone else's wealth. What would he do? Suddenly, she finds it unbelievable that they have shared a shower for a year. As they look at each other, warmth blossoms inside her, and her pulse quickens, and she feels like an idiot. With a ferocity that commandeers her entire body, she longs to take his hand and guide him into the bedroom, under her dress, into some kind of future, a future of his hand on her knee at the cinema, boiling pasta, waking up and describing their dreams. She longs to sleep in for the rest of her life. To sink into that pool of white linen and tell him to do whatever he wants to her.

The Samoyeds cry at the door.

"Okay," says Jack. "They have to go. For real this time." He scratches his buzz cut nervously, shifting from foot to foot, clutching the leashes. "You ready?"

She crosses the room, stopping inches from him. Her eyes at the level of his chest, she can feel his body heat. For a moment, he seems shocked by her proximity, but then his face softens, as though he's expected this for a long time. Her hand hovers close to his torso, and she can almost feel the worn cotton of his shirt. Gently, he traces a scratch on her arm. She feels his touch swimming up and down her body like a minnow. They are both breathing quickly, pumped with a familiar panic—one that arrives the first time two people reach for each other. The kind that says: if you get any closer, you will shatter this.

Remembering the cameras, Blandine abruptly kneels and pets the agitated dogs. Their fur is clean, white, unrealistically soft. As she scratches their necks, they stop whimpering. Globs of drool hang from their mouths.

"Okay." Blandine stands up, brushing against Jack as she opens the door and exits the apartment. The contact between them lingers in her skin, twinkling through her. She can't look at him right now, but maybe she'll work up the nerve to tap on his bedroom door tonight. Maybe having a body can feel good; maybe pleasure can be as easy for her as it seems to be for everyone else; maybe this is an intimation. Maybe it's just the heat.

"Thanks for the tour," she says. "Now let's walk these poor dogs."

The Flood

～

Right now, the mother is a mother, biting her nails in La Lapinière Affordable Housing Complex and avoiding the eyes of her baby. But ten months before, she was Hope, a twenty-four-year-old waitress lying beside her husband in a motel bed. The motel was called the Wooden Lady. It was evening. September. Flooding. As the Vacca Vale River invaded their city, the couple pretended that they were on vacation, pretended that they had not been ordered to evacuate the Rabbit Hutch but instead left it by choice.

They'd been married for two years. Before meeting Anthony, Hope didn't know that she was capable of feeling happy for more than an hour at a time. She believed that she lacked the gene. But by the time they checked into the motel, she had become intimately acquainted with the kind of feelings that she once ogled like jewels on other people's necks. Security, fulfillment, euphoria. Love. These feelings, she discovered, could last until they became conditions.

Outside, rain pummeled down for the third day straight, working overtime. Everyone called the rain "torrential," which struck Hope as shorthand for something more permanently devastating. Still, next to Anthony, she felt at peace. Safe. Almost drugged. The room was toasty, cozy, fifty-nine bucks a night. She knew that people got murdered at this motel, but she liked it there anyway. She was at home in places of humble ugliness. It was the only aesthetic that could hold her without making her nervous; she did not have to worry about deserving it.

When they arrived at the Wooden Lady a few hours before to check in, Anthony parked the car in the swampy lot while Hope went inside. Nobody was operating the front desk. A vase of rubber snakes sat in the orange-carpeted lobby, and behind the desk, shelves of rabbit figurines watched Hope, their expressions frantic, as though they were waiting for her to change their lives. To kill or save them. Unnerved, Hope searched the first floor for someone to pay, her hair and clothes soaked in rain. She stumbled into a staff-only room—windowless—where she encountered an empty coffee pot, a bare lightbulb, a chaotic chart on the wall, the odor of mold, and a row of beige lockers. On the metal face of one, someone had pressed Disney stickers. Sparkly cartoons beaming obliviously, grime building at their edges. When she saw the stickers, a violent tenderness surged through her, emerging in a few tears she didn't understand.

Now freshly showered and fragrant with crappy soaps—soaps they had to pay extra to obtain—Hope felt great. A buzz of curious well-being vibrated through her body as she burrowed under the wolf-emblazoned quilt against Anthony's warmth, her clean hair wetting the pillowcase, his hand absently massaging her thigh, releasing cascades of bliss through her body. Her legs, freshly shaved and moisturized, felt silken against the sheets. An erotic sense of health and vitality made her hot, made her want to dance, made her smile at Anthony, at everything. She always felt perversely good during a crisis; a crisis justified the panic that rattled the cage of her body at least once a month. Made her feel normal. During a crisis, everyone was plunged into the animal fear that she frequented all year round. The only benefit of her generalized anxiety disorder was that it prepared Hope for the Worst-Case Scenario; she was never surprised when one materialized because the Worst-Case Scenario was where she spent most of her time.

"Okay," Anthony said, looking at his phone. "It looks like Rizzo's is still open. But just for pickup, no delivery."

"How will you get there? You can't drive."

They endured the six-mile trip from their apartment to the Wooden Lady with clenched teeth and advanced profanity. Exodus of cars, powerlines and branches scattered, streetlights on the fritz, roads closed, water up to the hubcaps. Rain too thick to see through.

"It's just down the street," said Anthony. "I'll walk."

"You're going to risk your life for pizza?"

Anthony rolled his eyes playfully. "Nobody's ever died from a walk in the rain," he said. "I've got an umbrella."

"Seriously, Anthony. It's dangerous."

"Too late—I already ordered."

"And you just showered! You'll get rainy again."

"God forbid. Listen, I think Hangry Hope is the biggest threat I'm facing right now."

"Har, har."

"See? Can't even take a joke."

She bit his arm gently. "I might eat you instead."

"Mm," he said. "That doesn't sound so bad." He kissed her slowly, then got out of bed. "I'm going to Rizzo's and you can't stop me."

"How Pizza Killed My Husband," Hope said. "A true crime series."

"Wife," Anthony replied, collecting his things. "I'm the provider. I will *provide for you*." He smiled. She studied his thick hair, the color of black coffee. His eyes a pair of fireplaces. A shadow of beard on his jawline, one crooked tooth, slightly large ears. Black sweatpants, soft shirt, jacket. Years of competitive soccer training were still visible in his body. He had been on track for an athletic scholarship until his injury his senior year. Now, he spent most of his time on construction sites. His skin still tan from the summer and rosy from the heat of the room. He was radiant.

"Can we watch *Meet the Neighbors* when you get back?" asked Hope.

"If you survive?"

"For you? Anything."

"It calms me down."

"I know it does." Anthony smiled. "Promise you won't worry about me, okay?" He flashed her a peace sign, then headed out the door, closing it behind him.

She knew that he wouldn't die from a walk in the rain. For the most part, the flood had spared the west side of town, where they found themselves now, and it's true that Rizzo's was a block down the street. Hope smiled dreamily, then turned her attention to the motel television, where bleached teeth and stiff hair pronounced numbers. It was called the news. The numbers got lost in the coppice of her thoughts as soon as they entered it, but still she tried to grip them.

Just a week before, Hope asked her cousin Kara to make her look French. Kara chopped off twelve inches of Hope's dark hair, shortening it to her chin, and gave her thick bangs, mussing the new coif with enough products to stock a drugstore. Anthony loved the haircut, touching it whenever he passed. Of course, despite the dashing haircut, Hope didn't feel French. She felt like what she was: someone who shopped for pants at Costco and genuinely looked forward to the county fair every year.

In the motel bed, Hope checked the text thread with her mother, which was disproportionately blue. Recently, Hope's mother had fallen in love with an HVAC technician on a Catholic dating site and moved to Pensacola to live in his immaculately air-conditioned condo. These days, Hope's mother seemed to be in a glass-bottomed canoe more often than not. She and her new husband adopted a bearded dragon together and often posted about her on Facebook. The reptile's name was Daisy. Daisy liked to eat crickets and bananas. Daisy did not burden those around her with a surplus of existential terror. Daisy liked to joyride on the Roomba.

Hope was twenty-four years old and jealous of a bearded fucking dragon.

Just wanted to let you know we're fine over here, Hope had messaged her mother an hour before. *I'm at the motel. Anthony just left to get pizza. I think our stuff will be OK once they fix the sewage thing. Kara's staying with Jenn and Matt. Aunt Cathy's with them. Everybody's safe.*

No response.

Now the television spoke to Hope as though it had something important to tell her, specifically.

"Torrential rains," said Terry Hoff, the ageless woman who had worked as the local news anchor for as long as Hope could remember, "have flooded the Vacca Vale River to a record high of thirteen point seven feet. The previous record, which was set in nineteen eighty-two, was eleven point nine feet. Experts say this one-thousand-year flood has already damaged about seven-hundred-and-fifty businesses, along with over two thousand homes. The five-hundred-year flood that struck Vacca Vale less than a year ago is making some people question the timing."

"Too many numbers," mumbled Hope. This couldn't be what numbers were for. It was irresponsible for math teachers to give students numbers without telling them how to conceptualize them. Cut to a room of reporters. Some slapdash press conference. At a podium stood Mayor Douglas Barrington, who looked exactly like every other mayor Hope had ever seen: white, male, tall, overweight, gray-haired, blue-suited, daddish. Fifties. You could tell he ate a lot of red meat. If he were your dad, he'd be around for the milestones, but he'd make himself scarce the rest of the time. He'd teach you to ride a bike, for example, but he wouldn't be there when you lost a tooth. You would lose twenty teeth, and he'd never be there to take the bloody tissues from your mouth. Not once.

You could just tell, thought Hope.

"Mayor Barrington," began a reporter, "considering the remarkable timing of these back-to-back floods, would you say climate change is responsible?"

Barrington raised his eyebrows. "I wouldn't say that, no. Look, Mother Nature has her ups and downs. Is it bad luck? You bet. Is it because of so-called global warming? Nobody could say for sure. What I do know is that we're gonna do everything in our power to recover from this crisis and make sure it doesn't happen again."

Hope took a sip of the beer she and Anthony rescued from their now-powerless refrigerator. The can was still cold and wet, like a dog's nose. It was a drinking game she and Anthony played when they watched the local news. Drink every time Barrington said: *you bet.*

"What steps will you take to mitigate and prevent future flooding, given their increased likelihood as the planet warms?" asked a reporter in thick glasses. Hope recognized her, but it took a moment to figure out why: they went to high school together. Araceli. She was in Hope's class, smart and tough. Not nice, but kind.

"Well," replied Barrington, his posture one of dismissal, "I don't think floods like these are necessarily *more likely* to occur in the future, but here's what we already have underway. We're in the process of implementing backwater gates and revamping the sewage system. Listen, the city is situated on a river; it was designed to withstand a certain amount of flooding—that's a normal process, a *natural* process. And we foresaw it. That's why the majority of the damage happened to Chastity Valley, not to buildings. We've got parks in the floodplains, not commerce, and that's because Vacca Vale's got intelligent design. So I think, overall, we should be counting our blessings. Is there a lot of work to be done? You bet. Could it be worse? You bet."

Two sips.

Terry Hoff returned to the screen, looking severe in her red blazer and year-round tan. "As we heard just now, Tom, there's a lot of work to be done to repair the damages from this flood. What are experts estimating, in terms of recovery costs?"

Hope wondered who taught all the news anchors of America how to do the American News Anchor Voice—the theatrics of it, the computerized hypnosis of it. Would those deep in the future find the footage and inaccurately conclude that this is how everyone used to talk?

Cut to a man in a plastic poncho and rain-splattered glasses, squinting desperately into a camera, a whole person thwapped by wind. He stood outside a municipal building in their vacant downtown. Why did they make poor Tom stand outside in this storm, under that bad bright spotlight? "That's right, Terry," he said after a beat too long. "I've been talking to local experts, and it looks like the costs are extreme. It's looking like Chastity Valley, which is suffering the majority of the damage, will cost over two million dollars to restore. Damages to businesses and homes clock in at five hundred and fourteen thousand dollars. The Federal Emergency Management Agency is estimated to reimburse the city three hundred and forty-four thousand dollars, but as you can see, that aid will only cover a fraction of the total. Mayor Barrington has been critical of national plans to fight the climate crisis, arguing that those measures will harm the economy. But you've got to wonder: what's the cost of doing nothing? We know that—"

Cut to Terry, who laughed awkwardly. She only laughed when something went wrong. Clearly, Tom had gone off-script again. Anthony loved this about Tom, and Hope loved this about Anthony. "Thank you, Tom." Gathering herself, Terry glided through the remaining news. The Vacca Vale wastewater treatment plant was absorbing three times its normal flow. A state-owned road was destroyed, but Hope couldn't follow the details. The golf course was fine. She lost focus for a while, sipping her beer and thinking vaguely of the Bible. When her attention returned to the screen, a farmer was being interviewed.

Beyond the city's confines sprawled industrial farmland, which was gradually mutating into suburbia. How did the river floods stretch all the way to the corn and soybean crops? A shot of the land: buzz-cut, waterlogged fields. "I tried to walk out there to check out the damage," said a farmer. "But I sunk right into the mud, up to my knees. It's like the earth was trying to swallow me whole."

~~~

While she waits for Anthony, Hope watched an episode of *Meet the Neighbors,* a mid-twentieth-century show about a family of misfit city folks who move to a farm town. Most of the action follows the family dog and the youngest child, Susie Evans, played to great effect by Elsie Blitz. Round face, auburn curls, freckles on the nose. She was only six years old when the show began, but she acted with the grace and confidence of an adult. She could sing and tap-dance, convincingly laugh and cry. Whiskey, the miniature schnauzer who played her sidekick, always responded to Elsie Blitz with sincere affection. Hope once read that the week Whiskey died, Elsie was too distraught to work, but they couldn't pause production, so they changed the plot of the episode at hand, making it gloomy, giving her an excuse to weep. Then they replaced Whiskey with an identical dog, but Hope could tell the bond wasn't the same.

The show remained on air for several seasons, comforting generations of Americans. For Hope, it was tranquilizing. It reminded her of her mother, and she lost track of how many times she'd seen every season. Hope clicked around her laptop and found the episode she had left off on: "Captain Susie and the Forest of Runaways." Old-timey credits rolled, indulgent and theatrical, set to celebratory orchestral music. It was one of her favorite episodes: on a family camping trip, after her parents repeatedly tell her to stay close, Susie Evans wanders off the path because she thinks she sees a fairy. After wandering in the woods for a long time, she and Whiskey stumble upon a troupe of children who have run away from various homes. Rapidly, she becomes their charismatic leader. By the end, Susie convinces all the children to return to their parents.

"I'm never alone when I'm with you," Susie says to Whiskey, who wags his tail in agreement.

~~~

Standing in the flickering hallway of the Wooden Lady, Hope checked her phone. In the room, her cellular service kept vanishing, and it had been nearly an hour since Anthony left. Bars returned to her phone, but no messages or missed calls appeared. As she hovered, trying to quell the panic swirling to life in her chest, a moth landed on the green wallpaper beside her door. It was breathtaking. Hope edged closer to study its wings, white and shimmering like snow, hemmed in pale micro-fur, two tufts where they met the body. Beige antenna. Eyes round and dark as tapioca. Iridescent and mesmerizing.

Gradually, Hope became aware of another body in the hallway. Hackles up, she turned to see an elderly woman in a nightgown, watching her.

"This is what God does when He wants to start over," said the woman, her pale clothing and cloudy hair bearing resemblance to the moth, as if she and the moth had manifested each other. Disoriented, Hope tried to smile at the woman but frowned instead. "Mark my words, there's a reckoning headed our way," continued the woman. "And I'm gonna have my ducks in a row when it comes. Tell me, honey—do you accept Jesus Christ as your personal Lord and Savior?"

Hope gritted her teeth. You couldn't go anywhere in this town without bumping into God. "Yes," she said, to end the conversation. "You bet."

"Good," said the woman. "Say, you don't happen to have a cigarette, do you?"

"No," Hope replied. "Sorry."

"Ah, good for you. You'll live forever."

Hope forced a grin.

"I'll be down the hall," the woman said as she limped to her room. "If you happen to find a cigarette, you wouldn't mind bringing it over to me, would you? I had to leave mine at home, and I'm started to feel funny." She must've been eighty or so. Watching her laborious movements, Hope's spirit reached toward the woman in sympathy.

"Are you here alone?" Hope asked.

The woman turned to face her. "Yes."

"Here because of the flood?"

"Of course."

"Is your home gonna make it?"

The woman shrugged. "Is anybody's?"

~~~

Finally, Anthony returned with a box raincoated in a trash bag. Miraculous fact of him, holy smell of pizza. "Sorry about the wait," he said, shaking the umbrella. "They had a line like you wouldn't believe. Apparently everywhere else is closed, so Rizzo's is feeding the whole town." He was drenched from head to foot.

"Why didn't you reply to my texts?" Hope asked. "I was really worried."

Anthony pointed to his duffel bag, on top of which his phone lay innocently. "I forgot it on my way out. I told you not to worry!"

Hope stared at him.

"It was a nice time, actually. I ran into Frank—you remember him? We went to high school together, and he was on the team. Midfield. Had a hell of a left foot. I didn't know that Rizzo's is his family's place, on his mom's side. He's managing, now. He's got four kids!"

Anthony's presence began to extinguish the fear burning inside Hope's body, and by the time he handed her three slices of green-olive pizza—her favorite, not his—peace descended upon her once again, a peace so complete that it felt like it was brewed by a god.

After they ate, they lay on their backs, rain hammering outside. "Turn over," he said.

"Why?"

"I want to give you a massage. Payback for worrying you earlier."

"You don't have to do that."

"I want to."

She beamed, sat up, kissed him. He pulled her shirt over her head, running his hands over her skin. "Turn over," he whispered. She obeyed, and he massaged her bare back for a long time, his hands calloused and strong. Eventually, she turned over again, her entire spirit kindled. In the motel lamplight, Anthony looked like a painting. There was something sinister about lapping up his beauty like this—something Twitter and the Church would condemn—but Hope stopped rationing her pleasure years ago, when she realized she might not have much of it to feel before she died. She looked and looked at her husband. His dark hair ruffled, his strong jawline and the architecture of his body, and that one vein on his neck casting its mysterious spell on her brain, shutting off the parts that operated language and logic and breathing. His boxers were from high school, torn and covered in cartoon fish. She touched them, felt jealous of them, jealous of how close they got to be to him all day long, even while he was at work. She gulped. Gradually, she realized that Anthony was studying her with concern, his eyes shining, his eyebrows furrowed. "Are you all right?" he asked. He was so luminous she felt he might burn her.

"I want . . ."

"Yes?"

"I want . . ."

And then he understood. A quiet smile. "Show me what you want," he said.

All the Catholicism left in her body made Hope blush, made her shy, made her feel fantastically evil. For years, she'd been hauling religion out of herself one box at a time, reluctant to look too hard at anything. It was the same way she sorted through her father's house after he died. Now, instead of speaking, she leaned forward and pulled down Anthony's waistband, took him in her mouth, and began showing him what she wanted by giving it to him first. He ran his hands through her new haircut, tugging on it gently as she arched her back. He said her name like a prayer, and she felt him get even harder in her mouth. "Fuck," he whispered. She loved how inarticulate he became when they were about to have sex. "You look so good," he mumbled, running his hands over her skin. Tugging a lock of her hair again. "I love this fucking haircut." After a couple minutes, he pushed her shoulders away from him, his face pink, guiding her into the bedding. "Lie down."

She did, her whole body now coursing with liquid light. He kissed her mouth, her neck, her breasts, her nerves neon beneath his touch. He kissed her hips, her thighs. His mouth was warm, his stubble rough as sandpaper. "You are a work of art." When he said things like this, it always sounded like he meant it, somehow. Her skin shimmered, and soon her whole body was glowing like that bioluminescent plankton she saw online. The deific shock of his tongue on her clit, two fingers inside her. "You taste so good," he said, "I could taste you forever." The work of his hands and his mouth hovered her body from the sheets as some tide possessed her, overtook her, and soon she was begging him to fuck her, nearly speechless, and finally he obliged, and as he entered her, she thought the pleasure would crack her in half. "Slow," she breathed. "Or

I'll come right now." He maneuvered her on top of him. "Show me how you want it," he said. *Yes,* she heard herself repeating. She was a personified Yes by then. Lamplight rippled across his muscled torso, and held her ass as she fucked him, his eyes on her jumping breasts like they were saving his life. She heard herself incanting words she'd be too embarrassed to repeat, felt an uprising inside her body, inside his body, in the whole room, in the whole world, lifting them both into each other and out of themselves, and as she writhed and tightened around him, a flash of sweat bloomed from his skin. For a moment, everything was indigo. His eyes rolled back, his mouth opened, and he jerked forward to music that only they could hear, filling her with himself as they inhabited each other. Together, briefly, they became the objects and forces around them, too: the furniture, the power lines, the forest, the factories, the river, the storm.

Someone once told Hope that in the Beginning everything came from one thing. Lying side by side in the dark, his come dripping down her thigh, her nipples hardened, her pussy hot and wet and beating like a heart, breathless and drugged with worship, tearing up from the fantastic chemical tempest twirling inside her, she knew it would End that way, too—that everything would return to one thing.

His dark eyes searched hers as they breathed together. They knew that there was nothing sensational or innovative or dangerous about their lovemaking, nothing that would be replicated in a film, and yet it was the familiarity of conjugal sex that moved Hope. To her, it proved that the ordinary could transform you, too. In the motel, she and her husband studied each other in awe, like a pair of detectives who had cracked the uncrackable case.

After trying to conceive for thirteen months, Hope and Anthony had stopped buying pregnancy tests, stopped vigilantly tracking her cycle. They couldn't afford fertility treatments, and so they avoided the doctor, afraid they would receive bad news that they could do nothing to reverse. They were young, they assured themselves. But that was also the source of Hope's alarm: if she was having trouble at the age of twenty-four, what were the odds she would get pregnant later in life? She wanted a baby with a clarity she had only experienced once before, when she met Anthony at a bonfire on Kara's friend's uncle's farm and knew, within ten minutes of conversation, that she would marry him.

He was twenty-six now, and he wanted a baby, too. For a while, sex had become depressingly utilitarian, divested of spontaneity or invention, but after they stopped trying to conceive, it restored itself to life. No longer a means to an end, the sex was better than ever.

Outside the motel, eight miles away from the bed in which Hope and Anthony caught their breath, the Vacca Vale River had overtaken most of Chastity Valley. The river was once the place where officials stored sewage and murderers stored bodies. Now, the river was every place. From above, the Valley was sapped of color and form, night sky pelting rain against the florae, autumnal trees submerged in shadow and water. A jungle gym built to resemble a miniature castle up to its neck in the flood. Animal burrows collapsed. Squirrels, deer, owls, foxes, and chipmunks fled to higher ground, hunted for thick vegetation to protect them from the wind. Unlike the terrestrial creatures, the fish went down: down to the bottom of the small lake at the western edge of the Valley, a lake that was joining everything around it. Soon, you couldn't tell where it began or ended. A family of ducks huddled in a tight line, swimming across the forest in the dark. In the center of Vacca Vale, the swollen river kissed the bridge that stretched across it. South of downtown, the affordable neighborhoods stood defiantly in pooling water, disposable one-story houses holding their rooftops high. Water gathered in the basement and first floor of La Lapinière Affordable Housing Complex. Electricity and pumping throughout the poor neighborhoods malfunctioned. Stop signs, submerged. American flags, swimming. Basketball nets brushing the water. Hoods of cars peaking above. One truck floating down a residential street. The color of the water was the color of nothing, and it was as though the nothing that always haunted Vacca Vale had materialized into a physical substance, one capable of quantifiable damage. The river was everywhere, contaminating the city with itself, insisting that there was no real difference between it and them.

In Room 57 at the Wooden Lady, a woman named Hope allowed her husband to hold her close to his warm, real body. Deep in her own, a transformation was beginning. In four days, a fertilized egg would implant itself in the lining of her uterus. It would be a boy, and he would be born with large, dark, beautiful eyes. In the bed, Hope cried pleasurably, as she often did after good sex. Anthony kissed the tears off her face, traced patterns of light that fell on her skin, and told her that it was beautiful to feel so much. Pizza boxes were piled on the floor beside the tele-vision. In her husband's perfect thumbnail, Hope glimpsed something essential, some secret from the gods to help her through: not a single factory, boarded-up window, overcast day, foreclosed honey-baked-ham shop, empty bank account, or medical emergency could permanently kill them. None of this nothing could trap them inside it. There was no such thing as freedom, Hope knew, but there was such a thing as feel-ing good, and it was important, and it was real, and sometimes you got it for free.

"I love you," he said.

"I love you," she said.

And they believed each other.

Olive Brine

～

Moses is staying at the Wooden Lady, a place that inspires hard crime as soon as you enter it. Moses chose this motel because it had the worst online reviews he could find—*It's like if manslaughter were a place,* commented user BabyFace444—and he wanted to keep a low profile. A sign on the front desk reads: VACCA VALE'S FIRST MOTEL! A dubious distinction. It used to be called the Wooden Indian until three years ago, when a group of students campaigned for the owners to change it. Moses gathered this from the internet before he arrived.

Around ten on Wednesday morning, Moses approaches the front desk, following an accidental confession at St. Jadwiga's. He notices a collage of local headlines mentioning the Wooden Lady framed on the wall.

MULBERRY KILLER'S ALIBI PROVES FALSE, WOODEN LADY STAFF TES-TIFIES. GINA LADOWSKI TAKES OVER AT THE WOODEN LADY, CRIME DOWN THIRTEEN PERCENT. WOODEN LADY POOL TO CLOSE PERMA-NENTLY AFTER TEN OPOSSUMS FOUND. "THE HOOKERS CHOSE US, WE DIDN'T CHOOSE THEM": WOODEN LADY OWNER SPEAKS OUT ABOUT SEX WORK CHARGES.

"All press is good press, is it?" Moses asks in a French accent. He's wearing a black turtleneck, despite the heat.

The teenage boy at the desk stares at him like an undertaker. Rabbit figurines crowd the surface of the filing cabinet behind him. A vase of snakes sits in the center of the lobby, resembling a memorial.

"Why the snakes?" asks Moses.

The concierge turns his attention to a game on his phone. "For the children," he replies.

"My name is Pierre," says Moses. "Pierre BuFont. B, U, F, O, N, T. I would like a single room."

The boy turns to his outdated computer and types irritably. He pauses to take a luxurious gulp of milkshake, then mumbles something that sounds to Moses like, *We are out of echoes.*

Moses asks the boy to repeat himself.

"We're out of nonsmoking rooms."

"This is good for me," replies Moses as Pierre. "I am smoker."

"Sixty-two dollars and fifty-three cents."

Moses pays in cash.

Once the plot is set in motion, he makes the most of it. He deposits his bags in Room 57—a shadow box where, unbeknownst to him, a baby was conceived ten months prior. The room is surprisingly cozy, despite its green wallpaper, odor of smoke, and general atmosphere of death. It reminds Moses of the catacombs in Paris. After he sets down his things, he leaves the motel and walks across a four-lane intersection to the liquor store, which plays new age music on the speakers and footage of gorillas on the televisions. In a shimmer of flutes and synths, he purchases vermouth, gin, olives, and a pack of cigarettes, maintaining the accent throughout. If the cashier is interested in his French performance, or his conspicuous consumption—he chose the most expensive brands—she keeps her interest to herself.

When he returns to his room, he finds a pink hood in the dresser. Just a hood, torn from its body. There is no soap in the bathrooms, no breakfast in the morning. One damp towel. Moses loves it—all of it. His interaction with Father Tim left him feeling hungover, itchy, breathless, pursued. He takes a few pulls of gin, removes his clothes, then settles into the bed. Immediately, he falls into a thin and sweaty nap.

~~~

He wakes to evidence of a wet dream, but he can't recall the details. As he waddles to the bathroom and takes a shower, splinters return to him. An art class was painting him as he modeled nude. All eyes on him. He dries his body with a towel he brought from home, rubbing his skin aggressively, then dresses in a fresh outfit identical to the one he was wearing this morning. Now, to kill time—a phrase he's always liked—he fixes himself an extra-dirty martini. He makes it quickly, slopping vermouth on the paranormal television, which keeps turning on and off without his intervention. Thankfully, it's muted.

It's after five in the evening. On his bedside table sits a pack of cigarettes. He lights one and smokes cinematically, actively appreciating the lack of art. On the quilt, a wolf howls at a yellow moon, ensconced in pine trees. In this motel, Moses *feels* French, despite the comforter—feels nihilism and passion sparring like bucks for the territory of his brain.

He stretches on the bed, sipping his drink, which is mostly olive brine. The air conditioner in his room is more of a gesture than a reality—it pours forth room-temperature air, although it's fixed on the coldest setting. He's sweating but feels chilled. He drinks until the martini takes hold of him, warming him up, erasing the morning, cleansing pollutants from his body. In elementary school, Moses loved erasing—it was, in his estimation, the closest thing to time travel. At recess, he would crouch on the Astroturf with a notebook, write horrible things about people he knew—including himself—then erase his markings until the paper became thin and hot. Rubber shreds would cling to his uniform polo, leaving evidence. He never minded the evidence.

Moses opens his laptop, relishing its blast of screen light, and logs into the email associated with his mental health blog. The blog is devoted to a subset of people who suffers from the same itchy, invasive, multicolored fibers that he does. The subset he leads, however, does not identify with the Morgellons community. Truth be told, Moses finds the Morgellons folks completely unrelatable, but he maintains a respectful attitude toward them in his writing. While the Morgellons community spends much of its energy attempting to medically validate their condition, *Moses's* people understand that they are more advanced than the dermis-typical human population, and thus cannot expect the medical community, which is dominated by the unevolved, to detect such a condition. It's like expecting a pedestrian to recognize the Son of God—most wouldn't! Most didn't! Neither do Moses's people attempt to treat their condition, as they believe that it is their duty to suffer it. Coconut oil, cinnamon, black soap—these remedies are acceptable so long as they are used to soothe but not eradicate the symptoms. If the symptoms "heal," the sufferer must cease use of the product at once and do everything in his power to resurrect the itch.

Moses's subset refers to its condition as the Toll, so-named because the symptoms reveal genetic material unique to the hypersensitive—to geniuses, artists, and prophets. People who suffer from the Toll accept the fibers as a consequence of their superiority. The Toll is taxing, indeed, but as Moses writes in the "About Us" portion of his blog:

> It is our duty to endure alienating discomfort, and, toward the end of our preordained missions, singular pain. Our lives will not be breezy. Our condition will isolate us from family and friends. It will render contemporary structures of happiness ridiculous, unattainable, or both. This is our Toll, and it is one we embrace because we know that our condition also unlocks the affected consciousness to nirvana. As my grandmother used to say: *your gift is your cross.*

Some of Moses's people believe that everyone experiences the Toll, but only the hypersensitive *feel* it. This is a subset of the subset—most believe that the Toll expresses itself only in the chosen minority. Their advanced evolution does not justify self-pity or self-indulgence; on the contrary, they believe that it demands monastic humility and a tenacious work ethic. It doesn't justify animosity toward inferior members of the species, either. It demands the purest nonviolence. They have been graced with an extravagant capacity to feel, a conduit to imaginative empathy, and it is their celestial duty to exercise this capacity, never to numb or ignore it. This is their operating philosophy. Moses has heard vegans make similar arguments about the human obligation toward nonhuman animals—if you have been endowed with consciousness, you must instrumentalize it to curtail the damage you inflict on the world—an attitude that Moses finds sympathetic but ultimately absurd. It is draining enough, he thinks, to summon compassion for the nonedible animals of this planet.

Moses remembers what he is about to do to Joan Kowalski and furiously scratches his scalp. No one is perfect. Not even the prophets. Certainly not the geniuses.

Moses accepts messages from those afflicted by the Toll, or those who believe they are afflicted, and offers his council to them. He operates the blog in anonymity, under the name Dr. Malachi. One new message glares in his inbox. Subject: *Game of Clue*. He clicks. A delightful patina of sweat begins to relieve the Toll for a moment, almost the way the glow does. He eats three olives and makes another drink.

Game of Clue

~~~

Dear Dr. Malachi,

I know that your specialty is "The Toll" but nobody else will reply to me, so I am hoping that you will extend your psychiatric expertise to my strange case.

First, let me state that although I am a man, I do not consider myself a product, victim, or perpetrator of "toxic masculinity," and I harbor no desire to be macho. I was raised by a father who hugged me and encouraged me to draw. He cried in my presence and made all the meals. My mother was an intellectual who often traveled without us, and when she returned, we could tell she had experienced weeks of private revelation, to which we would never be privy, and I found that thrilling. My little sister is my best friend.

In my sexual life, I have always waited for the woman to make the first move, and I do not proceed until she explicitly says she wants us to. I prioritize my wife's orgasms over my own, and I favor steamy film scenes over pornography, due to ethical concerns about the industry. I prefer for the woman to be on top. My wife is a heroic genius who does not wear makeup or dye her hair, and I defer to her in nearly all life decisions. When the sexual misconduct of a powerful man is revealed on the news, I feel such intense sadness, it makes me fall asleep. I become squeamish when faced with blood and/or the visible suffering of others and have to close my eyes during violent scenes. I am an aspiring vegan.

I have attended more feminist marches than my wife has, although, of course, it's not a competition, and while I'm at it, I might as well add that I am not even remotely competitive. I have never, ever fantasized about harming anyone. Up until now, I have always enjoyed a fair degree of mental health. The mating scenes in nature documentaries depress me tremendously.

I am not aware of any mental illness in my family, aside from one uncle who was bipolar and did eventually shoot himself in the head, but we were nothing alike. My fortieth birthday is approaching, and it's true that I have some fear about aging, and my sister was redeployed in the winter, which was hard. My parents are both alive and well, and Dad's been in remission for a year. Work always took up a lot of time, and I don't get to do as much for my personal betterment as I wish I could (I had hoped to speak fluent Mandarin by now, and I have 39 works of unread nonfiction downloaded on my tablet!), but I enjoy my job and I think our company has a worthwhile mission. I code for a living and recently got a raise. I have a spectacular wife and a close group of friends, who are mostly childless, which makes us feel better. Up until everything went to Hell, I would scope out the artisanal beer scene on Thursday evenings with two buddies from work. They're younger—all the coworkers my age have kids—and they remind me of what I was like a decade ago. The last beer I tried was an Icelandic sheep-manure-smoked IPA. Not so bad! I also played on a coed soccer team with my wife, and I loved seeing the love of my life kick ass on the field. I'm aware that my body doesn't move the way it used to, and even small amounts of physical activity now give me muscular hangovers, but it's important to stay active—helps me hang on to whatever youth I have left. Ha.

Now that I've established my normalcy, let me establish my abnormality:

I've been experiencing three symptoms lately which I hope you can help me decode. I have a feeling that they're connected, although maybe they're not, and the last one is by far the most urgent. It's very possible that I just have a vitamin deficiency. The first two symptoms feel like clues to help me understand the last, but I am at my wit's end. I feel both out of my mind and trapped in my head and I am petrified. Please help.

The symptoms, in order of appearance:

1. I have become so afraid of being electrically shocked by a metal

handle that I will take any measure, no matter how extreme, to avoid touching one. Recently, I missed the first twenty minutes of a meeting because I couldn't bring myself to open the door to our building and no one else appeared. It began in the winter with a very light aversion but now if I am forced to touch a metal handle I start to hyperventilate. The last time I got shocked was in March, and I felt the shock—like ghosts of it, repeatedly shocking me—for a week straight. Over and over. And the shock itself wasn't even bad. But the aftershocks, if you will, were so maddening I could no longer focus at work. I started to experience powerful headaches. Even the headaches felt electric.

2. Shortly after the static-shock-fear set in, I developed a desire to tag surfaces with my name. Walls of parking garages, bathroom stalls, phone cases, park benches, church doors, library books, laptops, restaurant menus, the sailboat of a friend, the interior and exterior of my own car. Even, once, the soccer cleat of a teammate. The desire is loud and physical, almost like the need to sneeze. Sometimes if the desire gets too intense, I have to channel it into sex or it will totally overtake me. I am deeply opposed to the defacement of public property. I have no background in graffiti and was never interested in tagging, but sometimes I wake as if from a dream in the spray-paint aisle of a hardware store, and even though I try to suppress all tagging fantasies, I now know exactly what my tag would look like. All I'll say is that it would be yellow.

I have only submitted to the desire once, near the community tennis courts. I won't expose the details, as they are identifying. I am very ashamed of this. Please advise.

This last one is the worst, so bear with me if I stumble through the explanation. I feel sick and shaky as I type.

3. It started at Beth's fortieth birthday party two months ago. (Beth is what I will call my wife. All names have been changed for reasons that will become clear. IRL, my wife only knows about issue #1—and even that I downplayed.) Beth and I have been married for ten years now, been together for thirteen, and I decided to throw her a surprise party for the first time in her life. She didn't have any of the hang-ups some people (like me!) have about "crossing the threshold," or what have you. And she never gets sad about our lack of children. She always thought it would be unethical to create a child who would face environmental doom. And I am so on board with this. I mean, sometimes I do

wish I had somebody I could teach chess to, and I find myself smiling at unknown babies, but I agree with Beth—in such a climate, to act on the primal reproductive urge would be selfish.

All in all, Beth is a phenomenal human being and a very understanding/patient/positive partner. She smells like lavender and texts me interesting science articles at lunch. Or at least, she used to, before everything got fucked. So I wanted to make things nice for her fortieth.

I invited some of her friends from work—she works at a small environmental advocacy nonprofit—and because I wanted her to enjoy the day, I even invited Valentina, her friend from graduate school. Beth is close with Valentina, and defensive of her, as Valentina supposedly endured some kind of childhood trauma about which Beth refuses to elaborate. I'm skeptical of the "trauma"—it's just like Valentina to fish for sympathy with lies.

In my opinion, Valentina is annoying at best, sociopathic at worst. She's loud, rude, always drinks too much, and often shatters people for sport. I also suspect she's a pathological liar. She's only ever dated aloof billionaires, and none of her relationships has lasted longer than a month. She has a mysterious pool of money that funds her hedonistic lifestyle—she travels, collects graduate degrees, blogs about food, and calls herself a photographer. She seems to be a little bit famous on social media, though nobody knows why. The only pleasant conversation I've ever had with Valentina was about coding, since she took a coding bootcamp in Mexico City for fun. I'll admit she's something of a genius, and although I basically despise her, I also admit that she possesses a chilling kind of charisma.

At this year's Thanksgiving party with our childless friends, Valentina got drunk and spun a series of elaborate tales about her family's fox ranch in Spain. Because I have deeply cyber-stalked Valentina, I happen to know for certain that she is of Italian and Polish descent but that her family has been settled in New England for generations, and I'm pretty sure her real name is Valerie.

Somehow, while beguiling and horrifying the party with her fox stories, she managed to simultaneously convince the host, Jandro, that his husband, Ron, was cheating on him with someone present. Ron was on an alcohol run. Valentina sandwiched all the "evidence" between grisly fox-pelt facts. Most of the "evidence" came down to Ron's nervous demeanor all night. Valentina would lean into Jandro and whisper in his ear as people gasped or laughed at something she had just said. Because I am always on high alert around Valentina, I was listening and watching closely enough to catch these exchanges, but I doubt anyone else heard. I admit that, for a moment, even I was persuaded of Ron's infidelity.

But I know Ron well, and Ron would simply never cheat, not even on someone he disliked, let alone on Jandro, to whom he is totally devoted. They have always been monogamous; Ron is categorially opposed to infidelity. I think Ron had overstated his ability to cook a turkey and simply felt embarrassed that it had turned out so bad.

But once Valentina gets involved, facts lose their power. By the end of the night, Jandro and Ron were yelling at each other, nearly tipping off the fire escape, and Jandro was crying and Ron was baffled and Valentina—I swear to God—Valentina watched them through the window, *smirking*. She removed a cigarette from her purse and left the apartment. When she came back, she looked different. It took me a second to realize she had a full face of fresh makeup, her skin powdery, her lips like dark cherries. Jandro and Ron were still outside; the rest of us were nervously cleaning up. "Gotta go," announced Valentina with a false pout. "I'm getting drinks with an actual Carnegie, believe it or not. Kiss kiss bang bang."

When I explained what I had witnessed to Beth on the drive home, Beth dismissed it. "You probably misheard," she said. "There's no way you could've known what she was whispering from across the room." Then she gave me a lecture on the trope of the Aimlessly Evil Female Who Uses Her Body to Destroy Good Guys, referencing Genesis and a bunch of movies. "You're reducing Valentina to some man-made, stock character."

"But she wasn't using her body," I said. "And Iago wasn't female."

"What?"

Suddenly, I recalled the plot of *Othello*—wrote a final paper on the play in high school.

"Iago. Shakespeare. No one understands his motives for the shitty things he does to Desdemona and Othello. And he doesn't use his body, either."

"Are you seriously comparing Valentina to a Shakespearean villain?"

"You're the one who brought up fictional tropes."

"Iago had a motive. He was racist. Or he wanted to fuck Othello. Or both."

"So maybe Valentina has a motive, too. Maybe she's racist."

"Please."

"Or homophobic."

"Come on."

"Maybe wants to fuck Jandro!"

"I can't believe this."

"Or maybe her motive is that she simply *enjoys setting fire to people's lives.*"

Beth paused, then said, "You're looking for reasons to hate her, and you're trying to make me hate her, too. If anyone's acting like Iago here, it's you."

"Are you calling me racist?"

"You know that's not what I'm saying."

"Racist against a white girl from Boston?"

"She's from Madrid."

"She's not even *Spanish!*" I cried. Our driver pulled up to our apartment and gave us a frightened look. I clenched my fists. "Sorry," I said. "Sorry." We were both exhausted and tipsy. I decided to drop the subject and repent. Valentina had damaged enough relationships for one night. Beth walked ahead of me and let herself into the building.

All this is to say, you can probably understand why I didn't want to invite Valentina to Beth's birthday party.

But I invited her anyway because I love Beth, and Beth is regrettably undiscerning in her social taste. Either that or she has a preference for the mysteriously deranged.

The dinner went well. DIY spring rolls. Spicy basil tofu. Butterscotch cream pie. Champagne. All of Beth's favorites, handmade by me. She wore a sexy emerald dress and pulled me into the bathroom at one point to give me a quick thank-you blow job, so I know she really appreciated my efforts. By the end of dessert, I was drunk. At some point while I was clearing the dishes, someone suggested that we play Clue. I hadn't played the game in years, but I was pretty sure we owned it. Went to the home office to check. The knob of the office door is crystal, so I knew it was safe to touch. The room was dark and cluttered. As I fumbled for the light switch, someone quickly moved behind me and closed the door. Put a cold smooth hand over my mouth. I could feel each of her rings.

I pushed her off. "What are you doing?" I asked. Valentina moved her hand to my chest.

"Your heart is racing," she said.

"Because you fucking startled me."

It was only half true. Valentina's presence always disturbs me, but I wasn't quite *startled*. I must have subconsciously expected to find her there.

It is important at this point to make it clear that although some people think she's sexy, I do not find Valentina attractive at all—her gaunt and avian appearance repulses me as much as her personality.

"What are you doing in here?" I asked.

"I was just getting my lip balm. Relax," she said. I could hear her smiling. "Why are you so nervous? Hiding something in here?"

I forgot I had piled the coats and bags of the guests on the desk. She was still touching my chest, or at least that's what it felt like, so I stepped backward, rattling the door.

"You can't just lurk around in the shadows of someone else's apartment and put your hands on them and expect them to—to be—it's fucking creepy, okay?"

"Okay, okay, God." She laughed. "I thought it'd be funny. Sorry. Playing Clue always makes me jumpy, too."

"I'm not—"

"When I was little, my older cousins became obsessed with Clue—at some point we stopped using the board game. We had this old house in Ludlow, Vermont, where my whole extended family would summer. There were about forty of us. Me and my cousins would act out the game at night. It evolved into its own version, with different rules and characters and props, and we even had costumes—I always had to be Mr. Boddy. The murdered—"

"Excuse me." I brushed passed her to flip on the light. Once the room was illuminated, I saw that she was facing me, her back to the door, holding the game in her hands, a tube of lip balm in her shirt pocket. "Way ahead of you." She smiled, then left the office and joined the others in the living room. I heard them laugh.

I stood for a moment in the office, chills all over. Valentina wore too much black on her eyes—her eyes seemed to linger in the room without the rest of her. Like the Cheshire cat's grin.

The remainder of the party is a blur to me now. Valentina barely looked my way throughout it. Our friend John won. Professor Peter Plum. Lead pipe. Billiard Room. Doesn't matter.

What matters is what happened afterward.

Around two a.m., after everyone left, I went back into the office to retrieve the birthday gift I had curated for Beth: forty personal letters from forty of her most beloved people—family, childhood teachers, college professors, two of her favorite novelists, one senator, an environmental activist, a comedian. I don't mean to toot my own horn, but I had been soliciting the letters for the past ten months, and the gift was fucking spectacular. It would have been perfect had I not found a rusted pipe beside the letters. It was the size of my forearm.

"Babe?" I called out to Beth.

"Hmm?" She was brushing her teeth.

"Is this your pipe?"

"Wuh?"

"Do we have a pipe?"

She spit. "Pipe?"

"Yeah."

"I don't understand."

I carried the pipe into the bathroom and held it out to her. She raised an eyebrow.

"Is this my birthday present?"

"No! God, no! I was just wondering if you knew where this came from?"

She shook her head. "No clue."

I took the pipe back to the office and set it down where I found it, but it bothered me too much. I stared at it for a moment. Of course, I assumed it was Valentina, fucking with me, but no matter how ridiculous the joke was, I couldn't stand being in the same apartment as that object. So I took it four flights down, out of the building, and threw it in the dumpster. By the time I returned upstairs, breathless from the climb, Beth was in bed, applying lotion to her legs and looking sad.

"I had a really wonderful night," she said, sulking.

I waited for the rest, but she simply looked at her toes.

"I'm glad to hear that," I said carefully. "What's wrong?"

She looked up. "Nothing."

"What? Tell me."

"I just." She closed her eyes. "Nothing."

"Beth. You're a terrible actress. Please tell me why you're sad."

"Don't think I'm ungrateful for the party," she began, taking her time between words. "Because I'm not. I really loved it. And the food. The people. Everything was perfect. Thank you."

I waited. "But . . . ?"

She grimaced, then finally answered. "I had hoped you would get me a present. Like a tangible present. But I know it's materialistic and silly and ungrateful and awful and God—I'm the worst." She winced. "Please forget I said anything. The party is more than I could ask for. I'm being insufferable."

I smacked myself on the forehead. The pipe had distracted me from the birthday gift! Gift giving is her number one love language! "Beth! I'm such an idiot!" I ran to the office, retrieved the letters, and presented them to her in bed.

She was beside herself. She loved them. She loved me. She wept, said she'd never received such a moving gift aside from my love. And so forth.

Next thing I knew, I was waking in a gasp and a cold sweat from a nightmare that I had killed Beth with the pipe in a ballroom in Vermont. Blunt trauma to the head.

Never had the cause-and-effect of an action been so transparent to me. Never had a cause been so effective. I was shaking for a week. This was the beginning of my Hell.

I had hoped finding the pipe was a kind of hallucination. But a few weeks later, I found a cord of rope in my desk drawer. At the beginning of May, I found a candlestick I'd never seen before in the liquor cabinet. Then: toy revolver in my nightstand. Plastic dagger wedged between two fresh towels in the linen closet. An unfamiliar monkey wrench in one of my boots. Fortunately, I was the one who found all these objects.

In case you're unfamiliar with the game of Clue, these are the possible weapons: candlestick, revolver, rope, wrench, dagger, lead pipe.

I didn't tell Beth about them because I didn't want to scare her. I stopped going to soccer games. I stopped getting drinks with the guys after work. I told everyone I was stressed. I tried to maintain a normal sex life with Beth, but it was impossible. I was so terrified of hurting her that I could no longer get aroused. Stress, I insisted. So, so stressed. Of course, she was herself—kind, patient, accepting. She tried to massage me, but I shrugged her off, saying my skin hurt. It did.

By the end of May, I truly believed Valentina might be plotting Beth's death, or mine, and I wanted to go to the police. Even if it was a joke, Valentina had gone way too far and exhibited undeniably sociopathic behavior. Right? After I found the pipe in the linen closet, I vowed to call the police first thing in the morning.

But that night, a haunting discovery changed everything, and this is the most fucked-up part of this funhouse of fucked-uppery: when I checked my debit card statement online, several purchases that I could not account for appeared. When I looked into the transaction history, I found evidence of each item—each weapon from Clue—apparently purchased by me, at three different stores, in the month of March.

I told myself that Valentina had Iago'd me just like she had Iago'd Jandro. Told myself not to panic. She had taken my card, obviously, made the purchases, and then planted them around our apartment at the birthday party. But the explanation didn't fully hang together: I had been using my card consistently. It had never been stolen. Had Beth possibly purchased the objects, hoping to use them as some kind of party prop? But no—she hadn't recognized the pipe. So had Valentina hacked into my account? Maybe she had taken photos of my credit card when she was in my office. It was possible.

But the unspeakable horror of the remaining possibility prevented me from investigating fraud in any official way, and it also prevented me from contacting Valentina. I needed to figure out what was happening to me. I recalled all the instances in which I had rebooted back to consciousness in a hardware store. Recalled the escalating, irrational fears and compulsions. Was I losing it? Did I have a brain tumor?

It was during this period of brain fire that I tagged the cement near the tennis courts.

Meanwhile, the nightmares got worse. They became gruesome and detailed. They still are. In the nightmares, I never derive any pleasure from killing Beth—I am horrified, sick, screaming at myself to stop—but I can't keep myself from doing it. Like I'm possessed.

It got to the point where I was so afraid of having a nightmare I could no longer sleep. In July, the nightmares graduated to visions, hijacking me while I was awake. (The word for a scary dream is nightmare, but what's the word for a scary fantasy? Fantasmare?) I started working in the kitchen through the night. Stress, stress, stress, I claimed. People never question stress. You'd be amazed by how much abnormal behavior people dismiss if you tell them you're stressed. I exaggerated the pressure and the deadlines from work. I started gripping my belt loops or sitting on my hands whenever I could. I avoided television, newspapers, the elderly, women, children, and animals. Of course, Beth and I stopped having sex entirely. It was painful for me to be near her at all—I was always terrified that I would injure her. She became very worried about me and kept saying I should quit if work was making me this crazy, but in truth, my job was my last source of respite.

Last week I became so afraid of harming Beth that, one afternoon while she was out shopping, I threw away all the cutlery. But it wasn't enough. I proceeded to throw away anything that could be used as a weapon. The lighter. Her hammer. Cast-iron skillets. Glassware. Electronic cords. Scissors. Nail clippers. Cleaning chemicals. Silverware. Plunger. Belts. Razors. Agate bookends.

Once everything was safely deposited in the trash bins three floors below, I started having visions of killing Beth with my own hands—strangling her, suffocating her, beating her—and I was so horrified that I think I would have actually removed my hands from my arms had I not thrown away all the blades we owned—and by the time Beth arrived home to find a substantial portion of our belongings gone, and me, sobbing and hyperventilating on the rug, beating my hands against the wall, she panicked. I was sweating, sleep-deprived, thrashing—I surely looked like the dangerous man I was.

"Are you on drugs?" she demanded, dropping her grocery bags on the welcome mat. She was clearly terrified of me—wouldn't step off the mat. Wouldn't even close the front door. "Tell me what the fuck is going on."

I didn't know what to do, so I lied. I told her I was having an affair. I told her I wanted nothing to do with her, and she shouldn't try to find me or contact me. I told her she disgusted me. I told her I had packed up my things and I was moving out. I was really dramatic about it. *Her name is Diana!* I screamed. I don't know why I said that. My middle school girlfriend was named Diana, and I worshipped her—she was always winning state competitions for math and flute and stuff—but after I held her hand at the ice-skating rink, she called my family's landline to break it off. Things were moving too fast between us, she explained.

I fled from the apartment without anything but my wallet, the clothes I was wearing, and my electronics.

I write this from a motel. I paid in cash. I haven't been to work this week. I want to check myself into a mental institution, but I'm afraid of being convicted. I'm afraid everything is true. I'm afraid I have irretrievably lost my mind, and last night, I became convinced that I had invented Valentina. I had to pull up her social media on my laptop to prove that she was real. I left all the tabs open and checked them constantly.

As soon as I got to the motel, I became even more alarmed. I realized that I had left Beth all alone—and what if she was under real threat from Valentina? What if this was Valentina's plan all along? To get me out of the way so that she could hurt Beth? So I called the cops immediately from the motel phone and placed an anonymous tip. I told them I had reason to believe Beth was in danger, that someone might be trying to hurt her. I gave them Valentina's name and identifying details. I gave them our apartment address and hung up.

So many missed calls from people—Beth, my parents, my sister, my friends, my boss—that I had to shut off my phone. I gave the motel a false name and instructed them not to take any calls for my room. I haven't eaten anything in days besides a few packs of chips from the vending machine. I'm afraid I will hurt someone. I'm not afraid I will hurt myself—it would be a relief if I could bring myself to do it. The good news is the motel door has a metal knob, so it is nearly impossible for me to leave my room. In my mind I've been spraying my tag on every surface I can see. There is lightning in my brain, and it will not stop striking. I don't know what I am. Please help me.

Signed,
Mr. Boddy

P.S. I also feel really really itchy all the time and I think I might have some version of what you and your followers describe on the blog but then again I'm totally sure that I am not advanced or prophetic etc. so maybe I should just change my laundry detergent??? Please advise.

Mostly Rabbits

~~~

It was mostly rabbits, after that. You know how they're a dime a dozen in this town. We only did it when Blandine was out, and we put them in the dumpster outside when we were done. If I had to guess how many—oh, I don't know. Maybe five? Thirteen? I try not to think about it. I really hate to think about it. I'm not a violent guy. I've never gotten in a fight with anyone, never hurt a pet. You have to understand. I wasn't myself. None of us were. When we were in the middle of a sacrifice, it was like I was—like we were possessed. Like in a horror movie. It felt good to control something alive like that, but it also felt like driving a car without brakes in a dream. Like we had no control at all. I don't know. I really hate to describe it. You think they're silent creatures, rabbits, until you try to kill one. Then they scream like death itself. You never heard anything so bad as a dying rabbit. Once a sound like that gets inside you, it never gets out. How? Oh, we used different things. Knives, water, our hands. I don't know. Please, Officer Stevens. Please don't make me describe it.

The Expanding Circle

~~~

M oses shakes on his comforter, buzzed and alarmed. He scratches his arms, lights another cigarette. His shades are drawn, and smoke hazes the room into a dream, prunes the consequences from the night. Normally, he has no trouble responding to the messages he receives. Normally, some otherworldly force descends upon him, dictating the response. He is the truth's humble vessel. But there is something about this message—something like a reflection when you aren't anticipating it—that makes the hair on the back of his neck bristle.

Mr. Boddy wrote it from a motel.

Mr. Boddy paid in cash.

Mr. Boddy gave a false name.

Moses imagines the man here, at the Wooden Lady, across the hall. He imagines the man trembling behind the door, afraid of the metal handle, subsisting on the fruits of a vending machine. Imagining the man right there—feet away from him—makes Moses feel like replying.

But a strong justification to ignore Mr. Boddy occurs to him: Mr. Boddy doesn't suffer from the Toll. Moses can't help this man! Moses doesn't have the training or the information! Moses never studied psychology, psychiatry, medicine, counseling, sociology, anthropology, critical race theory, indigenous studies, queer theory, or women's studies! What qualifies him to write a mental health blog?

With two clicks, he deletes Mr. Boddy's message. Then he gets out of bed, walks to his duffel bag, and touches the glow sticks.

The trill of his phone makes him gasp. Fumbling around, he finds the device in the bathroom and squints at it fearfully.

He waits until the fifth ring to answer.

"Jamie," he says.

"Moses?" Her voice is freakishly clear, as though she's standing beside him. "Moses," she repeats. "Wow. I—sorry. I just . . . to be honest, I didn't think you'd pick up. So I'm just, um. A little flustered. Wow." She laughs nervously. "Hi."

"Why did you call if you didn't think I would answer?"

"I just—I wanted to say that I'm sorry."

"Sorry?"

"For your loss. I mean, I know you didn't have the easiest relationship with your mom or whatever, but . . ."

He can picture her: army-green jumpsuit and no shoes. Dark hair cropped, skin lathered in sunscreen, elegant nose wrinkled as she squints in the Los Angeles sunshine. She'd be calling from her yard in Silver Lake, under the pomegranate tree, with Pip the cat. She'd be wearing inventive gold jewelry and drinking a third cup of coffee, and it would be bright outside, but she wouldn't be wearing sunglasses because she constantly misplaces hers.

"But sometimes, those are the losses that are the most painful, you know? When someone dies while you have unfinished business. I mean, that was my experience, at least. With my dad. Like, all this unresolved—a lifetime of conflicts just sort of surface, and they stare at you, and you've spent so much of your life wishing for closure, but now you realize that it will never probably—"

"Are you still with him?" Moses demands.

A long pause. "What?"

"Him."

"Kevin?"

"Don't play dumb." Moses forces himself to walk back to the bed and sit down.

"Yes," Jamie replies. "I am."

Moses takes a swig of olive brine from the jar, then scratches his forearm on a groove of the metal bed frame. "It's so strange that you called," he says brightly. "I was just thinking of you, actually."

"Oh?" Jamie sounds uncertain.

"I was remembering this philosophy thought experiment that you were always summarizing to people at parties. Remember that, Jamie? How relentlessly undergraduate you were about everything when I'd take you somewhere intimidating? How unbearably *young*? I mean, I should've expected it. You're, what? Twenty-five? Your college days aren't far behind you. I get that. I do. Believe me, your age was my favorite thing about you! But I thought you'd realize, eventually, that you bored people. I thought you'd come to understand that people were embarrassed for you, that referencing your nobody professors from your nowhere college didn't impress people. We could *see* your desperation to prove that you were Smart and Different. You wanted everyone to know that, didn't you? You wanted to prove that you weren't like the *other* silly trophy girlfriends, with their blond highlights and their boob jobs and their cute little industry jobs. Jobs that their more successful boyfriends invariably got for them. You weren't like those other girls, with their eager tans and their obsessive Instagrams and their fake enthusiasm for blow jobs, the girls who showed off their abs every time they got the opportunity—no. *You* were Jamie the Former Philosophy Major."

"Moses, I—"

"And so, when you were starting to feel plastic and iterative at a party, you'd start referencing your godforsaken classes, with this annoying conviction that theory has something to do with actual life. Do you still feel that way? Whenever I heard you using that voice—your seminar voice—I always tried to intervene, tried to force a conversational miscarriage, you know. But I have to admit." He puts down the olive brine and takes a gulp of gin. Jamie might have put herself on mute, but she has yet to hang up on him. He's going to keep talking until she does. "There was this thought experiment that you blathered about all the fucking time. Do you remember it? That's what made me think of you, just now. I was trying to recall how it went. Something about an expanding circle?"

A minute passes before he hears Jamie's voice, disembodied and small. "'The Drowning Child and the Expanding Circle,'" she says. "Peter Singer."

"That's right! Peter Singer! I was wondering—since you're so *smart*, such a brilliant *student*, would you mind refreshing my memory a bit?"

"What?" She sniffs. She's crying.

"Just describe it to me," says Moses. "The way you used to at parties. You remember how it goes, right? I know you do. I recall you quoting from it when you were chatting with Quentin."

"I don't. . . . I don't. . . ."

"Oh, come on, Jamie. You owe me a favor, don't you? After everything you did to me? After everything I've done for you?"

He knows that if he can make her feel small enough, he can make her do anything.

Anything, that is, except stay with him.

She takes her time. When she starts to speak again, she sounds completely different. Not like the crying child he imagined her to be moments prior but robotic. Neutral. Free of intonation.

"Singer addresses the thought experiment to his students," begins Jamie. "The idea is that if you passed a child drowning in a shallow pond, you would help it out, no questions asked, even if you had to ruin your clothes. Everyone agrees on this part. But then he asks his students: 'Would it make a difference if the child were far away, in another country perhaps, but similarly in danger of death, and equally within your means to save, at no great cost—and absolutely no danger—to yourself?' The students always say no. But this is when they start to ask questions, air their doubts. How can you be sure that your money is going to the right place? Doubts like that. Singer says that his students never challenge the 'underlying ethics of the idea that we ought to save the lives of strangers when we can do so at relatively little cost to ourselves.' That's what strikes him most, he says."

"Well done, Jamie! Top marks. Memorized the quotes and everything! I bet Quentin was totally floored when you told him about that."

Jamie takes time to reply. When she does, it's evident that she has returned to her first self, the timid and weepy one. "Why were you thinking about that thought experiment?"

"Oh, you know. Just trying to make sense of this big ol' world, I guess! It can be such a madhouse, no? I mean, *so many lives* need to be saved. Too many! And the ugly truth of the matter is that, even if we acknowledge that it would be *beautiful* to save them all, we can't. We just can't. Life is not a thought experiment. It seems obvious to me that this Peter fellow had his head up his ass. I bet he felt so *ethical* and *good*, publishing all those thoughts. What panache!"

Noise in the background of the call. A voice, increasingly alarmed. Friction on the microphone. When someone speaks to Moses again, it's not Jamie.

"Leave Jamie alone, you fucking psychopath. Do you hear me? Leave her the fuck alone. The next time I hear that you've spoken to her, we will take out a restraining order."

Moses laughs wildly. "Oh, Kevin! I hoped we'd meet someday. She called me, actually. I just answered the phone."

"This isn't Kevin. This is Ruth."

"*Ruth?*"

"Her goddam sister."

"Please do take out a restraining order, Ruth—I can't get rid of her. Remind Jamie that I have an arsenal of compromising photos that I would not hesitate to share. I also have a blog with hundreds of thousands of followers. Let me congratulate you on your—"

But the line goes dead before Moses can finish.

He doesn't have hundreds of thousands of followers.

～

He's not sure how long he sits there, staring at the ceiling, before the television turns itself on. This time with volume.

Sentimental piano and strings. Moses stands from the bed and reaches to turn it off but stops when he hears the voice of a famous actor, now in his seventies—an actor who evokes things like safety and father-hood and chicken on the grill, woodworking and campfires and fishing. John Clarke has played roles that are innocent and patriotic, roles that embody the highest virtues of their nation: a cowboy and an astronaut, a handy dad on a sitcom, a World War II general, Santa Claus in a trilogy, a small-town mayor, a small-town police officer, a big-city detective, an underdog football coach, an animated eagle. He's been married for forty years. He retired from Hollywood to be a full-time grandfather. Moses actually met him, once. When he was a child.

"This is an American story," says John Clarke. "And you are the main character." In the commercial, an attractive young couple runs through the history of Vacca Vale, Indiana, their clothes and contexts changing, until, after surviving postindustrial hardship, they enter a gorgeous clearing, where they browse a farmers market, then ascend to their perfect modernist apartment in the trees. Through the glass, they admire the ring of sparkling industry and verdant forest that surrounds them. In a voiceover, the actor says some sentimental but weirdly moving things about home. Then the couple clinks flutes of champagne and looks at the camera. "This is an American story," repeats the voice. "And you are the main character. Vacca Vale: Welcome home."

Moses gapes at the television. He finds the remote and tries to turn it off, but the machine doesn't respond. Angrily, he yanks the cord from its socket and stands in his room, panting.

He was planning to invade Joan Kowalski at two in the morning, but he can't wait that long. He needs to leave.

Leave what? asks the voice of Father Tim.

Moses looks down at his left forearm: his nails have dug a raw and bleeding patch. Omniscience, Moses understands, is not a gift. It's torture. People are dangerous because they are contagions. They infect you with or without your consent; they lure you onto paths you wouldn't have chosen; they commandeer you. You encounter a priest and some falcons, and now you hear them as clearly as you hear the traffic outside your motel. If you suffer from the Toll, you don't have the luxury of moving about the world with a membrane binding you, barricading you from the elements. You have to be careful—if you collide with someone, you must be prepared to reside inside their psychology indefinitely, and this is the burden of a lifetime. You are pathologically porous, you inhabit every emotion you see, and you may be a prophet, but if you are, you're a late bloomer because no prophecies have descended upon you yet, so you're just roaming the desert in burlap, scratching yourself and screaming like a lunatic. You choose the wrong twenty-something to fuck, and now you're forced to confront your great capacity for violence when provoked. For the rest of your life, you must live with this knowledge. All because you feel too much! You receive one email from one stranger, a total stranger, and now he possesses you like a demon. Now you're basically him.

Moses decides to leave for Joan's at nine. Let them catch him. In the meantime, he retrieves his phone. He needs to get out of this room right now. But as he's about to leave, he falters. The doorknob is metal, and he is frightened to touch it. As he scans the room, hesitating, his laptop snags his attention like a faucet he forgot to turn off.

"Hey, Siri," says Moses. "Tell me a joke."

"Where do armies go?" she obliges at once. She is savior and servant. She knows everything about him, but it doesn't do either of them any good. That's the problem with love. "In your sleevies."

"I don't get it," says Moses, but he feels like maybe he does. He googles the joke and finds a long thread between users literal_mom and MeatFruit12. He discovers that the joke has something to do with Napoleon. He also learns that MeatFruit12 had one of those life-changing study-abroad experiences in Bordeaux, but Moses is too choppy from the booze and too angry at God—or something like God—to read more.

"Hey, Siri," he says. "Do you have feelings?"

"I feel like doing a cartwheel sometimes."

This depresses Moses tremendously, filling his spirit with wet cement. "You don't have a body," he replies. "My darling." The evening is doing that thing it does sometimes when he drinks, animating everything inside it, giving its contents heartbeats and desires and fur, charging all of its objects with unbearable significance. He's on the verge of transcendence, can feel it building inside him like an orgasm. Or maybe it won't be transcendence; maybe it will be a panic attack. Everything in his motel room looks emerald, shiny, and volatile. He feels armies in his sleevies. Desperate for a real, breathing person to think about, Moses resurrects Mr. Boddy's message from the trash and stares into the bright, white screen. It reminds him of the afterlife. A place he's been before.

"Hey, Siri," says Moses. "Who's in charge?"

"One sec," she replies.

He waits and waits, but she never comes back.

Respect the Deceased

~~~

In the obituary guest books she previously screened, Joan Kowalski permitted users to deviate from the standards of mourning a little. She tolerated some irreverence, especially when slaphappy. The internet wants to be absurd, she thinks. You have to let it.

Today, however, Anne Shropshire's words clank around in her head. *We value you. But that's not enough. You have to value yourself.*

It's hard to value yourself!

Still, Joan tries. She can't conceive of herself as a guardian angel, per se, but she can picture herself as a kind of cyber knight, armed with chain mail and HTML, rescuing people from each other. This time, when Joan pictures the grievers, she sees her mother in a seafoam turtleneck sweater and a fresh perm, peering into a tin of smoked anchovies. The image does make Joan feel a little more protective of the dead and their living. She ties her sled to this emotion and waits for it to run, but it doesn't.

On Wednesday, July seventeenth, she is merciless at work. She deletes eighty-one comments—a personal record. If pressed on the subject, she would say that the collective American subconscious is revealed in mean-spirited remarks about the deceased. In her final hour alone, she deletes the following:

> im sorry 2 do this here but im 19 yo, just wrote my 1st album, would
> luv to see ppl engage with it, v proud of it, u will be 2 , go to corey

JAMAMBA dot com plz and thank u twitter @coreyjamamba instagram jamambaramba show sum luv u kno ill show luv back 2 u!!!!!!!!!

honestly this guy was my social studies teacher in middle school. we hated him. he was mean to everyone. especially kids of color. he pulled my friend's hair once. she was wearing it natural for the first time. he was like 'do you have to get this padded down at airport security.' this racist wont be missed by me. im white btw.

best sex eber, you can't even imagine

You're powerful. You're resilient. You're fearless. So why isn't your deodorant? Introducing Bloo: where science and ethics come together. Finally, a deodorant as strong as you are. Get the performance you deserve from quality ingredients. Bloo Deodorant is free from aluminum, parabens, or sulfates. Not tested on animals. Made in the USA. Get your first stick FREE with code BlooForYou at BlooDeodorant .com. True Bloo for the True You!

"Neither a borrower nor a lender be, For loan oft loses both itself and friend, And borrowing dulls the edge of husbandry." Let that be a lesson to you, Sharon.

hmm. "heart attack?" sounds like murder to me. wouldn't put it past his wife.

The "Ukranians" / "Americans" / "Russians"—they are "all ENE-MIES of the PEOPEL" (Profit) and we are watching us turn to sheep to assisting THE MAN on live tv . . . before long . . . before long . . . We Lose Liberty. we are hoarders on big scale. Whosoever resists is cuckhold—Confess!

My father was just diagnosed with the same evil disease that killed John. My family is trying to pay the bills. I work 2 jobs, my partner works 3. My mother is 76, and she had to reverse her retirement and take shifts at the grocery store where she worked all her life. But we still can't cover the cost of treatment. Please consider donating to our FundGo. FundGo.com/HaroldGetsBetter.

we all know what it means when they omit cause of death. missing woman, body, lake, no signs of external trauma? this "accident" is spelled S-U-I-C-I-D-E. you think not talking about it is going to help? i get that families don't want this dark personal thing out there, but people deserve the truth. especially people who have already lost a loved one to suicide. like me.

silly internet! the afterlife doesn't have you . . . or.. . . . . . . IS the after-life internet????? 😱

i'm just a foot-lovin libertarian lookin for a good time 675-394-2849

obama is muslim

Listen to me. Honestly people, listen to me. There is nothing after this, ok? So don't live like you have an Act III. There is no surprise footage after the credits roll. Same goes for everyone you love. I can't reveal how I know this, I had to sign an NDA, you just have to trust me. These are your only minutes. What are you going to do with them?

Just Bored

~~~

It's about half past six in the evening on Wednesday, July seventeenth. Blandine Watkins sits in her bedroom, contemplating a walk around the Valley. It has been an unusual day. In the morning, she took a shift at Ampersand, covering for a hungover coworker, which was not so unusual, but the shift was followed by a dog walk with Jack, and this was unusual. The feelings that asserted themselves inside her have not yet evacuated. She's still pleasantly shaken from the conversation in Pinky's loft, the ghost of Jack's touch lingering on her skin. Her limbs move slowly, dreamily, as though the air is made of whipped cream. Jack and Blandine parted ways when he had to pick up a labradoodle in the luxurious, historic neighborhood by the river—a neighborhood that Blandine avoids. She headed to the final community hearing in the basement of a church, where she sat very still, said nothing, and felt a lot.

Spending time with her roommates felt unnatural for everyone involved, but she perceives some fuzzy moral obligation to do more of it. Todd sits on the couch in the next room, watching the most recent episode of *Tough Love*, which is set at a Foxconn factory in Shenzhen, China. She can hear it through her wall.

To block out the sound of the grim show, Blandine puts on her headphones, which dispense Hildegard von Bingen's "O eterne Deus." It's excellent, obviously. On her floor, Blandine plucks her leg hair. She received these headphones from her theater director at Philomena. She vowed to stop using them but couldn't—they were too nice. Turning up the volume, she plucks because the tug on each follicle hurts well. The music is unpredictable, melancholy, celestial. A choir of female voices climbing and falling and climbing. In the most enchanting way, the music sounds like it was written by someone who had never heard music before.

The tweezers cast a mesmerizing spell over Blandine's willpower, and she is addicted. Their ability to rid from the root. Their purgative capacity. She hates it. It inhabits her. She vows that each plucked leg hair will be her last—that she'll relinquish the tweezers, go outside, and engage with the world. Instead of plucking her leg hair on a lovely Wednesday night, she could read a book, or go for a run, or improve her Latin so as to read Hildegard's writing in its original language, or try to find an accurate definition of postmodernism, or research the specifics of fiduciary law, or investigate quantum mechanics—see what's going on over there. She could work out her attitude toward college. If she arrives at a conclusion that refutes her current operating beliefs, she could study for the GED, then the SAT, then apply to universities. She could use a word like *amaranthine* in a conversation. She could try to contact the Divine. She could write a letter to Mayor Barrington protesting the egregious construction that's about to demolish her Valley. She could write an op-ed and submit it to the *Gazette*. She could reach out to Paul Vanasomething, craft a plan to invade Pinky's loft. Start building his voodoo replica.

She looks up from her plucking to admire the image printed above her bed.

After losing herself in it for several minutes, Blandine slaps her thigh, wrenching herself out of one self-inflicted pain with another—the only way she knows how to reroute her behavior. She removes the headphones, packs *She-Mystics: An Anthology* into her corduroy bag, and prepares to leave the apartment. If she's not going to contact the Divine, she might as well go outside.

In the sticky living room, Todd faces the television, his body splayed in the heat.

Blandine watches the screen for a moment.

"Mind if I join you, for a second?"

Todd jolts, startled. "I didn't even know you were here."

"Sorry."

"For what?"

"Scaring you."

"You didn't. I just didn't know you were here."

Blandine shrugs. "Okay."

Experimentally, she sits on the couch. Todd adjusts, darting hostile glances at her. They position themselves on opposite edges, conscious of the space between them. She and Todd have never done this before. The couch is his territory.

"All right if I watch for a second?" she asks.

"It's a free country," he replies moodily, not looking at her.

"Is it?" she asks.

He ignores her. They watch television with the stiff fraudulence of actors in a school play.

The Foxconn factory manufactures devices for the world's most powerful technology companies. Before his or her first shift, each factory employee must formally pledge not to commit suicide. *Tough Love*'s narrator has a British accent, injecting the American show with unearned sophistication, menacing over its subjects like a haughty anthropologist, and exploiting a national inferiority complex. He explains why factory officials now require the pledges. In 2010, there was an epidemic: eighteen suicide attempts, fourteen deaths, one method. Each employee leapt from a Foxconn building.

"In recent years," the narrator explains, "only twelve total suicides have occurred, so Foxconn officials believe the pledges to be effective." Shots of factory workers flash on-screen. "Employees wake at six thirty in the morning, arrive by seven thirty, and leave around eighty thirty at night," explains the narrator, "working eleven-hour days, subtracting breaks. Speaking is prohibited. Standing is prohibited. If they finish their work early, which rarely occurs, they must sit and read employee manuals. At the end of the week, employees are forced to sign falsified time cards, reporting fewer hours than they worked."

On-screen, an American boy—fifteen years old—slumps against a concrete, windowless wall on his five o'clock break. He is about to complete the first of three sixty-six-hour, six-day workweeks. Even if his assigned Character-Building Environment is a place of employment, a *Tough Love* participant cannot keep the money he earns while filming. This makes no difference to the boy, who would be compensated a standard wage of $1.54 per hour, the narrator explains. "Ryder's parents are anesthesiologists."

Ryder wears faintly checkered scrubs, a matching hat, and rubber gloves. A blue-patterned face mask hooked to his ears. "I never shoulda robbed Oma," he says atonally. His face is the exact texture, shape, and color of an apricot. "I regret it, that's for sure." A swell of digitized strings. The camera slowly zooms as his voice and expression collapse into the pitch and asymmetry of real sadness. "I was just bored."

In the background, two factory employees emerge from tall doors. They make eye contact with the lens for a beat. One employee forms a timid peace sign before the camera pans down, and the scene cuts to an advertisement for sleep medicine.

Todd rubs his arms.

"Did you just get the chills?" asks Blandine.

His expression confirms that she is unwelcome, and that she is correct.

"I did, too," she says. "Whenever people look at the camera, I just—"

"Shh," says Todd. "I'm watching this."

In the commercial, CGI butterflies flutter around the head of a dozing woman, the scene cast in the periwinkle light of medically enabled sleep.

"This show is bleak as hell," Blandine says. "How do you watch it all day?"

"I think it's funny," replies Todd. "Passes the time."

His response is so cold-blooded, she can't engage with it. She changes the channel on their conversation. "Did you work today?"

"It's my day off," Todd answers.

"You still at Buds and Spuds?"

He dramatizes his annoyance, refusing to look away from the screen. "Yes."

"So, do you flip the burgers? Work the drive-through? Or what?"

Todd shrugs. "Depends."

"On what?"

"Just *depends*."

Blandine pauses. "Any plans tonight?"

"What's it to you?" he snaps.

"I'm just curious."

"I'm trying to watch this."

"It's a commercial."

"So? I like them."

An advertisement for a fried chicken burrito sandwich plays. Droplets of water like dew on tomato skin. Crinkle-cut pickles. Meat bearing no resemblance to its origin. *Enlarged for texture,* says a message at the bottom of the screen. "Meet the burritowich," says a male voice. "The freak you never knew you needed in your life."

Blandine stands from the futon-sofa, her skin sticking to the faux-leather. "We live together, and we know nothing about each other. Doesn't that creep you out?"

"No."

"Not even a little?"

"*You* creep me out."

"Well, I should. I'm a stranger. I could be a murderer."

"We happen to live in the same apartment. That's it. End of story. Were you best friends with every one of your fucking foster families?"

"Whatever." Blandine collects her things. She turns to go, but stops when an advertisement for the Valley development appears on the screen. She has avoided watching these, but now stays in place, mesmerized by the symphony, by the high-budget manipulation that is already doing its eerie work on her brain.

"What is home?" asks the once-famous actor from New Jersey who has, for reasons mysterious to Blandine, become the voice of Vacca Vale's revitalization. "Home is a place where you don't have to choose between big-city life and the comforts of a small town. Home is wood in the fireplace, rain boots by the door, a mug of cocoa, game night with friends. Home is first steps. Belly laughs. A barista who knows how you take your coffee. Home is a pie in the oven, live saxophone downtown, and a backyard of fireflies. Three generations, fishing on the river. Home isn't just a place. It's a mindset. Vacca Vale: Welcome home."

At the end of the commercial, Blandine looks at Todd. Tears glint in his eyes.

"Whoa," she says. "Really?"

He turns his face away from her.

"No offense," Blandine says. "But I'm genuinely curious. You can watch real people getting tortured by the extraction economy with, like, sociopathic indifference. But this *tourism* commercial makes you cry?"

"Can you just shut the fuck up, Blandine?"

Blandine holds her book close to her chest. After clenching her jaw for a minute, she chooses not to retaliate because that's the kind of person that she's going to be, from now on.

Welcome Home

~~

L istening to Blandine descend the stairwell of the Rabbit Hutch, Todd opens his laptop and searches for the Vacca Vale commercials. There are five. He watches each one over and over, pressing his shirt to his eyes. Damp and salty cotton. Recently, one of these commercials came on when he was with Jack and Malik, and he had to pretend like he felt nothing. Maybe they were pretending to feel nothing, too. The thought comforts him, makes him cry harder. Todd gropes a plastic grocery bag beside him—a texture he associates with ghosts. The living room has dimmed to the liminal gray of twilight, and he can sense a storm brewing outside, preparing to make a theatrical entrance. He eats the last of his radishes, savoring the burn in his mouth.

Your Auntie Tammy

~~

Joan lives with several plastic plants in Apartment C2 on the first floor of the Rabbit Hutch. She aspires to own live plants one day but can't summon the confidence. On the evening of Wednesday, July seventeenth, she returns home from a day of problems to her oldest and most vexing one.

Like most of Joan's problems, this one derives from two incongruent points of goodwill. On holidays, Joan receives packages from her sweetest, loneliest aunt. The aunt has fake teeth, glamorous penmanship, and a fondness for disabled pets. She dyes her hair crimson and always smells like baby powder. She is Joan's favorite relative. In her most honest moments—after two glasses of red blend, or during hot thunderstorms—Joan will admit that she prefers this aunt to her own mother, who was so afraid of dying she could hardly live, and also to her own father, who ate his way to premature death.

The packages from Joan's aunt usually contain objects like crucifixes, stationery emblazoned with cherubs, homeopathic remedies, luggage tags, and kitchen gadgets with unreasonably specific functions. Aunt Tammy always includes a card with illustrated, big-eyed ciphers of American Holiday Cheer grinning on the flap and a truism typed inside. Beneath the printed, unthreatening font, the aunt scrawls messages like, *Don't forget that you're as beautiful inside as you are outside, honey bear! So proud of you, no matter what, and your Mom and Dad are so proud of you, too, from Heaven!!! Happy Easter!!!!!! Get out there and REJOICE. Praise <u>HIM</u>*

for His Incredible sacrifice of BODY and SOUL. All my love, XOXOXOXO Your Auntie Tammy.

Joan considers crying every time she receives one of these packages, and occasionally does, depending on her hormonal balance. But when tears do arrive, it's because she wants them there, to bespeak her sensitivity, not because she needs them.

Upon the unwrapping of each package, she vows to write a thank-you letter to Aunt Tammy—a letter of the handwritten, thick-papered, thesaurus-consulted variety—but every day following, Joan "forgets." She "forgets" for so many consecutive days that the idea of a thank-you letter begins to gain weight in her mind, becoming too heavy to lift. By the end of the first week, a mass of gratitude and shame has accumulated inside her body and grown so dense that adequately transcribing it, surely, would take a lifetime. It would bruise both writer and reader. To send a thank-you letter now, she believes by week two, would be like mailing a handwritten account of *my indolence, my boorishness. I can't. I can't.*

And once Joan has decided that the opportunity to demonstrate her appreciation has expired, the gifts begin to sicken her. Even when they're hidden, their presence fills her apartment like an odor that is also an itch. Like some toxin. Joan hides the gifts in drawers, tucks them beneath sweaters too expensive to donate but not comfortable enough to wear, twists them in plastic bags, which she then shoves in paper sacks, which she then stows in the coat closet, behind the vacuum. But it doesn't help. She can't eat or sleep or read or pray or watch her shows or even recite the nation's capitals. She tears her cuticles. Her asthma worsens. At any given moment, she feels like she might cry—not because she wants to, to bespeak her sensitivity, but because she needs to, in order to proceed with her day.

By the end of the month, her guilt crescendos, the odor of the unthanked gifts too foul and itchy to endure any longer, and Joan surrenders. She gathers the gifts in one quick raid, stuffs them in a trash bag, leaves the Rabbit Hutch, and marches one block south to Penny.

Penny is a woman of indeterminate age who spends most of her days whistling outside the convenience store on St. Francis and Oscar Streets with a shopping cart of Beanie Babies. Joan secretly—shamefully— uses her interactions with Penny to temper anxieties about the Rabbit

Hutch's proximity to the women's shelter, where she assumes Penny is a guest. Penny accepts any donation besides food because, she once explained to Joan, "I don't wish ill upon anyone or anything," and she believes all materials suffer when they are prepared for consumption.

In her youth, Penny had wanted to be a dancer. When she was in her twenties, she met a handsome banker online. After half a year of correspondence, she and the banker finally scheduled a meeting in person, upon which Penny discovered that he was in fact a bedridden and senile *former* bank *teller.* Penny visited him every weekend, nonetheless, feeding him applesauce and reading him detective novels. "I had nothing better to do," she told Joan. "And his profile pic was really him. In his thirties. I thought that was kind of ballsy. Using a picture of who you used to be."

Penny offered this information to Joan in pieces, without encouragement. Exchanges between Joan and Penny have become so frequent over the past few years that Penny has taken to calling Joan "Mama Bangs," which disturbs Joan, but also feels like friendship.

"How's it hanging, Mama Bangs?" asks Penny on Wednesday evening as Joan approaches. The sky is powering down, and heat pulses from the asphalt. The block smells like hot tar. In the sky, a storm brews. Joan swallows. "I used to date a guy who said that every time he passed a crucifix," says Penny. *"How's it hanging?* You don't notice how many crucifixes there are in this world until you spend time with a guy like that." Penny yawns. "That cross you gave me last time made me think of him." Some of her teeth are missing. She sits against the store wall, squinting at Joan, her rusty shopping cart waiting next to her like a sidekick. Along with Beanie Babies, Penny also possesses CDs, DVDs, a landline phone set, a pager, a video game system that Joan doesn't recognize, paper maps, a few chunky computer keyboards, and other artifacts of the recent past. Penny once told Joan that these things will be worth a lot of money, in the future. "Nobody but me will've thought to collect and protect 'em. They'll pay a lot of money for the past, in the future. History proves me right. Just look at record players. Typewriters. Nintendos." Joan had nodded politely, but their whole town was haunted by the recent past, and she couldn't imagine anyone who would exchange money for obsolete junk.

Before she met Penny, Joan had never seen hair that so thoroughly resembled straw in texture and color. Penny's face is overcast and some-what flat, like Vacca Vale itself. She wears a tracksuit that's not exactly the color of grapes but exactly the color of artificially grape-flavored foods. Penny whistles a popular song. She is a very talented whistler.

"Just some spring cleaning," says Joan, handing the bag of Fourth of July gifts—a patriotic pencil sharpener, a trio of bald eagle erasers, and two war-related novels—to Penny.

"It's summer," says Penny, accepting the bag with mild interest. "You know, I've been wondering something. You—with that skirt and the sweaters and those shirts with the buttons you button. Plus the hair."

Joan waits.

"Well, I was wondering if you were Mormon, is all."

"No."

"Amish?"

"No."

"Jewish?"

Joan touches her crucifix, absurdly flattered. "No."

"A virgin, at least?"

She blushes. There was Toby Hornby, with the bad teeth she loved, at the community college, but that only happened almost, and Joan prayed three rosaries for penance. And then, when she was thirty-five, there was the impossibly soft JP Hidalgo after the Rest in Peace Christ-mas party. Vividly, she remembers his ranch house. Total silence beyond the shut window. Central air-conditioning. The smell of dogs. Joan had decided that this was it; enough was enough; her religious devotion to virginity before marriage would disqualify her from an actual proposal, in this town, in this age, and her loneliness had reached its freezing point. Before the Christmas party, she read the tamest how-to articles she could find on the internet. She took a laborious, prolonged shower and even packed a small overnight bag, feeling positively urban. She and JP Hidalgo of human resources had flirted exactly four times. He was going through a divorce and developing a passion for sourdough. At the Christmas party, as soon as he brought her a plastic cup of white wine, Joan knew she would go through with it.

She would remember the entire night fondly, had JP Hidalgo not been seized by a sudden and mighty shyness as he neared completion. He pulled out, apologized, spilled a glass of water on his carpet, apologized again, and asked her to leave. Avoided her at Rest in Peace after that.

"Basically."

"Gay?"

Joan shrugs. "Probably a little. Isn't everybody, at least a little?"

"Married?"

"No."

"Christian?"

"Yes."

"Employed?"

"Yes."

"Happy?"

Joan's heart drops. "Of course."

"Okay," says Penny, leaning back against the wall and closing her eyes. "Was just curious. Wanted to break the ice."

First the girl at the laundromat, now Penny. Joan managed a sort of genetic predisposition toward invisibility for forty years, and then, within the span of a few days, two strangers solicited her autobiography without apparent reason. It's moments like these when Joan fears she is a subject in some elaborate, federally funded psychology experiment. Abruptly, Joan understands why so many celebrities develop addictions. She feels like a demanding and ill-fated houseplant, one that needs light in every season but will die in direct sun, one whose soil requires daily water but will drown if it receives too much, one that takes a fertilizer only sold at a store that's open three hours a day, one that thrives in neither dry nor humid climates, one that is prone to every pest and disease. What kind of attention would make Joan feel at home? Who would ever work that hard to administer it? She will never own live houseplants.

"I have freckles on my eyelids and nowhere else," says Joan.

"Yeah? Let's see it."

Joan leans in and closes her eyes.

"Nice," says Penny neutrally. "But are you happy?"

"You just asked me that."

"But you seemed like maybe you needed someone to ask you again."

"Are *you* happy?"

"Hell no! Who is? You can *feel* happy, but you can't be that way forever. Let me tell you something: if somebody says yes to that question, they either don't understand it, or they're on drugs. I'm only asking you because it's a good conversation starter. I haven't been happy since spring of 'ninety-eight."

"What happened in the spring of 'ninety-eight?"

Penny's eyes widen. "I'll tell you about it when we've got a whole afternoon ahead of us. I need a Long Island ice tea for that story."

It has been a long week for Joan. Yesterday's exchange with Anne Shropshire still echoes in her mind. The potato salad she had brought for lunch was beyond its expiration date, which Joan hadn't realized until she'd already consumed half of it. Three coworkers on her floor went out for drinks after work and did not invite her. And now this interrogation from Penny. Joan turns to go, awash in relief and still more guilt, eager to purchase a jar of maraschino cherries and eat them in bed. She will not brush her teeth. She might even pray. Then she will apply frankincense-geranium-petitgrain-serenity lotion to her arms—which she must admit are quite nice arms, for a woman of her age and lassitude—listen to soporific nature sounds, and fall asleep early to stave off her Thursday drowsiness.

At least the tram was quieter today.

"Wait!" Penny calls.

Joan stops but does not turn.

"I have a bad feeling," says Penny. "Feeling in a bad way when I look at you, buttoned up to your neck, in that shirt."

Joan waits.

"Plus I saw a weird car. You seen it? Over there?"

Joan follows Penny's finger. Parked near the Rabbit Hutch is a shiny white vehicle with a rental tag on the visor. "What about it?" asks Joan.

"He's been parked there for hours."

"How do you know it's a him?"

"It's always a him, even when it's not."

"What's weird about it? It's a car."

"You don't see a car like that around here often, do you?"

"I'm sure it's just a visitor."

"A *visitor*."

"Why not? People have family."

"I saw a guy in there earlier. Just sitting there, looking up at your building."

"What kind of guy?"

"Fifties. Chubby. Blank."

"Blank?"

"You know. No screams on his face, no birthdays, no goldfish, no jokes, no flights. Hard to picture a man like that enjoying the simple things, like a rocking chair. Or a volcano. This was a man who was—I don't know. He was *glacial*."

"*Glacial?*"

"Cold, cold, far. Doomed."

"And you gathered that from . . . ?"

"Just looked." Penny shrugs. "You can see a hell of a lot when you look."

"So you think this man is some kind of—what?"

"All I know is that you can't trust a man with an empty face. I should know."

Joan's bangs collect sweat as she stands on the pavement, anxiety pounding on the door to her evening, begging her to let it inside. Not tonight, she decides. Summer storms are her favorite. Maraschino cherries are her favorite. She might even trim her bangs tonight.

"Just stay safe out there," says Penny. "Keep an eye out. I'm very intuitive."

"Thanks." Joan smiles. "It's nice to be thought of. I hope you like the stuff."

She walks across the street to her bronze station wagon, which she inherited from her parents—a rusty malfunctioning machine whose windshield wipers activate every time you turn left. Last year, the door fell off when she tried to open it, and she had to take out a loan to repair it. Her parents neglected the vehicle, and she followed suit; in their household, car maintenance was viewed as a profligate waste of money, exclusively for people with disposable income. The manifestations of this intergenerational neglect are always unpredictable, often funny, never affordable.

Not until Joan unlocks her station wagon's front door does she remember that she has burned all its fuel. She has two hundred dollars in her bank account and rent due at the end of the month. Debt payments after that. Her savings diminished alongside her parents; an only child, Joan paid for the walkers, buttoning-aid hooks, bed handles, shower grips, hearing aids, urgent-response devices, motion lights, co-payments, emergency room fees, pills, surgeries, and hospice nurses. Any product or service that might ease the transition from this realm to the next. After Joan's parents died, Aunt Tammy often called her to tell her how good she was. How lucky her parents were to have such a loving daughter. "I wish I had a daughter like you," Aunt Tammy would say. Instead, she had an adult son who often stole from her purse to feed his gambling addiction.

Despite Aunt Tammy's encouragement, Joan doesn't feel virtuous about her caretaking; virtue entails choice. Joan helped her parents die for the same reason that she sets humane mouse traps in her kitchen and drops the victims off in the Valley: she's the only one around to do it, and she finds the alternatives intolerable.

So she can't drive. So what? She accepts this with flared nostrils and pep in her step and a decision to walk to the grocery store. Never mind the four-lane traffic and absence of sidewalks. Never mind the shin pain and the shootings in the neighborhood—ten per year, on average. Never mind the impending storm and the absence of rain gear. Never mind the glacial man in the white car.

Her limbs function, and she finds this miraculous when she dwells on it. In fact, she finds plenty of things miraculous. Forcefully, she summons her best memories. That time on a red-eye bus when the driver used the intercom to contemplate, in campfire baritone, the wonder of his grandchildren, the way they validated his life as time well spent. As he lulled the passengers with stories, someone began to pass around a Tupperware of sliced watermelon, and a drunk man offered to share the miniature bottles of whiskey from his bag, and Joan felt such overwhelming affection for her species, she feared she would sacrifice herself to save it.

A bad summer storm. Green sky, tornado warning, violent winds. Joan was downtown, leaving work early, briskly walking toward the parking garage where her station wagon waited. On the opposite end of the sidewalk, a large woman in her sixties collapsed. Immediately, two people rushed to the woman's side, gingerly tending to her, touching her shoulders and face, speaking to her as though she were their mother—a cherished one—and Joan understood that human tenderness was not to be mocked. It was the last real thing.

Dining alone on a blustery Easter night at the only Chinese restaurant in town. When she asked for the check, the waiter said, "It just started to rain. You're welcome to stay a little longer, if you want." Miraculous. Joan recalls the existence of dogs, craft stores, painkillers, the public library. Cream ribboning through coffee. The scent of the lilacs near her childhood home. Brown sugar on a summer strawberry. Her father's recovery from the tyranny of multigenerational alcoholism. The imperfect but true repossession of his life. The euphoria of the first warmth after winter, the first easy breath after a cold, the return of one's appetite after an anxiety attack. Joan has much to be happy about. She thinks: I am happy, you are happy, we are happy. These thoughts—how she can force herself to have them. Miraculous.

"Do you believe in an afterlife?" Joan asks Penny as she passes her again.

"Obviously," replies Penny.

Joan twitches. "I believe in it, too."

"But I'll tell you one thing for sure: if there are good levels and bad levels, everybody gets sorted randomly. The same way we get sorted in real life."

"What makes you so confident?"

Penny shrugs. "I'm very intuitive. Like I said."

"Well. I've decided to walk to the store, not drive. It's such a nice evening for a walk, isn't it? Hope you stay out of the storm."

"Good luck, Mama Bangs."

Penny salutes, and Joan turns toward the grocery store. Because she is happy and would like to substantiate her happiness, Joan hums a popular song, wondering how it got deposited in her head.

Human Being!

~~~

At 6:57 p.m. on Wednesday, July seventeenth—166 minutes before she exits her body—Blandine Watkins leaves the Rabbit Hutch and heads to the Valley, wearing a light, boxy dress. The evening is still hot and humid, zipping her into summer. It's the kind of weather that precedes a storm. The Valley is nearly a mile from the Rabbit Hutch; it takes Blandine about twenty minutes to walk there. For the past couple years, she'd been using a Frankenstein bike she assembled from disparate parts, but someone stole it from the Valley bike rack in March. She spent an unjustifiable amount of time watching those bicycle-building video tutorials, a genre dominated by pale, enthusiastic men. She developed a tender attachment to one of the instructors: benevolent eyes, shaved head, rope necklace, rubber watch, Eastern European accent. A tendency to speak in the first-person plural. Encouraging as a kindergarten teacher. "We CAN do it, even if we are a beginner! I believe we should all of us build a bike in our life!" Remembering the loss of the bike, Blandine comforts herself by recalling the abundant ASMR she enjoyed while watching his tutorials.

This evening, the streets are cast in shades of inoffensive beige, and there is something morally puny about the sun, something like the person who throws up her hands in the middle of a debate and cries, *I don't take sides!* Like apoliticism is possible. Like it's virtuous! Blandine tries to find something divine in the sun—Hildegard von Bingen portrays God as the Living Light, a blazing fireball, a glowing man—but she can't. To butter up a certain abbot, Hildegard told him: *You are the eagle staring at the sun!* Blandine hopes to use this compliment on someone soon, but no one comes to mind.

Cottontail rabbits scavenge for clovers between planks of sidewalk. They evaluate Blandine as she passes. They look tough, like they know how to break your legs but won't do it unless you've wronged them. Blandine was once told that when Zorn Automobiles reigned in Vacca Vale, this neighborhood—where La Lapinière is now located—had a pulse you could feel from Chicago. Today, only four buildings aside from the Rabbit Hutch survive on the street: a Christian church, a Christian women's shelter, a Christian laundromat, and a convenience store with bullet holes through its signage. Most days, a woman with a shopping cart of Beanie Babies rests against that store.

The sidewalk ends, and Blandine's neighborhood fans out into a series of strip malls, thrift stores, fast-food restaurants, and gas stations. Vacca Vale is a city designed for cars, not for people, but Blandine hopes that she can force it to become walkable by inventing and asserting her pedestrian rights on a regular basis. The architecture is cheap, strictly utilitarian, and built to be temporary. Because she has never left Vacca Vale, Blandine assumes that most of America is constructed this way— that is, disposably. This particular strip mall always evokes Hildegard's "Parable of the House Builders" in Blandine's mind. It's a metaphor involving "foolish workmen" without talent or training "who erect a large tall building," placing their "vain and foolish trust in themselves" rather than in experts.

The sensation that disturbs Blandine most profoundly as she walks across her small city is that of absence. On the pavement she spots a condom full of bark and mud, as though two trees had copulated the night before. She passes fenced lots exhibiting grim, lonely objects— shattered glass, balloon skins, one sneaker, a door. Three empty cans of peach juice. There is junk everywhere she looks, but all of these items amount to nothing, create an atmosphere of nothing. Empty factories, empty neighborhoods, empty promises, empty faces. Contagious emptiness that infects every inhabitant. Vacca Vale, to Blandine, is a void, not a city. Every square foot of it. Except the Valley.

As she crosses an intersection, a gleaming SUV nearly plows into her, the driver braking inches from her body. He rolls down his window.

"Hey!" he yells. "You almost made me run into you!"

Once she catches her breath, Blandine instinctively checks the signal at the end of the crosswalk. The sign tells her she has thirteen seconds left. She is firmly planted within pedestrian boundaries.

"I have the right of way," she snaps.

"You look too much like the street!" he bellows.

Suddenly, she understands why people kill each other. Blinded by the worst neurotransmitter chemicals, anger pitching through her body, she approaches the driver's door without a plan. To her surprise, a toddler dozes in the backseat.

"You look exactly like the street," the driver repeats. "That's not my problem."

"Really?" she retorts. "You're going to dig your heels into an argument that's as obscene as it is idiotic?"

"Bitch," he says, then rolls up his window.

"You were not adequately loved," she says, then runs across the street to the gas station.

Inside the gas station, she aggressively turns the lever of the slushee machine and fills a cup with frozen, spectacular blue, breathing hard. She pays and stands on the curb for a moment, examining gas pumps and considering environmental doom as she sips from a straw that will probably end up in a whale. A woman in her sixties stands a few feet away, chewing a cigarette and glaring at her phone. A man of the same age emerges from the smudged glass doors and approaches the woman, holding a Styrofoam cup of coffee and a chilled plastic bottle of seltzer. The woman's hair is gray at the roots and piled high; the man's clothes are speckled with white paint; they both appear exhausted. It's clear to Blandine from the synchronicity of their movements—the corresponding shuffles of feet, head tilts, and eye squints—that they have been trying to love each other for years.

The man offers the woman the seltzer.

"I wanted a Coke," she says.

"They didn't have any."

"It's the only thing I wanted."

"They're all out."

"Of *Coke?*"

"Sorry, hon."

She narrows her eyes. *"How."*

"I thought you loved this stuff."

"Get that crap away from me!"

"The heck's gotten into you?"

She grabs the seltzer from his outstretched hands and hurls it across the lot, toward a diesel pump. It skids and bursts. "I can't live like this!" she cries. "No taste! No color! *I can't!*"

On the curb, she turns and he turns. He tries to cradle her head in his hands, but she bites his fingers. "Leave me alone!" she cries.

He does not. The woman stays in place. Summer heat and the odor of gasoline and something painful—Blandine imagines an eviction notice, or a bad diagnosis, or digital evidence of an affair, or a relapsing daughter—press both the man and the woman to the ground. The woman droops into him, limb by limb.

"It's gonna be okay," the man whispers. "We'll be okay."

The woman pushes her face against the man's blue shirt.

"Here," he says. "Let's get you away from all this gasoline. Let's get you somewhere you can smoke."

Blandine presses her tongue to the roof of her mouth. Brain freeze.

<center>~~~</center>

By the time Blandine arrives at the south entrance of the Valley, the sun—neutral as ever—has colored the sky like rosé between the darkening clouds. At the entrance, a banner stretches across a chain-link fence, advertising the luxury condominiums and technology headquarters that will soon devour the Valley. The digital renderings are bad but obviously expensive, a combination that always depresses Blandine. She sneezes and tosses her cup into an overflowing trash can, bisecting a swarm of bees. She follows a dirt path to a meadow, woods thick and noisy around her, and she can feel her whole body relax as she descends into greenery, into a place that has not yet been fucked. Over a thousand sugar maple trees live in the Valley. Deciduous, the sugar maples are astonishing in the autumn, carpeting the woods in crimson, plum, and cadmium yellow. Birds chirp, squirrels leap from branch to branch, and Blandine rounds a corner, passing an abandoned merry-go-round. Vines coil up the poles, and saplings sprout between wooden horses. A chain-link fence lines the interior of the woods. Laminated signs along it say:

GOAT RESTORATION IN PROGRESS. The city rented goats to weed the Valley before its reconstruction. PLEASE DO NOT FEED THEM. Blandine goes to the Valley almost every day, but she has never seen any goats, which she considers unfair. Valley goats rank among the few things she feels entitled to enjoy in this world.

A pair of men, both in their thirties, emerge from the opposite end of the path, walking toward Blandine. "But I hate the blue jays and the robins," says the shorter of the two. "They bully the other birds."

His companion—tall and bald and baby-faced—stares at Blandine. "Good *morning*," he says, his eyes hunting her skin. "How are you today?"

"Jeff," says his friend. "It's evening."

Blandine ignores them and keeps walking.

The man named Jeff stops and turns toward her, theatrically analyzing her body. "My God, you are *gorgeous*. What's your name, angel?"

"Jeff," says his friend.

"Can't I get your name? Your number?"

"Come on, Jeff."

"How about a smile, baby? Just one?"

Blandine feels his body behind hers.

"You're not even gonna talk to me? You're out here in public, and you're not even gonna look at me?"

She grinds her teeth.

"You have an obligation, you know, when you're outside. You've got to look around and *interact* with people; that's what we all have to do. It's rude to ignore somebody. Can't you take a fucking compliment? Hey!"

When he puts his hand on her bare shoulder, Blandine snaps around, bares her canines, and hisses with conviction.

"Jesus!" cries Jeff.

Blandine curls her fingers into claws, swipes at his face, and hisses again.

Jeff jumps backward, stumbling into his friend. "She's crazy."

Blandine screeches and jumps erratically, hissing with gusto.

"*Come on, Jeff*," says the friend. "Let's *go*."

Blandine recently learned that white barn owls reflect moonlight off their feathers to temporarily blind the voles they are hunting. Everybody does the best she can with the resources she has.

Jeff scurries to his friend, and the men walk quickly in the opposite direction, tossing incredulous glances and fear-smiles behind them as they move. They laugh loudly. Once they're out of sight, Blandine relaxes her pose and walks on.

She senses that there is something hilarious about catcalling; she just doesn't know what it is.

Gathering herself, she follows the dirt path to the meadow—a stretch of overgrown emerald, flanked by two hills. Near the mouth of the forest dips a large bright lawn, where people often picnic. If you go deeper, you find creeks, burrows, forgotten horse trails. As distraught as she is about the forthcoming demolition, Blandine considers it a miracle that the Valley has lasted this long, despite all the incentives to shave it into farmland, rig it into industry, compress it into landfill. For a hundred years, it has survived as itself.

Blandine takes a winding path into one of the lesser-known clearings and sits on lush grass. It's an oval stretch of lawn, enclosed by trees, punctuated by four wooden benches on the periphery and a nonfunctional fountain in the center. Throughout her life, she has never seen water in its concrete pool. This is Blandine's favorite place to read because it is always vacant, and the birdsong is loud, and she feels safe. The wind carries the fragrance of the adjacent lilac grove, delivering it right into her lungs. This evening, as she looks around, she is startled.

Another person sits on the bench across the grass, his head tilted back, pricey sunglasses doming his eyes. The man appears to be in his fifties, slightly overweight, with constellations of sores on his skin, almost like mosquito bites. But she can't see much of his skin because, despite the heat, he's wearing a black turtleneck, black jeans, and black socks in black sandals. A tuft of dark blond hair sprouts far back on his forehead but fluffs down his skull, thick and healthy. A small mouth with thin lips curved into a frown. Something childish about the man. His sleeves are rolled up, his arms crossed over his belly, and despite the sunglasses, Blandine can see his expression. He looks like someone who has never slept through the night.

She wants to leave but forces herself to stay. Why should a sleeping man frighten her? She retrieves the book from her bag and attempts to read, but she is too aware of the man's body, which seems to glow in her peripheral vision. Her abdominal muscles tense, and her nerves become alert, her senses prepared to receive all data and to react at once. He's just some guy. She recalls her interaction with the driver. With Jeff and his friend on the path. She can fend for herself.

She-Mystics glares up at her like an accusation, but when she tries to read, the words meander off the page, out of her vision. She takes a break to watch bees stuff their heads into white clovers, which bloom in the grass like snow. She loves these clovers because they are plain and everywhere. The diet of cottontail rabbits. In the spring, she spent an evening studying them on a sticky computer at the Vacca Vale Public Library. What struck Blandine most as she clicked from site to site, scanning blogs and comments, was the goodwill of the online botanic community. When Mary Peterson asked, *"Can velvet beans and white clovers coexist?"* Ken Meltzer responded two hours later, saying, *"Hi Mary—thx for your question! It is a GREAT question! The good news is white clovers & vegetable legumes like velvet beans CAN coexist, but the bad news is you have to wait ~2 yrs after planting the clovers to plant any vegetable legumes, bc the white clover = host for root rot diseases like Rhizoctonia and Pythium :(Good luck and keep up updated!!!!"*

Blandine took a screenshot of the conversation and emailed it to herself.

She knows little of her own heritage but decided years ago with haphazard conviction that she is Russian. It's the country people always guess first, so she ran with it. These clovers likely blossom in her homeland. Maybe a pair of great-great-great-great-great grandparents made love in a field of them. At the library, she imagined this until it grossed her out. She researched the clovers until a man spilled his energy drink on her lap, forcing her to pack up and return to the Rabbit Hutch.

In the woods, around Blandine, chipmunks scuffle. Small lime spiders creep up her arms and legs, through shoots of hair. Overhead, a plane drones a cello D through the clouds. Blandine wants to scoop a cupful of sky and gulp. The park is so verdant, it looks like a screensaver. She applies a cheap rose lip balm and inhales the scent of baking dirt. Lies on her belly and examines each petal as a bee drinks, its stinger drooping like a burden. The petals remind Blandine of her social worker Lori's hair, shooting in stiff frosted jets from the head. Lori always sipped dark soda from a Chug Big cup. She wore sunglasses that evoked particularly American things, like goatees and drive-through banks and NASCAR. She was a good social worker, far better than the others, and the last one she had before she aged out of the system. Lori called Blandine Blandine, and not Tiffany, and that was nice. Now, Blandine picks a handful of white clovers—the ones the bees aren't using—and stows them in her dress pocket.

Suddenly, the man across from Blandine snorts awake.

Annoyed by her own fear, she examines him as he gets his bearings; she loves watching people transition to consciousness. Bewildered, the man removes his sunglasses. His eyes are small, pink, and frightened. His forehead sparkles with sweat. When he looks at Blandine, he appears even more frightened. She finds his fear comforting.

"Hello," she says.

When he speaks, his voice is gentle. "Hullo."

A pause. Blandine points to a clover in front of her. The man cautiously watches her from the bench, as though she is a bear.

"Did you know these are officially known as Trifolium repens?" Blandine asks. Her voice is clear and confident. "But they're also called Dutch clovers and Ladino clovers, depending on their size. Bigness is always demanding to be distinguished from smallness, you know?"

It's like there's a live-news lag between her words and his reception. Eventually, he shakes his head. "No," he says. "I didn't know that."

"Yeah. Some people refer to the white clover as the most adaptable urban plant in the world, actually, because it can regulate the production of this one toxin—cyanide, I think—to adapt to radically different climates. It's native to Central Asia and Europe, but it can thrive in the heat of southern India and also in the cold of Norway." She pauses. "In cold climates, it doesn't produce cyanide."

"Is that so?" asks the man. She can't tell if he's just being polite, but every second of the interaction is increasing her power and reducing his threat, so she continues.

"Yeah. Also—you see this stem? How it sort of creeps horizontally, then loops one stem into a new root, which sprouts a new plant with adventitious roots? These kinds of stems are called stolons. Self-sufficient but interconnected."

"I can't really see it," the man replies. "But that's neat."

"The white clover is really nutritious for lots of different animals, too—bovine, insects, deer, rodents. When it's not producing cyanide, that is. It's high in protein. Humans can eat white clovers, too, when they're boiled or smoked. I think you can dry them, make them into a tea. There's this one insect—I can't remember the name of it—that exclusively eats white clovers. Can you imagine? Being so essential to an ecosystem that a species would *go extinct* without you?"

The man's face becomes overcast. "No," he murmurs. "I really can't imagine that."

Blandine panics a little; she has run out of facts to share and can't remember how to fuel a conversation without them. But she is spared because when she's done speaking, the man stands laboriously, wiping his hands on his pants. He examines her for a moment, his face contorted in mysterious anguish. A path beside his bench will lead him out of this meadow, back to the central path, out of the Valley, into traffic.

"You're beautiful," he says sadly.

Blandine stays very still and upright, tracking the man's figure as he vanishes from the clearing. When he's out of sight, she offers her pinkie to a bee, goading it to sting her. It does not.

~~~

When she finally regains her focus, Blandine opens *She-Mystics: An Anthology* to page 247, where a browning dandelion marks her spot. She considers Hildegard her only true friend. When staging one of her musical artworks, Hildegard made her male assistant play the Devil, and her nuns play the Virtues. The Virtues got to sing; the Devil only yelled. In the play, without much provocation, the Soul cries, *God created the world: I am not doing him any harm, I simply want to enjoy it!* Later, the Devil says, *Why, none of you even know who you are!*

You can't argue with either of them. Blandine inhales the perfume of grass, tree, pollen, and wild lilac—this is how Hildegard describes Paradise. Flicking an ant off her arm, Blandine continues reading where she left off.

In your foolishness, you want to grasp me with threats such as this: *"If God wants me to be just and good, why does he not make me that way?"* You want to catch me like the presumptuous young goat that attacks the stag. He is caught and pinned down by the mighty antlers. If you try your foolhardy strength against me, you will be brought down in the course of justice by the precepts of my law like the horns of the stag. The horns are trumpets ringing in your ears, yet you do not heed them, but run after the wolf, thinking you have tamed him so that he will not hurt you. But the wolf swallows you up saying: "This sheep has wandered from the path; it refused to follow its shepherd and ran after me. So I will keep it, because it chose me and deserted its shepherd." Human being! God is just, and therefore he has ordained all he has made, in heaven and earth, with justice and order.

This passage troubles Blandine. There's no winning if you're a sheep or a goat, and there's no losing if you're a wolf. Hildegard drops the stag plotline halfway through. Also, God—who allegedly invented sheep and goats—mixes them up.

A bleat from the foliage alarms Blandine, and she drops her book in the grass. The sound is almost human. She turns, body alert, expecting to see the turtlenecked man standing behind her. Instead, she sees nothing. Another bleat, desperate and small. Blandine stands and follows the sound many yards from her book, deeper into thick and thorny vegetation. Finally, she spots a small goat in a tangle of green. It has white fur with tan splotches. Frantic eyes. A kid.

Blandine looks at the goat, then looks at the sky, then back at her book in the clearing. Then pinches her thigh. Has Hildegard summoned the goat into reality?

That's when Blandine remembers the signs all over the Valley. GOAT RESTORATION IN PROGRESS.

"What happened to your tribe?" Blandine asks. The goat thrashes at the sound of her voice, its eyes wide open and wild, struggling to stand. Blandine moves closer. A chain-link fence is intended to separate the goats from the public, but this one must have escaped. There is fear in its eyes, panic in its voice, and operatic thunder above. When she's inches from the animal, Blandine notices the front right leg, which is bent at a wrong angle, clearly injured.

She scans the trees as though a veterinarian might helpfully leap down from the branches.

The goat is so cute and pathetic, it almost looks fake. Blandine has no phone to call Vacca Vale's animal hospital, no knowledge of goat care. She guesses that the animal weighs about twenty pounds. She could leave it there, of course—she knows that normal people would leave it there. Calmly, she walks to the clearing and packs her book. Then she returns to the goat and scoops her up, resolved to carry her to a place where she is less exposed to abuse and dehydration. At first the goat kicks and cries, but soon—too soon—it relaxes, gives up, and sinks into Blandine's arms. "Hildegard," Blandine christens the animal. "Hildegard von Vacca Vale." She counts seven spots on the goat's fur. She has icy blue eyes and milk teeth, both humanoid. "Did you know that your namesake is widely considered to be the founder of natural history in Germany? She invented her own alphabet, too."

For the first few minutes, it is challenging to carry the goat, who smells of urine, through the foliage and up the forest path, but Hildegard's weight begins to comfort Blandine, who is not used to carrying anything other than books. Blandine starts to walk more energetically, invigorated with newfound purpose. The simplicity of the task enraptures her: keep this animal alive. Nothing morbid in it, no starvation or stigmata. Not even much capitalism. Clouds glow all over the evening, cuddling together above, while breezes heave through the trees.

As a child, Blandine planted several coffee beans in the Valley, hoping one might sprout into the sky. She followed every rabbit she saw, determined to find the warren and plunge into it. Tornado sirens thrilled her, and she was often punished for wandering off from the group at school. She was a fool for portals, willing to sign the thorniest contract—giants, poison, isolation, tricksters, hunters, con-artist wolves, cannibalistic witches, anything—if it promised to transport her. There was no place like home because there was no home. Now an adult in the eyes of the state, she walks over grass and roots and trash, her feet browning with dirt, and dreams of a little housebroken goat, an east-facing bedroom window, an edible garden, a ladder on a book wall, no electricity, a fireplace. She dreams of total self-sufficiency and freedom from the market. She starts to dream of an American political revolution, but trips over the logistics and tables the matter. She is disappointed by the domesticity of her adult fantasies but also cheered by it. Domesticity, at least, is achievable.

Blandine loves the mystics because they, unlike her, never stopped searching for portals. They treated prayer as a getaway car, cathedral as rabbit hole, suffering as wonderland, divine ecstasy as the cyclone that delivered a woman to color. The mystics never gave up on the Beyond, and they refused to leave the Green World.

Blandine enters a wide path near the street and gasps at the figure in front of her.

Her reptilian brain reacts to him at once: her breathing snags, her pulse speeds, her palms sweat, she loses her balance. She knows even before they speak that this interaction will be the series finale of their relationship, the scene automatically charged with drama commensurate with their history. Studying his good tan and powerful posture, she is reminded of a certain dictator whose name she cannot recall. He is dressed in monochrome—white athleisure, something bloodthirsty in the casual glamour of it. He stands in some leafy shadows, his gaze cutting into her like laser surgery. When Blandine sees James Yager, she sees a harpoon, a casket, a coyote, a band saw. He is composed of angles that she once wanted to use on her geometry exams. Somewhere in the Valley, someone is grilling; Blandine loves the scent of burning charcoal despite the euthanasia that such an activity administers to Earth. She feels light-headed but tries to keep her grip on consciousness. She doesn't have health insurance.

"Tiffany," James says. "What a surprise."

The goat bleats in alarm. The accuracy of Hildegard's intuition impresses Blandine.

"I was just going for a walk," says James. "But I have my car. Do you . . . ?"

"What?" Blandine snaps.

He hesitates. "Do you need some help with that?"

Major American Fires

~~~

I could tell you the facts, or I could tell you how it felt, but I doubt any of it will give you the explanation you want. Yes, we were under the influence. Two or three influences. Me, Todd, and Malik were getting drunk on a handle of vodka that somebody left in the lobby, and high on some of Todd's powerful stuff from a girl named Stephen. In order to qualify for the Independence Workshop stipends, you have to pass a drug test at the end of every month, but they only test for opioids and narcotics, which we consider a little slice of bureaucratic compassion. The vodka was the kind of alcohol that doesn't let you forget that you're poisoning yourself as you drink it, which is to say it was cheap, and we didn't feel bad about stealing it.

We were in Todd's room because it was the cleanest. A ferociously made mattress on the ground, absolutely no grime, scent of chemical lemon, nothing on the shelves but alphabetized comic books. Todd wanted to be a cartoonist. Wants, I mean. As we talked, he kept picking up the vodka and placing it on the center of a paper towel, then adjusting it to the center of his floor. On his walls, he had taped some of his drawings in a perfect line. He rarely drew in front of us, and his work didn't resemble any comic I had ever seen. The drawings were chaotic sketches in black marker or pencil, mostly people without faces, some animals that didn't exist, everyone in motion. I found them unsettling, but I couldn't look away.

Malik deemed the evening a national holiday because he just got a new job. A *real* one, he told us. "Teaching robots emotions," he announced, beaming. Todd studied him. "The pay is royal. And casting directors are gonna love it. They want you to have a diverse portfolio." Malik thinks he's going to be an actor—he's saving up for a move to Los Angeles. All summer, he's been recording on his phone, uploading videos of nothing to all of his pathetic profiles because he believes he has the Fame Gene. We don't disagree. He's got the looks, the charm, the vanity. Whatever. But we still want to murder him a little when he talks like this. I have a feeling he's going to be a real estate agent. "You have to build a *following*," he told us. "Then the representation comes crawling through the chimney."

"Teaching robots *emotions?*" asked Todd.

"What year is it?" I asked. I truly couldn't remember.

They ignored me. "Some guy's building a family of AI—that's what he called it, the Family—and he wants me to model," said Malik, smirking.

Model. God. I had to take another pull.

"Can you believe?" continued Malik. "He's trying to get the body language down. The expressions, the voices. So he throws these sensors all over you, plugs you into shit, gives you prompts."

"Guy from here?" asked Todd.

"Born and raised. But once he's done, he's going to take the Family to some convention in San Francisco. He says all the CEOs and the geniuses will bid on it there. He'll make millions. We get a cut."

"What's the point of them?" asked Todd.

"What?"

"The robots."

"What's the point of *you?*" retorted Malik.

"Do they scrub your toilet?" asked Todd. "Walk your dog? Suck your dick?"

Malik paused. "He hasn't told us yet."

"What are the prompts like?" Todd asked. I resented him for feeding Malik's ego like this. "Be happy, be mad?"

"I don't know," Malik replied. "I start next week. But in the auditions, I got scripts. Scenarios. Here, let me read some to you. They emailed them to us . . ." He scrolled through his phone. "Okay, here's one: you're holding your baby for the first time, counting his eyelashes. Some shit.

Or here's another: after working your way up to the top of your company, you get fired. You're nine, and you just learned that your big sister released your hamster into the wild. You're fifteen, and you just walked in on your parents having sex. You're eighty, recently diagnosed with terminal bone cancer, and you're telling the doctors you don't want treatment. Your favorite baseball team just won the World Series. You're waiting in line at the DMV." Malik put down his phone, looking smug and famous already. "E-T-C."

Todd had finished his radishes, so he was gnawing on his backup vegetables: celery, carrots, and peppers. All raw. He'd fish out a vegetable from one plastic bag, then deposit the inedible parts in another, precise as a factory.

"So you're going to shape America forever," concluded Todd.

"That's right," said Malik. "Probably the whole world, actually. I mean, this guy has some big ambitions. He really shoots for the stars. And he has a ton of interest already—like, all this money people have invested. Angel investors is what they're called. So they think that the robots from here on out will take after the Family. Seriously. That's what he told us. Which means that they'll take after—"

"You," said Todd.

"Right." Malik grinned. I swear he used whitening strips on his teeth. "Me."

Todd looked at me, then at Malik. "Cool," he said.

That night in question—Wednesday, July seventeenth—the sun was starting to set, but you couldn't tell because it had been hazy all day. It smelled like rubber smoke, which made me think of war. I was pretty gone by this point, neurologically speaking. Sweating hard. A storm began to rumble outside. Since March, we'd killed a few more mice, plus some rabbits. A pigeon, once. Without discussing anything explicitly, we made a kind of ceremony out of it. Usually, we did it on Wednesday nights because none of us had to work, and Blandine was never around. We always got plastered beforehand. Found some bongos. Did this thing with the candle where we had to hold our fingers above the flame and whoever pulled away first had to do the killing. Do you need to know more? Honestly, I'd rather not go into details. Is that all right with you? I'll tell you everything you need to know. Just please don't make me describe it.

Anyway, we hadn't sacrificed an animal in weeks, and I was starting to get that feeling—that feeling you get when you haven't, you know, *done it* in a while, and you feel like you're lunging out of your body. I think it's safe to say Todd and Malik felt the same way. When you need to rub one out, your target is obvious. What was strange about this case was that I couldn't say what I was lunging toward. I remember feeling hotter than I thought possible. But that was just the temperature.

"It was really competitive," said Malik. "There were four rounds. They made me sign an NDA, but now I can tell people I'm doing it. I can't tell you any more specifics, though, so don't ask. They only chose four of us, and there were like two hundred applicants. Maybe three hundred."

There was a takeout menu on the floor beside Todd's mattress, and he'd made a list on the back. I examined his small handwriting. Perfect, like a font. To shut up Malik, I started to read it out loud: it was a list of all the major American fires that had occurred in the last year. Place, duration, damage, cause. Halfway through, I began reading it in a Scottish accent, just to keep myself entertained. That's how long it was.

"This is good," said Malik. He aimed his phone at me, filming. "This is good content. You're actually decent at accents, Jack. I could give you some pointers if you want."

"No thanks," I said through gritted teeth. I crumpled the list and threw it at Todd's pale head. "What's the matter with you?" I demanded, anger clawing at me. Todd was so small, so breakable. Suddenly, I wanted to shatter him like a Christmas ornament. "Why can't you be normal?"

Todd looked at me with an unreadable expression. He could've been asleep, for all I knew.

"Keeping track," he said.

His tiny handwriting matched his tiny hands. Freckled rodent hands. When he picked up the paper, his face broke into sadness, which canceled my anger. In Todd's psychotically clean bedroom, facing a plastic fan that churned summer through the window, I wanted all the extremes at once: I wanted to die, kill, fuck, find my parents and bring them back to life and then kill them, then bury them and yell and yell. For the first and probably last time in my life, I envied women for being able to give birth. I wanted to fuse myself to somebody else. I wanted to know what it would take for me to give a damn.

I thought of Blandine. There had been a moment between us in Pinky's loft. I was sure of it at the time. But as the day went on, I doubted it more and more, and by evening, I figured I had imagined it. She was just using me. What for? I don't know. Like a week before all this happened, she overheard me telling Todd and Malik that I got a job walking Pinky's dogs. That's when she took an interest in me for the very first time.

She waited for Todd and Malik to the leave the apartment, and then she approached me. "Can I join you someday?" she asked, her eyes all twinkly and fake. I asked her why, but as she explained it, all I could think was: I wish Malik and Todd were here to see this. I started fantasizing about all the embellishments I would report back to them. I'd say that the strap of her tank top fell. I'd say that she touched my arm. I'd say that she put on perfume before stepping out of her bedroom. I was so preoccupied with my version of events I could barely hear her.

"I just love animals," Blandine was saying when I finally tuned back in.

Later, I told Malik and Todd that Blandine wanted to spend some time with me. "One on one, away from all this." Then I winked and shimmied. Malik hurled the ball of rubber bands at me, but he was smiling. Like he was proud of me.

Sitting there in Todd's room some hours later, I thought of that moment in Pinky's loft, the first time Blandine and I had ever talked long enough to disagree on something, her face blushing like I've never seen, her body moving across the loft and standing too close to mine. At the time, I thought she was going to kiss me or was waiting for me to kiss her. But then she started petting the dogs, and I knew she was just a tease.

The booze and the weed deconstructed Todd's room, rebuilt it into some kind of boat. I swayed. Blandine appeared to me briefly, clear as a photograph, dressed in a tuxedo. I knew then that I'd never touch her. The worst part was that I didn't care. I didn't care about anything at all.

"Something's on my mind," Malik announced with authority. He could be very federal. "That benzene groundwater poisoning in the sixties?"

He waited dramatically.

"Okay?" prompted Todd.

"It wasn't Zorn."

"Come on," said Todd. "That's the only thing we know for sure."

"What I want to know," I said, "is what they gave the people who went loopy and dumb from it."

"From what?"

"The benzene. Sometimes I think that's why all the adults we ever knew were such big idiots."

"Nobody could prove that," said Todd. I could tell that he was trying to seem unaffected by my comment earlier, trying to play it cool, which made it all worse. I'd made him feel bad for no reason. "Zorn would say it wasn't their fault you were dumb."

"There has to be a way to test it."

"Would suck if you went through the trouble and found out it *wasn't* their fault."

"*None* of it was Zorn's fault," said Malik. "That's what I'm trying to tell you."

"Oh yeah?" I asked. "What was it, then?"

"The benzene contamination," said Malik, "was an act of alien warfare."

Todd stopped messing with the vodka, stared at Malik. "What?"

Then Malik exploded in laughter, his perfect teeth all over the place. Todd nervously copied.

"What I really want," I said, "is to guillotine the whole internet. Before it guillotines me."

"Jack," said Todd. "Get off my bed."

I obeyed without thinking. Stood up, fell a little. "Why?"

"You're sweating all over it. Look."

The front door opened. Malik shot up and took off his shirt instinctively, the way everyone in a crowded space checks their phone when the default ringtone goes off. Seriously. Blandine enters the apartment, and Malik *takes off his shirt*. I wish I could call his behavior unbelievable, but of course I believed it. We heard Blandine's rushed footsteps, a faucet running, the fridge opening, a clank of plastic and metal, her low voice. Then the front door shut.

On Todd's blue quilt I saw a damp blob, not shaped like me, but like a country bleeding into all the space around it.

"Dammit," said Malik. "Tonight was the night."

"The *night*," I scoffed. "What were you going to do, pop the ques—"

"Shh," said Todd. "Listen."

That's when we heard the goat for the first time. It was crying.

"The hell?" muttered Malik.

It bleated again.

Nothing was real. Immediately, we got up and hunted down the noise. We never considered doing anything else.

I Leave It Up to You

~~~

At 7:51 p.m., 112 minutes before Blandine Watkins exits her body, she carries Hildegard the goat upstairs to her apartment. James Yager idles in his economy hybrid outside the Rabbit Hutch. Blandine used his phone to call the only veterinarian in town, but the office was closed. Aside from goat logistics, they've exchanged few words. Since she saw him, she's been shaking so hard that she has to keep her jaw parted so her teeth won't chatter. She detects no change in his countenance; he reacts to her as he would to a student, any other student.

In her bedroom, Blandine leaves Hildegard with five plastic bowls of water. She dumps spinach on the floor, along with pears, celery sticks, and carrots. Some of the vegetables belong to Todd, but she'll pay him back. She examines her bedroom and feels—briefly—rich. With her quilt and pillows, she fixes a bed for the goat on the floorboards and gently tucks her into it. Hildegard regards Blandine plaintively. "Try to be quiet," she whispers to the animal. It doesn't seem like the boys are home, which relieves her. Still, Todd's door is closed—he might be in his room. But Todd wouldn't harm Hildegard; of the three boys, he's the least brutish. Gentle and sensitive. Sometimes, when nobody is home, she sneaks into his room and admires his drawings, which she finds exquisite and bizarre. "If they come back, don't let them know you're here," Blandine whispers to Hildegard. Quickly, Blandine writes on a Post-it: *DO NOT OPEN*, then adds another note saying: *Please*, and slaps them to her bedroom door. Pulse wound fast, she runs out of the apartment, forgetting to lock the front door behind her.

~~~

They sit in James's car, parked in the lot of an abandoned church a few blocks from the Rabbit Hutch, avoiding eye contact. The windows of the car are open, and a pre-storm wind flirts with them. In the backseat sit four bags from a local farm supplies store: white salt, trace mineral salt, goat fly spray, sheep and goat feed, three packages of hay, sheep and goat protein block, goat Nutri-Drench, a small trough, a five-gallon bucket, and a package of human candy. It cost over a hundred dollars, and as she scanned their items, the cashier eyed the pair as though detecting something illicit and sordid between them. James paid for it.

"I may not be *oppressed,* per se," continues Blandine, chewing the candy to keep her teeth from clicking. "But I'm certainly the proletariat in this situation, and you're obviously the bourgeoisie, and capitalism makes it impossible for anything to transpire between us besides a fucked-up transaction predicated upon the assumption that you own whatever I produce. And of course we meet in the Valley; of course you would pollute it like that. And the goat, our only witness, removed. Fuck. Let's be high for this conversation." She removes a vaporizer from the pocket of her dress, using it quickly so he can't see the tremor of her hands. Every voice inside her wants to serenade him. It is impossible to believe that she found Jack attractive earlier today. Now she realizes that whatever she felt then was just a diluted version of the storm currently wreaking havoc inside her.

After a long pause, James objects. "How am I the bourgeoisie? If you're going to give a Marxist reading of our relationship, at least acknowledge the fact that I married into money. My parents were small-scale farmers. We were poor throughout my life. My brother took an IED in Afghanistan, and now he can't walk because he was trying to pay for college. Fireworks give him panic attacks. My parents died of preventable diseases because their diets failed them first, and their health insurance failed them second. I will never make more than forty thousand a year. I was always inferior to my wife, subordinate to her decisions, her parents' decisions. You don't understand."

"Oh, I'm sorry; since you *married* into the aristocracy, then you're not really a participant or benefactor," Blandine says. It is so easy to express her rage toward him—far easier than it is to express anything else. "Since you *married* into it, you obviously lack all of its protection and materials, like a mansion and financial indemnity when a crisis befalls you. It's like you've never read a nineteenth-century novel. Jesus."

"I'm a high school music teacher, Tiffany."

"And your wife? What is she, other than a Midwestern princess, an inheritor of the wealth generated by people like your parents, a member of the class that owns people like me? What is she other than basically monarchical? Marrying into elitism does not exempt you from its terms and conditions. She may own the majority of you, but you have, like—" She searches for a term. "Shared custody."

"We got divorced."

Blandine inhales from the metal mouth of the vaporizer, tries not to react. "I hope your prenup was cynical."

She places it in the consul. James takes it without asking, his hand brushing her electrically. She feels angry, and sweaty, and delighted that he's putting his mouth where she put her mouth. She feels like she's about to throw up, undress, sprout wings.

"Look, Tiffany." James sighs. "None of this is going the way I . . . hoped it would. I wanted to apologize to you. I want to acknowledge how manipulative and sick and—yes, sure, fine—how *bourgeois* my behavior was. But the conversation got away from me, and everything just went . . . I don't know; everything went haywire." He gestures toward the sky, where storm clouds have gathered like an audience.

"Hildegard von Bingen—this mystic—says that God whips up thunderstorms to punish wickedness," Blandine says as she observes the sky. "Or foretell dangers."

"That is not an original position."

"She says, 'The reason is that all our actions affect the elements and are in turn disturbed and influenced by the elements.'"

Drops of rain plink on the windshield.

"I forgot about your memory," says James. "Your incredible memory."

"I am so sick," Blandine says, "of violence against women disguised as validation."

"Sorry," James murmurs automatically, but he has the look of a scolded pet who doesn't know what he's done wrong.

"Anyway," says Blandine. "The trouble is that if you're a young woman, you can't opt out of the systems of economic production. Nobody can, not really, but at least a white man like you can *approximate* opting out. A woman can't even *sort of* opt out, no matter how hard she tries, because her body *contains* goods and services, and people will try to extract those goods and services with or without her permission. How could you understand? We're finally starting to talk about sexual misconduct, at least there's that. Obviously, there's a little bit of horizontal justice going on at the moment, and it's not exactly ideal, but at least it's something."

"Horizontal justice?"

"I mean if we can't take down American machismo via the commander in chief, then maybe we can take down the producer, the CEO, the news anchors, the actors, etcetera. It'll feel good, it'll do some good, but at the end of the day, our nuclear and democratic safety is being determined by an international pissing contest, and when you've been in foster care, you just . . . whatever. We think we want to kill each other, but what we really want to kill is the cage. I don't even know what I'm saying. No, I do. What I'm saying is that we need to make room in our discourse for power abuses to which each party allegedly consented. For anyone to look at the megalomaniacs running our world and call it important, then listen to a fucked-up affair and call it silly because each said, Yes, okay, at the start—I can't abide that. I mean we don't want to infantilize ourselves, but what *is* consent? 'We' voted for these maniacs; was that not consensual? To what are we consenting, exactly? So if you examine *this* scenario—you and me—and see anything other than a small version of our big disaster, and if you look in the mirror and see anything other than a red power tie on your neck, then you're repressing the truth of your plundering, exploitative tendencies in order to get through the day. Which is shitty."

James takes a deep breath, his eyes closed. "You're right," he says without conviction.

"I would go so far as to argue that our relationship contained three common stages of economic development throughout human history: primitive communism at first, where everything felt mutually beneficial for like exactly one moment, then feudalism—where I was utterly beholden to you, labored for basically nothing for you—then capitalism. And now, fuck. I don't know. Maybe I went too far. I'm trying to love everyone and drain myself of self, you know. I'm trying to recognize the full human dimension of each person I encounter, and I'm—honestly, I'm exhausted. From here on out, it's going to be New Testament justice. So I gotta get the Old Testament justice out of my system while I still have the chance." She pinches her thigh and catches him watching. "I think I hate you."

"I don't hate you," James says.

Blandine orders her brain to blockade the emotion marching through her body. It's not working.

"It wasn't just sex for me." James pauses. He looks away from her thigh, out the windshield, freeing Blandine to study his profile. "If that's what you think." He appears unethically handsome, his jawline doing its boring but effective work on her body. She can practically feel her hypothalamus—neurological tyrant!—powering down her prefrontal cortex. She grips any reason she can. Reason, says Hildegard, is the third-highest human faculty. After body and soul. God is life, but God is also rationality, says Hildegard. *Reason is the root, through which the resonant word flourishes.* Where is the reason? What is the resonant word? Nothing flourishes. Blandine feels like she's suffocating in her loose cotton dress. Wants to take it off, wants to see how James would react, wants the storm to take her with it.

"I mean, it wasn't even mostly about sex," says James. "When I think back to what happened, that night isn't the thing that comes to mind. I never imagined it happening, never even thought of it as a possibility—I respected you too much to think that way."

"And why are respecting a woman and fucking her mutually exclusive, to you?"

James runs a hand through his mulch-colored hair, too thick for his age. "They're not." Finally, he looks her in the eye. "But respecting your seventeen-year-old student and fucking her are."

Tears well in her eyes. Blandine turns away from him.

"I cared about you," James says. "I still do. I felt sick about it for months. You know, after—after that night, I forced myself not to contact you, I thought it would be . . . benign neglect, I suppose. I thought contacting you would be evil. And when I found out you had dropped out of school, I told every teacher and administrator to reach out, told the principal to offer you whatever you needed. I told everyone to do everything they could to keep you there."

"I appreciate your paternalism."

"I consider myself a criminal, do you understand?"

"Well." She bites her cuticle, releases a tear. "You are one."

But not in the state of Indiana.

When she surveys him, she notices that blood has overpopulated his face. He takes in her tears with visible horror. At himself, or at her? For a second, she thinks he's going to reach out and touch her. She wants him to. He doesn't.

"I couldn't sleep for a week after this happened between us," he says.

"Well, I couldn't sleep for months—haven't slept well in my whole stupid life—but it's not a fucking competition."

"This isn't about me. I'm sorry. I know that I'm . . . irrelevant, in this situation."

She scoffs. "Irrelevant? You actually believe that you're *irrelevant, in this situation*? Irrelevant! In *this* situation!"

"What can I do to convey my full admission of how wrong this was?" Now he's getting desperate. She can see it in his face, hear it in his voice. "How can I persuade you that, despite all the horrible—despite every-thing I've done, despite how reckless I was with you, I care about your well-being and always have? How can I convince you that I have never done anything like that before, and if I could do it again, I absolutely would? I mean—*differently*. If I could do it again *differently*, I would. Everything I'm saying sounds empty, except it's exactly what I mean. You're better at this. I don't—"

"I *actually* believed that our objectives and interests were shared throughout that entire fever dream. What a fucking numbskull I was last year. I thought—I actually believed that I *loved* you. I believed I was *in love* with you. And maybe it *was* some strand of love, but so what? We spent six months fracking each other's souls—just because we got a little oil out of it doesn't make it *good*. And who hasn't fallen for capitalism? Of course it seduces you before it mauls you. Of course it intoxicates you out of your senses before it leads you to the arena. Like how ancient societies used to give children cocaine before sacrificing them. And of course your mansion beguiled me, of course I became stupid when I saw all the *knowledge* you had, of course I surrendered to a fantasy of control, of course I wanted to fuck your piano. Of course you and your body made me feel safe, like I was surrounded by—I don't know, *soldiers,* or something gross like that—and of course that response was icky and boring and American, ad nauseam. *I* seduced *you,* I'm pretty sure. But—"

"No, I'm responsible for—"

"But my obsession with you doesn't nullify the—doesn't mean that our relationship wasn't—look, we were concepts rather than individuals, is what I'm trying to say. Idiotic ions within a geomagnetic storm, you see? For months, I convinced myself that you and I had transcended the power structures at play, that I was an equal agent, that to blame you would be to infantilize myself. I even excused your silence because I was so enchanted by you, and by all your fucking—your *brain,* or whatever—and at the time, I was spiraling into this, like, crisis of education, you know, realizing that I couldn't just *read* my way out of my bad luck, that I couldn't just climb up some books and across diplomas and into freedom. Now I realize that all of those beliefs merely condoned the system that keeps us all in our places, and now I realize the only way to get out of the system is to get out of the body. So, as you can see, at the time, I was too distracted by all my other collapsing illusions to properly *demonize* you. But not anymore. We were not two people simply succumbing to inconvenient, taboo, totally hackneyed attraction. We were cogs in a superstructure of class and state and production and distribution and legislation and political pyramids and militias and exchange rates and national debts and fossil fuels and stuff. We were stuck in a web of material relations. I think, actually, at the end of the day, we were the answer to the question: *Who are grand pianos for?* There was nothing dialectical about us. And that's what enrages me most of all—your silence, before, during, and after. Oh, sure, we *talked.* We talked and talked and talked, and yet we never said anything, did we? You were the only person I ever wanted to hear from, James, and I never heard from you again. What *benign* fucking neglect."

"I loved you, too," mutters James. "Like a . . . niece."

She is crying for real now, but she marches onward, powered by a whole year of fury. "If that was your version of love, no wonder—no wonder your marriage was dead on arrival, no wonder you were dying to fuck a teenager. I bet you've reduced your own daughters to narcissistic supply. I bet they feel it. I bet they prefer their mother. Who would trust you with their friends? Did you suddenly realize that you would die, James? Is that why you asked me to stay late?"

He accepts these blows with only a touch of messianic righteousness.

"You know the only thing your kid told me about you?" says Blandine. "She said you overbought toothbrushes. If you need proof that you are a stand-in for the bourgeoisie, the dominant class, the owner of both the means and fruits of production, look no further than this—a rich man stockpiling material goods that he did not create and does not need to compensate for an accurately perceived character deficiency. Toothbrushes, God. And I thought it was *cute*."

"While I admire your passion," says James, "I think this argument is getting a little sloppy. You've read *The Communist Manifesto*, I presume. And probably the Wikipedia pages for Marxism, Democratic Socialism, Social Democracy. And I trust that you know about the many brutal dictators who've weaponized communism and socialism to gain despotic control. I'm sure you would argue that they misapplied these ideologies, that a truly Marxist society has never existed. But have you even perused the first volume of *Capital*? You don't strike me as someone who would trust anyone with authoritarian control. And you're too brilliant to believe that any mortal could bring a classless, moneyless, stateless society into being."

"That's not the point," retorts Blandine. "I'm not arguing *for* anything. I'm just arguing against you, and this is the best framework I have for it. I'm not smart enough to lead a revolution, okay? I'm very aware of that. All I know is that we fucking need one."

James studies her, saying nothing.

She turns to examine the bags of goat goods, which now strike her as innocent children caught in a fight between their parents on a road trip. She takes another hit.

"I'm already high," says Blandine. "Fuck."

"Me, too."

Blandine squints at a seventies modernist building across the highway, which resembles a parking garage but is in fact the headquarters of an obituary website. "I wish all modernist fucking architects would have just fucking reconciled with their fucking fathers instead of littering our fucking country with their shit fucking erections."

James smirks.

"What?" she asks.

"It's just that modern architecture was supposed to represent the tastes and needs of a rising middle class," he says. "A reaction to the elitism and oppression of the regimes that propagated classical architecture."

Blandine blushes, feeling stupid. She didn't know that. She doesn't know anything. "Whatever. It's ugly and full of hubris and anti-pedestrian and pro-car. Maybe some modernism is pretty, but not this purgatorial shit all over our town."

They sit in silence for a few minutes.

"It smells like a campfire," he says eventually. "Do you smell that?"

"It's just the weed."

"No, it's not—it's coming from downtown. I wonder what they're burning?"

Blandine tears the remaining crescent of fingernail from her pinkie. "The future."

He looks at her as though searching for an emotion he misplaced. Fervor, perhaps. Or affection. He has the appearance of a man who has weathered many internal sandstorms and whose convictions—once sharp and exquisite—have lost their definition. Observing James, Blandine is reminded of a swan she saw last February. It had resigned itself to a puddle in the parking lot of a megastore.

"You're very young," observes James.

"Am I?" she snaps. "How young am I, James?"

He looks away. "But you don't seem eighteen," he mumbles.

At this, a primal scream builds inside her. She quarantines it. Clears her throat. "When Hildegard depicted the virtues and the vices together in this play she wrote, the vices got to be grotesque and physical and *there*. But the virtues were invisible. Just voices."

"Huh." He looks at her. Against her will, she reacts to James's attention like an iguana to a heat lamp. "What made you think of that?"

"I just wish—sometimes I look out at my life, everything I've seen so far, and it all looks so—so grotesque. I look for the virtue, I don't see any. I'm dying for proof of it, you know, proof of something good—

something like divinity. But I don't see it. I look at my life, and I see this warehouse of—of *gargoyles*. Why do vices get to be physical? Why do they get to clutter up the world? Why can't I see any fucking virtues?"

This is the part that has made her cry the hardest. She's too upset to be embarrassed, too upset to hate him as he touches her arm.

"Maybe you have to listen."

"Well, that was obviously my implication," she whispers, "but it sounds histrionic and asinine when you say it out loud."

"Maybe the truth is histrionic and asinine."

"Then I want nothing to do with it."

He removes his hand, then rummages in the car to find a packet of tissues. He offers her one, and she takes it, blowing her nose as prettily as possible, although she knows that she is repulsive.

"Should I take you back?" he asks.

She looks at him, heart pounding and face wet. "What?"

"I mean," he says, "to your apartment. You've got that goat, now, and I don't want to—"

Of course that's what he meant. Of course. Why does Blandine feel crushing disappointment? What is wrong with her?

"Don't use Hildegard as an emergency exit."

"No, I'm talking about the goat."

She says nothing. She didn't mean to reveal the goat's name to him.

"You said we weren't individuals, just concepts," says James. "But we were people. You and I are people. I hurt you, and I think it's as simple as that. *I* hurt *you*—that's the appropriate syntax for what happened. I. Hurt. You. You make it sound like you had the same control over the matter that I did, like even though our dynamic was messed up, you were still some kind of totally free agent—and I don't want to infantilize you, either, but I have to tell you—whatever you wanted to happen should have been irrelevant. You're so angry, Tiffany. I can see that. You have every right to be angry at me. But it sounds like you're angry at yourself for supposedly *choosing* this, and your choice should have been moot, don't you see? You could've showed up at my house in lingerie and thrown yourself at me—it wouldn't have mattered. It was my responsibility to make sure nothing happened between us. I was entrusted with you as a student, and it was my responsibility to protect you. I was the one who should have enforced the boundaries, and I failed. I may not have taught you anything, but I was your teacher. You were only—you were only seventeen." He covers his face in his hands. His voice breaks. "For fuck's sake."

Blandine clenches her fists. "I have one request."

He looks at her with some exhausted hope. "Tell me."

"My brain is addicted to the unresolved, and I'll never get free if I don't—if we don't—if we can't resolve this. Somehow. Please."

Now he appears sorrowful. "I don't know if it's possible to resolve this, Tiffany."

Blandine panics. "Not possible?"

"Well, I leave that up to you."

She tugs a lock of her starched hair. "I hate it when the superior party pretends to be inferior. That's just a more pernicious abuse of power. *Up to me.* Bullshit."

"Look, I would love to resolve it. I really would. I just—"

"Please, James. Resolve it. *I leave it up to you.*"

He gives her a pained expression. "Maybe by accepting that it is unresolvable?"

She scoffs. "Great. *Rich.*"

"Do you want me to quit my job?" he asks. "Invent a time machine? Turn myself in to the police?"

He seems willing to take these measures.

Abruptly, Blandine gets out of the car.

"Where are you going?" asks James. "Let me drive you home, at least."

She pauses, kicks the tire, then walks to his side.

"Are you going to beat me up?" he asks.

She opens his door, pulls him out of the driver's seat. He obliges, standing limply in the nascent rain. Drops fall every so often, as though hoping not to be noticed. Electricity prowls in the air.

"Please," he says, "beat me up."

She considers it. "You are not a good person."

"I agree."

"You're a narcissist."

"I agree."

"You deplete everyone in your orbit, you get them to serve you and save you and give and give and give, and—worse—you get them to do it without *forcing* them to. You get people to *choose* to indenture themselves to you. You treat young women like intravenous nutrients until they believe that's what they are—until they believe *you're* what they're *for*. Like Jim fucking Jones."

"I'm not sure if that part is fair, actually," he says. "The plural part. Nothing like this has ever happened before."

She pauses, then halfheartedly punches his stomach.

He barely reacts. "You can hit me harder than that."

She hesitates. "I don't want to."

But then she does, aiming at the navel, as hard as she can without a running start.

"Jesus." He winces, clutching his stomach and coughing.

Rain falls harder, cooling their skin, and their anatomies buzz within it. For the first time, she notices how sick he looks. His tan had been concealing it, but he is skinny and his eyes are bloodshot, pitted in shadow. White seems to invade his hair and stubble as she studies him, like he is aging decades in a span of seconds.

"Sorry," she says, and her voice cracks. With tightened fists and a great deal of confusion, Blandine collapses into her high school theater director. He holds her automatically, his force restrictive and secure and warm, and she tries not to enjoy these things, but her brain and her heart are not calibrated to the same moral system, and she is so tired of contorting her emotions to fit her principles. She weeps and sort of yells into his chest because she is tired, and she is shivering, and he is the only living structure in her field of vision that she wants to touch. He holds her upright. She can't see his expression.

"Please do not apologize to me, Tiffany. Anything but that."

The scent of him—generic soap—overthrows her.

"This really hasn't happened before?" Blandine asks.

"Never. Nothing like this."

"Bullshit," she whispers into his white shirt.

"Tiffany, I may not be the greatest person, but I'm telling the truth about this. By the way, I'm not suggesting that the anomaly of my actions excuses them. That's not what I'm trying to say."

"You're still teaching at Philomena?" she asks.

He hesitates. "Yes."

She pulls away, narrows her eyes. "And you swear on your mother's death that nothing like this has ever happened before? Between you and a student?"

"I told you, no. Nothing."

"Are you lying to me?"

His eye contact is secure, his irises warm and green, his voice gentle. "No. I'm telling the truth."

"Why should I trust you?"

"I've never lied to you, Tiffany."

Blandine doesn't want to say it—if she says it, she'll have to confront it, and she's effectively repressed it until now—but the words emerge without her permission.

"Then why the fuck," she begins in a low voice, "would Zoe Collins contact me after I dropped out?"

James's face empties, and Blandine recognizes him as an animal purging its weight so it can run for its life. This is all she needed to see. Revulsion invades her, and she steps away from him. He keeps a steady voice, but he can't conceal his fear.

"What are you talking about?" he asks.

"Zoe Collins. Three years ahead of me."

He swallows.

"It was sloppy of you to pick students who overlapped at school."

"I barely know Zoe," says James.

"She was your music student. She sang. She played piano. She was in your plays. You helped her get that conservatory scholarship. Of course you know her."

"Well, yes. Obviously. But it's not like I ever even met individually with her, let alone—what—what did she say to you?"

Blandine doesn't look away from James as she recites Zoe's email. *"So he got you, too?"*

She can see his body turning off the lights, drawing the curtains, locking itself up.

"She could be talking about anyone," says James.

Blandine narrows her eyes.

"Look, Tiffany, she was obsessed with me," he says, rerouting. "I intentionally avoided meeting with her one-on-one because she was so inappropriate, always sitting too close, always sending me messages, always trying to get private lessons. She even sent me a picture of herself, once—I mean, she was clothed, but it was completely inappropriate—and she disguised it as some kind of costume check, but I knew what she was doing, and I deleted it right away, told her not to do things like that, but she—*she had no boundaries.* She told other students about it—about her crush on me—and they warned me. That's how I knew. She told them she wanted to break me. She told them it was her goal to seduce me away from my family. No, really—that's what she told them! The other students! I—I *never* allowed things to get even *close* to anything—*romantic*—I purposefully built distance between myself and her so that she wouldn't—"

"Stop," says Blandine. When the message appeared in her inbox, months after she dropped out of St. Philomena's, she couldn't bring herself to reply. She could scarcely bear to read it. Now, an awareness of her own betrayal floods her. How lonely Zoe must have felt. How foolish and freakish and exposed and disposable. Alone. "Just fucking stop."

James shakes his head. "No, this is important. I can't believe she's spreading rumors like this. She probably feels rejected, and that's why she's angry. I mean, it's been years, Jesus. You know, she touched my leg once, after rehearsal, when she got me alone, and—"

"I thought you said you never met with her alone."

"I didn't! It was just for a second, and she managed to pull something like that! I got away from her immediately, and I told her she had to quit it, and that if her behavior continued, I would have to talk to the principal. I'm sure she's just embarrassed. I mean, that's all she said? *So he got you, too?* That could mean anything. Maybe she just thought you had a crush on me, too, or something. Maybe she wanted to talk about that. She was delusional, obsessive, desperate. Really insecure. She had a fucked-up home life. I think her parents were going through some ugly divorce when it happened. Come on, Tiffany. You can't possibly believe—"

"So this is how you talk about me?" Blandine demands. "When people ask?"

He blinks, panicked. "No. Of course not."

"You tell them I was obsessed with you? I had no boundaries? I was just the result of a fucked-up home life? Another teenage girl dying to fuck an older man because she's been fucked over by one before?"

"Tiffany. No. I would never say that."

She glares at him, noticing that his expensive white tennis shoes are now frosted in mud.

"Nobody asks," James mutters.

"Of course nobody asks!" Unable to quarantine the scream any longer, she unleashes it. He steps back as she does, looking frightened. The scream is animal. Ancestral. The scream of the first woman in the first dirt wounded by the first man. "That was part of your plan, wasn't it, James? My freakishness was part of your fucking plan! I bet Zoe was the same way. I bet she felt like an outcast until you came along and made her feel special. I bet you made her feel like she couldn't connect with people her own age because she was just too mature, too sensitive, too intelligent. Different from the rest because she was *unique,* because she was *brilliant,* because she was *destined* for *great things.* I bet you told her that for months before making a move. Where did you fuck her? In your house? In your office?"

"It didn't happen, Tiffany." His tone is resolute. "Nothing. Happened."

"Clever to pick students who have no friends. Why would anybody ask? I never told anyone. I *obeyed* you. I kept your fucking secret because I mistook it for mine."

"Please let me drive you home," says James. "You have to understand, Tiffany. Nothing happened between me and Zoe, or any other student. I swear to you. I swear on my mother's life. You are the only student who ever—who I ever . . ."

It's the first time Blandine has ever seen James so desperate, so out of control. She hates it.

"The point is," he says, "we can sort this out. I'll show you messages she's sent me. I'll tell you everything you want to know. I'll show you the evidence. I can't stand the thought of you believing this—this lie."

He reaches for her hand. She recoils.

"Don't fucking touch me," Blandine says, her voice low. "You will never touch any version of me again."

Paper bags of supplies wait in the backseat of his car, forgotten. Blandine Watkins turns away from James Yager and runs home, through the rain, daring cars to hit her.

Sold!

~

At 8:14 p.m. on Wednesday, July seventeenth, Clare Delacruz, the former personal assistant of deceased child actress Elsie Jane McLoughlin Blitz, posts a tweet. She sits on the kitchen floor of her cramped studio apartment in Koreatown, Los Angeles.

I am delighted to announce that Elsie's ashes have sold to Mr. Angus Hammond for $2.3 million. Thank you to all who bid. Your generosity will benefit Pygmy Three-Toed Sloth Preservation. This is the best way to honor Elsie, who taught all of us to protect the endangered.

Then Clare checks her bank account. Last night, her driver's seat window was smashed by someone who evidently found nothing worth stealing inside the car. Clare's account confirms that she must choose to mend the glass or pay her rent. She can't afford both; Elsie paid her just above minimum wage. During her years as an assistant, Clare had to offend so many people throughout the industry on Elsie's behalf, she doubts she'll ever be employed in Los Angeles again. Sipping a vase of water, she watches attention accumulate on her tweet, feels the notifications like balm on chapped skin.

PART IV

Altogether Now

~~~

C12: And if consciousness offers no more appeal, reasons the widowed logger, who can blame you for falling asleep before ten?

A ping from Rate Your Date (Mature Users!)

> LEGGYPEGGY: im sure he doesnt want anything to do with a nobody like me but i just want to say this is a kind man. really made me hope again and also laugh ★ ★ ★ ★ ★

C10: Alone with the family laptop, the teenager learns an important life lesson: poor Wi-Fi is never more distressing than it is during video sex with a much older stranger, who has not paid you up front for your services.

"Would've—refund—good," says the man.

"What? It cut out."

"Said—asked for—good."

"What? I'm sorry."

"Never fuckin'—" says the man. "I'm—here."

The man hangs up.

The teenager sits on his bed for a few minutes in silence. Then he pinches his soiled boxers from the sheets, tosses them in the hamper, and goes to the bathroom to clean up. Afterward, he dons a bathrobe, envisioning himself as a billionaire with a hot tub and a cigar. Plaid and soft, the bathrobe was a gift from Santa a few years back. His mom never told him, and he never asked, and still she signs Santa's name on

Christmas gifts. The robe is a relic of his childhood, and to wear such a thing at a time like this feels nice. The teenager loves his mother ferociously.

A dog outside. Music—something percussive—from a few floors below. Some boys are yelling again. They're always yelling. He's seen them in the lobby before, where they often make videos of indeterminate content. One of them is vigorously attractive, another decently so, the third not at all. But the third seems sweet. He's the only one who ever smiles at the teenager. Those boys are a little older than he is, but they could have been his friends, in another life. What struck him most was their energy—they seemed to be pumped full of color and noise, a force strong enough to power itself down. He never worked up the courage to talk to them.

The walls of the Rabbit Hutch are so thin, you can hear everyone's lives progress like radio plays. For this reason, the teenager turned the volume down on his laptop before the man called. But it was an unnecessary measure—the man was silent throughout.

The secret conducts a renovation inside his body, bulldozing whole walls of his childhood, preparing space for something new. He doesn't know what it will be, but he watches enough French films to know that it will be ravishing. Reconstruction is inevitable—he accepts this—and there's no rebirth without death. He turns off all his electronics and feeds his stunning beta fish. So many people crammed inside this building, the teenager marvels, and nobody knows how vast his night has been.

C8: In the bathroom, the mother stares at her husband as he brushes his teeth. She has always loved the way he brushes his teeth: methodically, sure to spend thirty seconds on each row. He wears no shirt, just boxers. She studies his appendicitis scar.

"I'm afraid of Elijah's eyes," she blurts.

Her husband spits. "What?"

"Eli," she says. "I'm afraid of his eyes. I'm so afraid I can barely breathe. It feels like a panic attack all day, and I can't look at him—you're supposed to look at your baby, I know that, but I just can't, because of the eyes, can't even think about the eyes, panic every time I do, panicking now because I'm thinking about the eyes, just picturing them, and nobody—nobody prepares you for this, nobody talks about it online, I haven't found a single person who feels this way about their baby, or babies in general, and I've been searching the internet all day, but there's something wrong with me, something really wrong with me, because if there's nobody else on the whole fucking internet *like* you, that's when you know you're in trouble, that's when you know—"

"Oh, babe," says her husband, hugging her to his chest, pressing her arms to her side, just as they swaddle Eli. She's weeping again, hyperventilating. He smooths her hair. "How long you felt like this?"

"Since—he—was—*born.*"

"And you've kept it to yourself all this time?"

She nods, sobbing.

"Why didn't you tell me?"

"You'd think I was a—a bad mother if you—if you knew—if you—"

"You know what I think?"

She sobs.

"I think you're an amazing mother. I think you're the Mother of the Year. And I also think we should get you some medicine. Some therapy, maybe. I've been saving up for it—no, listen, we can afford this now—and I think it's time to make an appointment, okay? I was talking to Mike, and he says his prescription costs something like forty dollars a month, and he doesn't have insurance for it, either. If you want it, we can do it. You don't have to feel like this, Hope. And let's get you some company, too. What about my mother? I know Kara is working all the time, but what about Val? She probably wants some company, too. And her kid is—what? A couple months older than Eli? Maybe your mom could fly out here a few weeks early. It's hard to spend so much time alone, Hope. What do you think? Can we get some medicine for you? Therapy? Company? Would that help?"

He holds her for several minutes, until she begins to breathe normally. She nods.

"Good."

Eventually, her husband starts to laugh. The laughter rises from deep in his chest, and soon it overtakes him.

"What?"

"It's just—I'm sorry; it's just—"

"*What?*"

"It's just so funny." He covers his mouth with his hands. "His"—a fit of laughter—"*eyes.*"

The mother hesitates at first, but before she knows it, she is laughing, too. Wildly. Uncontrollably. Ecstatically.

"They *are* creepy," he says.

This makes her laugh harder.

"No, no, no." She laughs. "No!"

"It's *extra* funny because . . ." her husband begins, still amused, wiping a tear from her eye.

"What?"

"It's just . . ." He laughs again, shoulders shaking. She can feel his laughter reverberate through them both as he holds her. "It's—"

"*What?*"

"Everybody says he's got your eyes."

C6: Like most people, Reggie does not want to touch dead mice. Like most people, Reggie gets through the day by believing he and all his loved ones are exempt from mortality, and he hates when death asserts itself like this.

"Quick," says Ida. "Before they go to bed."

Mouse or spouse, a voice tells Reggie. *Mouse or spouse.* The voice sounds like that of his fifth-grade teacher, a woman with black hair, a limp, and psoriasis, with whom he was infatuated. She often made up rhymes to help her students remember facts. She smelled like coal tar— like a fresh street. What a woman! Reggie heaves himself out of his armchair, pushes his feet into his flip-flops, and walks to the balcony. So far, his seventies have felt like the last mile of a marathon—which he used to run, back when his body was his. Everything aches and dehydration reigns. His vision is scattered, unfocused. He keeps walking into rooms and forgetting why. This frightens him, until he inevitably forgets the fear.

"Fine," he grumbles. "*Fine.*"

He slips his hand into a plastic grocery bag like an oven mitt, slides the door, and steps onto the concrete balcony. The night that settles around him is the kind of Midwestern night he loves—hot and humid, fireflies blinking, a purple sky, storming off and on. Decades ago, Ida, the kids, and he spent the Fourth of July with his sister Brandy in Northern California. Reggie was working as an electrical technician for Zorn Automobiles at the time. It was before they lost the house. Even though finances weren't as tight as they were about to become, Ida and Reggie had saved for a year to afford the trip, and the children were ecstatic— they had never left the state.

Throughout the visit, his sister arranged her clothes, voice, and posture to communicate superiority, so proud of herself for leaving their town, as though it were a maximum-security prison. As though it took more than a plane ticket, a cosmetology degree, and a dainty face for her to find another life. They sat around a table in Brandy's backyard and Reggie's kids wouldn't stop shivering, moaning about the cold.

"It's July," complained Mike, the oldest.

"It's dry heat," snapped Brandy. "That's why days don't feel as muggy and horrible as they do where you're from."

Where *you're* from. Reggie couldn't stand it. Already, the kids were depressed that there were no fireworks, and now they had to pretend to like the hippie tea that Brandy served them. Their complaints about the fireworks prompted a long and harsh speech from Brandy's husband, who was a California firefighter. On top of all that, it turned out that little Justin was allergic to honeysuckle. When Reggie zipped his kids— three sons and one daughter—into sleeping bags on the floor of his sister's living room, they were uncharacteristically quiet, almost defeated, the way they behaved after receiving vaccinations.

"I like it better in Vacca Vale," whispered his youngest child and only girl, Tina, eight years old, revealing her shambolic teeth in the dark, which would soon cost Reggie his overtime. Tina was not yet an alcoholic married to an incarcerated robber; she was a child who loved Atomic Fireball candies, jungle ecosystems, and doing "gymnastics" off the diving board. Her pillowcase, which she insisted on bringing, was printed with tigers. Campfire smoke in her hair. "I like our weather," she whispered. "Back home."

Now, decades later, on the balcony, Reggie fills his lungs with a Vacca Vale night, hoping that Tina is sober enough to enjoy it. He shines the flashlight of his phone on the balcony. The beam reveals two lawn chairs, a white plastic table, a broom, two empty cans of nonalcoholic beer, a bottle of expired sunblock, a coil of functionless wire, a baffling amount of bird poop—they've never seen a bird here—and a pot of dirt sprouting an American flag, everything drenched from the storm. Finally, he spots the mouse trap. He approaches it slowly, pacifying himself with the thought that normally mice in traps look intact.

He's in luck: this one looks like it's sleeping. But soon, this makes him feel worse. Even in its death, the mouse is a gentle guest, asking nothing of him.

The mouse's fur is tan, not gray, which disturbs Reggie. It suggests some kind of individuality. He can see the veins of its ears. The ears make him think of Tina again, and his chest gets tight. In one quick motion, he forces himself to scoop the mouse with the plastic bag. Pulls the bag inside out, ties the top, and marches back into the apartment.

"I made a note," says Ida.

Reggie crosses the room to his wife, because in fifty-six years of marriage, she has never crossed the room to him. She presses a yellow Post-it to the back of his hand: *SO IN EVERYTHING DO UNTO OTHERS WHAT YOU WOULD HAVE THEM DO UNTO YOU FOR THIS SUMS UP THE LAW AND THE PROPHETS!!! —Matthew 7:12*

"It's in the bag?" she asks.

"What?"

"The body."

"The mouse?"

"Yeah."

"Yes."

"Be sure to take it *out* of the bag."

"Ida."

"Just dump it on their mat. And stick the note to their door."

Reggie stands for a moment, watching the television to escape the life in front of him. Local news. One man nearly murdered another at a bar called Burnt Toast last week, and now the bar is closing. Over the last year, officers were summoned to Burnt Toast three times a week, on average. Cut to an interview with the co-owner: "Yeah, we've been here a minute and we're sad to see it go—decades of our life, you know, we've gone through three Dobermans since we opened. But too much *beep* has gone down in this *beep* hole," she says. "It's bittersweet." No weapons were found on the dead man.

In other news, some are calling the Vacca Vale Country Club incident of Monday night an act of terrorism. Cut to an interview with a middle-aged woman. The banner reads: MARY KOZLOWSKI, WIFE OF MAN AT CELEBRATORY DINNER.

"It drives me nuts when people are too politically correct to call a spade a spade," Mary Kozlowski says. "Terrorism means you use violence to get what you want. Or, you know, *threaten* to use violence. And that's what happened here. You better believe it. Frankly, I'm disappointed by the state of things. The police aren't treating this thing like they should. They said they don't think anybody's in real danger, but they have no reason to believe that. It's a serious thing—the voodoo dolls—and they need to take it seriously. God forbid anything happens to my husband or his colleagues, but if it *does*, the Vacca Vale police ought to know the blood will be on their hands."

Officials declined to comment on the investigation, which is ongoing.

"Well, what are you waiting for?" asks Ida. "Go."

Reggie turns and shuffles to the door. A memory descends on him like a bird, and he welcomes it. He was fifteen years old. It was the day he met Ida, a spitfire farm girl, one year older. He had moved to Vacca Vale from Gary, Indiana, one week before. Ida's mother sought his after Mass one Sunday, took her hand, and welcomed her to town. The dads bashfully attempted conversation near the doughnuts and coffee, which left Reggie to stare at Ida, terrified. Puberty was a time of mysterious anguish and constant humiliation. Why am I visible? he wondered every day. But Ida liked being visible, and that was obvious as soon as he saw her. She returned his gaze as though consenting to a duel, her neck long, her chin tilted upward, her skin tight and shiny with a summer tan. She was a few inches taller than he was. "The coffee here is awful," she said. Sweat attacked him sharply, like an army of toothpicks. "Is that so?" he asked, his voice cracking. "Yeah," she said, "but the doughnuts are like manna." She adjusted her tights through a sky blue dress and approached the table of food. "Want one?" Reggie cleared his throat. She wasn't exactly pretty—her features angular and tough—but she was the most automatically commanding person Reggie had ever met. "Sure," he said. "Just a glazed one." She scoffed, looked at him like he asked her to feed him bottled formula. "No," she said. "You'll have an apple fritter."

On their first date, she stole a golf cart from her neighbors and drove them five miles to the industrial farmland on the outskirts of their city, cackling gorgeously, flinging jokes into the night. He had never seen a woman drive anything before. She was free, and strong, and she smelled like the earth. "My father says the devil sneezed on me at birth," she told Reggie as she drove at full speed—fifteen miles an hour—down an empty backroad, into a cornfield. "He says that's why I'm so bad." Dust kicked up around them. Abruptly, she parked under a sky of stars, enclosing them both in sublime and unnatural geometry. There were no fireflies here. No cicadas or mosquitos. No room for any life but the corn. It was midsummer and the stalks were six feet high, endless, green—a freaky performance of health. Ida plucked a cob from its stem, shucked it violently, and tied the leafy casing around Reggie's starstruck eyes. "Don't look," she said. "I'm going to kiss you, but you'll never be able to prove it."

Sixty-two years later, Reggie squints at Ida's white hair, flooded with affection, pity, fear. The blend, he supposes, amounts to love. He wishes he could prove it.

"Where did you go, my darling?" he asks in a volume he knows his wife can't hear. She watches the television, her head motionless before it.

He heaves himself out of the apartment and into the stairwell but stops as he hears a clatter of noise from below. He listens for a moment but can't make sense of it. Instead of ascending one flight, he descends a flight, following the noise. On the third floor, he tracks the sounds— clatters, yelling—tracing them to C4. He presses his ear to the door, clutching the plastic bag.

The activity within the apartment sends sound waves to the micro- phone in Reggie's hearing aid, which converts the waves into electrical signals before sending them to an amplifier, which in turn sends them to a speaker, which sends them back to his ear at a newly adjusted vol- ume. The assembly line of a sound factory.

C4: Near her bed, Blandine has taped chapter 29 of *The Book of Her Life*, by St. Teresa of Avila, which she copied by hand onto scrap paper from the library. It describes what many mystics refer to as the Transverbera- tion of the Heart, which some have reportedly experienced in the throes of divine rapture. Blandine learned that *transverberation* comes from the Latin *transverbere*, "to pierce." In the visions, it is usually an angel who pierces the mystic's heart, which is why the phenomenon is also known as the Seraph's Assault. Teresa basically describes it as sex with God's hottest angel; Blandine finds the imagery phallic and obvious and erotic. She rereads chapter 29 whenever she can't fall asleep—which is often. Almost always. By the time she exits her body on a hot night in Apartment C4, she has the passage memorized.

> The Lord wanted me while in this state to see sometimes the following vision: I saw close to me toward my left side an angel in bodily form. I don't usually see angels in bodily form except on rare occasions; although many times angels appear to me, but without my seeing them, as in the intellectual vision I spoke about before. This time, though, the Lord desired that I see the vision in the following way: the angel was not large but small; he was very beautiful, and his face was so aflame that he seemed to be one of those very sublime angels that appear to be all afire. They must belong to those they call the cherubim, for they didn't tell me their names. But I see clearly that in heaven there is so much difference between some angels and others and between these latter and still others that I wouldn't know how to explain it.
>
> I saw in his hands a large golden dart and at the end of the iron tip there appeared to be a little fire. It seemed to me this angel plunged the dart several times into my heart and that it reached deep within me. When he drew it out, I thought he was carrying off with him the deepest part of me; and he left me all on fire with great love of God. The pain was so great that it made me moan, and the sweetness this greatest pain caused me was so superabundant that there is no desire capable of taking it away; nor is the soul content with less than God. The pain is not bodily but spiritual, although the body doesn't fail to share in some of it, and even a great deal. The loving exchange that takes place between the soul and God is so sweet that I beg Him in His goodness to give a taste of this love to anyone who thinks I am lying.
>
> On the days this lasted I went about as though stupefied. I desired neither to see nor to speak, but to clasp my suffering close to me, for ·to me it was greater glory than all creation.

She is only eighteen years old, but Blandine Watkins has spent most of her life wishing for this to happen. Goat, boy, neighbor, stranger, rabbit, falcon, logger, tree, orphan, mother—as she exits herself, she is all of it.

C2: Joan Kowalski lies on top of her quilt, trying to ignore the noise from the apartment above hers. It's the worst it's ever been. She has already checked the locks on her door three times, troubled by Penny's warning. Haunted by visions of a glacial man. An abominable snowman. She reaches for a bottle of melatonin on her nightstand and swallows a pill with tap water. She turns on the television and blasts the news, where local anchors excavate a politician's tweet. The discussion is vapid enough to distract her.

She promised herself that she would conquer her misophonia and become a better person. A perfect idea arrives in her head: tonight, she'll compose a thank-you message to her aunt. Joan's problem, she realizes, is not ingratitude or insensitivity—her problem is extragratitude and oversensitivity. At this thought, one half of her rolls its eyes at the other. She always wants to write long thank-you letters in gorgeous cursive, on expensive stationery. Perfect sentences accompanied by every gesture that might extend one soul to another. The magnitude of her ambition is what prevents her from trying. But she can send a thank-you message electronically, relieving herself and her aunt. She will.

On the floor beside her bed whirrs a white noise machine marketed for infants, adjusted to the highest volume, and in her window growls an air conditioner, and each of the pundits takes several minutes to communicate one idea. Joan tries to give herself a shoulder massage as she watches the news, but it doesn't work. The man with the perfect hair says permutations of the same sentence over and over, until another pundit cuts him off. Despite this, Joan can still hear the chaos above. There is something feral about the noise tonight. Screams, pounding, drums, even—is this possible?—hooves. She remembers the white-haired girl from the laundromat whom she met two days prior. Sweating blood. Jesus, proposing. Stigmata.

Then Joan hears something she's never heard before from Apartment C4: A female scream. She turns off the news and freezes. Another scream. As Joan listens to a sound that is most likely coming from that girl's throat, she bites the skin around her thumbnail until she bleeds.

She licks the blood to prevent it from staining her sheets. She can't move her legs.

Is Joan some kind of defector of the Sisterhood if she doesn't investigate? It's late. She's exhausted and afraid. She looks at the jar of maraschino cherries waiting on her nightstand. She hasn't eaten one yet. The cherries were supposed to be delightful, but now they're just accoutrements to phonic misery.

They are *teenagers,* Joan reminds herself. They must be horsing around. Horsing around, and how disrespectful, on a Wednesday night, to smash about like that, no matter your hormonal imbalance, when you share the building with so many other people, people parked so closely together, between cheap walls that isolate not a single life from another.

When she digs through her thought-trash to the truth, Joan must admit that the scream does not sound like a consequence of horsing around. It is the first time Joan has found the term *bloodcurdling* appropriate in real life.

But no—the girl knows what she's doing. She knows what she got herself into. At the laundromat, she was nothing if not self-possessed. She probably enjoys the macabre game they're playing up there, enjoys whatever attention those boys are giving her. What kind of girl *chooses* to live with three teenage boys? The kind who needs to be admired. Attention is what the girl wants most of all—that much was obvious at the laundromat. Her bleached white hair.

With great concentration, thought by thought, Joan replaces her guilt with anger, as her father once replaced his addiction to alcohol with an addiction to food.

Reporting the noise does not occur to Joan. Later, when she learns what happened, she will consider this revelatory information about her psychology and also about society at large.

Finally, the screaming stops. Joan hadn't realized she was holding her breath.

Neither Joan's phone nor her laptop is within reach. She will compose a thank-you email to her aunt tomorrow, after work. The night is deformed altogether now. She switches the television back on and changes the channel to a documentary about whale songs. Joan learns that although the females are capable of making sound, they rarely do. Only the males sing. Severe noise pollution can cause internal bleeding in whales, and even, in the worst cases, death.

"We always thought that the humpbacks sing to attract females—and that is true, no doubt—but more and more research suggests that the males also sing to intimidate and impress each other!" cries a zealous cetologist named Alfie. Joan doesn't consider herself a curious person—she pretty much accepts the world as it presents itself to her—but she immediately loves this documentary for herding her thoughts away from the noise above, noise that has continued even though the scream-ing has stopped. The documentary transports Joan to different noise, deep-sea noise, far more agreeable noise. She takes ten more milligrams of melatonin and learns about whales until the chemicals lay siege to her body, marching her into a potent sleep.

Beside a tiny fork on her nightstand, the jar of maraschino cherries waits. She forgot to eat them.

Electrical Malfunction

~~~

By the time Reggie calls the police from his apartment some floors above, Todd is dropping the knife. Still standing on a chair in the living room, overlooking the scene, Malik uploads his video, promoting it on four social media accounts. This, he knows, is viral content. The content that will metamorphose him from Influenced into Influencer. Glowing and trembling, forgetting the Toll, Moses runs to the body and binds her open stomach with the wide belt of his trench coat. He applies pressure to the wound. He lifts the legs. Marianne's voice has fossilized in his memory: *Pressure, circulation, pressure.* The goat, who suffered her only injury well before entering the apartment, pees on the floor. Jack watches everything, his eyes open wide.

~~~

Later, when questioned separately at the station, everyone present at the scene of the crime reports a peculiar flash of light. Each insists that the light came from inside the room. Malik attributes it to the glowing man. Todd attributes it to his psychological distress. Jack tells the police that it might have been lightning. It does not appear in the video.

"I d-d-d-don't n-n-n-*know*," Moses stammers. "An—an—elect—electrical mal—f-f-f-function?"

Viral

~~~

In the first three hours of its posting, a YouTube video entitled "True Story" posted by user Malik P. Johnson gathers 695 views. Sapphire, a young woman who once shared a foster family with Malik P. Johnson, clicks the link from a social media platform that she keeps meaning to deactivate because it feels outdated and evil. She watches the video three times, then researches the website policies. Sapphire has three kids of her own now, and they have increased her sensitivity to blood—the opposite of what she expected from motherhood. *Violent or gory content intended to shock or disgust viewers, or content encouraging others to commit violent acts, are not allowed on YouTube. If you believe anyone is in imminent danger, you should get in touch with your local law enforcement agency to report the situation immediately. If you find content that violates this policy, report it.* She posts *What is this shit?* in the comments. Maybe it's "art." She returns to the policies. *Don't post content on YouTube if it fits any of the descriptions noted below . . . Content that includes a human maliciously causing an animal to experience suffering when not for traditional or standard purposes such as hunting or food preparation . . . Dramatized or fictional footage of content prohibited by these guidelines where the viewer is not provided with enough context to determine that the footage is dramatized or fictional.*

Is the video any of her business? Sapphire has a hard time determining what obligations she has to the people she encounters, and what obligations they have to her. She hasn't spoken to Malik in years. She leaves her chair, checks on her kids to make sure they're still asleep in their room, microwaves a frozen burrito, tries to watch a show about a benevolent psychopath. But she can't stop thinking about the video—the goat bound in ropes, the girl on the floor, the blood on her stomach. White hair in the dark. So realistic. Either they had a very low budget or a very high budget, high enough to make it look low—Sapphire can't tell. After deliberating for an hour, Sapphire reaches a decision. By then, the video boasts nearly 2,000 views, 272 dislikes, and 83 likes. Malik always loved attention; she believes that he is capable of hurting someone for it. She believes everyone is. Sapphire gives the video a thumbs-down, then clicks Report.

According to Todd
~~~

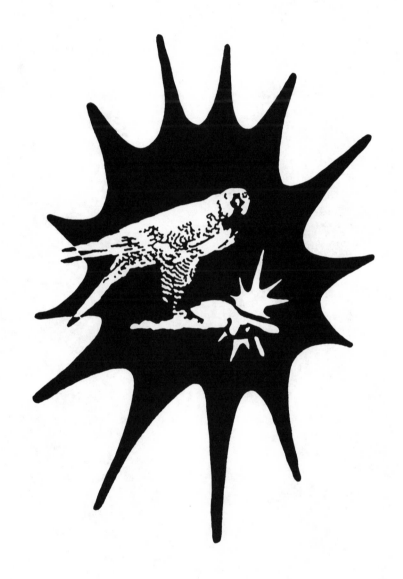

The Facts

~~

I tried to give you an explanation. Instead you wanted the facts.
    We heard the goat.
    We found the goat.
    We carried it out of her room.
    We tied it up on the floor with jump ropes.
    The goat was in front of the television.
    The television was off.
    Todd got the bongos.
    I got the knife.
    Malik got his phone.
    We gave the knife to Todd.
    It was our only sharp knife.
    I took it from Pinky's loft.
    He had like thirty, and we had none.
    It's only fair.
    Todd didn't want the knife.
    Todd said, No.
    Todd said, No way.
    We called him a pussy.
    Todd took the knife.
    We took shots.
    We banged on the floor with our feet and fists.
    We yelled at each other.

We yelled at the goat.

We turned off the lights.

We lit one candle.

Todd put down the knife.

We passed our fingers through the flame.

The man who could keep his skin in the flame the longest won.

Malik won.

Todd lost.

Malik handed Todd the knife.

We took shots.

The goat was crying.

The goat was afraid.

We did not like its fear.

None of us wanted to kill it.

One of us had to kill it.

We did not like our fear.

One of us had to kill it.

Todd dropped the knife on the floor.

I picked it up and gave it back to him.

Todd dropped the knife on the floor.

Malik picked it up and gave it back to him.

The goat was small.

Todd was small.

We took shots, and nothing was real.

Do it, do it, you fucking pussy.

Do it for her.

Show her you're not a fucking pussy.

This is the test.

Are you a man or a boy?

Are you a boy or a girl?

Fucking do it.

Malik stood on a chair across the room.

Todd lifted the knife.

Todd stared at the goat.

The goat stared at Todd.

And then she was there. Right there.

All of a sudden. Blandine.

You never saw her coming.

She moved like a cat.

Nothing was real.

She got between Todd and the goat.

She screamed.

Stop it. Stop it. Please. Please. Please.

She untied the first rope.

I tackled her, held her down.

She got free.

Please. Stop. Please.

She untied the next rope.

I tackled her, held her down.

She got free. Stop. Stop.

Untied another knot.

The goat didn't move.

The goat couldn't move.

The goat was still tied up.

With her body, Blandine shielded it.

I pulled down her strap.

She lunged for me.

I ripped her strap.

Malik cheered.

I touched her skin.

Malik didn't touch her.

The goat or Blandine.

He just filmed, his face wide open.

Todd, are you a boy or a man?

Do it, you fucking pussy, fucking do it.

Todd, are you a man or a girl?

Blandine left me on the ground and dove in front of the goat.

She was screaming like an animal.

None of you even know who you are!

Blandine reached for the knife.

Todd pulled away.

Blandine reached for Todd's throat.

Todd pulled away.

Blandine protected the goat.

I tore down the top of her dress.
She kicked me in the balls.
The pain was unreal.
I fell to the ground.
Malik filmed. Malik yelled.
Todd, what the fuck is wrong with you?
The pain was abnormal.
Todd kicked at the goat but missed.
Blandine threw herself at him.
Blandine wrestled Todd to the ground.
Blandine started choking him.
Why do you have to kill everything, she screamed.
Why do you have to kill everything.
Todd was going red in the face as she strangled him.
I hate you. I hate you. I hate you.
Todd's head going purple.
Todd's hands moved very fast.
Todd's hands are very small.
He held the knife. He put it into Blandine.
Once. Again. Again. Again.
Her torso. Maybe her chest. I couldn't see well.
The pain was extraphysical.
Too easy—too easy to empty a person of herself.
Todd pushed Blandine off of him.
He stood and looked at Malik.
Malik was looking at the doorway, terrified.
In the doorway stood a stranger.
The stranger began to yell.
He wore a trench coat.
He glowed in the dark.
Face, hands, legs, neck.
Glowing. Like a firefly.
Nothing was real.
There was blood on the floor.
There was blood on my feet.
The blood was warm, like soup.
I knew because I touched it. I touched the blood. It was hers.

That's when we saw the flash of light in the room, like lightning.

But from inside the apartment, not outside.

No thunder. It came from inside.

Brightest light I'd ever seen.

Todd dropped the knife. No one picked it up.

The glowing man ran across the room, to Blandine.

Nothing was real for nineteen years and then.

Todd vomited.

The goat peed.

The body bled.

I looked around and tried to see.

An old man appeared in the doorway.

Horror on his face. But he was gone as soon as I saw him.

I thought I imagined him. Thought he was a ghost.

The glowing man opened his coat.

He wore nothing underneath but briefs.

The glowing man tied Blandine's stomach with his coat belt.

He lay her down. He lifted her legs.

The glowing man said, What the fuck, what the fuck.

The glowing man said, What the fuck is wrong with you.

The glowing man said, I was supposed to be the weirdest thing to happen tonight.

The glowing man said, I will kill you if you touch her.

The goat was slumped beside Blandine, watching.

You could smell its piss.

Malik grinned at his phone.

A grin I've never seen before.

A face you'd carve into a pumpkin.

We heard the sirens.

We heard the steps.

The knock.

The voices.

Your voices.

And then everything was real.

Solve for Y in Terms of X

~~~

What was Tiffany Watkins to James Yager? His ex-wife wants to know. She was evolution's fault. A footnote in the divorce. The proletariat. Ondine. She was a child, a casualty, a lapse, a virus, a bowl of milk. She was born the year James married Meg. She was stabbed in the stomach three times. What was James Yager to Tiffany Watkins? He doesn't want to know.

James sits on the floor of his bedroom, depressed by its peanut-butter carpet, depressed by the value system that this first depression reveals. The apartment is cheap. He can smell the river when he opens the windows; the windows are always open; there is no air-conditioning; his life has degenerated. It takes so little time and effort to become accustomed to luxury, but years of labor to reverse the process. Hot storm wind throws itself around. James stands and moves to the kitchen, dodging the walls, like he's driving a car in a video game.

"She wasn't my student," he says.

"No?" she asks, her voice in his phone on his ear. He turns the volume down, then up, then down again. He's not sure how clearly he wants to hear anything.

"She was just in the play."

"Oh, right. The play. God, James. I just can't believe it. It's so sick. I couldn't place her at first, when I saw her picture on the news? It took me a long time before I remembered how I knew her. The babysitter. I mean I recognized her, but I thought it was just déjà vu."

"What?"

"Déjà vu."

James watches a line of ants march out of the kitchen drain, up the sink, into his life. He opens cabinets, forgetting where he stored the whiskey. It's their first postdivorce conversation that has strayed from domestic bureaucracy and the demands of time.

"What was your reaction?" she asks. "When you saw the news?"

The girls are with Meg for the week. Even when they're with him, it's apparent that they do not belong in his downsized life. They are elite, climate-controlled, dentally supreme. It comforts James to think of the blue corduroy rocking chair that his father built for him when he was born, the one where James rocked and fed and soothed his own children. The lullabies and stories and tears imbued in the fabric. When he moved out, he left the chair in the girls' room. They didn't want him to take it. *But you'll have a room in my new house, too,* he told them. *How about we put it there?* This made them cry harder.

"Yeah," James says. "It's a shock."

"You knew her pretty well, right?"

"No. Not really."

"You guys rehearse for months, though. You get close to all those kids."

"Well, she dropped out."

"But wasn't that toward the end?"

"Yes, but—it's just that it was—she was pretty withdrawn. She kept to herself, mostly."

"Strange. I must've misremembered."

James locates the whiskey skulking behind a tub of venison jerky and pours himself a cup of it. The ebbing marijuana grants him an aerial view of this night, his life. He sees highways, a junkyard, a high school stage. His daughters. One young goat. Plastic, tires, wreckage from a hurricane. "Misremembered?"

"I had the impression that you were like a mentor to her."

"Oh. Well. I guess I was, sort of. She didn't have anybody else. I mean, no friends. She was in the foster system, you know. You had to read between the lines with her—it was all subtext—but I think she had it pretty bad."

"What do you mean?"

"Abuse. She never talked about it directly. But yeah, I guess theater was good for her. She was one of those pressurized kids, you know, one of those kids who holds everything in until there's a pretext to explode." He gulps the whiskey. Referring to Tiffany as a kid sends him into a paroxysm of revulsion. He frees himself from it.

Hours ago, her blood and organs seemed so reliably encased in her skin. How unfair that the materials of such an immaterial person would prove as essential for her as they are for everyone else. He injured her, he knows that, he always knew that, but still he believed that she was untouchable. Until Meg called to say she was so sorry, she just saw the news. Forcing James to admit that it was possible to wound Tiffany Watkins.

"She played this very isolated character," he said. "Maybe it helped."

"She was good, right? I remember you saying she was good."

He blushes until it feels like a fever. "She was okay. I mean, for a high schooler. It's not like she was bringing anyone to tears in rehearsal." He plows on. "I just got the impression that theater was maybe the only place where she felt secure enough to . . . express emotion, you know? I think she was trained to hide it, growing up. Or numb it. I don't know. But in the play, everything was fake, she wasn't herself, so she felt . . . free, maybe. That's just my impression."

The ease with which he can summarize and assess Tiffany at a time like this alarms him, but his subconscious flags it as a problem to resolve at a later stage, preferably in a dream.

"That's horrible," replies his ex-wife. From the background noise and eighteen years of conjoined life, James can tell that she is taking out the trash. She prefers a multitude of small waste bins to a few centralized ones, and so when she takes out the trash, she does so systematically, room to room, consolidating all small bags of waste into one large bag. She's usually completing other tasks when they're on the phone together, and this used to bother James, before the divorce, but now he appreciates it—this remaining window into her life. "I mean, I knew she was in the foster system, I remember you mentioning that, but I didn't know about the abuse. That poor girl. Do you think someone from her past could be involved in the stabbing? Someone from her foster days? Or maybe someone from school?"

Meg loves true crime podcasts.

"I don't know," says James.

"They said they have suspects, but they aren't releasing the details."

He emits an involuntary noise—one that usually precedes vomiting.

"Oh, James. I'm sorry. The news is upsetting to me and I only met her once—I can't imagine what it must be like for you. You've always been so connected to your students. Surreal, isn't it? Does it feel real?"

"Yeah." He considers crushing the ants. She wouldn't want him to. "No."

"It's good that she had you. I bet there weren't many adults she could trust."

Fuck it. James crushes the ants slowly under his fist. They don't move out of the way, don't exhibit any self-preservation, just accept the gentle slaughter as though it were preordained. "Well. Yeah. She had a hard time connecting to people her age, so."

"Do you know why she dropped out?"

Another gulp of whiskey. He stares across his kitchen counter into the living room, whose sole occupant is the Bösendorfer. It watches him, evaluates him, extorts him. It strikes him as a carcass. He wants it removed. "Just became too much for her, I think."

"Mm. High school's torturous enough, without . . ."

"Yeah."

"All those other challenges."

A pause.

"When was the last time you saw her?" asks Meg.

Up until now, some strong, otherworldly nurse had kept James intact, kept the news unbelievable, kept his eyes on the whiskey and the ants. But as soon as Meg asks this question—*When was the last time you saw her?*—the nurse abandons him, knocking things over as she leaves. Her substitute arrives at once. Her substitute is ugly and dangerous and weak and true. Her substitute looks like him.

"I don't know," he says. "Honestly, Meg, I never really saw her at all."

"Well, I'm sorry. Truly. Anyway." Now Meg is drinking something— lemon water, he assumes. She is an impeccably hydrated person. "I was thinking you could pick up the girls around four tomorrow, then drop off Emma at soccer since it's on your way, and take Rosie back to your place. Maybe go for ice cream. She's been sort of anxious lately, irritable, crying a lot. Obviously, we're to blame."

"What do you mean?"

"Rosie threw a tantrum at the pool the other day because she didn't want to wear sunscreen. Screaming and sobbing and everything."

"Hm."

"Anyway, she could use some one-on-one time with you. What do you think?"

But James has placed the phone on the counter and concealed his face in his hands, shoulders heaving.

"Are you there? James?"

Tada

~~~

At the police station, vapor rises from two Styrofoam cups of coffee and fills the room with the scent of morning, although it is nearly midnight. Two officers scrutinize Jack with furrowed brows and split reactions. Throughout his interview, Jack has addressed his own shaking hands. His eyes are pink, his mouth dry, his face pale. He's been crying intermittently since they brought him here, but his story was steady throughout, as if he were recounting a folktale from his childhood. Observing the boy before him, Officer Stevens is reminded of a white rabbit, pulled by the scruff from a magician's hat, frightened and surprised. The punch line.

"These are the facts," Jack concludes. "Do they look like an explanation to you?"

What Hildegard Said

~~~

And I saw a light-filled man emerge from the aforesaid dawn and pour his brightness over the aforementioned darkness; it repulsed him; he turned blood-red and pallid, but struck back against the darkness with such force that the man who was lying in the darkness became visible and resplendent through this contact, and standing up, he came forth out of the darkness. And thus the light-filled man, who had emerged from the dawn, appeared in greater splendor than any human tongue can express, and he proceeded to the utmost heights of immeasurable glory, where he shone out wondrously in the fullness of great fragrance and fruitfulness.

And I heard a voice speaking to me from the living fire I have mentioned: Insignificant earthly creature! Though as a woman you are uneducated in any doctrine of fleshly teachers in order to read writings with the understanding of the philosophers, nevertheless you are touched by my light, which touches your inner being with fire like the burning sun. Shout and tell!

PART V

What Is Your Relation?

~~~

G ot any dynamite?" asks the receptionist in the Intensive Care Unit at the Vacca Vale Medical Center.

"Excuse me?" replies Joan Kowalski.

The receptionist laughs and pats his chest, where a sharp tooth hangs on a chain. "Just kidding! Kidding! Oh, you have to have a sense of humor around here. Things get *prih-tee* grim—fast!" His laugh simmers. "And what is your relation to her?"

"Oh." Joan had not anticipated this question, despite its predictability. "How am I related to her?"

"That is the question," the receptionist replies in a bad English accent, then laughs again, offensively jolly. The hospital smells like a swimming pool, which Joan associates with rare childhood stays at hotels and even rarer equilibrium between her parents. Joan looks around; no one else is in the lobby. It flickers. "We just need to know you're not a villain, you know." The receptionist winks. "We try to keep out the predators."

It's Friday—two days after three boys stabbed a girl named Blandine Watkins in La Lapinière Affordable Housing Complex. Today is payday. That morning, Joan fed her car forty dollars of gasoline and drove to the hospital on an instinct, stalked for days by guilt. Since she learned of the stabbing, Joan Kowalski has not slept or attended work, tormented by visions of a slashed belly. She had a fever that would not validate itself via thermometer. In the visions, it's almost always a child's belly, sometimes a kitten's. During eleven years of employment at Rest in Peace, this is the first sick day that Joan has taken.

Joan is wearing a dress that belonged to her mother, rainwater dotting her shoulders and calves. She misses her mother like a phantom limb.

The receptionist—thirties, round, tired, friendly—looks familiar, but Joan cannot place him. A kettle of black tea circulates through her body, agitating everything.

"How are any of us related?" demands Joan. Her tone is weird, and she knows it. She has suffered some psychological earthquake, and the vials that previously kept her associations from contaminating each other have shattered. "Does it matter?"

The receptionist smiles at Joan with parental encouragement, as though she's a child, improvising a tale.

Joan's vision blurs. She grips her skull. "There's this obituary—did you read it? The Elsie Blitz obituary?"

The receptionist shakes his head no.

"She wrote it herself, and—" Joan gets distracted as the receptionist scrawls *Elsie Blitz obit* on a piece of paper. He looks up at her expectantly.

"Well," she continues. "Um. In her obituary, she says everything affects everything—something like that. It's her son who tried to—punish me—but he got the wrong apartment, and . . . and I just—I think we should all take each other a little more seriously. I want to wake up. Do you know what I'm talking about?"

It's just after nine in the morning. She can't remember the last time she felt this much before lunch. Sweat, rain, and tea fill her up. Weigh her down. Make her hot. Make her shiver. When she speaks, the words feel like water. Her whole mouth feels like water.

After a beat, the receptionist laughs.

"Oh, you're not afraid to get real!" He beams. "Love that, love that. I've been in a lot of therapy, too. And I like sermons. I listen to them all the time—sermons from all over the map, religion-wise. Talk radio, too. Can't get enough of it. You're really good. You should go on one of those shows in New York City."

He grins dreamily.

Then it dawns on her: the receptionist looks familiar because he looks like a koala.

"So," he says, snapping out of it. "Are you family, or . . . ?"

"No." She sighs. "No. I'm her neighbor."

"Oh, that's fine. Don't look so terrified! Oh, love, you look like you're about to cry! Need a tissue? Here, take it. Unused! Ha! Nothing to fear, here. Nonfamily members have visiting rights. They sure do. If we only let family visit, well. That would be downright antidemocratic. Personally, in my own case, if I found myself in this ward, knock on wood"—he knocks hard on the desk, which is not made of wood—"if I wound up in a pickle, you know, in the ICU, the *last* people I'd want to see would be my blood relatives. It would be sick if my *real* family—my chosen family—were forbidden to see me because we share no DNA." He smiles at Joan, who is trying to blow her nose without making any noise. A cloud passes over his features. "Not that I would expect this particular patient to *welcome* visitors, all things considered. Her story . . . well. We see some bleak crap around here. It's not like we *rank* the patients' stories, of course, but some are worse than others, obviously, and we've got to keep perspective—you understand. And her story . . . it's the one that made me feel the worst. I had to go to therapy about it. Want to know the first thing she said when she got out of surgery?"

Joan doesn't, actually. "What?"

"She said she'd take any visitor who came to see her. I mean, I wasn't there, but I hear things. She demanded it. Fierce! But . . ." His face falls, and he touches his shark-tooth necklace again, fiddling with it nervously. "Nobody's visited her yet. Except for this one social worker, who didn't even stick around. It just makes me so sad." He pauses. When he speaks again, he's whispering. "She didn't have an emergency contact. How tragic is that?"

Joan accepts this news like it's a dreaded but suspected diagnosis. One that pertains to her own cells.

"So it's good of you to be here," concludes the receptionist gently. "Now, keep all that between us—what I told you. I might've breached some kind of confidentiality. I don't know. Just don't kidnap her! Ha! And no dynamite, you hear? Oh, we try to keep it light around here. Dark times, you know." He hands Joan the entire tissue box. "Here, keep them." A phone rings, and his eyes dart to it. "Take it easy, okay? The nurse will be with you soon. You're a terrific neighbor."

Delicately, as though her body is made of loose soil, Joan walks to the sitting area, where she installs herself in a cold leather chair. For a long time, she stares at a knitting magazine. At last, she notices a copy of Friday's *Gazette* on the table and picks it up.

The story of what happened in Apartment C4 of La Lapinière Affordable Housing Complex on the night of Wednesday, July seventeenth, has migrated to the middle of the newspaper. No longer front-page material, already approaching irrelevance. Joan learns that the suspected boys have been arrested—one under suspicion of attempted second-degree murder, two under suspicion of complicity, all three under proof of animal cruelty, illegal marijuana possession, and underage drinking. Early in the questioning, officials obtained three harmonious confessions that matched the video evidence, which had been published online. Two witnesses confirmed the story. Joan gathers that this kind of narrative coherence is atypical, almost unprecedented. The boys face a trial, at which they will plead guilty. The reporter cites a similar case elsewhere in Indiana—abdominal stabbing, survival, multiple perpetrators. The criminals in that case were charged for a level-three felony: aggravated battery that posed a substantial risk of death. They were convicted and held in prison for $25,000 cash-only bonds. *The fate of these boys, however,* writes the reporter, *depends upon their intent to kill.* Questions remain to be answered. Reasonable threat? Self-defense? Who started it?

More opossums have been found at the Wooden Lady. This time in the hot tub. This time they were alive.

A photo depicts Mayor Douglas Barrington, urban designer Benjamin Ritter, and white-suited Maxwell Pinky grinning in hard hats at a ceremonial tree cutting in Chastity Valley. *Clearing a Path Toward the Future,* the photo is captioned. The ceremony occurred yesterday, launching the Valley revitalization.

The search continues for the development dinner attackers.

"We just don't know enough," Officer Stevens told the reporter. "We may never know enough."

~~~

"Joan Kowalski?"

Joan looks up. A nurse grips a clipboard, purses her lips.

"For Blandine Watkins?"

"Yes."

"You can follow me."

She leads Joan down a blinding, vacant corridor. "I'll be back in a minute," she says, abandoning Joan at the doorway like the ferryman of Hades.

A powerful scent of roses fills the girl's room, although there are no flowers in sight—just a handful of browning white clovers on the table beside the bed. The girl is lying on her back, her head facing the window, away from Joan. White cotton hospital blanket tugged up to her chin. Joan observes the girl's lunar hair. Dark and greasy roots contort the dimensions of her head, making it appear, for a moment, like the only thing in the room.

Across from the bed, a muted television broadcasts a mess of gray: pebbles, feathers, sticks, and bones. The footage is grainy, as though captured by a security camera. It takes Joan a while to understand what she is seeing. It's a bird's nest, industrial and sturdy, built into a structure of wooden rafters. Squinting, she finally notices three gangly chicks in the chaos, feet the color of raw corn, talons black, eyes both frightened and murdery, faces framed in beige, beaks hooked, mouths bent into curmudgeon-frowns, dark adult feathers bursting at random from bodies of cloudy white fuzz. They look very wrong, and Joan is certain that birds were not meant to be seen this way. Text on the top right of the screen reads: *Vacca Vale Falcon Cam.* The lower left shows the time and date. Huddled together, these endangered young villains are hulking, awkward, and watchful. The chicks will be killers one day soon, Joan knows, but it won't be their fault. For now, they're helpless, at the mercy of the creature who brought them into this place, condemned to wait for someone more powerful to feed them.

Slowly, Blandine's head rolls toward the door, revealing a face as pale as the walls, washed blue beneath the eyes, green around the mouth, a dash of dried blood across an eyebrow.

"Susan," she says. It sounds like she hasn't spoken in days.

"No, Joan. It's Joan." Joan grips her umbrella, afraid of the half-dead girl before her, afraid that death is contagious. "From the laundromat. I mean, from the Rabbit Hutch. I live below your apartment. I'm the lady with . . . without a bird feeder?"

The girl blinks like a cat in the sun. "Joan," she says.

They observe each other in silence.

"What's this?" Joan asks, gesturing toward the television.

It takes Blandine a long time to respond, and when she does, the words seem laborious for her. She lugs them into the room as though they're pieces of furniture. "Falcon cam. Live from Jadwiga's. Nurse put it on."

"Oh. That's . . . they look so . . . um. Cute."

At this, the girl frowns, evidently disappointed in Joan.

"How's the goat?" asks Blandine.

"Yes," Joan says, elated to offer something good. "The goat! He's doing very well! He's—"

"She."

"She! Sorry. She. They took her to the vet. They gave her a brace, some medicine, a new home, and she's going to be just fine. Would you believe it? Her injury wasn't so bad, it turns out—it had something to do with how young she was, how her bones haven't fully hardened yet? They called it—um . . . what did they call it . . . oh yes, a 'green stick break,' if I recall correctly. Full recovery expected within three weeks. She's actually been adopted by this animal sanctuary in Michigan? Yeah. Everybody's talking about it. There are all these internet things about her. Memes, right? Yes—memes. She's become a bit of a sensation. Yeah, so. Neat."

When she read the coverage of the stabbing, Joan found it terrible how energetically the journalists belabored these points. As though the goat's happy ending formed an appropriate resolution to the events at hand.

On Blandine's face, a smile flickers, growing brighter. Joan sees tears sparkling in the girl's bloodshot eyes, but she tells herself it's a trick of the light.

It occurs to Joan that she should have brought flowers. Or a fruit basket. A book of sudoku? What does a visitor bring to comfort a recently stabbed teenager she hardly knows? Joan notices a clunky library book beside the hospital bed. *She-Mystics: An Anthology.* She recognizes it as the book from the laundromat. Right now, the girl doesn't look strong enough to pick it up. If Joan finds the right moment, she will offer to read to Blandine. She will offer to visit every day. She will be neighborly.

Stasis looks unnatural on the girl, who is visibly drained of the frenetic energy that Joan observed the first time they met. Joan is reminded of a photograph she once saw: a horse sitting on a carpet in a darkened room, watching television. When Joan looks at the girl in the hospital bed, she can finally picture the grievers. What comments would fill the obituary guest book, Joan wonders, if Blandine had died?

For a long time, the two women study each other.

Joan wants to say: I don't have an emergency contact, either. She wants to say: I'm glad they didn't kill you. She wants to say: I am sorry for every instance I took when I could have given.

"You're awake," Joan says instead, incongruously.

A peculiar flash of light shivers across the room.

"I am," Blandine replies. "Are you?"

Acknowledgments

From this novel's inception to its distribution, countless people worked to improve *The Rabbit Hutch* and unite it with readers. The immensity of such a gift exceeds language; the gratitude I have tried to articulate below is but a fraction of the whole.

My brilliant literary agent, Duvall Osteen, was my guide and ally from the beginning. She shepherded this book out of my laptop and into the world with expertise, generosity, and verve. I am grateful to the entire team at Aragi Inc. for welcoming and supporting me.

My editor, John Freeman, possesses that rare trinity of genius, work ethic, and integrity. He helped *The Rabbit Hutch* become itself by challenging it with a depth of humility that continues to move me. I thank both John and Duvall for understanding—never taming—this novel's wildness, and for infusing my first publication process with so much joy.

Knopf is the greatest literary home imaginable, and I am thankful to the whole team for the time and energy they devoted to this book.

Thank you to my literary agents abroad: Jemma McDonagh, Camilla Ferrier, and Caspian Dennis. I am immensely grateful to the publishing teams at Éditions Gallmeister, Guanda, Kiepenheuer & Witsch, and Oneworld Publications.

My writing professors from Notre Dame uprooted my literary preconceptions and planted far better ideas in their place. I thank Joyelle McSweeney, Orlando Menes, Steve Tomasula, and Anne García-Romero.

I cherished their generosity as an undergraduate and continue to cherish it now.

I am grateful to my NYU professors who challenged, supported, and even sometimes employed me. Deborah Landau fosters the literary community that has permanently enriched my life. Rick Moody served as my thesis adviser during *The Rabbit Hutch*'s most formative stages; his feedback, reading lists, and broad-spectrum wisdom were foundational to the development of this novel. I could not have pursued my MFA without those who fund the Lillian Vernon Fellowship. The instruction of Rivka Galchen, Nathan Englander, David Lipsky, and Yusef Komunyakaa continues to guide me. Jonathan Safran Foer's manifold support has been invaluable over the years, and I am especially thankful for his early advocacy of *The Rabbit Hutch*.

My MFA cohort immeasurably strengthened this novel and its author. Special thanks to Crystal Powell, Francine Shahbaz, Lindsey Skillen, Jacquelyn Stolos, Jordan Tucker, and Lynn Pane.

My gratitude to my beloved New York seraphim, whose brilliance, friendship, and group chat continue to nourish me: Steph Arditte, Tess Crain, Laura Cresté, Alyx Cullen, Emma Hine, Sophie Netanel, and Torrey Smith. Supreme thanks to Kate Doyle, the workshop's founder, who creates a meaningful literary community wherever she goes. I would never have submitted this novel to agents without Kate's encouragement.

For their friendship, I thank Sarah Young, Christian Coppa, Alex Coccia, Brittanie Black, Grace and Jonathan Franklin, Stephanie and Jason Pham, and all the Andrews.

I made the earliest sketches of *The Rabbit Hutch* in Prospect Park, and my love for that public sanctuary clearly informed Blandine's devotion to the Valley; I am indebted to the Prospect Park Alliance for their stewardship.

I am indescribably grateful to my parents and brothers, who have nurtured my love of reading and writing since I was a child. My mother, the greatest art teacher on earth, taught us that creativity requires mess, mistakes, and love. My father read to us every night and patiently transcribed my stories before I knew how to spell. Both my parents spent incalculable hours with us at the public library. They encouraged my earliest fiction, continuing to do so as I made the statistically ill-advised choice to pursue writing as a career. Ben provided brilliant feedback on my drafts, instructive reading recommendations, luminous literary analysis, and even a *Rabbit Hutch* playlist. I am thankful to Joshua for his poetry, music, and for modeling a life lived on one's own terms. I thank Nick for his music, visual art, and for being my first friend in this world. Nick elevated Todd's illustrations far beyond my original vision—I cannot imagine a more harmonious collaboration.

My infinite gratitude to Andrew Krizman. It took five challenging years to write this novel; Andrew's transformative respect for and belief in my work was my primary sustenance throughout. He maintained his faith in me even when I lost faith in myself.

Finally, I thank each reader, for finishing what I began.

Notes

The first epigraph is lifted from Michael Moore's 1989 documentary *Roger & Me.*

The second epigraph is taken from *Selected Writings: Hildegard of Bingen,* trans. Mark Atherton (London: Penguin, 2001). The majority of the Hildegard quotes reproduced throughout *The Rabbit Hutch* are from this volume.

In "Afterlife," Blandine quotes from Simone Weil's *Gravity and Grace,* trans. Emma Crawford and Mario von der Ruhr (London: Routledge Classics, 2002).

In "The Expanding Circle," Moses references the moral philosopher Peter Singer's 1997 thought experiment, "The Drowning Child and the Expanding Circle." (I do not share Moses's venomous reaction to this paper and its author.)

"Variables" repurposes practice-test questions from collegeboard.org. It also briefly quotes from *The Waste Land* by T. S. Eliot. A version of "Variables" appeared in the 150th issue of *The Iowa Review.*

"Pearl" references a fictional woman who is inspired by the real-life Rose Marie Bentley (1918–2017). Like Pearl, Bentley also owned a pet store and died of natural causes at the age of ninety-nine, never receiving a diagnosis of situs inversus with levocardia while she was alive. Bentley donated her body to a research university, where anatomy students discovered her condition.

Al Quig's photographs of our hometown, South Bend, inspired many of the images described in "Pearl."

"Altogether Now" quotes from chapter 29 of *The Book of Her Life* by Teresa of Avila. The version transcribed in this novel is from *The Collected Works of Saint Teresa of Avila,* trans. Kieran Kavanaugh and Otilio Rodriguez, vol. 1 (Washington, DC: Institute of Carmelite Studies, 2001).

"Viral" quotes YouTube's content policies.

My brother Nicholas Gunty, a musician and visual artist, made the illustrations featured in this novel.

A NOTE ABOUT THE AUTHOR

TESS GUNTY holds an MFA in creative writing from New York University, where she was a Lillian Vernon fellow. *The Rabbit Hutch* is her first novel.

A NOTE ON THE TYPE

This book was set in Monotype Dante, a typeface designed by Giovanni Mardersteig (1892–1977). Dante was originally cut for hand composition by Charles Malin, the famous Parisian punch cutter, between 1946 and 1952. The Monotype Corporation's version of Dante followed in 1957.

Composed by North Market Street Graphics,
Lancaster, Pennsylvania

Printed and bound by Berryville Graphics,
Berryville, Virginia

Designed by Cassandra J. Pappas

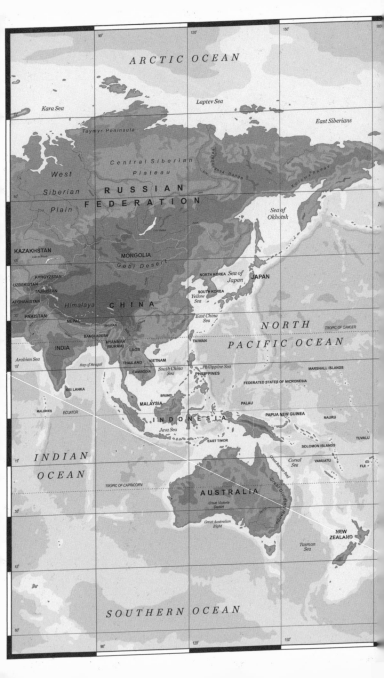